1 BECOMING

LOIS A WITTICH

authorHOUSE®

AuthorHouse™
1663 Liberty Drive
Bloomington, IN 47403
www.authorhouse.com
Phone: 1 (800) 839-8640

Published by AuthorHouse 06/15/2015

ISBN: 978-1-4969-5512-8 (sc)
ISBN: 978-1-4969-5511-1 (hc)
ISBN: 978-1-4969-5510-4 (e)

Library of Congress Control Number: 2014920856

Print information available on the last page.

This book is printed on acid-free paper.

CHAPTER 1 ENCOUNTER

Heads turned as a stunningly beautiful, raven haired young woman swayed sensually into thte main hall of an upscale nightclub in downtown Austin, Texas. It was, without a doubt, a truly breathtaking moment.

Carrying herself with poise and confidence, her shapely, well-toned body rippling seductively beneath a turquoise-green, spaghetti-strapped dress she must have sprayed on, she made her way through the crowd. Free from the bitch chemistry common in so many women, she quickly struck up a conversation with two other young women. Charming them with her genuine caring she shared her excitement for the upcoming evening, her thick, waist-length hair flouncing in emphasis. Her fair complexion colored with the blush of anticipation as they chatted, her Scottish flavored English accent becoming more pronounced the more animated she became.

Still in lively conversation, the three were headed for the restroom to 'powder their noses' when she felt a presence to her right and stopped. Sitting alone, just inside the entrance of the adjacent sports bar, was the most physically striking man. His broad shouldered frame, long legs, glowing skin - more deep mahogany than black - and an aura of raw power tempered by an underlying compassion charged her body with a kaleidoscope of emotions and a physical jolt so powerful she gasped. It would prove to be a transformative encounter.

Sensing her pause he tilted his head and faced her. His large almond-shaped dark-brown eyes, flecked with amber highlights, locked in a stare with her startled green ones. Instantly opening to each other they both softened their gaze. Penetrating the surface reflections they explored the depths beneath, bypassing the superficial to completely receive the core of each other. Simultaneously feeling an eternity elapse, the delicate charging of body hair the only evidence of the energy coursing between them, they forged a body link, a cell-for-cell fusion that transcended falling in love or becoming soul mates and restructured their capacity for intimacy, passion and communication. Shyly, their eyes disengaged

Calling over her shoulder, "Go ahead girls, I'll see you later," she walked over, reached out and offered him a delicate well-manicured hand. "I'm

Shauna." Reviving the intense eye contact, he replied, "Gifford," and slowly took her hand, enveloping it with his huge palm, enclosing long slim fingers in a warmth that aroused her instantly. She tugged his hand and as he rose to his full height gave thanks for every fraction of her five foot eleven inches - plus the extra five inches her stilettos added. Looking up, thinking, *he must be seven feet at least*, she was captivated by the beauty of his head, so smooth, free from creases, lumps or bumps.

It's perfect, she thought as she took note of the extremely short buzz cut, like a shadow, carefully sculpted to continue down both sides of his face and around his jaw to join the thin lines from the ends of a well-trimmed mustache; the little tuft under his bottom lip and thick dark eyebrows. *Such an intriguing work of art - a study in shades, textures and precision! But those lips! Large and fleshy with that line in the center where the two halves of the upper one come together like the prow of ship!* She had to admit she would like them pressing against hers.

Tearing her eyes away, she focused on the room behind him and noticed a group of guys at the far end, rowdily following a game on the flat-screen behind the bar. Judging by how tall they were, she guessed they might be members of the local Austin Acers basketball team and the man beside her one of their team mates. And then wondered why, if that were the case, he was alone and seemingly so preoccupied. Mentally shrugging, knowing she'd find out soon enough, she turned and pulled him gently out of the bar. A little surprised by her uncharacteristic forwardness, at least when it came to approaching men, she was determined to enjoy this new moment to the full, and all the next new moments as they arrived.

Leading him into the nightclub, she checked him out from the corner of her eye as he walked beside her. Swaying from side to side, his arms swinging with the movement in a jaunty, relaxed amble, his lightweight clothes outlining his body making it obvious he dedicated himself to maintaining a highly machined physique, he was a gorgeous feast of masculinity.

Apart from sharing names, neither had spoken. Neither seemed uncomfortable. Nor were they particularly aware of, or concerned by, the impact they were making as the rapidly growing crowd that was restless with anticipation seemed to stand aside to let them through. The people pouring into the club, scrambling to get as near to the stage as possible before seating themselves at the closely packed round tables, paused to let them pass, almost without thinking. It was if the two were preceded by a force field that gently opened a pathway before them

Unerringly leading Gifford to the only empty seat at a table near the stage, Shauna invited him to make himself at home. Saying she had things to attend to but would be back, she left him to make her way on stage. A quick look over her shoulder caught him perfectly relaxed. His long legs dressed in black dress slacks were sprawled to either side of him. A silken, burgundy shirt unbuttoned halfway, showed off his hairless, muscular chest, further enhanced by a discrete gold necklace that glittered under the recessed ceiling spots. He certainly stood out from the crowd and she definitely liked what she saw she decided, before turning to disappear into the backstage darkness.

Moments later a small group of musicians took their places center stage. As the club lights dimmed to a soft, restful glow and the stage lights brightened, a pronounced hush fell over the audience. Out of the silence began to flow the sweet sound of stringed instruments in harmony. The melody slowly built to a soaring crescendo that warmed the heart, released the senses and lifted the audience above their cares. No wonder it was a packed house.

As the climax subsided, a tall, slender yet curvaceous woman in a shimmering, silver-studded, floor-length gown slowly emerged from the back stage shadows. Joining the ensemble, she began to sing. A thunderous applause filled the club, bringing a smile of appreciation to the singer's lips. With her stunning appearance and unique mezzo soprano voice, the acknowledgement was not surprising. Singing in Italian, her every note crystal clear and edged with a subtle yet palpable vibrato, she moved with grace and a total focus to weave a spell of sound and gesture that captivated the audience, seeming to draw them into a collective participation. She in turn was lifted to new heights by the experience of being so received in sharing her love of performance and her voice seemed to dance along with the waves of music - rising, falling, intertwining - increasing the impact on her mesmerized listeners.

Gifford was sat bolt upright. Ever since Shauna had appeared he'd been transfixed. Surprised, stirred and excited he allowed her voice to penetrate him and felt his being shift with the strength of their connection, a new collective power . . . He and Shauna! He felt fresh and alive.

Several waitresses were going from table to table quietly asking if a Gifford Jefferson was in the house. When approached and asked, he mutely nodded, yes. Receiving the message that his buddies in the sports bar next door wanted to move on and were trying to locate him, he asked the waitress to let them know to go on without him, and he'd call them in the morning.

He had no desire to be further distracted from this performance he wanted to be so completely immersed in.

Earlier that night now felt like another lifetime ago. Gifford would have been the first to drunkenly call for a move to new hunting grounds. That's one reason why he had a stretch limousine and driver on tap. It was a babe magnet and an essential seducers accessory. But Gifford's normal thinking process had been short-circuited. Not that he fully grasped what was happening or how rapidly he was changing. *Man, I have no idea how to deal with what I'm feeling right now.* But he was stirring, like he was finally waking up. Feeling good - happier and lighter than ever before - and so connected with this woman he'd just met! Aroused, he covertly scratched his crotch and readjusted. *Have I really been so asleep? Living such a small life? And now, suddenly, I'm changing? Becoming more aware, more alive, more conscious? It can only be because of her. I have never had such thoughts before: to even wonder if two people in total agreement can become so much more as individuals when they are with each other than they could ever be on their own. This is not at all like me and yet it feels so right, so liberating.*

His body quaking, he nipped his speculations in the bud to turn his full attention to the continuing performance again. Shauna was part way through an operatic version of a classic rock hit that had him immediately enraptured along with the rest of the audience. As she fell silent to allow the orchestra to build tension for the final passage, she gracefully made her way down the ramp and slowly glided towards the table where Gifford sat. Locking eyes with him, she sang the last lines in English:

"You know it's true.
Everything I do,
I do it for you."

She held the last note until it was nothing more than a poignant and lingering memory. Rooted to the spot, eyes still locked on Gifford's, her breasts heaving, threatening to spill from her exquisitely tailored gown, she radiated pleasure. Abandoned in her excitement, she was electric.

As the audience rose for a standing ovation, Gifford, appreciating her honoring, patted his thigh, indicating she had a place to sit. As it was the intermission and every other chair was occupied, she acknowledged the applause before accepting his offer. Placing her arms around his neck she swung onto his lap - a conversation-stopping maneuver she managed with aplomb.

Gifford sensually kissed her long, gracefully curving neck until she turned her head and met his lips. A shiver thrilled through her as they gently collided and melded into each other's energy fields and she felt Gifford to be like herself. Knowing her mind could talk her into or out of anything, she had become increasingly reliant on her feelings for guidance and with her whole body informing her brain, not just her brain commanding her body, she tuned in to her hyper-sensitive awareness – an awareness she would soon find out to be both unique and revolutionary - seeking an explanation.

But she was too distracted. Aroused to the tips of her being, feeling Gifford right in step, she continued their kissing as they explored the uncharted territory of each other. Feeling a new life stirring beneath her, becoming enlarged and firm, she whispered in his ear. He laughed and said in his soft bass voice that he was going to be fine. She sighed. She had to leave her deliciously stimulating perch and finish her performance. Sliding off his lap she could see that what had been trapped beneath her was now a little more obvious, but hopefully only to the inquisitive, well-directed eye. Shauna could feel his warmth lingering along her buttocks as she redirected her attention to the performance and disappeared backstage once again.

With the musicians in position and the audience resettled and ready, Shauna re-appeared front center stage lit by a spot. A collective gasp swept the room at the sight. She was wearing her now signature gown that left little to the imagination: dazzling, fire engine red with a neckline that plummeted to her waist and an open back that plunged equally provocatively.

Red was, for sure, her trademark and Gifford who'd been cooling down was suddenly hot again. The red second skin clung to her curves ensuring all eyes were fixed on her every move. She had the audience's full attention without even opening her mouth. Unique, faux-peacock-feather stilettos barely showed but added an exotic contrast when they did. Her hair, now free from hairpin prison, cascaded over her shoulders to her waist, accentuating her beauty with attractive ringlets that framed her face. A strong scent of newly minted pheromones wafted across the stage signaling her readiness for just about anything and she sensed the uneasiness and disapproval of a few in the audience. Unconcerned, she flicked her hair back with a toss of her head, turning it into a gyrating mass of wavy commotion.

An infectious smile started working her lips at the enthusiastic applause that had followed the initial gasp. Glancing at Gifford, excited to sing and poised to perform as never before, her smile smoldered. Behind her the musicians started softly. The angelic trills of the harp began to tenderize the listening hearts before the violins slid in and then the whole ensemble, building the music to a crescendo before quietening to allow Shauna's first flawless notes to soar, free from distraction.

Infused with a new power and vitality, her previously spectacular voice now pierced the shadows within each person, bringing light and the hope of a better tomorrow to everyone who would open. As she sang, she slowly made her way down to the floor where the audience sat absorbing every nuance, and threaded through the crowded tables, almost having to slide her feet because of the gown's tightness. Lightly touching the occasional patron as she passed, spontaneously sensing who was welcoming and who was not, she completed her foray and returned to the stage just as the last note faded.

As the program drew to its close, Shauna, having given her all throughout, was joined by a tenor and chorus. From the first note a new intensity was evident and the fusion of music and chorus so hypnotic that it was hardly noticed when Shauna joined in. As she sang louder and louder, her voice merged and soared in a musical hide-and-seek, back and forth in a tapestry of sound that brought many to tears until, just when it felt like the majesty had peaked, she placed her hand on the Tenor's heart and he unleashed a sound so high, rich and pure, it seemed to transcend all earthly constraints. The music followed him, propelling him to further heights and he placed his hand over Shauna's heart in return. The minimalist gown left him with a handful of breast and Shana, anticipating his embarrassment, quickly took his hand and held it against her shoulder, thinking; *I guess we should have scheduled a dress rehearsal.*

As the number continued, it was like stepping into another world - one of unlimited freedom and opulence and untold joy. The music would ebb and SWELL . . . ebb and SWELL . . . ebb and SWELL . . . like a wave birthing across the ocean, growing more and more powerful, climbing to a lofty crest and then curling down and into itself to once again become part of the ocean. To ebb and SWELL, ebb and SWELL all over again - repeatedly.

Finally, the last note resounded. It lingered. Stretching outward it wrapped itself around everything, finding its way through whatever and whoever it encountered, soaring through the walls of the club across the planet and into the solar system and beyond. Like a bright light eliminating darkness it flooded every crevice, shadow and wide open space. Becoming a mere reverberation it would live on in those who had allowed themselves to be penetrated, continually calling for them to listen and hear it, whether they were awake or asleep, urging them to spread their neglected wings and fly: to not look back or stop their new lightness of spirit.

Shauna, almost overwhelmed, aware that she had never come close to such an irresistible performance before, could feel the pulses and vibrations blossoming throughout the room as many responded without knowing what was happening. Well, it was they who were happening. Gifford and Shauna locked eyes again in a shared biology of togetherness and she knew it was this that had powered her extraordinary performance. Their skin glowed and they sensed a new awareness and sensitivity in heeding the call within their own selves; plugging in to a new quantum energy they had unleashed and made available for anyone to run with if they cared to.

No one stirred. Not a sound, not a cough, not a movement, not a whisper. The whole room, including the performers, was frozen in time. Then, as if at some unseen cue, the audience rose to their feet in unison with thunderous applause. It went on and on and on and on. Shauna acknowledged the Chorus, the musicians, and the Tenor, and received an enormous bouquet from the club owner before performing two encores which received equal acclaim.

Eventually the audience accepted the performance was over and began gathering their belongings, reluctantly preparing to leave, many also taking with them everything they had experienced, an indelible memory. They'd been branded for life with a new inspiration.

Eager to enjoy more personal connections with her admirers, particularly those who had come long distances to hear her, Shauna made her way down the ramp as quickly as she could to greet those who were closest. Some of the other performers followed her, while others packed up or headed backstage. Gifford, a very important question rattling around in his brain, was uncharacteristically nervous in spite of this experience with Shauna - in fact, because of this experience with Shauna. And the more he tried to shake off the nervousness the more nervous he became. *What was that about attracting what you focus on the most?* He started towards her, zigzagging through the thinning crowd, arriving behind her as she was deep in conversation with a fan. Pausing, his forehead glistening with a thin film of moisture, he realized just how important she had become to him in such a short time. *Damn nerves!* He thought, feeling like a teenager about to ask for a first date, his anxiety apparent. *What the hell is happening to me?* For the first time he felt someone else's wellbeing more important than his own self-centeredness. Becoming aware that he'd been digging his fingernails deep into his palms, he quickly opened his fists - just in time.

Shauna turned to face him, having felt his approach. One look and she could feel his turmoil. Only inches apart their body heat leapt the gap and she flashed him a bright smile, reaching up and kissing him quickly on the lips as a group of enthusiastic admirers closed in. Gifford took her hand and Shauna excused herself as he piloted her away from the crowd. "I am feeling kind of crazy with a whirlwind of pleasure you seem to have me bewitched and yet I feel you so pure of heart and delectable and your singing took me to places I've never been before if you know what I mean I just want to be with you." He could hardly recognize himself speaking. "I want you to come home with me. I hear it's raining heavily and I have a driver and limo out front, curb-side . . . I really would love for you to come." Touched by the vulnerability in his last admission, fully aware of the perspiration claiming his forehead and his nervous fidgeting as the words had gushed out, she considered her reply.

Not entirely surprised by the invitation, he wasn't the first to have asked, she was at first concerned by her response. She'd never accepted such an invitation before nor even been tempted, yet here she was not just contemplating the possibility, but actively relieved to have been asked. She knew to go with her gut feeling not with what her mind might tell her, just as she had when she'd first approached him - to not be led by what things might look like or her past experience, but by what she really felt. Gifford could barely endure the wait.

Finally, she said: "I feel I can trust you. I sensed how different you are when I first felt your presence. But I've never done anything like this before. I mean . . . I do desire to experience you closer; to feel everything; to move through whatever we may face . . . and I am feeling we'll be together in some way because we already have an intimacy unlike anything I've ever experienced . . . So . . . yes, I would love to come home with you."

A joyful Gifford scooped her up and twirled her around before gently setting her down again on her peacock stilettos. Shauna continued. "Before we go though, I want to visit with a few more people and speak with my assistant. Then I'll get my purse and we can leave. I'll be as quick as I can." And she disappeared into the throng of people lingering around the edge of the stage.

Waiting, Gifford watched as Shauna's audience made their way out and the club was transformed for the after-performance dance and drink crowd.

His impatience was morphing to anxiety when the sight of Shauna coming towards him diffused his tension. Still in her performance gown but with a large purse slung over one shoulder, she looked flustered from attending to business but oozed sex from every pore. *Her luminous smile would heat up Antarctica,* thought Gifford, becoming throbbingly hard as he thought of being alone with this, dare he be so cliché, 'Sex Goddess'. He'd spent his time waiting, fantasizing about later while wondering just what he'd let himself in for. Now, seeing her, almost literally in the flesh, his fantasies and doubts both vaporized in a flash.

"Let's get out of here," they said in unison, laughing, appreciating another cliché. Hand in hand they headed for the front entrance, Gifford slowing to keep pace with her. Neither of them had any idea what their coming together had set in motion.

CHAPTER 2   HOME

When Gifford and Shauna reached the main entrance the front doors were wide open revealing chaos outside. People were milling about peering through the pouring rain while waiting for their cars, and those already driving were in gridlock, wipers slapping, trying to maneuver and be on their way.

That the valet parking service was understaffed and dysfunctional wasn't helping. Nor was the fact that many were in a semi-daze. Coming from such a sweet, powerful experience - like heaven on earth for some – to once again face the cold, wet reality of everyday existence that offered a menu of anxieties. *How many,* Shauna wondered, *would remember tonight's performance and in the night upon waking from a dark dream feel the craving for a higher life she knew her performance had evoked?*

A stocky guy with a powerful build alighted from a black stretch limousine parked curbside to the right of the entrance canopy. He looked to be in his thirties, perhaps a little over six feet, with a military bearing, a short haircut, and a clean shaven, average-looking face. He made a quick dash for shelter near Gifford. "I got here almost an hour ago anticipating this mad tangle. After I get you in, I'll signal the officer handling this mess to help get us out of here." Gifford thanked him and introduced Shauna. "Troy, this is Shauna." *What a looker!* Thought Troy. Then Gifford continued. "Troy's been with me since forever. He's my driver, bodyguard and handyman." Shauna could sense Troy was devoted to Gifford but wondered why Gifford needed a bodyguard.

After a whispered exchange with Troy who opened the large umbrella he'd brought with him, Gifford asked Shauna to hang on, and quickly went to the car, Troy sheltering him on the way and helping him into the back seat. Returning to escort Shauna, Troy got his umbrella tangled under the entrance canopy and lost his cool as he fought to straighten it right way out. Seeing the fiasco, Gifford immediately sprang out of the limousine, totally focused on helping Shauna and before she knew it he had scooped her up and with giant strides had reached the limo. Setting her down on the sidewalk so he could climb into the car and pull her in beside him, he realized what he had done. "Oh shit! What the hell?" he blurted as he noticed the water swirling around her ankles. *Bye, bye specially made stilettos,* thought Shauna. "So sorry, Babe. I'll make it up to you." he said, flustered. "Not to worry, my pet," she said, briefly laying a hand on his hot cheek.

Having untangled the now broken umbrella, Troy was holding its leaking cover over both his charges as Gifford turned to ease backward into the rear seat while at the same time pulling a compliant Shauna and her unyielding gown with him. To speed up the process, Troy used his free hand to grab Shauna around her legs and lift her horizontal to feed her into the car. So Gifford pulled and Troy pushed as a not exactly dry Shauna, completely at the mercy of these two chivalrous, good intentioned, but surprisingly fumbling incompetents, entered the limo head and breasts first. A perfect plan, expertly executed?

Having provided Gifford with a face full of breasts as she entered, Shauna, once seated, bent to take off her soggy, ruined shoes. Though she was acutely aware of giving him another eyeful she didn't want wet shoes rubbing against her feet. *What the heck! He'll see much more of me tonight!* Off came her shoes as her spectacular body was once again exposed to his ravenous eyes

As Shauna and Gifford turned up the heat, Troy eased the limousine away from the curb and, catching his police friend's eye, prepared to inch his way free of the chaos.

Gifford was focused on settling Shauna beside him while touting a rock-hard erection. Once settled he hesitated for the briefest moment before reaching for Shauna's hand and gently placing it over his hardness. Shauna tilted her head to fix him with her intense green eyes, aware of his increasing arousal as she did so. Her eyes plumbed his depths while she gently rubbed him through his pants, surrendering to her own lust. Pussy lips inflamed, clit engorged, pelvis gyrating, her arousal ripped through her body. "Oh, Baby, what a sensual power you're awakening in me," she simmered. *I'm so inexperienced except when it comes to knowing how to please myself. If only I could rely fully on my instincts and intuition. What have I gotten myself into so deeply - and willingly? Right now I'm jumping off a steep cliff with no landing in sight.* She was exposing a side of herself she rarely displayed and shyly averted her gaze. "What is it, Love?" inquired a surprisingly tuned in Gifford. "Nothing!" Shauna flushed as the empty word slipped out.

Unlike Gifford, she had never experienced such a rapid, all-embracing sexual response before. She'd never realized she was capable of such an erotic uprising. She zeroed in on Gifford's top lip. So close. His breath on her face intoxicating. His unique aroma disorienting. She inhaled deeply as she gently guided the tip of her tongue to the 'prow' of his upper lip. Unable to suppress a groan from deep within, she felt a spine-tingling charge flow between them, as if a long-broken circuit had finally been reconnected. *How could such a simple, delicate touch inspire such feeling?*

Gifford remained transfixed, allowing her to follow her fancy in hot anticipation of what she'd do next. Shauna took her time, slipping her tongue into Gifford's mouth, exploring tenderly the delicious, moist, intriguing hollows and swells. Gifford could not restrain himself. He tightly embraced her, pressing into her and began to ravage her mouth with his tongue, teeth and lips. Her desire soared as her writhing groin sought more and more of him. Shauna was desperately rubbing her sex against him, seeking his inflamed erection, preparing for orgasm. She felt her sex-juice soaking clear through her panties.

She began to struggle for breath. She couldn't. It was difficult to pull back from him, he was so strong. She thought she would faint, but Gifford got the message. She inhaled deeply as he relaxed his embrace. Tears sprang to his eyes as he realized what he'd done and he bowed his head to hide them in her lap. She caressed him whispering, "I like a man who can cry," and eased them into a more comfortable position. "No harm done," she added, "but for future reference: I refuse to be loved to death." And she laughed gently. "You know, Mr. Gifford Jefferson, I feel I'm already addicted to you. But let's cool down and enjoy the ride home, shall we?" and she shushed him with a finger to his lips. They both gradually settled down, sitting in a comfortable silence, neither of them feeling either guilty or repentant.

Appraising the limousine's interior, Shauna decided she liked the masculinity. Glossy, black with silver trim, tinted windows and the smell of leather. A mirror-backed bar area split a long, leather seat on the left. To the right, two short, white, terry cloth robes hung above the seat just beyond the door she'd been manhandled through. *Nothing like being prepared for a rainy night,* she mused, listening to the rain on the limo roof and squeezing even closer into Gifford's warm body.

Waking to Gifford asking if she'd like a drink, unaware how long she'd been dozing, she thought a moment. "Do you have Baileys? If so, I'd like mine plain, thank you." *Highly unlikely,* she thought as he rummaged in the bar. "Voila! Behold! A bottle of Baileys!" he exclaimed enthusiastically. Shauna smiled, *Kind of like pulling a rabbit out of a hat.* Pulling out two crystal glasses he poured Baileys in both. *Another surprise*, thought Shauna. She let the thick sweet liquid slide down and warm her inside, giving her a slight buzz and pulled Gifford closer. Tilting her head to reach his lips, she arched her back, unthinkingly lifting her breasts.

Fumbling her glass to the floor she once again reached for his upper lip and sucked on it. Her breasts pressed into him as she made love to the lip that so fascinated her. She grabbed and sucked, searching with her tongue, expertly caressing the object of her latest obsession. Switching her attention to Gifford's lower lip she began to squirm with the need for sexual release. Feeling Gifford's crotch begin to stir again, his cock growing even larger, hardening and jerking within the confines of his pants, she released his lip. He was moaning a short breathy staccato beat, turning her on to the point where *OH MY GOD! Here we go AGAIN?* And she wet herself once more. She knew her panties wouldn't absorb it this time - and she'd so not wanted her dress to join the sorry shoes. Already beyond being surprised by her fast sexual release, Shauna suspected she'd be reaching climax in no time at all. Their sexual journey seemed to have started in overdrive and quickly become turbo-charged.

Gifford unearthed his head from where he'd buried it between her flawless breasts under a drape of long black hair. "I hate to suggest this, Shauna, but I don't want our first time to be just a 'quickie' in the car. We're very close to arriving home anyway so can we wait?" *Gifford, dear Gifford.* The hot proximity of Shauna's lust was burning his skin and melting his resolve. *Shauna Oh Shauna!* But she was on a train that had already left the station and was roaring and howling down the tracks. Where . . . were . . . her . . . brakes? SCREEEEEEEEEEEEEEEEEEEEEEEEEEEEEC H! She almost heard the sound in her ears and wanted to cover them as she went speeding on her way to a throbbing, all-consuming climax.

Cooling down with thoughts of being submerged in a tub filled with ice cubes, Shauna was relatively composed when Troy lowered the privacy panel and she could see a massive, block wall of chiseled white stone through the windshield. *Signaling 'home', no doubt.*

The car was idling in front of a pair of huge black wrought iron gates that were slowly opening inward. Wrought iron carriage lamps to either side illuminated part of the property through the light drizzle, a lingering residue of the earlier downpour. To the left the wall dipped down to a small gate and then seemed to go on forever. To the right she could see an end where it

13

probably angled back around the property. This was no humble home. This was an opulent estate.

The car passed between the gates onto a driveway of white gravel, the floodlit front of the house clearly visible as they approached. The right side, adjacent to the driveway, must have been at least three stories high, the left side, perhaps two stories and the center section, one. Facades of geometric patterns decorated the different levels and a few sections that cantilevered out. *A la Frank Lloyd Wright*, thought Shauna. A huge rectangular porte-cochère, supported by equally proportioned white marble columns, protected an impressive main entrance. Several wide, shallow white marble steps led up to massive black double doors featuring stained glass inserts. The all-white exterior was saved from its starkness by the judicious use of well-chosen plantings. Arranged artistically to soften the geometry of the architecture, they were lit by their own discrete uplighters that emphasized the elegance and modernity while bringing out the cacophony of colors in the flowers. *Someone has a green thumb,* thought Shauna. *I wonder if it's Troy.*

The limo slowly bumped onto a wide cement pad and stopped at a side entrance of large, white, double doors. Shauna could see that the cement extended maybe another eighty feet before it reached a large garage building. Troy got out of the limo and walked back to ceremoniously open the door for Gifford and Shauna. *He looks cute,* thought Shauna. As Shauna swiveled her legs towards the door, Troy took her hand and helped her out. Gifford scooted after her, uncramping himself as he did so, unwinding to his full height, and lifting Shauna into his arms with one sweeping, sure movement. Gifford could feel Shauna's dress where she had wet herself. A smuggled smile tweaked his lips - for his mirth only. He carried her through the entrance doors onto a wide balcony just inside. A gasp and a "WOW!" involuntarily escaped Shauna as she surveyed the seemingly endless living space.

She was poised above a magnificent foyer of black and white. It was void of knick-knacks and any clutter. *Whoever has to clean probably thanks their lucky stars.* It had the vibe of a single man, divorced or a bachelor. *Most likely the former,* she speculated.

Troy left to take care of the limo, closing the entrance doors behind him. Gifford gently swung Shauna from side to side so she could more fully assimilate the grandeur of his home. Shauna however was immediately captivated by the breathtaking chandelier. Suspended maybe thirty feet above the foyer floor, it was more or less at her eye level as she lay in Gifford's arms.

The spectacular mixed bag of intertwined shapes and colors, that must have been close to eight feet high and almost as much around, immediately identified it as the work of Dale Chihuly, the famous one-eyed glass blower. It was breathtaking and Shauna immediately asked Gifford to turn it on. He did. She excitedly declared it to be a sight far better than the giant Christmas tree they displayed in New York. The whole foyer area had come alive. The light made the glass clusters dance and pirouette, blink and dazzle, in, around, on, above, below themselves. It was as if this creation of Chihuly's had taken on a life of its own and was performing for their enjoyment.

Gifford, struck by Shauna's reaction - it was infectious - told himself that he needed to cherish more what he had, to not be so numb, to not take things for granted. How many times had he walked through the foyer and not noticed, had not stopped to be charged by the beauty and inspiration – or to be refreshed?

Shauna indicated to Gifford that she'd like them to descend the gently curving, staircase of polished white marble, which led to the enormous, spectacular, minimalist-designed, circular foyer below. Set in the curved wall at the foot of the stairs they were descending were two doors, *presumably a closet and a powder room*, thought Shauna. Then came the black entrance doors she'd seen from outside. Beyond those, an enormous white, marble-topped table was set against the wall that curved round to a sister staircase to the one they were on. This ascended to the living area across from and one flight up from where they'd entered. On the table by the entrance sat an elegant, dark gray, soapstone sculpture-vase containing a tall arrangement of bird-of-paradise flowers. "Look at me. Look at me" they seemed to shout: just because they were neither black nor white.

Shauna asked Gifford to set her down on the foyer floor where her eye had been attracted by a circle of polished black granite chips with iridescent blue flecks set in the middle of the white marble. Extending her foot, testing the slick, coolness of the polished marble - it felt so good - she walked slowly out to the black granite circle and caressed it with her toes. Gifford watched her adoringly. He was enraptured by her presence. Shauna began swaying, perhaps inspired by the chandelier above. Moving to an inner sound of pure pleasure she abandoned herself to another kind of time and zone - a time away from ticking clocks and scheduled agendas, where a moment of sexual ecstasy can feel like almost forever.

Gifford could feel the inner energy of Shauna moving within him, just as he had earlier. Unbelievable! He wanted to join her but the moment's hesitation was all it took to stifle his will and he remained rooted to the spot until his intrusive self-consciousness and self-doubt subsided. He suddenly intuited something very important about Shauna. She not only had a healthy self-confidence, but more vital, and the key, he saw, to unleashing an unlimited whole body sexual ecstasy over and over, was that she totally loved and treasured herself first. She felt herself whole and pure. Not perfect. Pure. *Yes. Pure.* Gifford determined right then to release anything that had ever kept him suppressed, to give himself, with Shauna's help, to a complete unlimited intimacy - first with himself, and then with her. *Fuck it. Of course!* And right now he wanted to be everywhere she was as she now played with herself.

She had slipped her hands beneath her gown and was stroking her breasts, caressing and tweaking her nipples until Gifford could see them standing proud. He wanted to suck them. She tilted her head back, sliding one hand to her throat and neck and the other over her pubis, pressing as hard as she could, her pelvis in constant motion. Gifford wanted to do the pressing so much his groin was bursting. Shauna began groaning from deep in her throat, becoming louder and louder until the sound echoed around the vast chamber. Her breathing became more rapid and raspy. Her circulation flowed faster. Her nervous system caught fire. She continued her dance of ecstasy, running her tongue over her upper lip, totally focused on her own pleasure, happy, happy, happy. No one could steal happy away from her, except herself.

Eventually emerging from her trance-like state, she headed for the stairs up to the living room. She felt like a queen climbing the long, elegant, gently curving staircase. Gifford followed in hot pursuit, experiencing a rapidly increasing, barely controllable lust. All he'd been thinking of since she'd taken off on her abandoned flight-of-foyer fancy was stuffing his cock into her – repeatedly, uncompromisingly! His untamed, animal instincts were raging, almost unchecked. He wanted to take Shauna to a place of erotic bliss where she could not contain herself or ever again experience such sexual excitement without him. *Man, I need to cool it*, he cautioned himself.

At the top of the stairs, a vast living room spread out to the left encompassing what seemed like dozens of entertaining areas. What a sight. At least twenty feet high, it was a geometric delight furnished in black and white and shades of grey - *So many lovely places for making out*, thought Shauna. But it was three graceful lamps that really caught her eye. They had small circular bases from which sprang arrays of slender tubes that soared elegantly towards the tall ceiling in different directions, bowing over the room, hovering above the seating areas. Each tubular stem ended with a tiny halogen light. Shauna asked if they were custom made. Replying that he didn't know, they had come with the house, he thought: *Yet another example of what I don't value and just take for granted in my own home.* Shauna explained that she had studied architecture and design while in college and loved discovering the new. Brightening each time he heard her Scottish tinged English and the different way she pronounced certain words, Gifford realized it helped him get back on track, to actually be one hundred percent present with her in the moment. *So much for sexual fantasies filled with conquest,* mulled Gifford inwardly.

Three enormous floor-to-ceiling glass panels spanning the whole of the curved far wall snagged Shauna's attention and she made her way over to look out. She could see few details in the darkness. An 'L' shaped pool stretched along the deck with a fountain at the far end, a scattering of white, wrought iron, glass-topped tables and matching padded chairs, and a large barbeque and bar area with a terrace beyond Shauna smiled affectionately at her tour guide, imagining the parties that undoubtedly took place in this 'bachelor' setting. *It looks like it could accommodate at least two basketball teams plus wives and playmates.*

Gifford, drawn to her, cupped her chin, tilted her head back and kissed her ravenously. "You're like an adorable little kid," he breathed, as his heavy-lidded, lust-filled eyes looked down at her approvingly. Turning away from the storm raging outside, well aware of the tempest raging beside her, Shauna gazed back over the living room, taking in the formal dining area now on her right. It featured an enormous teak table with easily twenty white chairs tucked around it in front of a wall with an archway that Gifford explained accessed stairs that led down to the kitchen and up to five bedroom suites.

Her curiosity peeked Shauna asked if anyone else shared his home. Sighing, slightly frustrated, Gifford explained that Troy stayed in one of the upstairs suites and Garcia, his Mexican-American housekeeper, in another, the three others being used for guests. He then asked if she'd like anything before he sent the chef home. When she said no, he used the house intercom to thank the chef, Mark, for waiting and released him for what was left of the night.

Gifford, now the picture of patience, explained how Mark was his seventh chef in five years. "He always seems so dedicated, both to his work and to me, but there's something I can't quite put my finger on. Nothing he's done or said, just a feeling. I mean, he always makes sure to only serve fresh, organic foods so I can perform at my best, insisting on buying the food himself." Thumping his well-muscled chest and giving Shauna a wink, he finished with a grin. "He knows how vital I am to the team," Her peals of laughter hid her desire to rip off his shirt and go flesh exploring. Noticing her gazing intently towards the archway again he added that he'd give her the full tour in the morning.

A little disappointed, but understanding, Shauna, still not quite ready to leave this stark opulence turned her attention in the other direction where a wide marble staircase with a polished teak handrail led upward beside a huge fireplace that dominated that end of the room. She strolled across to take a closer look, leaving Gifford to readjust his bulging crotch.

Three five foot square glass panels framed with thin strips of titanium protected the fire bed and gave the impression they were floating in space. The hearth, faced with polished white marble tiles, grouted black, contrasted with the mantle above, which rose at least another five feet and was faced in polished black granite tiles, grouted white. Stood on top of the mantle were three, impressively large, modern African sculptures - two naked women and one naked man, hand chiseled out of dark colored stone. Aware of Gifford excitedly edging his way towards the staircase, she assumed it led to the master suite where she would soon launch her maiden voyage with him. Impishly patting a glass panel, Shauna commented, "This fireplace is monolithic. I'll bet when you fire this monster up it will fail every deodorant test!" And there was Shauna's infectious laughter again.

What am I going to do with her? At this rate will I ever find out what it's like to be with her? Gifford couldn't help but smile though, flashing his perfect set of sparkling white teeth - not unnoticed. *One minute I want to pounce on her and unmercifully ravage her, inside and out. To fuck her till she screams for me to stop. I want to own her, to possess her, to eat her up. And then into the mix comes a desire to softly yield. To please her. To lead her through an intimate, tender exploration until she erupts uncontrollably! I go from one extreme to the other. The fucking teeter-tooter is driving me crazy. She's got me stirred and confused and completely conflicted . . . Must be why I go for one night stands - fuck'em and leave'em.?*

And then she melted. Closing the short distance between them she rushed into his embrace, plowing her body into his while raining kisses all over his chest. He was stoked like a furnace and Shauna felt her own heat rising to his hardness. This promised to be a far more intense experience than either of them would have imagined. Gifford gently lifted her as she wrapped her arms around his neck. He quickly ascended the stairs to the master, expertly negotiating two stairs at a time, while a wide-eyed Shauna had the brief ride of her life, firmly clutching fast to a wild, sexually-charged, stallion.

CHAPTER 3 THE FIRST TIME

At the top of the staircase Gifford, hands full, paused to allow Shauna to open the double doors to the master suite. While both of them were simmering with anticipation and all Gifford really wanted to do right then was to meld Shauna's body with his, he paused again. Hesitant with indecision he tenderly lowered her to the floor. Her bare feet disappeared in the thickly textured, cream carpet that covered the immense lounge leading to the bedroom ahead.

Shauna impulsively moved towards the open doors opposite to get a look at the bedroom proper, arriving just as a short, roly-poly woman hustled from the room, peeking over a large bundle of white satin sheets tucked under her chin so she could see where she was going and supported by hands carrying several spray bottles of cleaning liquids. Both women were startled by their sudden near collision which, for Garcia, irritatingly interrupted the almost hypnotic reverie she'd fallen into, as she so often did when working alone. Garcia quickly composed herself, greeted the unexpected Shauna and proceeded across the lounge and down the stairs, acknowledging Gifford with a curt nod as she passed him. Gifford explained to a flustered Shauna that he had called Garcia from the club and asked her to clean the master suite and change the linens. "It's not the first time I've interrupted her sleep and so far she seems to be OK with it. I don't do it that often and she says she's able to get back to sleep pretty fast." Shauna had no desire to know how many women Gifford had feathered his nest with but he went on. "She insists on being called Garcia, and besides keeping the place clean and tidy, doing the laundry and taking care of household shopping with Troy, she trims my face and head," and he flushed. "Having married at an early age and raised eight children, she relishes having her own space but insists on taking care of me. I know she's overly protective and sentimental, but she has a huge heart, and she gives relentlessly of herself. She really is a treasure and I think you'll love her when you get to know her."

Distracted by the encounter, listening to Gifford, Shauna turned to scope out the lounge. To her left, a large refrigerator, disguised as an armoire, stood beside the open bedroom doors. To her right stretched a huge window wall that echoed the one in the living area below. In contrast to the geometric sharpness of the rest of the house, the lounge was cozy and warm. An eight-seat sofa, fronted by a large, glass coffee table, dominated the space with its size and plumpness. Surrounding the sofa were equally large chairs and several loungers, each one beckoning a 'try out'. A scattering of end tables and table lamps completed the arrangement.

Gifford walked to the window wall and slid open one of the glass panels so they could hear the rain and feel the now refreshingly-cool, moisture-laden air of the subsiding storm. He turned on the outside lights. Shauna was instantly drawn to the spectacular view - soft recessed lighting on both sides of the glass panels illuminated another huge deck with a lap pool glowing with underwater lighting. Quickly joining Gifford, she marveled at how this second deck was apparently suspended over the one below, balanced she knew not how. Shauna was immediately consumed with questions, eager to know how such a majestic architectural feat had been achieved.

Gifford wrapped his arms around her shoulders, gently pulling her against him and slowly sliding his hands under her gown he fondled her breasts. Feeling his intense heat fueling her own, Shauna let out a soft whimper as Gifford, keeping his emotionally husky voice under control, explained a couple of features of the pool - anything to prolong this tactile exploration. Her short staccato rasps indicated he was having the desired effect. Totally absorbed in their mounting sensations, they continued their pool gazing; giving to prolonging the delicious foreplay. Shauna was fixating on the feel of Gifford's tremendous erection pressing into her butt, especially when she slyly pushed back, trying not to be too obvious.

Extinguishing the exterior lights, Gifford led Shauna back toward the dimly illuminated master bedroom. Just two small ceiling lights cast soft shadows throughout the massive room. A deep penetrating hush seemed to suffuse the whole environment, embracing the two lovers. Gifford held Shauna close, one hand cupping her ass, the other resting between her shoulder blades. He whispered. "I want us to make limitations intolerable so that nothing will ever suppress anything we feel for ourselves, each other, or our sexual pleasure together. I want everything with you . . . to inspire you as you do me. To pour into you as I feel you pouring yourself into me . . . I feel as if your being here has answered a call I didn't even know I was making . . . I feel lustful, yet gentle. That I can become the person that I'd forgotten I used to dream of being?"

"Oh, yes!" replied Shauna. "I adore how you're so open and in-tune. For the longest time, I have longed for a different kind of intimacy without having any real idea of what I was calling for. And now, here you are, exceeding every desire I've ever imagined . . . Whatever transpires I feel we are exactly what we each need to create an unlimited oneness. We have everything we need to have everything we want. And, Baby . . . you're so bloody sexy!" Radiating at full power she added huskily, "Let's find out what's a Wow and what's a whimper."

Taking her at her word, he found the tag to her gown's zipper hidden under her left armpit and slowly - ever so slowly – pulled. Turning her to face him he took both gown straps in his deft hands and gently slid them over her shoulders until, suddenly and unexpectedly, gravity took over and the inevitable occurred.

The gown plummeted to the floor around Shauna's feet and she was left standing naked except for a red thong. Both were a little startled by this almost instant disrobing. Gifford's mouth opened and his eyes flitted across her entire body, finally settling on her large breasts with nipples encircled by an unusual color blend of brass and pink. As Gifford stared in fascination, her nipples began to harden, enlarge and stand erect. For a moment Shauna felt self-conscious at being so quickly exposed with her nipples giving away her desire to fuck hard and fast.

Shauna's blazing eyes watched as he then shed his clothes too. Huge powerful shoulders with an array of small tattoos, a broad chest, impressively tight abs and small waist, the suggestions of a wonderful ass, large muscular thighs and a glorious hard on that finally came into view as he dropped his shorts.

Naked, he returned his gaze to her. Perfect breasts, narrow waist, smooth hips, thighs, ass and pubis and long elegant shapely legs tapering to delicate ankles and beautiful feet had him mesmerized. As they appraised each other, Shauna's pussy, throbbing with the need to be filled, was sending waves of heat seeking to draw him closer. Gifford licked his lips, a little dry-mouthed and a little wolfish, and Shauna reddened before he said, "You are truly magnificent. Your beauty, your body, your talent. But it's what I have felt from you and within myself these last few hours that I cherish the most. A freshness, a different joy, a different intimacy. Your remarkable power and inspiration for change. You are a phenomenal person and I'm sorry your unveiling was so abrupt. It wasn't my intention."

Reassured, it was just what she'd needed to hear - to feel vulnerable yet safe - she suddenly began to shiver and automatically wrapped her arms about her, hiding her breasts from Gifford's insatiable eyes. "Are you cold?" he asked with concern.

Replying shakily, "I'm . . . I'm . . . All . . . right," she unfolded her arms and placed her hands on his chest before moving to trace a couple of his shoulder tattoos with a finger. Her touch made him ache for more. "It's just that for a moment I had some foolish doubts arise. I haven't had much experience and I started to question whether I would meet your expectations."

"Oh, Love. No matter what happens, you couldn't possibly disappoint me. What I have with you now is more than I ever expected, anything else will just be icing on the cake." And he gathered her in his eager arms to carry her to the bed.

Roughly ten feet square with a white headboard and white satin bedding it was a fitting stage for what was to come. Spreading her out full length he lay on his back alongside her, both radiating intensely, a slick film of moisture covering their skin, glistening under the soft glow of the low-key lighting. Shauna turned on her side. Looking at him intently she said, "Just so you know, I've only had three partners - all clean, conservative and totally wooden in bed and I made sure I was tested after each one, so you're safe." Although he'd never had a woman be so forthright before, he wasn't surprised that she would be. Although he had to admit it hadn't been top-of-mind for him. "Well, I've been with more than three women. But I do have standards and I always use condoms, much as I detest them. I'm also checked every month as part the team's health program so you're safe too." "I hate condoms!" she exclaimed with a passion. "Just the way they feel in me. That's one of the reasons I'm on the pill. I want the real thing - slippery, juicy, friction-free sex." And she reached for his erection to gently spread the copious pre-cum over the head, marveling at how smooth and responsive it was.

As she caressed the sensitive ridge, he arched his back and sucked in a huge breath, his member becoming even bigger and darker, arousing them both even more. Wrapping her fingers around the shaft, she slowly began to stroke it. Moving to sit on her haunches, she took the large, sensitive head into her anxious-to-be-filled mouth. Inspired by her scorching need her tongue knew exactly what to do, driving him to crave the release of ramming inside her.

Sweating profusely, hips pumping wildly, balls swelling tight with mad expectation, he begged, "Shauna. Please. Stop! . . Let me . . . be the one . . .

to give pleasure tonight. I want everything with you . . . to be different, to be . . . the giver for once. I've always been the taker, you know . . . getting what I wanted and then turning my back . . . to fall asleep." Eyes glazed over, he struggled to spit out the words as Shauna held him in her mouth.

Slowly she slid him out and moved to take him in her hands. Gently grasping her wrists, careful not to hurt her, he stopped her. "I want to put into practice what you have been showing me about us: that we are one. When I stimulate you to orgasm I'll be right there with you. Neither of us knows what's in store because this is all new to us, but I know it will be more of everything than either one of us has ever experienced." And he grasped his loaded, straining testicles to head off an immediate orgasm. The intense sensations surging throughout his body were making him light-headed and blurring his vision. Lust laden he lay on his side stroking her skin, taking the time to come off the boil, his prick twitching and swaying as he cooled down, driving Shauna wild, desperate to have him inside her.

"Lay back, my Precious, and let me find the wild, raw you within. Direct me if I need it. Lead me to what heightens your pleasure. Tell me when you're close so I can join you." Crying at his tenderness, she blurted, "Baby, I'm so fucking close right now and feel you're that way too, SO FUCK ME NOW!"

But he hadn't even started. Holding her gaze he stroked her mound and gradually slid off her thong as she frantically bucked, stoking the fires raging in them both. He was already pouring with sweat as if he'd been playing ball for an hour.

As her swollen sex came into view, neatly trimmed, close-cropped, dark bushy curls hiding the heart, he broke eye contact, feeling the urge to lick, suck and probe. To open her tightness, stretch her ready for him. His cock jerked at the thought. Upper thighs throbbing she humped the air and spread her legs, wordlessly begging for penetration.

True to his word though, he continued to stroke, lightly fondling the tender skin of her outer lips, enjoying the feel as she arched her spine and thrust out her breasts, her darkening nipples straining to be nuzzled, nursed, caressed and, oh so gently, nibbled. Licking her lips, breathing heavily, Shauna was on the brink already. *Perhaps I'm better than I thought.* But then, he was ready to explode too!

Resisting the urge to give in and plunge deep and pump her full, he kept her humming forward, tenderly stroking around her pussy, repeatedly teasing her pubic hair and inner lips, lightly touching the scalding flesh, driving her crazy for some sort of release. Ready for both penetration and orgasm,

Shauna was writhing and groaning uncontrollably, zoned out, closing in on an ecstasy beyond her experience, and close to taking Gifford with her.

"I'm going to open your sex to get you ready." "Yes!" she almost screamed, and gasping for breath every few words continued, "Your . . . beautiful cock . . . is so long, it will be . . . knocking on the door . . . to my womb . . . Just take it slow . . . be patient . . . as I . . . stretch to . . . take you fully." "Maybe if I don't thrust hard or penetrate deeply," suggested Gifford. But Shauna was insistent, "NO, no, no . . . we're to have . . . the full-out, unlimited pleasure we want . . . no compromises . . . no holding back."

Both were so close to climax: heat soaring, hearts pounding, sweat pouring. Channeling his lust he finally covered her body with his, spreading her legs even wider and nudging his erection against her pussy. Immediately her body shuddered and her eyes lost focus at the feeling of his cockhead, impatient to feel him inside her. But he held off, instead lustfully suckling her mouth, pressing his tongue tip between her lips before thrusting it full length and ravaging her with an unleashed passion.

When she gagged and coughed he drew back, wiped the sweat from her face, apologizing silently and returned his attention to her pussy. Teasing her entrance with deft fingers he refocused her toward a pulsing orgasm. Her churning vagina had sapped her will, undermining her desire to wait for him as the ecstasy raged through her body echoed by the incoherent jumble of sounds pouring from her mouth.

Her frenzied climb to climax was testing him to the limit. She was ripe. Her lips swollen huge and her exposed clit projected large. He swirled two fingers just inside her and then slowly introduced a third that became swallowed. Unable to hold back, she clamped her legs around his waist, forcing his fingers deeper and frantically huffed, "I . . . have . . . to . . . cum."

"Yes, Love, Cum, Explode." And he massaged her clit while pushing his fingers even further into her convulsing sex. Within seconds he could hear her fingernails clawing the sheets as she let loose a torrent that swirled around his fingers before pouring onto the bed. Miraculously his own load was still intact and, lifting his erection, he whispered, "See what's in store for you next?"

He eased aside the damp hair plastering her face and with a sure hand gently pulled on a nipple, fascinated by how long it would stretch. A still smoldering Shauna let out a slow, low groan as she sluggishly released her legs from his waist and went limp. At full arousal he teased first one breast and then the other, leaning over a sated Shauna ready for signs he could start again. He sucked on a nipple, swirling his tongue around and around then gently catching it between his teeth and pulling. Adjusting his balls which were demanding relief, he repositioned a reviving Shauna.

Lifting her legs, one over each shoulder, he lowered his head and burrowed his tongue through her silken hairs to lick her erect red cherry. Groaning and humping his face, she surged towards another orgasm. Speaking so husky and slow he barely recognized her, she growled, "I want you in me this time . . . I have to be fucked by that amazing cock of yours . . . or I'll go fucking crazy!" Raising his head, his mouth and cheeks covered in sex cream, he grinned. "You smell so delicious, Love. I could lick and eat you 24/7." "Just fuck the hell out of me!"

Obliging, he spread her raised legs even further, and placed is rod at her fiery hot, steamy opening. Tenderly nudging it around her opening, meeting her clit with the head, he slowly pushed in, sending pulses of unbearable pleasure buzzing through her. Writhing in abandoned ecstasy as he continued to pierce her she screamed, "NOW! Plunge in now!" And he thrust hard, reaching his limit before slowly backing out: teasing sweet agony, again and again until his whole body coiled for release and she yelled, "Here I come." "Me too!" he gasped, with a last thrust, balls slapping her crotch. Shuddering uncontrollably, they erupted in unprecedented bliss, jetting stream after stream, both soaring on a wave of ecstasy and they fused as one.

The ongoing implosion took them to new heights and created new dimensions as time space bent and folded, coming back on itself, creating a new matrix for creation - pulsating, throbbing - causing distances to close, motion to slow to a near standstill, and time to cease. Unknown worlds loomed large – worlds of pure electricity and life force energy, super-charged, ready-to-be-explored, where human footsteps were as yet unknown, worlds awaiting human fusion. But the fusion of human bodies would remain limited to a sexual ecstasy unless the old ways of stunted intimacy were shattered and a total oneness became the center of the universe.

"What the fuck?" blurted Gifford, shaken and disoriented. "Did you feel that?" "I certainly did," she replied, dazed. Sensing they'd glimpsed a new life in waiting, she was wondering why and how, and what it would take to break through. Or had this been a one-time event?

CHAPTER 4   PREPARATION

Shauna lay sprawled face up on the master bed. After a day of shopping, when they'd put the previous night's phenomena on hold while Gifford bought her almost a whole new wardrobe, she was still trying to get her head around what had happened. They had glimpsed a new vastness. But was it one they had created or one that had been waiting for them to find? No closer to any answers, she stretched, luxuriating in the afterglow of Gifford's lavishing, feeling the first stirrings of her monthly visitor.

Her breasts felt bloated and heavy and she could feel the pressure in her abdomen. Fortunately, it felt like a few days before she'd start bleeding and she was wondering how to broach the subject with Gifford of having sex during her period. Some men liked it, others would avoid it and others kept themselves totally ignorant of the process. She wanted him to enjoy it, just as she always did.

Coming out of the bathroom wearing just a loose pair of basketball shorts he unceremoniously collapsed on the bed beside her, flipping his phone onto the nightstand and laying a leg over her. Gently stroking the side of her face he said, "It's Mark's day off so I've made reservations for eight at the Hyatt. They have a great revolving restaurant with a spectacular view. It's known for its steaks and sea food and I'm hankering after a porterhouse. I'm guessing you might prefer their salmon or lobster. I've only eaten there once but I really liked it, and with you I'm pretty sure I'll love it. They also have a live group so we can get in some dancing too, if we feel like it."

Touched by his sensitivity, his clothing suggestions had been spot on as was his sense of her food preference, she quickly stripped off her tank top and hugged him, naked breasts to bare chest. Pulling off his shorts and throwing his leg back over her, his largeness pressed against her hip. Inching under him she held him close as he rocked back and forth slowly massaging her pussy, stirring an exquisite pulsing that fired their pleasure.

She trusted him. Even with her life, she realized. She would go with him, wherever that might take her. And she saw that same kind of vulnerability in him. But there was more, something new, different and much more powerful, that drew her into him deeper still. It was as if his intensity was so strong, that he was collapsing into himself and drawing her with him into his center to merge together till neither could tell where either started or ended. The deep calling to the deep, and the deep answering! She felt a pressure transforming their bodies that felt familiar, as if they'd been there before and were meant to be that way. In a new and different physical dimension not subject to what had been known or discovered. And somehow the trigger was sexual. She felt excited and fearless about 'going-with-the-flow' of this new adventure.

They made slow and gentle love. Soaring to a pleasure and intensity that melted every physical, biological and psychological boundary, they transformed in a seemingly endless simultaneous orgasm. The generated power spread instantaneously beyond the known and unknown - perhaps beyond existence itself – as, oblivious, they became bodies of pure, electro-magnetic light unleashing an unspeakable joy.

They perceived themselves as a single galaxy within the cosmos, their atoms re-arranged, creating a different dimension from within their own bodies. With no reference points, they were unable to quantify anything. Shauna wished she'd paid more attention to Einstein's theory of relativity, but then, it was only a theory. What they had to go on was their combined intuition and the strong connection between each other - two, yet one. *Were they the first?* She wondered. *Did it matter?* At least she now knew the first time hadn't been a fluke.

Saying, "We can rest for a while before we need to get ready for the evening," he kissed her softly. Twined together, they quickly drifted off to sleep.

Garcia woke them. "Come on sleepy heads. Rise and shine." Groggy with sleep, pulling a sheet over their nakedness, Shauna thanked her and asked for a few minutes. Garcia skipped into the master lounge and they stumbled to the bathroom.

Hastily showering, Gifford, a towel around his waist, moved to the closet. Shauna, a towel around her head, soon followed. Darting into the closet she slipped on her bikini pants, grabbed her outfit and returned to the bathroom. Hanging the clothes on a towel hook she sat ready for Garcia to create magic. Taking her time, Garcia tamed Shauna's hair and applied the barest hint of makeup. "My, Oh my!" exclaimed Shauna having watched the whole process in the mirror. She hurriedly stepped into her dress to complete the picture, which set Garcia clapping with pleasure.

Popping his head out of the closet wondering what the excitement was about, Gifford gaped at the vision before him - Shauna all dolled up and oozing sex. Her hair, sophisticated and alluring, complemented her smoking hot outfit. She was wearing the dress he'd picked out on their earlier shopping extravaganza: short, black, with spaghetti straps that flared to hold her perfect, bra-free breasts and set off by open mesh stockings and patent leather high heels. Breathless at her beauty he lifted her up and twirled her around, kissing every inch of skin he could reach. Prying herself loose, she admired him in return. So cool in a soft yellow turtle neck, tan tweed jacket, brown dress slacks and casually elegant brown leather shoes burnished to an expensive glow. From his neck hung a simple gold necklace that accented the wardrobe and echoed the flecks in his eyes. "Oh, Baby, you look so handsome!" she said and spun around slowly, "And behold your handiwork and generosity!" lifting the dress to show off what was underneath - a radiating sex in sheer black silk.

Ducking back in the closet, he returned with a simple, black, velvet covered box. "You're not quite complete without these." Opening the heavy box, her expression was priceless - a proverbial Kodak moment for anyone who'd been around long enough to know what that meant. Inside lay a platinum necklace, matching earrings and a chunk of platinum bracelet. They were exquisite. He picked up the necklace and placed it around her neck, kissing her nape as he did so. Then threaded the earrings through her lobes and slipped the bracelet on her wrist to complete the ensemble, standing back to admire her perfection. Overwhelmed, Shauna's tears flowed, requiring Garcia to make some final adjustments to her makeup.

Stroking the necklace, loving the feel of the beautifully sculpted metal against her fingertips, she fell into Gifford's ready arms and they embraced for a long time before she kissed him hard on the mouth. "You make a one-in-a-million couple. Go have fun. OK?" blurted an emotional Garcia. "Vamonos," laughed Gifford, adding, "Thanks Garcia. You did great."

Shauna, in a last minute scramble, grabbed her purse and new black jacket and they hastened down to the side entry where the limo was waiting, door open, a smiling Troy ushering them in. "Great evening for an outing," he said, ironically, given the continuing downpour. *Man, do they look great together*, thought Troy. *Thank goodness for the canopy in this weather.* Somehow, the contrast between the rain outside and the limousine's cozy, intimate interior set the tone for the evening to come.

CHAPTER 5   FEAST

They had a quiet, content, and relaxed ride to the Hyatt, basking in the happiness of each other. Fortunately, the hotel had a large sheltered entranceway. No need to fret about the rain. Leaving Troy with the car, they crossed the spacious lobby to the bank of elevators. Shauna braced against Gifford and the elevator wall as they were shot to the top floor where they stepped into an elegant foyer with the glass-walled moving restaurant invitingly beyond. The maître d' greeted them warmly, prepared for their arrival – Washington, two at eight - and promptly led them to a narrow table set end on to the glass wall offering a spectacular panoramic view of Austin and beyond. Shauna was surprised that she had no real sensation of movement as the restaurant rotated - the center of its own universe.

Ignoring the people staring, Shauna was excited and felt a shiver of anticipation sweep across her bare skin. Gifford, like a true gentleman, removed her jacket and seated her. Removing his own jacket, he slid into the chair opposite. Gazing at her, he leant forward and touched her face lightly, whispering a finger across her lips and reviving their arousal. Both of them already hot-wired with their mere proximity.

A parade of waiters, wearing very noticeable white gloves, theatrically attended to their needs: water - ceremoniously poured into high stemmed large crystal goblets; place settings – fussing with the already impeccably neat arrangements; and drinks. Shauna was trying to decide if or what she would like when Gifford suggested a bottle of red wine. She told him she wasn't sure if she could drink more than one glass. Responding that they'd be making an especially long evening of it, he sweetly encouraged her. She acquiesced and after thoughtfully scanning the wine list, he selected a merlot. As Shauna didn't want an appetizer, they left it at that for the moment. Gifford beckoned their head waiter over to advise him that they were celebrating and would like to take their time over each course, beginning with the wine. Nodding in understanding the waiter departed.

Shauna, radiant and bright, leant forward to kiss Gifford on the mouth, repeatedly, each kiss longer than the one before. Becoming progressively more aroused, Shauna squirmed in her seat, her pussy tingling. Gifford sighed and whispered, "My Love, oh my Love, I just look at you and I get hard." "Oh yeah! Sure you do?" she said teasingly. "Hey, you doubt me? Put your hand under the table and check it out." Hearing the sound of a zipper and seeing him subtly shift in his chair Shauna reached under the table as directed, bumping into his hardened appendage. "You sure that's because of me, Baby?" she said, a sly smile on her face. "You better believe it!" keeping his voice down, "the rascal kinda fought his way out of my briefs and though I'm trying to coax him back in to save him from your wanton clutches it appears he'd rather be inside you." But he managed to zip up just in time.

The wine waiter set down the bottle of wine and Gifford went through the opening-pouring-tasting-pouring ritual with him before he left. The two clinked glasses firmly, holding hands while enjoying the first sip. Gifford rolled the wine around in his mouth, appreciating the many layered and full bouquet of this $600 steal – although who was stealing from whom he wasn't quite sure because it tasted phenomenal. Shauna took a small sip and swallowed, savoring the taste and smoothness. She didn't know one wine from another but could tell this glass contained a rare and delectable treat. She sighed. Gifford asked her how she liked the wine. "A perfect introduction to what promises to be an exceptional evening." She took another sip, enjoying it slide down her throat as she tilted her head back.

"You know, since soon after we first met, I've had such a desire to call you 'Chip'. I really have no idea why, it's just something I've been feeling. I mean, it's not that I don't like Gifford, it's just that you feel like a 'Chip' to me." Her green eyes stared into his as she took another sip of wine, making love to the edge of the glass with her tongue - a sensual touch that did not go unnoticed.

"Well Love, you are full of surprises. If you think I'm a 'Chip' I guess I'll get used to it. In fact, I rather like it already."

"So what do you think about what we're experiencing when we make love?" she asked. "We're obviously releasing or touching something previously beyond human imagining - at least as far as I'm aware. It's as if when we make love we access a different part of ourselves, a part that we need each other to get in touch with. And I have a feeling that not just any two people could do it, that maybe this is why I was drawn to you, and why you are responding the way you are, that this is why it's necessary for us to be together." And she stopped, aware that in speaking she had perhaps exposed some of the answer.

"You're awesome . . . The way you just put it out there. Listening to you I can see how what happened makes sense and I'm wondering whether, now that we have a possible explanation, that if we make love with intention, we could direct or magnify the effect."

"I think you might be right but I also suspect that it could make it more elusive. Kind of like when people try to get pregnant they can't. As if making love with a purpose other than enjoying each other changes the chemistry and they can't conceive."

"So? What? You think we should just continue to make love and see what happens?" "You have a problem with that?" she asked with a grin. "No. But now the genie's out of the bottle, I don't know if we'll be able to." "Speak for yourself. When I'm in sexual ecstasy with you I'm not really thinking about anything, I'm just feeling. And that might be the real secret. Not the intention to achieve a result but to feel everything right down to the microscopic. The more we feel, the more we open, the more we let go, the more likely we will soar." "Sounds good to me, Love. Let's dance."

As she nodded an enthusiastic yes, Chip stood, checking his crotch to make sure he was decent. Helping her out of her chair he led her, arm in arm, to the dance floor. Facing each other, a handsome couple in the mix of dancers, but a couple with a difference - exchanging high-frequency pulses, they glowed from inside. Only one other person seemed to sense their difference. In his early fifties, confident and debonair, he was sat at a distant table between two garish young women who, oblivious to anything or anyone else, were fawning over him.

Chip and Shauna came together, melting the space between, he, his hands on the curve of her buttocks, she with her arms around his neck. Almost in a trance, eyes fully engaged, they started a slow sway to the music. Slowly rotating his hardness against her stomach, his balls pressing her mound and setting off her clit, he bent to carefully kiss her exposed cleavage and neck before kissing her lips. What bliss! When the music eventually ended, they made their way back to their table to order their first course and cool down. Or not.

As they were seating themselves, their waiter appeared with menus. At first shocked by the prices, Shauna acquiesced when Chip, sensing her discomfort, suggested she order whatever she wanted; perhaps the lobster *and* the salmon. Taking him at his word, she ordered tomato bisque followed by a house salad with half portions of the lobster and salmon as her main course. Chip chose Borscht followed by a house salad and a medium rare porterhouse.

Chip reminded the waiter that they'd like plenty of time between courses and topped up their wine glasses. Shauna practically drained her water glass in one long swallow. "Wine makes me thirsty," she said. "So does being aroused." She laughed, making Chip grin. "I'll have to keep you plied with water then, my Love."

"I've been meaning to ask you what was going on when I first saw you by yourself in the Sports Bar. You seemed so sad, depressed even . . . and alone. How come?"

"Wow. That seems like another lifetime ago. I already feel like a totally different person." Chip paused, choosing his words carefully. "I divorced a few months ago - something I'd never considered possible until it happened. I loved her but now realize I took her for granted. I treated her almost as an afterthought. In fact I thought of her as rather dull and predictable day after day. To be truthful, I was an asshole. I was married to basketball - my buds, the players, the coach and assistants, the competition, the game itself, the money, the celebrity perks, the endless females 24/7 during the long season - until I'd destroyed anything there'd ever been between us. And there was certainly nothing of value for her to want to hang on to. She ended up with custody of our two kids and I was denied visiting rights. Although I thought that was harsh I can see now why it turned out that way. Having met you I'm glad everything happened the way it did - every bit of it. If I hadn't gotten that wake up it's likely I would never have been open to this change you have caused. To ending the deep sleep, self-pity and small life I had unknowingly been wallowing in. I had no real purpose beyond basketball. I didn't really know anything about how to care for someone or how to really love and receive being loved. I wouldn't be sitting with you right now if you hadn't been who you are and felt me the way you did and taken the risk. Thank you." He leaned over and kissed her.

"You know, Chip, it was your time to wake up. You heard the call and responded. And I am so thankful." She kissed him back, long and pleasurably.

Taking another sip of wine, she asked, "Why do you have a body guard? I mean, it's great that Troy does so many different things for you, and doubtless does them well, and he's obviously devoted to you: but why a body guard?"

"Well. There were a few times when I felt my life was threatened. Nothing concrete, just a strong sense of being followed, stalked even. The cops did some investigating but never came up with anything. I got the feeling at the time that they thought I was just some Prima Dona spoiled SOB. So I remedied the situation in my own way to give myself some peace of mind. The sense of a threat has disappeared but I've gotten used to Troy and what he does for me. And I like him. Anything else you'd like to know, Miss Interrogator?"

"Well, this is very personal, but since we're not going to have secrets, here goes." She took a deep breath and continued. "My best guess is that in one or two days my period will start and will last for about six days. The first two days I usually bleed heavily but then the flow tapers off to nothing till the following month. What I was wondering is whether you would have a problem having sex with me or if you would like to cum in me while I'm having my period?"

Silence. Not uncomfortable. And then. "Well, my love, I've always stayed away from women at that time of the month - even my ex-wife. I don't really know why. Hell, I only have the vaguest idea of what goes on and finding out has never been high on my list of priorities. I guess I'm both ignorant and a coward."

Leaning forward she took his hands in hers, "Baby, there's no need to be hard on yourself. I've never had sex during my period either. But I have a burning desire to feel you inside me when I'm that hypersensitive and so lubricated. For you to feel me and me to feel you, in a whole new way."

"Look, Love, I want to experience everything with you. So, of course I'll be with you in this. I want whatever you want and I don't want to miss out on, or pass up any part of you. But is there anything I should know so we can both have the best together?"

"Thank you. Thank you for being so willing to expand our intimacy." Idly caressing his hands as they held each other across the table, she continued softly. "I'm sure you're aware women experience some pretty drastic changes – mentally, physically and emotionally – but we don't all experience the same changes or to the same degree. Many women hate having periods, others experience depression or lots of cramping, and some consider it a major nuisance. But I've never experienced any of that. I went from being a tom boy in my youth to loving being a female and developing fully. What happens for me is that a few days before I feel my body preparing, like now. I feel bloated and more emotional. Over the next 24 hours I can expect my uterus to start

33

cramping, usually a sign that I'll start flowing soon, and the inner lining of my uterus, with blood and mucus, will begin to discharge. I'll become more sensitive and unbalanced emotionally as my brain is flooded with chemical changes leading to mood swings that can sometimes be wild." Keeping her eyes on Chip, thankful for how engaged he was, she carried on, doing her utmost to share her experiences with him as tenderly as possible. "And then, my love," almost whispering . . . "and then . . . and then." She hesitated. "My breasts, and particularly my nipples, become swollen and very sensitive to touch. My vagina becomes extra sensitive too. The lips, ripe with blood, sometimes feel like they're ready to burst. And right now I can't tell you how turned on I am with you. Really, I can hardly wait to feel you all over me and inside me. There's no place on either of us that can't be aroused." While speaking she'd become increasingly restless and dropped her head knowing she had that tell-tale look in her eyes. Releasing a hand from his she took a sip of wine.

"Are you close to an orgasm?" he asked quietly. "I certainly feel something building in me, a disturbance that's much more than just feeling horny." And he pulled her up and led her toward the men's restroom. Crossing paths with the waiter carrying their soup, Chip said, "We'll be right back." And they carried on.

Entering the restroom he said, "I figure there'll be less chance of being disturbed in here than in the women's." And they crammed into one of the stalls and locked the door. Agreeing not to stimulate each other but to let whatever they were both experiencing to run its course, they arranged themselves. Shauna sat on the toilet, her panties down and legs apart, while Chip stood in front of her, pants unzipped, prick exposed. She felt herself roaring over the edge as he began groaning, involuntarily thrusting and swiveling his hips, his prick dancing violently. Clutching her breasts, her orgasm ripped through her full force while his gigantic erection, directed between her legs, spurted with his own run-away orgasm. Sweating profusely, mouths gaping soundlessly, they released an erotic energy that broke any attachments they had to an obsolete reality. Breaking any ties to outmoded laws, theories, myths, patterns and beliefs that, yet unproven, still subconsciously had ploughed ever-deeper ruts through their brains and reinforced resistance to change.

Merging together, willingly and freely, without physically touching, they felt the strongest frequency they had yet transmitted. It poured out to destinations beyond all physical boundaries and those of their imaginations. They were caught up in a hurricane of transmissions, receiving even as they were sending, being pummeled in the small stall space by glimpses of other dimensions and other-world pulsations. Their atomic structure was once again being altered – being made lighter, brighter, less subject to gravity.

"We're obviously preparing for something greater than even we were imagining," said a shaky Shauna. "All we can know for sure," added Chip, cleaning himself, "is that it's our sexual oneness that's the trigger." Dabbing at her damp skin and wet pussy with toilet tissue, Shauna pulled up her panties and slowly stood up, testing her legs. Taking her hand he whispered, "I'm starving. Let's go enjoy."

They were finishing their soup when Mr. Debonair, the man who'd felt their unique vibe while they'd been dancing, approached their table. So confident, a real smoothie with fancy clothes and a billion dollar haircut, he leaned into their space and introduced himself as Harvey Sexton. "I was very taken by your intimate dance earlier and it would be my honor and pleasure to have a dance with you my dear . . . if that's all right with you, sir." Just a smidgeon away from condescending. "It's up to the lady . . . sir." responded Chip in a pleasant enough tone. "I'd like to finish my soup first, so why don't you come back in about fifteen minutes and I'll be ready to dance with you then," said Shauna. "Of course," said Harvey, bowing elegantly, if a little ostentatiously, before turning to leave.

"I wonder what he wants," mused Shauna. "As long as he has honorable intentions. And if he doesn't, well, I feel sorry for him. He doesn't know how well you can take care of yourself," said Chip. "Just so we're clear here. It's you my beautiful man that I'm looking forward to dancing with again!"

But it was Mr. Harvey Sexton who came back ever so punctually. Shauna was ready. For what, she wasn't exactly sure. Good thing she trusted her feelings. Before joining Harvey she leaned over to briefly lock lips with Chip then led the way to the dance floor.

Harvey's moves were crisp and sure and ate up more and more of the dance floor as he glided Shauna around. *Watch out for the moving target,* thought Shauna as most of the other dancers made room for their whirling

trajectory. Pulling her closer he said, "I don't know your name." "Shauna."
"Good. Well, I'm a sex coach - an excellent one if I might add – and when I
saw you dancing with your boyfriend, I knew right then and there I had to
meet you. So here we are. I would like to talk to you and your boyfriend about
a business proposal I have for you. May I suggest getting together, possibly
at your place?" And he moved his hands to clench her butt. Decidedly
disconcerted by the assumption of familiarity, particularly when he started
rhythmically moving his pelvis closer and harder into her, she backed away
saying calmly, even sweetly, but firmly "If you wish me to continue dancing
with you, please have a little respect and take your hands off my ass."

Harvey immediately complied and they resumed as before. *Besides,*
thought Shauna, *Chip, a boyfriend! What an unobservant observation! Which
is kind of weird because he seems so alert and sharp, like his eyes don't miss a
thing. Pity. He's not exactly handsome, but there is something that's attractive -
perhaps his strong sexuality. Of course, he could be all talk and no performance.
And he does seem very self-centered, narcissistic even . . . What the heck, why
should any of this concern me?*

Shauna was right. He'd missed it with her. Despite having an ulterior
motive for contacting her, an assignment from his associates, Harvey had still
pegged her as just a very beautiful, probably flighty, shallow and sex-oriented,
woman he was attracted to. Admonishing himself for almost blowing the
whole deal he urged himself to get back on track and don't underestimate her.

When the two dancers returned, Chip, who'd been appreciating the
panoramic view, looked at Shauna to get a read on how it went. She seemed
warm to Harvey but there were undertones - perhaps boredom and a lack of
excitement. Harvey, in contrast, was animated, talkative and full of himself.
"I bring your fair maiden back unscathed and no doubt ready for another
course. Here is my business card for you . . . and for you. As I mentioned to
Shauna, I have a business proposition I'd like to discuss with you both and
would appreciate the opportunity to get together with you." Chip looked at
the card, taking time to think. "We're having some friends over this coming
Thursday for a barbeque party. You're welcome to come. And bring a friend
if you'd like - or not. The party will begin at eight o'clock and will be dressy.
If you have another card, I'll write you my phone number and address." *Leave
it to Chip. He's so open and giving. I'm glad he took the initiative. Let's see where
this goes,* thought Shauna. The sexpert was noticeably excited and gobbled
up the invite like it was his last. "I'll be pleased and honored to attend and

I'll bring a lady friend. So I'll bid my adieus until Thursday. Fair lady." He almost bowed again then seated Shauna before departing.

"I'm glad you invited him to the party. I think there's more to him than seems immediately obvious," said Shauna. "Now I just want to enjoy the rest of the evening with you," and she raised her wine glass for Chip to clink with his.

CHAPTER 6   STIRRINGS

As they continued the meal they talked about their lives and passions. Chip asked: "How come you have so much understanding of love-making and sex, and yet have had so few partners - and apparently men not that sexually active or attractive?"

"Where should I begin?" She wondered aloud before continuing. "All my life I've felt different from most people - even when I was very young. My father left when I was only five years old and to this day I don't know why. Mother refuses to talk about it - no matter how much I beg her. So, I was pretty much a loner growing up in Scotland - half wild. We lived near the coast and I loved the sea, the endless waves, and developed a love of swimming, even though much of the time the water was too cold. I daydreamed all the time and my mother had a difficult time making sure I was in school. Eventually, out of pure frustration I'm sure, she found me a private tutor, an elderly gentleman from the village whom I became very fond of. Naturally curious and quick to learn, I loved music and began singing the local folksongs. Upon reaching puberty, the world of me opened up. I explored every part of myself, touching and finding out what gave me pleasure. I didn't know enough to call it masturbation. I called it playing with myself and I enjoyed it. Later, I used a mirror to visually explore myself and experimented with various touches, pressures and positions as I watched and monitored my reactions. I had no idea that what I was doing might be considered naughty, bad or a sin against God.

To this day I don't believe that something as beautiful as the human body can be dirty or tainted or a sin to enjoy. Why do we respond with such pleasure when we are touched in particular ways almost anywhere on our bodies if we aren't supposed to enjoy it? Why is sex or feeling sexy considered bad? Of course it's often abused and twisted but it's also almost universally suppressed or denied. I can't help thinking that the two polarities perpetuate each other. I mean, I think it's outrageous that there are masses of people on the planet who've never experienced minimal pleasure, let alone erotic ecstasy. Anyway, I'm not interested in dwelling on what isn't or in laying blame for what is. That only joins me to a world I feel no place in or affinity with. I love feeling good and attracting people who are like-minded. And, my Love, you are taking me to places I have never ventured into before. I feel so happy and enjoy you so much."

She paused for water and her eager listener waited with anticipation, completely captivated by her narrative.

"When I was about ten we suddenly moved to Wales to stay with one of my mother's aunts. I don't know why but I liked it there. That's when I got real serious about singing, joining groups and church choirs, becoming part of something greater than just myself. I often became swept away by the combined voices reaching for greater heights together. I took voice lessons from an extremely disciplined teacher, which was just what I needed, and went on to college, studying to become a music teacher. That was when I had my first sexual experience with a boy I knew from school. It was painful in every way and I was so happy I had my own methods to fall back on. I continued to explore myself and learn more ways and positions and methods for me to relax and be open to multiple orgasms. Now, sitting here telling you these things, I feel like I've been preparing myself for you.

"Anyway, to finish, I saved the proceeds of my occasional modeling gigs and moved to London where I rented a small flat. For me, it was a strange new way of living. I was industrious and determined to make a place for myself in the world of music. I had many breakthroughs, and could have had more if I'd been willing to sleep with this producer or that song arranger, but I had no desire to use my body like that. As it turned out, keeping my integrity, both personal and artistic, soon led to a lucrative recording contract which meant I didn't have to worry about money, quite an adjustment for me. I was nearing the end of a one year stint in Los Angeles, where I'd made a number of CDs, when my agent negotiated a very generous six month contract to come to Austin. I wondered why Austin but came anyway. Now I know why Austin. Gifford Jefferson is why!" Liking listening to her and the way she said his name he commented to encourage her to continue. "I understand *how* you landed in Austin, for which I am more than grateful, but for an artist of your stature, it's hard to see *why*."

"It's hard for me to figure out too. My agent doesn't always seem totally direct with me, although I've had no cause to complain. Anyway, I make sure to make every move and moment count, never being too sure what might be next. I'm thankful they like me at the club though, and the effects of my performances, like what happened last night, really fascinate me. You know what I'm getting at, right?" He nodded. "And once again, I found you!"

"So where do you live?"

"I've been renting a condo over on 143rd and Woodlawn. I share it with a girlfriend, Peggy, who followed me here from London. The space is OK and we enjoy each other - that is, when we're both home - she has her life and I have mine. I called her earlier to let her know about you and me and told her that I'd continue to cover my part of the rent for now. Having said that, it would probably be a good idea to get clear about you and me. There's no question for me that it's you I want to be with. I feel you so completely but know that whatever we have will be day to day, or week to week or whatever seems to flow. I can't allow myself to dwell on the past. It's dead and gone. Or live in a future fantasy. Now is all there is, and now is what creates the future. I have to be as clear as I can be about what I feel and want and refuse to be limited by past experiences or how I've internalized them. I'm totally responsible for what I create and need to know where you stand." And she reached across the table and took his hands in her own once more.

"I've been so caught up in your story, my Love. You *are* so clear. And I love that. How you speak, what you say and what you give yourself to keeps surprising and inspiring me - of course I want to be with you. Listening to you I see that creating every day to be greater and greater - with more joy, more love, more sex, more discoveries, a deeper passion for everyone - is the direct route to an easy and exciting living. And will be the only way we can stay together." Lifting her hands he pressed them against either side of his face and began crying, feeling the power of surrender. "I can't think of a time when I cried before I met you," he whispered. "Thank you," she whispered back, feeling their energy mingling at a different level. Minutes later, rearranged and revitalized they were ready to move and headed to the dance floor again.

Returning for their main course, Shauna ate slowly, savoring every delicious morsel. Chip attacked his steak with total enjoyment, taking a break to pour the last of the wine. The ever-attentive waiter quickly stepped in to ask if they would like another bottle. "This will do us," replied Chip. "Another bottle would put me on all fours and it's a long ways down," laughed Shauna, glad she only had a minor buzz.

Finished, their stomachs and well-being satisfied, they leaned back in their chairs, comfortable and content. Declining dessert, they ordered Gran Marniers instead.

This will be a new adventure, thought Shauna, as Chip instructed her. "Swirl it around the goblet and then enjoy it slowly. It's strong stuff and you should feel a warmth all over." It was the perfect punctuation for such a many chaptered evening.

Chip was generously tipping all the waiters just as Troy appeared. They acknowledged the manager and plummeted back down to earth courtesy of the Otis elevator company, Shauna clinging to Chip to keep her balance. The after dinner drink had swamped her sobriety.

Back in the familiar confines of the limo, she was soon asleep, a disheveled Chip removing her hand from inside his pants.

CHAPTER 7   WORKOUT

Shauna awakened to early morning sunlight playing on the bank of windows. Alone - she assumed Chip was working out - she lay quietly, noticing how she was feeling. She stretched and sleepily brought herself to a rocking clitoral orgasm. Taking a quick shower and running a brush through her hair to clear most of the tangles, she dressed for a workout and headed downstairs to find her Love.

Crossing the living and dining areas she took a quick look around Chip's office off the landing before heading down past the kitchen. At the bottom she passed a large entertainment room with the biggest TV screen she had ever seen facing three tiers of over-sized upholstered chairs and a bar with an old fashioned popcorn machine. She loved popcorn. Continuing on she aimed for the sound of weights being racked and rushed through the double doors to the workout room.

She ran towards Chip who was in between exercises and jumped on him, wrapping her legs around his waist and arms around his neck. Chip braced himself and cupped her butt with his hands as he carried her back to the doors to close and lock them. Shauna felt a quickening rush through her body, realizing that Chip was ready for her. "What took you so long, Love?" He asked. "I have to confess, Babe. I had to masturbate I'm so horny. But here we are and it seems we're going to have a different kind of workout - perhaps a work in," she replied.

Laying her on a thick floor mat he quickly slid his hands across her stomach and inside her shorts. Burrowing for her clit, he locked on to the wet heat emanating from her pussy and plowed right in. Fingered roughly she was instantly shuddering and squealing, desperately seeking release. Craving more she ripped off his shorts. He returned the favor. Fighting off her sports bra he massaged her breasts sending wave upon wave crashing through her. She fingered her clit, redirecting his attention and he willingly obliged, sending her ballistic. Disengaging, he lay back and she quickly straddled him, totally focused on release. Fully impaled, she matched rhythms until the increasing sensations drew them both over the top. Shauna was practically knocked off her perch as Chip blew - it seemed like he was releasing more and more each time – and they soared higher, farther, faster, flying outwards, launched into multiple dimensions, adding new sequences to their DNA to unknowingly begin creating the building blocks of a new universe and collapsing back into themselves instantaneously.

Shauna shakily rolled off to lie on the mat, throwing a leg over his hip, rubbing her wetness against him. They slowly calmed to a semblance of normal, feeling good, relaxed.

Cleaned up they headed for the basketball court which, as Shauna had expected, was impressive. She made herself comfortable in the bleachers and took a good look around. *Wow, even digital scoreboards.* Chip was grabbing basketballs and towels when a couple of his teammates walked in, dressed ready for action. About to introduce herself, Shauna was preempted by Chip who hollered, "Hey Bro's, this is the woman I've been telling you about, Shauna. Shauna, the long streak of piss is Ivan and the runt is R Jay, but don't let that fool you. He'll find the basket, even if he has to go through you."

After a greeting featuring knuckle jabs, high fives and low fives so complicated it had Shauna laughing out loud they started playing. Ivan, tall and surprisingly stringy for a pro basketball player, was swarthy with a broken nose and a buzz cut similar to Chip's. R Jay, in contrast, was probably a shade over six feet with a shock of red hair spiking every which way. Extremely athletic he also seemed very strong, matching his two bigger teammates blow for blow. With the fourth guy a no-show Shauna watched for a while, aware they were all showing off for her, and then jumped down to the court to steal the ball from Ivan. Surprised, they watched for a moment as she dribbled down the court before taking her on. Skillfully zigzagging, down the court, avoiding their lunges she made a perfect three pointer – nothing but net! A proud Chip asked where she'd learnt to play. Explaining she had started in school and carried on to play small forward on her college team, she also pointed out that it was a while since she played and if she could beat them it was no wonder they hadn't been doing so well. Fired up they ran a game of two on two, Shauna holding her own pretty well, as long as they didn't get overly physical. A close game, with Ivan and Shauna the winners, she left them to the locker room to head back upstairs to shower.

Hearing running feet behind her she took off, pretty certain it was Chip. Within a few strides he caught her. "Gotcha!" he cried triumphantly as he hooked his fingers in the waist band of her shorts. Her feet slid from under, crashing her to the floor. Surprised and immediately filled with remorse, he rushed to help. "Love, I'm so sorry. Are you hurt?" She turned away from him, shoulders shaking, crying quietly. Tenderly he cradled and rocked her gently, checking her over for bruising.

Hearing the thud, Ivan and R Jay had come running. "Is she OK?" asked Ivan as they arrived. But it was only her feelings that were hurt. With no experience of the rough and tumble of growing up with boys, she wasn't used to ending up on the floor, pants around her ankles. "I'm sorry, Babe. I'm used to being the one on top and here I am on my butt. I need to lighten up, be more playful, not take myself so seriously."

"And I need to be more careful." He responded, helping her to her feet. R Jay and Ivan, impressed by a softer side of him they'd never seen - they had history with him - said their goodbyes, R Jay adding that it looked like Shauna might be the best thing that had ever happened to him. Waving them off, he picked Shauna up and carried her to the master suite. Laying her on the bed he told her that he wanted to take her out later for a picnic in the wilds northeast of Austin. "It's so beautiful there. We can hike, have brunch and relax before the barbeque later. Mark can fix us food and I'll drive us in the Caddy. What do you think?" Replying happily, "It sounds delightful. Thank you." she lay still while Chip examined her more closely for any other damage. Finding none, he applied rapid healing gel on her knees, thinking, *she has to be tougher than she looks, that was quite a tumble.*

Leaving the city, the landscape changed completely. In fact, Shauna had flashbacks to her beloved Scotland. Rolling green hills for as far as the eye could see beckoned to them. Chip, following his GPS, turned onto a dirt road for the final stretch. The landscape changed again: more rugged with rocky outcroppings and jagged peaks.

A couple of miles and thirty minutes later, Chip stopped. Shauna leapt out, eager to merge with the surrounding scenery. Opening her arms wide she spun around and around before Chip scooped her up and spun her some more. A barely discernible path through hip high, gently waving grass led them forward. Dressed in shorts and loose tops, their exposed skin enjoyed the caress of the long grass and the cooling, gentle breeze. Relishing every step they relaxed into the balmy quiet, intensely aware of each other and the magnificence of nature as they climbed.

At the top of the steep climb, Chip pointed to a rocky outcrop leading to a grassy plateau offering a breathtaking panorama. "What do you think about stopping here for brunch?" "I Love it!" she cried. "It's sooo beautiful, but I'm in your hands."

Inching their way over the rocks and down to the plateau, they unpacked. As he spread out a tarp, two small pillows and a couple of towels, she thought, *Aha*. Wasting no time, she took off her clothes and proceeded to strip him too. He gladly let her before drawing her close to kiss her passionately. Still locked in their kiss, they felt their way onto the tarp. Lying on top of her, holding her hands above her head, he covered her with kisses.

He soon had her dry humping and spasming erotically under him, bringing her ever closer to another release. Stimulating her hyper-sensitive nipples, clit and lips, it wasn't long before she was begging him once again to come inside her. Quickly pressing his cockhead to her entrance, he plunged in fully, delivered two long thrusts and felt their combined explosion. So quick, so intense, so delicious. He rolled of, spent. Still catching her breath, she wheezed, "I so wish you could stay inside me forever." Turning his head he smiled and kissed her tenderly. Gazing at each other they rested, savoring the after pulses.

"What happened to our time-space experiences this time?" He wondered out loud. "Were we too fast? Was I too focused? Did I miss something? Did we?" "Chip, my precious Love, there's no need to question yourself or our love making. No two times will ever be the same and we can't measure them by what does or doesn't happen beyond our enjoyment. I'm so fulfilled and happy just to be with you. Today has been wonderful so far, just what we needed. I'm not missing a thing. In fact, I'm thankful for every variation. I want fresh and new all the time: with you and with everything. Sameness and repetition is a recipe for boredom. And so is measuring the present against the past. I've no intention of creating that with myself or with you." Taking his hand she watched her words sink in, his eyes filling, body twitching as he absorbed her. He felt her to be her words and knew he needed to be that congruent too. Shauna held him close, feeling her breasts sensitive, bloated and sore, cradling him, happy he could be so soft and yielding.

"Let's eat, I'm hungry. But first I could drink a river," she said, breaking the silence. Sliding across the tarp she opened the cooler and pulled out a couple of bottles of cold Evian. "Let's share," suggested Chip, opening a bottle and pouring it into a mug from his backpack. Taking it, she gulped down a good half and passed it back.

Making short work of the picnic, they packed up, made the trek back to the SUV and beat the afternoon business traffic, getting home just in time to get ready for the barbeque. Chip called Garcia to help Shauna, asking her to bring something to soothe sore breasts. Looking forward to being together with friends, they had no idea what was in store.

CHAPTER 8 ENDANGERED

Exiting the shower on their way to the closet Chip turned and looked at her, his deep love obvious, his lust becoming more so as his eyes roamed over her naked body. Shauna ran for the bed and took a flying leap, landing on her stomach, unraveling the towel from her hair to wrap around her body. But Chip came flying after her. He landed on all fours, pinning her to the bed and whisked the towel away. She began to struggle against him but he held her wrists down until she seemed to settle.

He began licking and pinching her tight butt, playing with her crack, licking and probing, plunging his tongue as deep as he could. Ass in the air, Shauna clutched the sheet, bunching it into wads, more and more excited. Flipping her he nuzzled her clit. She was already off in another world. Finding the cherry he paused, "Oh . . . My . . . God, Love! You're so huge and juicy. I love how you're always so ready and willing, to trust my movement." "Oh, Babe . . . of course! Now, please. Don't stop!"

More than happy to oblige, his every touch sent shudders of ecstasy rippling through her. Shifting himself to between her legs, lightly rubbing her, she writhed in anticipation of his entry. Taking his time, driving her crazy with lust and himself into wild arousal, he finally thrust deep inside. Her whole body quaked and arched. He held her spread legs and thrust slowly back and forth enjoying her ecstatic arousal and his own pulsating emotions until, in a flash of fission, their atoms fused and split simultaneously, imploding outwards, an infinity of particles, their bodies blazing again, transcending, a beacon for like-minded life that was ready to reciprocate, wherever it was.

Wrapped in each other, they blissfully powered down. "We're creating something more than ourselves. And it feels like just a beginning," commented Shauna almost reverently.

Entering the closet, Shauna asked Chip to help pick out something to wear for the barbeque as she'd never been to one before. Looking through her clothes he suggested she also wear the sexy black swimsuit under her clothes so she could use Coach's Olympic size pool and regulation diving board, remarking, "It must have come with the house as I've never seen him use it."

As they discussed clothing options Shauna could tell he was excited about taking her to the barbeque to show off to his buddies. Helping her into the swimsuit he said, "You look so good I can guarantee some of the women at the barbeque will be flashing green when they get a load of you!" She stood before the mirror slowly turning around - every view a new sexual delight. Walking in to help Shauna finish getting ready, Garcia gasped. "Oh, my goodness. I hope the swim suit goes in the same direction as you. You better check everything before you come out of the water. I wish I could be there to see the reactions to your 'coming out' party." Watching Shauna slip into olive shorts and yellow t-shirt she added, "At least wearing those you should be safe for most of the time." She then fixed Shauna's hair into a ponytail and handed her a pair of silver hoop earrings

Shauna stuffed bra and panties and a few other items into a carry bag as Chip, dressed in black spandex shorts, purple tank top and short gold necklace, made for the SUV at the side door. Shauna scrambled after him, athletic shoes barely tied, ready, she hoped, for anything.

From Chip's mansion to Coach's house was a short distance but the neighborhoods worlds apart. From large lush lots - almost gated communities in themselves - and wide tree-lined avenues, to cracked tarmac, dusty yards and ranch style, brick bungalows. Coach's was set towards the back of a bigger than average lot enclosed by a tall, wrought iron fence and approached through a similar wrought iron gate standing open in front of a very long cement driveway. Chip turned in for the drive to the house, passing the pool on the left. On the far side of the pool a group of mostly men sat under shade trees in wooden lawn chairs arranged in a sort of semi-circle facing them. Clustered close to the house women were sitting visiting and keeping sharp eyes on the children in the shallow end. Chip parked close to the house beside several other cars nosed in at an angle. It appeared they might have been the last to arrive.

Taking what they needed from the car they headed around the pool. Reaching the women, who were noticeably hot and sweaty, Shauna wondered why they hadn't joined the men under the shade trees or weren't in the pool or even wearing swimsuits – maybe, like her, they were wearing them under their clothes. Chip made the introductions, letting Shauna know they were the wives of some of his team mates. The kids were too busy enjoying each other and the water to take notice. If it hadn't been for Chip, the women probably wouldn't have taken much notice either. She could feel that most of them considered her a potential threat. *Ah, the female bitch*, she thought. *Wouldn't it be great if we could just be ourselves and not have this or that fear or sense of inadequacy or a need to be validated - if jealousy didn't have to raise its ugly head. Oh Well, it won't deter my enjoyment.* Chip just thought it was too bad they didn't appreciate the gift she was. Moving on they headed towards his buddies under the shade trees, squeezing each other's hands in perfect understanding.

As they got closer, a man in his mid-fifties rose from his chair with hand extended towards Shauna. "Welcome to our humble place. So glad you could make it. We were wondering if you were coming," boomed a smiling, robust Coach. "To miss you would have been a tragedy. You're every bit as gorgeous as I was told you were. What a pleasure." And he shook her hand in a mighty grip. *Whoa.* The handshake nearly brought her to her knees. She was strong but her hands were delicate. "Sorry! Forget my own strength sometimes," apologized Coach. "Hey, I'll get over it," responded a resilient Shauna, flexing her slender fingers.

Balding and not particularly handsome, Coach made up for what might be considered shortcomings with an outgoing personality. He was intense, loud and full of an energy that didn't quite mask the anxiety and stress she could sense from him. Shauna wondered if they were caused by the job, or something else. "Hey Giff, leave it to you to find such a great beauty. You're a lucky man because she must see something in you I sure don't," commented Coach and the guys hooted and hollered in response. "So I hear that we might have a new recruit for our team, that you're quite an expert with the basketball," he added. "Well, actually that's why I'm here today," replied Shauna. "The one big concern I have is whether you can actually afford me. But just in case, I brought my lucky pen with me." This set the guys off again, clapping, whistling, stomping their feet.

It sure seemed like she was going to be the star turn of the afternoon, at least among the men anyway. The two women in the group seemed less enthralled, maybe they didn't want their men heading for greener pastures. *Too bad for clinging vine*, thought Shauna, the woman introduced as Ivan's girlfriend, Ivan was already smitten. Shauna had immediately felt the woman's limpet energy and Ivan's confusion when introducing her.

"Come sit by me," said Coach, indicating a chair next to him. Shauna dutifully sat as directed and Gifford pulled up a chair to sit on her other side.

"So, Shauna, darling, I want you to promise me that you'll let me know the second Giff doesn't treat you right, you hear?" "Oh, you can count on it. In fact I'll wear a special whistle that I'll blow so hard the moment something like that happens you'll wish you have ear plugs. But I wouldn't hold my breath if I were you. Giff is wonderful to me." Impressed with her quickness and loyalty, the guys tried to ply her with beer and snacks, which she declined while asking after Coach's wife.

"She's up at the house fixing lemonade and should be down soon." he answered "Why don't I go see if she'd like some help." She leaned over and gave Chip a long kiss before standing up. "Nice meeting all of you," she said as she left them, swaying her gorgeous ass, pony tail swinging back and forth across her back. More than one man was wondering how she was in bed. One thankful and very happy man knew and was saying nothing,.

Shauna headed back round the pool and up the driveway. It was sticky-hot. The shade had made it bearable, but here on the cement it was miserable. Up ahead a woman came round the side of the house heading towards her. "Hello! Are you Joan?" called Shauna. Moments later they converged. Joan was lugging a large urn-shaped plastic cooler with a spigot and a stack of red plastic cups. Shauna felt an instant empathy. Haggard with straggly reddish-brown hair, probably in her mid-forties, wearing an unattractive house dress, as if she didn't take much care of herself, Joan seemed beaten down from a life of servitude and the opposite of domestic bliss. Introducing herself Shauna offered to help carry the load. Gracefully declining Joan asked her to go meet her two boys who were playing basketball in front of the garage beside the house. "I can't keep them off the court even though it's really too hot to be playing. They're really eager to meet you though, so maybe you can persuade them to join us by the pool."

"I'll see what I can do. But first, would you mind if I had some of that lemonade. I'm so thirsty, I'd really appreciate it." Hefting the cooler Joan offered it up for Shauna to grab a cup and pour. Gulping it down she asked if was Joan's own recipe because it was so delicious. "Sure is," said Joan and carried on towards the pool while Shauna, thanking her, went towards the house, soon hearing voices and the bouncing of a basketball against the cement pad.

Rounding the corner of the house, she saw three boys playing. Two, about sixteen and fourteen had reddish-brown hair and freckles and she figured they belonged to Joan. The third, blond and tall, she presumed to be a neighborhood friend. Stopping their play as she approached, wondering who she was, they were not too young to appreciate her attractions. "Hi. I'm Shauna. Your mother told me where to find you." "I'm Jimmy," said the taller son. "And this here is Eddie, my brother, and over there is Brad. He lives down the street." "Nice to meet you guys," said Shauna.

Suggesting a game of two-on-two, Shauna was teamed up with a reluctant Eddie. It didn't take long for them all to change their minds about playing with 'girls' as Shauna quickly proved her prowess. One game turned into four and they were soon joined by Chip and his teammates wondering what was taking her so long. Unable to resist, they all wanted to compete and with sides picked they went at it with much jostling, pushing, fouls and all around rough-housing. Shauna excused herself to head back to the pool. "Hey, Shauna, wait for us!" called the three boys. "We just have to get our swimming trunks on and we'll be right out." And they scampered into the house. In the meantime, Reduced by two a side, the guys carried on, showing no mercy. Shauna watched while she waited, glad she was out of the fray.

When the boys reappeared they escorted Shauna to the pool, Jimmy holding one hand and Eddie the other. Brad trailed behind bouncing a bright beach ball. As they approached the pool, Shauna was relieved that the pool was still mostly empty, the women and children having migrated to the shade area now most of the guys were playing ball. The boys jumped into the shallow end to play with the beach ball while Shauna continued to the diving board where she disrobed. Eyes were riveted to her as she stood, barely covered by the skimpy suit. She was too absorbed in visualizing her next moves to notice.

She climbed the tower and boosted herself onto the board in one quick athletic move, walked out to the middle of the board and tested it, bouncing several times. Padding back to the fixed end she stretched. Checking her suit was securely in place she then walked slowly to the water end of the board and curled her toes over the edge. Taking several deep breaths she lifted her arms straight out in front of her, hands together as if praying. Balanced motionless, she was a study in total focus.

And then she exploded into a perfectly executed swan dive. Gauging the entry just right, she pierced the water with barely a ripple. Bobbing to the surface quickly she was surprised by the applause - even the women had joined in.

Treading water, she looked around for Chip. He'd come running, along with most of the other players, as soon as R Jay had broadcast that she was on the diving board and he'd seen the whole thing. Running along the side of the pool he had taken off, diving in behind her as she was surfacing. Popping up nearby, so proud, he shouted. "That was spectacular! What can't you do?" And he swam to her side, asking her to repeat the performance so he could watch from head on. Feeling his erection nudging her thigh, she took a deep breath, lowered herself under the water, wrapped her arms around his waist and kissed his mashed erection straining inside his swim trunks and shorts. From the reaction, she suspected she may have added to his torture, stimulating more pressure and less wiggle room. Surfacing she said, "Sorry Baby, I'll treat you extra good when we get home." "Forget the dive. Let's go," laughed Chip. Remembering the audience who had now drawn closer, eager to know what was going on between them, Shauna quickly swam to the side, hoisted herself out and walked wetly back to the diving board while Chip swam to the other end of the pool. On top of the board Shauna went through her testing and stretching ritual before perching on the end of the board and curling her toes over the end once again.

On the other side of the neighborhood a man adjusted the rifle braced against the parapet wall of the highest section of the local mall. He had been there a long time waiting for the right moment to follow through with his assignment. Cocky, full of confidence, he could already hear the praise he would soon be receiving. Pressing his eye to the powerful scope he watched a woman in a skimpy, almost invisible black swimsuit preparing to dive. Having watched her first dive he'd been confident, given everything he'd been told about her, that she would dive again and there she was, about to prove him right. And then she was airborne.

The .338 Lapua Magnum bullet missed its target by a fraction of an inch, ripped through the water to embed itself near the base of the pool near the corner.

Unaware of any disturbance, Shauna simply misjudged the dive. Overshooting, she whacked the water on entry, rippling the surface across the pool, disturbing any trace of the bullet's trajectory and obscuring her track as she swam the length of the pool underwater to where Gifford was waiting.

On her entry several of the guys rushed to the pool edge to see that she was okay but the ripples and reflected sunlight obscured their view. R Jay ran the other way, towards Chip. Nearing, he shouted, "Where's Shauna? Where is she?" "What's up, Bro?" asked Chip, suddenly anxious. "I swear I heard a shot fired," replied R Jay as he reached him. Fear gripping his heart. Chip now heard the question roaring through his own head. *Where's Shauna?*

Blissfully unaware, intending to surprise him, Shauna was slowly drifting along the bottom of the pool, surface ripples hiding her approach. Reaching the steps beside where he was standing she pushed herself up and half out of the water gasping for air, glad for her years of training as a singer and her developed breath control. Chip and R Jay gulped with relief. Further along the pool the concerned men, seeing she was fine, drifted after the women marshalling the children to where the food was laid out.

Having watched the diver flip through his scope before his view was obstructed, first by the surface waves and glare from the water, and then by the people who rushed to line the pool edge, the marksman scanned the pool area for a full minute before hastily packing, convinced he'd scored a hit. Making his way down to street level, he strolled away, high on adrenaline and buzzing with the excitement of a kill. He'd been told by his boss to never call before nine o'clock, but he was eager to share his success and couldn't wait.

Helping Shauna out of the pool, Chip and R Jay hugged and kissed her fiercely, not realizing that her mistimed dive and her ability to swim the length of the pool underwater had probably saved her life. Chip signaled R Jay to keep quiet about what he'd heard. Judging by the reaction of everyone else now crowded round the barbeque pit near the house, apparently unconcerned, it looked like R Jay had been the only person to hear anything out of the ordinary - not that gunfire in Texas was that unusual. Watching as Coach made himself the center of attention, as usual, R Jay began to wonder if he'd been hearing things or had made something out of nothing. It sure looked like nobody else had noticed anything odd or out of place. Or maybe someone had and was keeping quiet.

Heading back to the house to clean up and change, Shauna stopped by the SUV to get her bra and panties before entering the side door. Jimmy and Eddie, looking dejected, were eating supper by themselves at the kitchen table. "Hi guys," said Shauna brightly, glad to see them. At no response she wondered what was going on but continued, telling them she'd missed them at the pool just as Joan appeared, dish towels in hand. Asking if she could use a bathroom to clean up and change, a tight lipped Joan showed her down the hall.

Struggling her way out of the swimsuit - it felt like Velcro sticking to her skin - she laid it on a nearby hamper to rinse when she got home.

Showered and dressed, she felt much better, made her way back to the kitchen where Joan had prepared a spread of food and another cooler of lemonade. "Can I help take some of this down?" asked Shauna. "That won't be necessary. Some of the wives are on their way up to help." "Can I say my goodbyes to Jimmy and Eddie before I go then?" "I'll say good-bye for you. They're doing their homework and aren't to be disturbed." Nodding okay, Shauna left, the tension melting away as she stepped outside

----

Dropping her swimsuit in the back of the SUV, she jogged toward the delicious aroma of beef mingling with chicken, charcoal-roasted, true Texan style. Arriving, stomach growling, she sauntered over to Chip. Relaxed, talking with Ivan, he motioned for her to sit on his lap. Obediently she did, wrapping her arms around his neck, kissing him slow and long. Food was not their only hunger.

Coach barked, waving her over, "Come on, Shauna, start us out here. What's your pleasure?" Trotting over she loaded a plate as everyone else stood up and tried to not mow each other down jostling for their own share.

Returning to Chip's chair, Shauna sat on the ground and ripped into her food thinking, *Looks like I'm going to waddle out of here.* With everyone munching away, Coach roared, "Everybody enjoying?" He was greeted by a chorus of compliments.

Suitably stuffed, Shauna struggled to her feet, sluggish from her feast, and began a slow circuit of the pool to work it off some. Soon enough, footsteps behind her heralded Chip's approach. She turned and he gathered her into his arms. Melting into him their haunches met. "Oh, Baby, is that new, or have you been hard all this time . . . on second thoughts, I don't believe I really want to know." "Let's go home," was all he said before kissing her passionately.

Saying their farewells, they confirmed their get-together later with Ivan and R Jay to watch a recording of yesterday's game and went looking for Coach. Distant and apparently disgruntled, he flipped on the charm to say goodbye to them before abruptly walking away. Glancing at each other, their one thought was, *Weird!*

CHAPTER 9 A NEW FORCE

They raced to the SUV, Chip arriving first, eagerly opening the door for Shauna. She piled in. Tilting the seat back, she made herself comfortable, allowing her tummy plenty of room. The sun had already set and daylight was quickly fading as Chip made a turnaround to head down the driveway, through the gate and towards home.

Shauna slid back, unbuckled her belt, unzipped her shorts, pushed them down past her knees, pulled aside her bikini panties and began to explore herself until she found her very wet, enlarged Cherry. Stroking herself, quickly becoming excited and humming, distracting Chip. "Fuck, Shauna! Are you trying to cause an accident?" He reached over and moved her fingers aside to deftly massage her clit. "What are *you* doing, Babe? That's dangerous! And I'm so HOT!"

Quickly checking the road he slowed the car, whipped down a deserted side street and parked. Slipping off their seat belts, he raised her left leg and hooked it over the back of her car seat, worked his way over the console hump, tugging down his briefs and shorts, aiming his throbbing erection for her pussy. Lying back against the door, surprised at his determination, increasingly turned on, she pulled her panties aside and he plunged in.

They forgot everything. All they knew or felt was the fever of a mounting orgasm. Automatically synchronizing they soared into new realms, unwittingly transforming their nervous systems to alter their DNA again, close to becoming completely new arrangements of physical matter. They were becoming a force of unlimited change that would make old systems and beliefs obsolete, revolutionize the universe and its context and bring an end to the scourge of death. Never having taken drugs, Chip wondered if the experience was anything like a 'trip'.

As they calmed down, the environment around them shifted back to what they'd always considered normal but were beginning to think might not be. "What pleasure and sensations . . . indescribable!" exclaimed a transformed Shauna. They held each other, their bodies so biologically united they felt as one. *This is true intimacy,* thought Shauna.

Not wishing to hang around and analyze their experience, so exposed and vulnerable, they cleaned up as best they could with just a box of Kleenex. Chip helped Shauna swab and get rearranged then packed away his happy limp prick.

It didn't take long before they were parked at the side entrance. Troy appeared from the garage and ran over to see if they needed help. "It feels like we've been gone for a couple of days," said Chip as they made their way to the bedroom. "Doesn't it though," agreed Shauna.

Stripping in the bedroom they went straight to the shower, gently washed each other, stood in a loving embrace, water pouring over them. Her breasts swollen and sore, pussy lips tender, Chip carefully toweled her dry before having her lie on the bed, legs spread wide. He gently applied ointment to her inflamed genitals and breasts, lightly rubbing it in. Finished, he lay beside her and they rested, delighting in the cool night air wafting through the open doors and caressing their naked skin. Taking their time they eventually dressed for their rendezvous with the guys to watch the game.

Ivan and R Jay, firmly ensconced in the front row, already had the recording set up and the popcorn machine going when Chip and Shauna got to the entertainment room. Pouring drinks and passing them round, Chip settled beside Shauna in the second row and Ivan started the game.

Snuggling up, Shauna made herself comfortable and promptly dozed off. Every once in a while she would hear distant cheering or chanting and feel the warmth of Chip's presence. Other than that, she was 'gone'.

Nearing the end of the fourth quarter Chip stirred, realizing that he too had dozed off. At the final whistle, Ivan and R Jay stood to leave, Ivan to pick up his girlfriend and R Jay to stop by his previous home and see his two kids. Separated for four months he was beginning to get used to the arrangement, but really didn't like it. "I'll see you bright and early tomorrow Bro," said Ivan. Nodding at the slumbering Shauna he continued, "She sure is a keeper." "See you tomorrow too, and say bye to Shauna for me." added R Jay.

The place was soon quiet and Chip took his time to bring himself around. Then, cradling Shauna in his arms, he slowly made his way back to the master suite.

As he lay down beside her, Shauna, said drowsily. "Hey, Baby, I have a singing lesson in the morning and we'll probably do some recording too."

"Wow!" said Chip, "Thanks for reminding me. With all the distractions I completely forgot that I'm flying to Dallas in the morning with Ivan. We're Free Agents, as of this year and we're interviewing with the Mavericks. Fortunately, Coach is letting us use the team's jet so we should avoid most of the early morning crush and be back sometime early afternoon. I'll have Troy pick me up and bring me to the studio as soon as we get in. I'll also have him take you to the studio after he drops me off at the airport first thing, and make sure Garcia's around to help you get ready." "Thanks, Baby, that sounds great. Carry me with you and be safe. I'll miss you." Holding each other close they kissed deeply and dropped into a deep sleep, unaware of the magnitude of coming upheavals.

Somewhere in the older neighborhood with the plain brick ranch houses on large lots, a phone rang. Heavy footsteps clomped to the office door. The door closed muffling the ringing and the subsequent sound of one side of an argument. The clock on the office desk read nine-four p.m.

CHAPTER 10 VISITOR

Still dark outside, Chip was dressing in the closet, thinking about his trip to Dallas. Shauna shifted in bed stretching out, now unrestricted by Chip's presence. A bed hog, she knew instinctively when to conquer new territory. Gazing down at her on his way out, having a deep longing to curl up beside her for a while, he whispered, "I love you, my Precious. See you later," and made a stealthy exit.

The sun was already filling the sky with bright heat when Shauna emerged from sleep with the familiar symptoms of what she called her 'visitor' - a menstrual cycle so regular, so on time and so uncomfortable the first day or two. Rising, a song in her heart, she went to the bathroom, inserted a tampon and slipped on a pair of panties with a pad inside. Grabbing a couple of Midol, she went back to bed. After all, they hadn't gotten to sleep till well after one o'clock.

With Garcia's help Shauna was up, dressed and feeling human, laying along the limo's backseat, so thankful for not having to drive. With her hands pressing either side of her stomach, trying to ease the cramping, she dozed off. On arrival at the non-descript office mall where the studio was located, Troy opened the back door to find a disoriented Shauna. He helped her out of the car and through the building entrance which opened on a long hall with businesses lining both sides to an open door near the far end on the left. Entering she was greeted by Richard, her voice teacher. "Hi there, Shauna darlin'. Good to see you. I've been looking forward to our session today." Thanking him, Shauna introduced Troy who, seeing she was alright, left.

A small setup, the studio was dominated by the control booth from where Richard directed operations. It ran almost the full width of the room at the far end with a door beside it that led to an office/storeroom with a couch, small table and a disorganized desk. A small bathroom occupied one corner. A few stools and chairs scattered the recording area in front of the control booth, where performers faced a bare wall - no distractions.

A tad taller than Shauna, Richard sported a mustache and goatee that matched his, as usual, shaggy and unkempt, sandy hair - he was constantly running his hands through it. Clear, pale blue eyes, his most striking feature, were enhanced by his careful choice of clothes - today a striped blue, white and gray long sleeve cotton shirt rolled up at the sleeves. If he was making an effort to look like a musician, he was doing a good job. A bit bland but caring, he was gifted, very knowledgeable and extremely creative. He had finally gotten into writing his own scores and, though he hadn't told Shauna yet, had written two songs especially for her.

Going to join him by the control booth, Shauna hugged him and they sat to discuss plans for the day. Opening her file folder she handed Richard a copy and they went through it: fine tuning a duet with the Tenor; the first practice of a duet with a new soprano; a couple of numbers with the chorus; and a couple of numbers for her new album with Richard. A full morning, maybe longer. Shauna hoped it would all go smoothly: that she would have the stamina to tackle it well, to be fully engaged with the people involved and the music they would make together.

The schedule had moved along well, everyone on time. The Tenor had greatly improved. The young soprano had needed more work to be ready for Saturday night's performance and would join Shauna for further practice on Thursday. The chorus singers were primed and ready. Everything was feeling great for Richard and Shauna as they laid down her voice tracks for the album. Holding her achy stomach, Shauna, headphones in place, waited for Richard's signal. On cue her voice rang out clear and on pitch, filling the studio with her rapturous gift that seeped around the aged soundproofing to filter into the corridor outside.

As she poured out her heart, the door to the building opened and a tall, limber black man strode into the long hallway. Looking cool, dressed in black, elegantly casual, a black derby sitting at a jaunty angle on his head, he stopped to listen. Following the voice down the hallway he peeked into the studio. Heart pounding strongly, he melted at the combination of sight and sound.

Shauna was looking at Richard who was looking at the studio doorway. Turning slightly, without interrupting the music flow, to see what was drawing Richard's attention, it took all Shauna's willpower to keep singing and not go running to the strikingly handsome Chip. You would have thought he'd been gone for weeks instead of hours.

Finishing the song she rushed towards Chip as he entered and and embraced him exuberantly. Introducing the men to each other she took a ten minute break and led Chip in to the back room. Heading straight for the couch she lay down clutching her lower stomach. Chip drew up a chair and placed his hands tenderly over hers. "Garcia called me, Babe, and told me that soon after I left, you started your period. She said you were very brave in getting ready to come here and 'face the music'. I'm so proud you let nothing stop you. I hate seeing you in pain though." Gently lifting the hem of her dress he saw the pad in her panties. Kissing her stomach, he asked, "Are your cramps bad?" She nodded yes. "I really don't want any clothes on, and would appreciate some help getting my bra off. It's hurting my breasts - a lot." "OK, but remember not to lean over too far or you'll show yourself down to those lovely red shoes. And by the way, you look so pretty in that outfit with your hair like that." Shauna let out a big sigh of relief and smiled as the bra came off. "I still want to rip off my clothes, but I'll wait till we get home, I guess."

"When we leave, let's go to the café round the corner. You've been here for hours and I bet you've not eaten. Garcia told me you had no breakfast and she was concerned. I'll also have Troy stop on the way home and get a couple of remedies Garcia says will help. We're going to pamper you so much you'll wish your period lasted all month." They laughed and he kissed her tenderly. "Thanks, Baby. Now I'm ready to finish. I'm particularly excited about singing this last song for you, personally."

As she sang her favorite song to him, holding his gaze, Chip was so moved he started to cry. A jealous Richard, having never heard her sing so devotedly, was angry. *I can offer you so much more*, he thought. *Thank goodness I have my music.*

As the last note faded, Chip stood and took her in his arms. Both, shaking and sobbing, were overjoyed with the depth of their intimacy.

Chip thanked Richard. "The pleasure is all mine," he replied. "I've never had a student like Shauna. She's so devoted and such a professional - in every way . . . and have you ever heard such a marvelous voice?" "Nope," said Chip. He then arranged for Richard to come to his house on Friday at one to discuss the possibilities of setting up a studio there. Giving Richard a kiss on the cheek, Shauna looped her arm with Chip's and they left to meet Troy with the limo out front. She suddenly remembered her bra and rushed back to retrieve it, rejoining Chip as he got to the mall entrance.

It was a real Mom and Pop café with small wood tables and uncomfortable wood chairs. As the three of them sat, Chip had asked Troy to join them, a young boy arrived to take their order. Taking a menu Shauna asked, "Could I please have a glass of lemonade right away? Thanks." She was overheating and could feel herself perspiring. The boy left while they decided what to order, returning quickly, much to Shauna's delight. She downed the glass and asked for another, ordering chicken noodle soup too - the only thing she could think of that might not upset her stomach. The food came quickly. Shauna dabbled with her soup, ordering a third glass of lemonade, her brow leaking. Chip and Troy quickly finished their meals as she downed the last of her drink and the three paid and left to head home.

Oh bliss. They had just arrived at the house, having made the stop on the way to pick up Garcia's suggested treatments. Chip had been exceptionally attentive, making her as comfortable as possible and having Troy turn the air to ice cold in the limo. Carefully picking her up, he carried her into the house up the stairs to the master suite and into the master bedroom, laying her gently on the bed. He joined her, kissing her eager mouth and neck.

A bossy Garcia knocked on the door on the way in. Already attached to Shauna and protective, she quickly helped her out of her clothes and readied to change her tampon. "I'd like to see how this works," said Chip tentatively. Garcia, shocked, her husband had never shown any interest, in fact, the exact opposite, shrugged and showed him what to do. How to remove the tampon from its wrapper, hold it for insertion and slide it in so that the plastic covering could be taken out leaving the absorbent core plug in place. Shauna asked if he'd like to do it and he said yes. Garcia had thoughtfully taken precautions and had slid a plastic sheet under Shauna who spread her legs and bent them at the knee to make it easier for Chip to pull out the used tampon. Probing for the string he couldn't find it and Shauna had to reach down and feel around before finding it stuck to the side of the crack leading to her anus. Taking his hand she guided it to the string and directed him to free it from her skin and pull it directly out. "Sometimes it needs a good tug because there can be quite a lot of suction." Slowly withdrawing the plug, he exclaimed, "My God, look at all that blood." And still more oozed out, dripping onto the sheet. "Baby, you know you don't have to do this, right?" she asked lovingly. "I wouldn't want to miss this part of you, Love," he replied emphatically. "Thanks Baby," said Shauna, leaning forward, begging a kiss from him a he inserted the new tampon.

Taking the used tampon for disposal, Garcia handed Chip a pack of baby wipes for clean-up. Returning she had Shauna sit back and relax so she could treat her swollen, tender breasts and cramping stomach, instructing Chip with that too.

Garcia guided him as he rubbed the oils together in his hands, then, with amazing concentration, very slowly and carefully placed them on a swollen breast. The three of them immediately felt the energy flowing between Chip and Shauna through his touch. "Looks like you have the healing touch," said Garcia, adding that she had been trained in Reiki, a hands-on technique for releasing physical and mental toxins. "I bet if we could measure right now we'd see the electro-magnetic energy you're transferring." "Whatever works," responded Chip.

Shauna settled into an even deeper relaxation as Chip and Garcia took turns working on her stomach. Responding to their combined touch she began to feel a whole lot better and drifted into a light doze.

Appreciative of Garcia's devotion, he thanked her, his hands still resting on Shauna's breasts, so warm and responsive and alive, although her nipples were too sore and tender for love making. Garcia went to draw a bath and he continued his visual exploration of Shauna's voluptuous form, intent on enjoying her to the fullest, as stirred as ever, undeterred by the effects of her period.

Opening her eyes to find him staring at her with caring, deep love and a hint of arousal, she smiled. Hearing Garcia call, as if from miles away, that the bath was ready, she perked up, asking, "Where do you have a bathtub?" "Aha," he responded smugly. "It's behind a secret panel in the bathroom. I rarely use it but now seemed like a good time." She showed every sign of being excited. "I'll go get in the tub and have Garcia help you join me. I'm not nearly as free as you in letting her see me naked." He smattered her with feather light kisses before leaving.

Entering the bathroom with Garcia she saw that the end wall had disappeared. It was now an arch through to a second room. Through the arch she was faced with a grinning Chip leaning back, posing in a huge white Jacuzzi tub, his lower half hidden below a layer of bubbles and rose petals. Removing her tampon she allowed Garcia and Chip to help her into the tub. She sat between his legs, resting back against his chest, holding her hair above the water. Garcia quickly pinned it to keep it dry. "Thank you so much, you really do think of everything," said Shauna. "You make her feel like a Princess. Nothing less will do," Garcia ordered Chip on her way out.

"You know, this is amazing. I *do* feel like a princess!" "Just you wait. The best is yet to come. Love, I promise you you're going to be purring for more," beamed Chip, "I figured we could take a siesta after this and then go out to eat, celebrate my initiation into the blooderhood." Shauna laughed. "Just how long do you think you can milk this menstrual thing, Baby?" "Just as long as I can milk you," he replied.

Kissing her repeatedly he gradually worked his way from her neck down her back, taking his time, gently stroking. Sliding his hands forward, he caressed her lower stomach and thighs. "I'll steer clear of your cherry for a while. I know you're just too sensitive," he said, lightly touching her pubic hairs. He returned to kissing her shoulders and neck. Tonguing her ears, guaranteed to arouse her, he felt her buildup, as she could feel his, stirring against her ass. Knowing he'd have to at some point, so now was as good a time as any, he helped her get out of the tub, shower off, and back onto the bed, where Garcia had replaced the plastic sheeting.

Making her comfortable, attentive to her every need, it wasn't long before they were pleasuring each other, accompanied by blood trickling onto the protective sheet. A husky voiced Shauna whispered, "Baby, I'm so aroused already you might have to tie me down when the fireworks come." She laughed breathily. He smiled at her, happy she was feeling so good, watching intently as her eyes clouded and lost focus with his rhythmic attention. With a slight repositioning he brought his cock to her pussy lips and pushed it inside, setting her off into spontaneous shudders. Making sure he stayed connected, he purposefully aimed at her G- spot, relishing the bloody flow that lubricated him so freely as she drifted into a new sexual dimension, twisting and bucking.

Shauna, in spite of turning tiger, managed to stutter out, "Are y. . . you . . . doing . . . OK . . . w. . . with all the. . . b. . . blood?" "Love, this is an adventure I was not meant to miss!" he said.

Breathing fast and heavy, sweat dripping, he hung on as Shauna, body gyrating continuously, arms flailing, sweaty and loud, held nothing back. Thrusting as fast as he could, climaxing just before a grunting, unintelligible Shauna surrendered, gasping as she ejaculated an arc of light red liquid. Chip ducked, reaching quickly for some wipes to block any further unrestrained flow from this G-spot phenomena.

As they both recuperated from joyful orgasm, they seemed suspended, not daring to move too much, wanting to contain any spillage, especially after his prick came sliding out, bloody. "You're like a blazing fire in there, Love." "It's said that a woman's vagina can sterilize anything," said Shauna. "I'm a believer," laughed Chip.

Using the hand held shower, Chip helped Shauna clean up, taking his time to spray her front and back, enjoying every moment. He finished by thoroughly washing her hair, and showering himself. He towel dried them both and retrieving a fresh tampon, almost expertly slipped it into her. "I never thought you'd want to do that, Babe, but it's a surprising turn-on when you do. I've got so used to doing it myself, I don't even think about it, how it feels, it's just a chore, a habit – certainly no fun." Chip was so pleased he'd got the hang of it so quickly. *I guess it's not complex but it is rather an intimate undertaking. One I wouldn't have thought of as being enjoyable before.* "Would you like a nightie, Love?" "Oh yuck, no, no, no." "I didn't think so."

Picking her up, Chip carried her to bed and helped her get comfortable before he finished up in the bathroom. When he came out, Shauna was on her back in her favorite position - the sheet off and her legs spread apart - sound asleep. Chip climbed in naked and lay down beside her. She sighed and rolled over to him. She cuddled against him with a contented look on her face. He turned his head and lightly kissed her on the brow before falling into a deep sleep too.

Later, over dinner at Houston's, Shauna asked about his Dallas trip. "Well, Love, there's not much to report. They looked us over but made no offers. We discussed possible terms, seems they're prepared to pay well for a six year contract. Of course, the money is tempting, but after ten years, I don't know that I want to live that life anymore - in fact it often feels like no kind of life at all. I even talked with Ivan about retiring." "That's quite a decision, Babe. A major change. Just know that whatever you decide, I'll be right here with you." He kissed her deeply and passionately - enough to cause her to wet her already wet self.

"I think I alluded to a clothing company when we were shopping and it's real. We design and produce men's sportswear. I started it with Ivan and R Jay about a year ago and it's been doing very well. We have an outlet in L.A. and plan to expand into a couple more locations, possibly start a franchise business. In fact I have to go to L.A. after the party on Thursday to discuss some proposals." "Oh, Baby, that's so exciting. Who does your designing and what kind of clothes do you sell?" Stirred by her excitement, he replied, "Our top sellers are sports themed tops and shorts. Then we have a range of street shorts and slacks, and we've got a deal cooking with a major shoe company that might sign on to provide an exclusive line of athletic shoes. In fact I have photos and videos at home that I can show you. We've been doing some of the designs ourselves but have hired two independent designers out of Los Angeles to help, and they're proving really prolific, which is great for us. We've also just got a new, very cool web site up and running for online orders. And obviously our reputations as athletes help with sales and marketing."

"That sounds great - adventuresome and bold - I'm so proud of you. Growing your own business is where it's at. And, let me volunteer my services, Baby. I covered design in college and loved it, still do, so maybe, after studying what your line looks like, I can submit some design ideas and you can see what you think. If you like them, they'll be my donation to your success, if not, no harm done, and I'll have had some fun." Touched by her unrestrained support, he kissed her before continuing. "The other plan I have is to install a recording studio at the house - primarily for you now, but also because I've been interested for a while in producing some up-and-coming rappers. I know two right now who I'd like to get my hands on before someone else does. That's why I invited Richard over Friday." Raising their glasses to each other, they drank, both content and happy - especially Chip. Talking with her he now had a more solid idea of just where his future could lead.

Troy picked them up and drove them home where Chip put a slightly tipsy, exhausted Shauna to bed.

CHAPTER 11 REBIRTH

Chip stirred and propping himself on an elbow looked lovingly at the sleeping Shauna. Feeling his gaze, she opened her eyes to find him inches away. *Sure is a good kissing distance,* she thought as she puckered her lips, inviting him to take advantage. Then, flipping the sheet off, she slowly kissed her way down his body. Not used to such tender treatment, he allowed himself to relax to her touch. She played with his nipples, his balls, his prick, teasing him to fullness. "You look so fucking huge today, Baby!"

She took her time, wanting to bring him to orgasm with her tongue, continuing to caress his thighs, balls and erection, his jerking more frantic. Suddenly sitting, he grabbed Shauna's hand and urged her into the bathroom. Having her bend forward hands against the wall in the shower stall, he removed her tampon. Running his hands all over her - waist, belly, stomach - kissing her ass, - dangling breasts swaying sensuously at random as her body shook, he caressed her close to climax. "Are your breasts all right? I don't want you hurting." Having difficulty talking, she barely managing to get out, "They . . . feel remarkably . . . good . . . thanks." "I saw you like this yesterday and so desired to take you from behind. Are you ready for that?" asked Chip with anticipation. At Shauna's nod, he grabbed her waist in both hands and with her help pressed home. Slowly he slipped in and out of a trembling, blood-rich, ever-contracting, and super wet Shauna. Sensing orgasm approaching, he increased his urgency until they lost themselves in a pleasure unlike even their previous. Her fiery cauldron consumed them. An accelerating, super-charged electricity propelled them into a sub-atomic world of random strings that gradually transformed with their combined presence into rhythmic, organized patterns, each string vibrating with a different shape, filling space-time to infinity. The two of them could have been anywhere in the universe or beyond, vibrating with their own uniqueness.

Recovering their senses, they cleaned themselves and went to collapse on the bed naked, exhausted, holding each other close. They slept.

Waking much later, Chip suggested another picnic, this time to the north-east. Always keen to be out in the wild Shauna was only too happy to go and he arranged supplies with Mark.

Clearing the city she felt intoxicated by the space. "You can really breathe out here . . . and feel so liberated!" she shouted joyfully. They had the windows down and were reveling in the fresh air streaming through. "Hey Babe, I had Peggy do a search online yesterday morning. She found out that when a woman has an orgasm during her period, pain suppressing endorphins are released and the cycle is shorter because the contractions during sex flush out the waste so much quicker. That's probably why my cramps went so quick and my bleeding has reduced so much," said a happy Shauna, continuing, "Thanks to you, Baby, for being so willing and caring." "I love it that you're super horny when you menstruate. Are we going to have a great day, or what?" he whooped with a devilish grin. Shauna felt her pussy prickle.

Arriving at their destination, a meadow split by a meandering stream, an enchanted Shauna sat almost hypnotized by the tumbling water, gurgling its way downstream. A naked Chip had a different kind of tumbling in mind. So willingly she guided him to pleasure her. Careful to treat her gently, he soon had them on their way to another explosive orgasm, and their bodies, now becoming progressively lighter, loosening the chains of gravity, continued their transformation of full out pleasure from traditional procreation to birthing a new reality.

Being so fulfilled by each other and the after effects, and being in such a fresh and wild environment, they ate slowly, enjoying the pleasure of being together unencumbered and free. Relaxing, talking: he mentioning a meeting with his agent in the morning so he wouldn't be able to go to the studio with her but would pick her up later; she suggesting dropping by her old apartment so she could get some of her things and retrieve her car, they whiled away the afternoon until, the light fading, they reluctantly dressed and loaded the SUV, hoping to reach the highway before it was dark. Having stayed longer than they'd expected, Chip skipped Shauna's apartment and drove them straight home. It had been a wonderful interlude, but their excitement and anticipation was for all the adventures to come. As it turned out though, it wouldn't always be that easy to retain an excitement and enthusiasm for the future.

Garcia must have been watching for the car in the security center because as soon as they entered the master bedroom, she was knocking on the outer suite door. Entering, carrying a letter, she immediately apologized. "While you were gone yesterday and then again today, a man came to the house asking for you, Shauna. I'm sorry I didn't tell you yesterday, but I got so involved with getting you ready I completely forgot. I didn't feel comfortable with inviting him in, so I kept him standing at the front door. Today though he gave me this letter, telling me several times to make SURE that you got it. So, here, I hope it's OK." "Of course it is," said Shauna, taking the envelope, thanking her. It was simply addressed: To Shauna. "Troy said he has a clear view of him on one of the security tapes and can print you a picture if you'd like," added Garcia.

"Please," said Shauna. Chip walked to the intercom and asked Troy to print out the picture. In the middle of reprogramming the security feeds, Troy asked if Garcia could come get it. The message relayed, Garcia left to get the photo.

"I can't think who in the world it would be or how they would know to find me here," said Shauna, a worried look on her face. "Look Love, try to relax. Let's not waste energy until we know what's going on. Maybe the picture will clear it up." And he led her to the bed to sit saying, "Whatever this is or means, we'll get through it together. Together we can get through anything, my Love."

Trying to reassure and calm her, he wasn't having much success. She was clearly becoming increasingly agitated by shadows of her past. Not believing how rattled she was, she suddenly exclaimed: "Stop this right now!" "What was that?" asked a disturbed Chip. Quickly apologizing she said, "I was speaking to ME," and then began crying. Chip held her, stroking her hair and kissing her tenderly. "Do you think it might be a good idea to just go ahead and read the letter?" asked Chip. "I should. I know. But I think I'll wait for the photo first. That way I'll know who it's from - face to face, so to speak," she replied.

It seemed like forever before Garcia returned clutching a small photo. She gave it to Shauna, Chip looking over her shoulder. At first Shauna was puzzled. It didn't help that the security photo was in black and white. Staring back at Shauna was a man in his fifties, maybe, with thick dark hair in desperate need of a cut. Closer observation suggested the man was prematurely aged with deeply etched lines in his forehead and on the outer perimeters of his sad, forlorn eyes. The color of his eyes was impossible to tell in the photo. It was also difficult to estimate his height. His nose was striking, well sculptured and dignified looking, and his mouth was full-lipped - even sensual looking - but downturned sadly. *Who can this be?* She wondered. It was Chip who filled in the blanks. "You certainly have the same thick dark hair, and the nose is similar, and those nice big full lips . . ."Suddenly putting her hand to her mouth, she gasped. "No, it CAN'T BE! WHY would THIS man be tracking me down after all these years?" "So Love, this visitor was . . . your Father?"

Shauna's hands were trembling as she sat on the bed, opened the envelope and pulled out the letter.

Dear Shauna:

I know it has been a very long time since you and I have had anything to do with one another. And rightfully so. However, no matter what I have done to you, or how bad I've been to you, it can no longer keep me from wanting, with all my heart, to find you. So this is what I have been trying to do for over a year now. I have traveled all over trying to find you, but somehow always arrive just a bit late after you have moved on. I now realize that my own life is in danger. I believe I was shot at a few days ago and am very wary now, especially about coming back to this house.

I don't know if your mother ever told you about me. This is difficult. Please forgive me for raping you as a child. You were so beautiful and alive I couldn't help myself. And please do not judge me too harshly. Your Mother found out and threw me out and I have done my penance many times over. I was also driven from the Ayr Sect, still a strong secret force in Scotland, where I had a powerful position. And I have been living in disgrace ever since.

Recently, there have been secret communiques from this part of America back to the Ayr in Scotland describing a suspicious super power seemingly being created by a perfect fusion of human beings. This power, if it truly exists, could be a threat to the Ayr, possibly to the world. Shauna, you can be sure this all will be well looked into.

All the powerful sects are power and money greedy, have been for centuries, and have been controlling worldwide commerce. They will stop at nothing to maintain and increase their control.

Your mother will be contacting you soon. She knows much more. How she will contact you I do not know. Heed what she has to tell you. I believe there are plans for your escape. This is my last contact with you. I must vanish.

Your Father

Silence . . . Deafening silence . . . The quiet of the grave . . . Shauna frozen in place . . . Her face without color, eyes fixed on nothing - her strange gaze all-encompassing, trying to process every little anything, pulling whatever she could from the innermost depths of her being – sorting – sifting – sense - no sense - logical – messy - without meaning – fragmented – nothing – everything - important - stupid. She collapsed into Chip, grabbing him tightly, snuggling up into a fetal position, trying to squeeze into the very skin of his body. Gently prying himself free he covered her with the comforter.

Wait . . . What? . . . What was that? . . . Something close by? . . . Something roundish? . . . SLOWLY . . . S L o w l y . . . NOW nothing . . . Nothing at all . . . NO FORM . . . NO DISCERNABLE MOVEMENT WHAT So . . . . . . Anywhere . . . covers dormant . . . No SIGNS . . . OF BREath . . . No . . . This life . . . cannot . . . be . . . so fragile! . . . Out from the lungs wheezes the plea of the heart so perfectly placed architecturally . . . designed to be the spiritual advocate of the human body . . . magnificent. Do we actually listen to our soul's pleas . . . Let go of our own control? . . . Are we linked to the real and practical functioning of ourselves? . . . IN whole and honorable ways . . . Are we ravenous . . . to be greater and greater . . . INDIVIDUALS . . . physically . . . bonded . . . together, tissue to blood to bone to organ . . . forever? Manifesting necessary changes as we live . . . IN CHARGE . . . not the same old . . . generation after generation . . . BUT MAKING IT EASY ON EACH OTHER . . . TREASURING EACH OTHER? . . . OR IS IT STILL . . . competition - mind so critical . . . judgments so stubborn . . . Cut anything . . . bigGER . . . beTTER DOWn . . . to . . . the status quo . . . KILL . . . ELIMINATE enjoyment . . . BUILD shRINes to . . . s u f f e r i n g? . . . Enough . . . ENOUGH . . . WAKE . . . UP!

Yes, yes it was. The slightest of movements from deep under the covers where lay the unyielding yet warm life of a quietly smoldering, small heap of glowing flesh. Suddenly, so suddenly, the embers combust into trillions of brilliant particles dancing, quivering tiny super-sub-atomic shapes and clusters darting faster than the speed of light. A small bright flare explodes from within the covers. A raspy hissing roar accompanies the escape of two vigorously beating wings-but-not-wings wrapping around each other atop a roughly featured sphere.

Abruptly, the multiple movements and sounds slow down fast, countless charcoal ash-feathers drift away exposing two arms crisscrossed in gracefully entwined stability above a sphere now mutating into an even more beautiful, animated, smiling then laughing Shauna - exploding with life and compassion. As she continues to rise from the filth, grime and ashes of a world filled with the devastation of separation which is death, she is washed cleaner and cleaner. She glows from within. Her resonating voice urges her to keep stepping up, up, up. She sits on the bed her legs raised at the knees buried under the covers. Chip appears to be Shauna appears to be Chip . . . indivisible, ascending, becoming what has never been before . . . that is, in full manifestation physically . . . knowing and claiming itself to be powerful, without limits and with completely new strands of DNA . . . new, pure, regal, thought patterns . . . the full intelligence of the body bonding organically . . . one's own body first and then with others who are also transitioning as they become exposed to new sounds, actions . . . Living amongst people with less and less death secreted in the body. Unending support! What Passion! What Joy! What Enormous Changes! What an Elixir of Nourishment! Is it a miracle? Or is it what humankind has always been? But buried under endless layers of artificial programing? Till now!

From deep within their very guts new ideas are being born, new ways of thinking; disrupting the old, passed-on leadership, threatening the few in power who want the people blind and ignorant. The inner deep waking of an immortal strand buried so deep and for so long beside the ever more dominant chain of death genetics was now stirring within the Shauna-Chip singularity and would eventually alter mankind, attracting more and more who would choose a higher life, triggered cellularly to directly experience what's unconstrained, and dare to question, dare to speak and act against the thunder of the herd, to risk everything in their passionate pursuit of becoming one with Shauna-Chip who, through their oneness and passion, would show them a new unknown path.

One vast universe was opening where a new mankind would shape its own destiny. Taking guts, total focus and a deep hunger to live and be open to all others of like-minded destinies, this new life would require a close support system that humankind has never actually lived. *Imagine a life without limitations! Where being born to live IS possible!* The destruction of the death lock in every individual was underway.

Shauna and Chip knew they were different, aware they had a purpose. What they didn't know was how it would unfold - or rather, how everything would so savagely be torn apart. Even in the vastness and depth of their own perceptions they still had a universe of unknowns yet to be revealed.

Would the mighty jolt reverberating throughout them both in her confronting the words of her long lost Father be enough? Or would it take an even greater upheaval to shake loose, from the tightly packed debris concealed deep inside their cellular structures, the self-awareness of who they each really were and always had been?

"I had the most bizarre dream. . . I was a blob of molten, spewing flesh and there was this huge ball with wings that became falling feathers and I began rising up - on and on - as the two of us became indistinguishable from each other. There were two of us but we both looked like me."

"I had the same dream! Only I'm not sure it was a dream. It seemed so real." "You think?" "Honestly, I really don't know." Shauna thought for a moment, then shrugged, slowly rose on all fours, slithered over to Chip and mounted him lustfully. Her bikini panties slightly scraped his vulnerable balls, sending an excited shiver throughout his body. He had been overwhelmed by what he'd seen but hadn't missed a beat, immersing himself totally in everything that had taken place. Now, to his surprise he sensed a lighter, brighter, more playful Shauna. She spread her legs wide apart to lower herself even closer, sliding her sopping pussy back and forth across his prick, weaving a moist web of desire to stimulate his arousal.

Twitching beneath her, his root grew larger, thicker and harder, squirming to get out from under, stand tall and claim the attention it craved. Slipping to one side, she grabbed it and sucked in, her tongue expertly teasing. Not wanting to come just yet, he slid from her grasp, grabbed both her ankles and flipped her onto her back. Willingly spreading her legs wide she opened. A flash of insight and he saw how she subtly encouraged him to vary his approach, to become more vulnerable and sweeter. To become a new lover they could both love. And he loved her greater for it.

He entered her with a finger, her eyes widening, her sensuous, full-lipped mouth forming an 'O', sucking in air. He pushed deeper and deeper, caressing and probing, till she was bright and flushed with an almost unbearable excitement. Feeling her just moments away he quickly straightened, rammed his rock hard swollen sex deep inside her. He was home. Plunging faster and faster, two frenzied lovers bonding as one in total synchronization, fragmenting as particles of light, flashing instantaneously beyond the visible, they disappeared.

Multiple energies racing through space-time infinity . . . Defying all known laws of physics. Beauty, astonishing beauty, untold beauty, unknown beauty. Not just light years of empty space. Untraceably zipping through life intelligences, endless, unknowable, electrifying originality in constant flux pulsing around them feeding a sense of powerful purpose, they glimpsed themselves in a myriad scenarios – fantastic, alien, inexplicable - a matrix of scenes strobing past inside and out in a continuous stream until everything went . . . **black**.

Disorientation. Where were they? Where had they been? It certainly looked like their bedroom. Everything seemed to be in its rightful place. The clock said it was still early. Until the hands started spinning in a blur, stopping at seven-thirty in the evening. Looking outside a mushy-headed Chip confirmed the sky streaked with the colors of dusk. *More weirdness.*

Lying in damp, cold, slimy sheets - wet through, right down to the mattress. Semen still oozed from her pussy. What a wonder he could produce so much. Calling Garcia to clean up for them, he said, "I hope everyone did the necessary ready for tonight 'cos we sure haven't done anything," adding that he wished they could have rescheduled the party and spent the extra time alone together before he went to Los Angeles in the morning. Promising to be back in time to hear her sing on Saturday he finished. "I'll miss you though, my Love." "Me too," she said.

CHAPTER 12   TREACHERY

Ready to party, they stood on the landing outside the master suite surveying the spectacle below. People everywhere. Spread out through the living room and across the pool deck and terrace beyond, lined up at the bar in the dining area. All talking, drinking, circulating; a constantly changing tableau. Tables buried under heaped dishes were as yet untouched, as if the guests were waiting for the hosts before eating, or perhaps just content to talk, drink and enjoy the buzz.

They slowly descended to enter the fray, beaming, glowing, waving and acknowledging their guests. Eyes fastened on the regal couple as they entered their first party together. As they joined the throng, working their way through the living room, Chip peeled off to get drinks and Shauna scanned the crowd for her former roommate, Peggy, seeking a familiar face amongst the host of people she didn't yet know. Not seeing her immediately, she began to circulate, intent on talking with every person, with or without Chip. Free to move as she felt, as was he.

Several chats later she spotted Peggy in a corner with a small group, delicately sipping from a glass of white wine. Shauna was happy to see her looking so good, slimmer, engaged, animated. Making her way toward Peggy, she continued her appraisal of the crowd and noticed Mark, the chef, in a waiter's uniform carrying a large tray of assorted finger food. As he threaded his way in the direction of Peggy, Shauna sensed a subtle attraction between the two and paused to watch. They began a whispered conversation, leaning into each other, periodically touching, lightly and casually - a familiarity that suggested they knew each other before tonight. *Mmm, interesting*, thought Shauna as Mark moved on to offer his delicacies to other guests.

Continuing on course, Shauna reached Peggy and they embraced affectionately. Peggy thanked her again for covering her financially and Shauna explained that since they'd spoken she had decided to live with Gifford and would be calling to arrange picking up her things. "Not that I have much. Nearly everything is yours and I appreciate that you shared it with me. I'll talk with Gifford about the fate of my car. Gosh, he takes such good care of me . . . and Troy drives me wherever I want to go. I'm getting spoiled." "I'm so happy for you Shauna, but I'm also a little envious."

"Well, my dear, as I was coming over, I happened to see the rather intimate connection you seem to have with our chef, Mark. What's going on with you two?" "Oh that," giggled Peggy. "We met at the gym about a week ago. It was almost like he followed me there." Shauna's curiosity was pricked. "What do you mean?" asked Shauna? "Well, you know, his coming up to me lacked a kind of spontaneity, like he was following a script - as if I was in his plans already kind of thing. But whatever, since then we've spent quite a bit of time together and I've enjoyed it."

Wondering, Shauna inquired, "Does he ask about me?" "Oh yeah. I like to talk about you anyway - we *are* the best of friends after all - and he seems to be really interested." "So what kind of stuff do you say about me that would be of interest?" "Oh, like how you and Gifford met - so magical and passionate - and what a hit you are at the club. And how since you've got together I've hardly seen or heard from you. It's like you're glued to Gifford at the hip or something." *Glued, yes*, thought Shauna, amused. *And you're right about the something, it's certainly not at the hip. But can you really be so enamored with me? I mean, I know you're somewhat naïve, but still* . . . And an uneasiness crept into the pit of Shauna's stomach.

A series of taps on her shoulder interrupted her train of thought. She turned to face none other than the sexpert, Harvey Sexton, in the flesh again, looking longingly at her cleavage. "Why don't you come up for air and give me a civil greeting?" laughed Shauna. Lifting his gaze, he said lustfully, "Better than bobbing for apples. But I digress. How is my favorite sex queen tonight?" He was impeccably groomed as before, his dark hair slicked back not one out of place, his clean-shaven face glowing as if polished. With his beautifully cut suit, aristocratic speech and bearing she found herself curious, struck, as before, by his magnetism. Maybe he really was a sexpert. And he swung a petite brown haired, beauty in front of her. "May I present my friend, Giselle. Giselle, this is Shauna." Seeing Giselle's discomfort, Shauna immediately sought to put her at ease, commenting on how pretty she looked and how happy she was that she'd come. "I see you have drinks, so why don't I introduce you to some people," she offered and taking Giselle's elbow led her to Peggy's group, Harvey in tow. Giselle started to loosen up as Shauna made the introductions and signaled Mark to come with the snack tray. As Mark approached, Shauna caught the tiniest of hints that he and Harvey knew each other, and more than casually. She couldn't quite put her finger on it. *How strange,* thought Shauna. But once again her mental musings were interrupted, this time by a voice she loved and a kiss on the cheek. "Crap, the bar line is impossibly long," said an exasperated Chip as he handed Shauna a white wine and hung on to his beer. "Sorry it took so long. Well, hi there Harvey. I'm glad you made it. Now, who is this?" he asked, extending his big hand to the delicate Giselle who took it by the fingertips as Harvey introduced her before swinging her back to join Peggy's group again.

Troy, elegantly dressed in a white tuxedo, opened the front door to admit a boisterous Coach and a few of his favorite player-sycophants. Their loud entrance into the living room drew the attention and Chip quickly went to greet them. Directing them to the bar he stayed to talk with a couple nearby.

Shauna, circulating in her quest to at least greet every guest, wandered onto the pool deck, surprised by the number of people already in the pool - not naked, but close. The two Texas size barbeque barrels were under siege and the delicious mixed aromas of roasting chicken, steak and pork soon had her salivating. Swallowing hard, realizing how hungry she was, she turned and headed for the dining room to grab something a little less greasy.

Mission accomplished she made her way to one of the large tables on the far side of the pool where people were feasting. "May I join you?" she asked, introducing herself. "Sure," said someone, although no one seemed to really look at her - as if she was a ghost. *Who are these people and how do they fit into Chip's life?* thought Shauna as she sat. *Perhaps I was too hasty in wanting to strike out on my own. I feel really out of place.*

Tuning back in she heard the tail end of a discussion between two women at the other end of the table, confirming with knowing nods that this woman who had dared join them was indeed a marriage breaker. Shauna gracefully stood back up. Picking up her plate, she made sure she was stable on her high heels - the wine had gone straight to her head - before declaring matter-of-factly that she had come on the scene long after Gifford's separation from his wife and that she and Gifford were so good for each other in every way, emphasis on the 'every'. With a bright, charming smile, she then made her departure. Hearing the sound of a woman's heels clacking on the deck behind her, she had the odd thought that it was one of the women from the table hurrying to stab her in the back.

Whipping round she confronted a woman obviously startled by the menace in her action. Seeing the woman just wanted to talk to her, Shauna relaxed. "Hi, you must be Shauna. I'm Jessica, I'm working with Gifford in L.A. and I just couldn't let you go without telling you how sorry I am that you were treated so horribly. I don't know who those two women are but the rest of us work with your husband and are currently expanding his line of sportswear into a line of casual clothing that we're all excited about. But that's neither here nor there. What is is that he's been so different over the phone recently, and meeting you I can see why. Anyway, we thought we'd surprise him by flying here for the party tonight, stay over at the Hyatt and do business with him tomorrow, instead of him having to make the trip to L.A. That way he'll have Saturday free and won't have to rush to be with you for your performance. In fact, a few of us might stay over to hear you too, which would be a treat for us if we can swing it." She took a breath about to continue when Shauna jumped in. "Thank you so much for the apology. I appreciate that. For the record though, Gifford and I aren't married, nor do we intend to be. I'm also happy you decided to come tonight and stay over so Gifford won't have to travel this time. He'll be happy about that too. If some of you would like to have dinner here tomorrow night and can tolerate leftovers you'll be very welcome." "Let me get back to you on that," said Jessica. "Would tomorrow morning be OK to let you know?" Shauna nodded yes and gave Jessica a warm hug saying, "I guess you must have come when we were getting ready. Running late, you know. Gifford will be so surprised to see you. I'll let him know you're here when I see him." And they went their separate ways, pleased to have met.

Scouting for somewhere else to sit and eat her barely touched plate of food, Shauna decided she might as well scope out the terrace beyond the deck while she was at it. She wove through the clusters of people juggling their food and drinks as they stood and ate.

Making a loop around a fountain and bird bath, out of the corner of her eye she noticed three figures in a tight huddle under an overhang of foliage near the house. Their furtive discussion seemed to her to make them more obvious than if they'd just hung out closer to the action. Curious she eased closer, identifying Mark, Harvey and Coach. *I wonder what they're up to – and how they know each other?* Cautiously moving closer still, using the foliage as a partial screen, she could hear their muffled voices as they argued heatedly, so engrossed they didn't notice her. Coach suddenly bellowed, "The only way to get this solved and done with is TO SEPARATE THEM. And the sooner the better." He quieted down and they continued their muted discussions, but she got bits and pieces, including, "Saturday night." They bumped knuckles to seal whatever agreement they'd come to. Shauna, fearing discovery, quickly and quietly removed her shoes for greater speed while balancing her plate and, with hands full, hurried to put distance between her and the three conspirators.

Disturbed and shaken, more ruffled than her blouse, she joined a couple at a table near the pool, seeking to regain her composure. Looking up from putting her shoes back on she noticed the couple appraising her with interest. She adjusted her blouse and pulled at her skirt which had taken a hike upwards as she ran. "Those stilettos can be such a pain," said the woman. "I'm Hedda McCormick and this is my husband Eddie. We couldn't help noticing you dashing barefoot in our direction. Is there a problem?" Shauna did some quick-thinking. "No, not really. I have this terrible fear of snakes - no matter what kind or size - and as I was strolling around the pool, I saw a grass snake and just picked up my shoes and ran. Thanks for asking though. I'm Shauna. I live with Gifford. It's a pleasure to meet you both." She so wanted to blurt out the truth - *there are three guys, so unlikely to be buddies, who seem to be planning to separate me and Chip. I know each of the men individually, but how they're connected I have no idea. And separation would be the worst thing that could happen. It's unthinkable. Even the thought is totally unbearable.* She thrived on the truth, but this time she knew it would cause more damage than good. She wanted to eat. She wanted to drink. She wanted the nightmare to go away, right now.

"Shauna, Shauna, Shauna!" She turned, knowing the voice and hearing the urgency in it. Running up, Chip exhaled, "I've been looking everywhere for you!" Acknowledging Hedda and Eddie with a nod, he continued, "I'm sorry to disturb you like this, Love, but I need you to come with me," and he took her hand. Helping her to her feet he guided her into the house. "I wish I knew how to make this easy for you, how to sooth your heart. I can tell you're already shaken up by something but we have to deal with this first. You can fill me in later."

"It's my Father, isn't it." It wasn't a question. Since reading his letter she'd had premonitions and a distinct feeling that whoever was after him would get him, sooner rather than later. "How did you know?" he asked, not waiting for an answer before continuing "I'm so sorry, my Precious, but he's been murdered . . . He was found just outside the front gate . . . a single bullet to the back of the head. According to the policeman at the scene he died instantly, so at least he didn't suffer." A tearful and shaken Shauna asked, "Who found him? Did anyone hear the shot?" "It was Troy. He was passing the open front door making his security round when he heard what he thought sounded like a silenced gunshot. He ran out to take a look around and saw the gate in the perimeter wall wide open. Hurrying outside he found your father sprawled face down." "A few more minutes, seconds, maybe, and he'd have made it inside," added a shook-up Troy as he joined them. I had my flashlight with me and scoured the surroundings as best I could, but no luck. The killer got away." "But we'll find him!" promised Chip. He gently engulfed the shaking Shauna, encouraging her to cry all she wanted, telling her that she was not alone, that he would always be beside her - no matter what!

After unscrewing the silencer and hiding it inside his waiter's uniform with the gun until he could dispose of them properly, Mark let himself back into the main kitchen. Located off the chef's galley it was on the far side of the house away from the scene. *Oh man! Do I ever thrill to the rush of a kill,* he rhymed triumphantly. Excited to atone for his screw up in missing Shauna, he was flushed and jittery. Knowing he needed to calm down, to act as normal as possible, he joined the other caterers.

"Those trays getting heavy for you man?" asked a nearby waiter. "You bet," said Mark. "I'm gonna make this my last round before I collapse," he added with a big grin. He wanted to be remembered in case he needed to account for his whereabouts. He loaded a tray and hefting it to his shoulder staggered as if the load was too much, eliciting a few laughs. Carrying the tray he went up the stairs to the dining room and looked for Peggy to seal his alibi.

Shauna and Chip stood near her father's body, eerily lit by a police cruiser's headlights and garish red and blue flashing light bars. Shauna was reluctant to go closer - agonizing, sobbing and in fear. *Did the assassination of her father this close to home have a special significance? Was it linked to the clandestine meeting she'd witnessed earlier?*

Chip held her shaking body close, softly repeating to her over and over, "I'm so sorry, I'm so sorry, I'm so sorry. We'll get to the bottom of this - we will, we will, we'll get to the bottom of it." And he rocked her in his arms, stroking her hair, pressing her against his body and softly kissing her. He felt impotent and useless.

While wishing he had the magic ability to make the pain go away, he encouraged her to keep pouring out her feelings, whatever that looked like. Reassuring her with his presence, he unknowingly gave her the best she could possibly get: one hundred percent of his compassion - unfiltered, undiluted, filling her being with living nourishment, the real deal, unavailable anywhere else. He infused her with what few knew they were starved of and even fewer knew how to share – his full self.

Chip knew that what he felt with Shauna was greater than any love that can so often be superficial, self-centered and suppressing. In stoking the fire of compassion within his own body, he stirred the power within Shauna, enabling her to not just endure the suffering and pain but to move through it quickly to a greater strength and purpose. As her thoughts, feelings, and mind-chatter began to slow and stabilize, she began to surface from the well of despair she'd dropped into. Her sobs became less soulful and less frequent until, with a deep shuddering gasp, her whole body relaxed.

Looking down at her, he could feel a new aliveness and tender passion igniting within her. She had shaken off what could have been an endless darkness. Her body electric had been recharged. She was waking up to a fresher and more alive Shauna. "Thank you my Love. I feel so much better because of you," she said as her eyes filled with tears of appreciation. "You've given me new life and I'll always be grateful." He marveled at how surrendered she was - nothing to protect, nothing to hide, no need to be right, no excuses, no critical mind, no ego. *What courage. To rid the body of everything that would keep it from what it needed most: other bodies,* thought a chastened Chip.

A second police car arrived and Shauna and Chip decided to leave the all-too-common scene of a life ended prematurely. Shauna thanked Troy and asked him to liaise with the police for them and to take another circuit of the grounds, "Just to make sure," before she and Chip headed back to the house and the party. The last thing they wanted was to be entangled in a gathering crowd of the morbidly curious.

Marveling at how Shauna had just taken charge so soon after her tragedy, Chip squeezed her lovingly, saying, "That's my girl." Looking up she said, "There's something I want to discuss which I think could be related to the murder, but it's only a feeling and I don't want to muddy the waters, so I'll run it by you later." "OK," he said, distracted by a bickering couple who passed them coming the other way.

On the terrace, unaware of the tragedy out front, the five man band was already setup and playing. A dance floor had been laid down but the guests, many of whom had already heard of the murder, seemed more interested in learning as much as they could about the incident than in dancing.

Feeling everything but determined to not allow their joy to be compromised, Shauna and Chip, proud of how well Troy and Garcia had organized the party and how well it had been progressing, were equally determined to make sure any disruption was minimal.

As they made their way out onto the terrace Shauna told Chip about her conversation with Jessica. Remarking that he'd planned to cancel his trip anyway because of what had happened he thanked her and said he'd arrange to meet them mid-morning for as long as was necessary, "until supper if need be." Revising her original thought, Shauna suggested that he took them out for supper instead of having them stay for left-overs. Agreeing, he asked her to be prepared to join them, saying, "I'll make reservations for seven-thirty."

CHAPTER 13 THREADS

As they stepped onto the dance floor, it was impossible to tell that either Chip or Shauna had just minutes before received such appalling news. Obviously lovers and deeply immersed in each other, they immediately attracted most everyone's attention as they took up a position directly in front of the band. The heat they were generating was palpable. Ignoring the beat of the music, they danced their own lovers wrap. One pair of eyes of the many looking on did so with envy close to hate. Their occasional kisses further enraged the already disgruntled onlooker.

"At the risk of upsetting you with all that's been going on, I'm totally hot for you right now and want to be inside you," whispered Chip.

"No need to apologize, Baby. I adore that you feel that way. And yeah, I want you inside me too," replied Shauna. Both with the same thought - *run to the bedroom and take it from there* - they continued their moving embrace.

As Shauna didn't drink for at least twenty-four hours before a performance, she was considering switching from wine to Baileys – she felt she deserved a drink or two. "Mind if I sit the next one out, Love? My feet could use a break from these shoes and I feel like having a Baileys. You could go see your business associates." And she pointed them out. "Sounds good," said Chip, sitting her down before taking off for the bar.

An ever-vigilant Harvey, seeing his opportunity, took it. Briskly making his way over to Shauna, who was gently rubbing a bare foot waiting for Chip's return, looking forward to her drink and its welcome buzz, he started right in. "Hi there, beautiful. Looks like you could do with a foot massage," quickly pulling up a chair he sat down facing her. "I'm real good, you know. I'm known as the man with the golden touch. Here, let me demonstrate." And he roughly grabbed the foot she'd been soothing. As he rested it high on his thigh Shauna moved her chair back squealing it across the cement. Harvey, assuming permission, started stroking her foot and working the pressure points. "Your feet are beautiful," he commented, aroused. To Shauna's surprise, he seemed to know what he was doing and she felt the pain leave as he relaxed her foot. She wanted to ask him how he knew Coach, but decided against it. *Better to let it play out.* "I would very much like to dance with you - perhaps shoeless?" he asked.

Lost in thought, she barely heard him and responded slowly, distracted. "Mmm, dance? Thanks Harvey, but not tonight. I don't feel up to it and I'm not in the mood right now. Perhaps another time." Chip saved her having to elaborate further by appearing with her drink. "Here you are, my Love. Sorry it wasn't quicker, but it didn't feel right to cut in line. I see you're receiving some foot care from our friend Harvey. How's it going, man?" "Great, great, and I hope you don't mind me treating Shauna like this." "Oh man, not at all. That's probably exactly what she needs. Besides, it's up to her to decide what's good for her or not, and she seems more than happy. So carry on. I'm off to visit with my business associates. I'll be right back, Love." And he touched her glass with his before leaving again.

As Harvey massaged her other foot, Shauna leaned back, drink in hand, and closed her eyes. Admitting to herself that she was enjoying his touch, she was also clear that her feet were all he'd get to touch of her. She'd instinctively felt he wasn't to be trusted, and that had been confirmed by what she'd seen and heard earlier. *I wouldn't trust him even as far as I could throw him,* she mused. *Which, I guess, might be quite a long way given his light frame. Maybe I'd send him right back to where he's come from. Oh-oh, bitchy!* Was the Baileys affecting her already? *Could it be I'm more susceptible after the earlier upset?* She promised herself to be alert.

Overcome with lust at ministering to Shauna, Harvey was desperately trying to think himself out of an erection, which if noticed would embarrass him no end, given where Shauna's foot was. Plopping down in a nearby chair and scooting it over beside Shauna, Chip surprised Harvey into a rapid shriveling. *Well that's that taken care of,* thought Harvey. "We're all set for tomorrow Love. They loved the idea of eating out and want you to join us. We're planning on starting early and working through a light lunch so we'll be finished well in time. Shit! I'll have to remember to call Richard in the morning and reschedule our one o'clock appointment." Shauna let out a gasp, putting her hands over her mouth. "Damn, how did I manage to completely forget my voice lesson with him today? I'll have to call and apologize. I know it's late but I might as well do it now, see if I can worm in an hour or so tomorrow while I'm at it. I certainly hope so. I could do with some extra practice to be ready for Saturday! I'm so damn embarrassed! Do you have your phone on you, Baby?"

After listening to a soliloquy of wrath from an upset Richard, a contrite Shauna asked him to help her out. "I know how hurt you are. Forgive me. I know there's no excuse for having overlooked you . . . Yes, yes, I know, I must have been in a dead zone," *or an extra alive one,* she thought. "Of course. I'll gladly pay for the time you wasted waiting for me to show up. I so regret this whole thing. But Gifford has to cancel with you tomorrow to host an important business meeting, so could I take his one o'clock place in your schedule? . . . No, no, he'll call you to reschedule." Eventually it got worked out with Shauna accepting a short session with Richard at twelve-thirty.

Seeing how wiped out Shauna was from the interaction, Chip immediately comforted her. "Lucky you can sleep in tomorrow if you'd like. I'd certainly advise it," he said while kissing her full lips which muffled his words but not his intention. Coming up for air he said, "I'm going to get more drinks, Love. Harvey, can I get you anything?" "Thank you, but no. I'll take my leave since I have a busy day tomorrow. It's been heavenly being with you, Shauna. I hope my touch helped you." "Yes thank you, Harvey. My feet feel rejuvenated." "Well," continued Harvey, "I'll get in touch with the two of you soon concerning my business plan. Good night and thank you." He stiffly took his leave, head up, very proper. Chip got up and bent to slide his lips down Shauna's cleavage. Saying, "I'll be right back," he set off at a fast clip. Shauna sat back and closed her eyes and attempted to quiet her mind. The party had proved an excellent distraction. It had been good for her to stay occupied instead of withdrawing into herself to be tortured by the jumbled thoughts and emotions thrashing around in her head. Her father's murder and the terrible words she'd heard: 'SEPARATE THEM'. *What a living hell that would be - absolutely intolerable. And what would I do, or be, without Chip!* She whimpered inwardly. She didn't relish recounting what she'd overheard, afraid that doing so would force her to re-live the fear and disorientation of her eavesdropping; would somehow make the experience more real.

Squelching her concerns, she composed herself as Chip returned. Taking her drink she took a quick sip then cuddled close when he sat. Looking at each other they sighed contentedly. Head on his broad shoulder she enjoyed the distinct smell of him. There was a comfortable silence between them as they drank, soaking in the closeness of touch and togetherness. Every now and then departing guests would stop by offering brief thanks and parting platitudes, seemingly hesitant to intrude on their intimacy.

"Love, do you feel like taking a last turn on the floor barefoot before the band packs up?" "Hey, anything for you." Shauna untangled herself, stretching tall and proud. A prolonged sigh escaped Chip as with the lightest of touches he sensually pressed his body into hers to meet the band's first few notes of the old Kenny Rogers' number, 'Lady'. They nodded to the band in appreciation before becoming lost in each other: to the body warmth, to the body scents, to the depth of their eyes, to the overflowing of their hearts, to the sexual spark of their bodies sliding together in harmony, the extra six-inch height difference of a shoeless Shauna generating a new set of sensations to explore and savor.

Lost in the moment Shauna recalled the song, 'I could have danced all night' which she'd recently heard on the radio. "Yes," she sighed. *Of course,* she remembered, *the song had been coming from the radio in the kitchen. I'd have thought Mark would be more into hip hop, or metal, or rap.* She realized how little she knew about Mark - in fact, almost nothing. Abruptly stopping that train of thought - *Not now!* - she brought her attention back to the moment. Looking at her strangely, Chip asked, "Where were you just now, Love?" "Drifting Baby. Just drifting. Enjoying being right here with you . . . nothing else . . . nothing greater."

"You're irresistible," said Chip, clasping her tighter, spinning her flamboyantly around the dance floor. At the end, the band applauded. The couple curtsied.

As the band started breaking down their equipment, Chip handed an envelope to the drummer. "You did a wonderful job for us so I've added a little extra. Thanks . . . and give me a few business cards I can spread around." The drummer laughed and said, "Hey, you refer people to us and we'll come and play for you for free." "Thanks, sounds like a deal and a very generous one," replied Chip, shaking the drummer's hand.

Turning to head back to the house they couldn't help noticing Peggy coming towards them as she waved and called out. "I'm so glad I've found you. I'm so excited! Mark said he'll come with me to see you perform on Saturday. He's going to have to leave early but I'm so happy he agreed to come, I didn't think it would be his kind of thing, you know? Anyway, thanks for a great time." And she went on and on, agitating Shauna, who was hoping she might let something slip that would shed some light on Mark or the conspiracy. Realizing her paranoia, Shauna relaxed and let herself enjoy Peggy's enthusiasm until she said her goodbye and quickly left.

Saying farewells to the few stragglers, Chip realized Coach had slipped out without a word. *Oh well,* thought Chip, *Don't sweat the small stuff.* Little did he know he would soon experience how full-out terrifying, sweating the big stuff could be.

"Psst, psst . . . psst . . . psst." Peggy turned toward the unexpected sound, peering beyond the faint glow cast by the gate lights to see Mark hiding in the shadows. "You scared me, Mark. What's up?" "I wanted to catch you before you left," he replied, drawing her beside him where they couldn't be seen. "I have a big favor to ask of you, Sweetie. It's a simple thing but very important to me. Will you help me, please?" He kissed her on the cheek and put one hand over her breast for a fleeting moment - just to seal the deal. He thought he had a way with women when in reality all he knew was how to prey on the weak and vulnerable. Peggy was a good sort but when it came to men, she was a pushover and had had her heart broken and betrayed many times. She always seemed ready for the next plunge into disaster. She took the small, well-wrapped package Mark held out to her. "Take this and hide it somewhere in your condo, somewhere you wouldn't normally think to look. We'll make a game out of it. Next time I come over I'll look for it. If I find it, you lose and will have to hide it again. If you win and I can't find it, then guess what we'll do? Indeedy! We'll leave the package where you hid it so securely and your prize will be a nice big fucking." He snorted a laugh. "This will be our little secret, OK?" She nodded silently, blew him a kiss, headed for her car. *Certainly is heavy for such a small parcel.* She wondered what was inside and why it was so important to hide it.

She turned the package over noticing how well wrapped it was. No use trying to take a peek either, it was sealed with a brand of tape that would only come off with a special solution. Besides, Mark might slap her around if he found she'd tampered with it. The thought sent a shudder through her. She wondered occasionally if she wasn't settling for less than she should be and why so many unpleasant things happened to her. On the drive back to her condo she thought about possible places to plant the package. *Of course. Perfect.* She could hardly wait to get home and hide it.

Their guests taken care of, Chip and Shauna did the rounds, thanking the band members a final time, the catering staff and Troy, and were asking after Mark when he came running up the stairs from the kitchen area, red-faced and breathless. "Sorry Sir. I was outside getting some fresh air - getting a little break from all the food. What can I do for you?" "It's what we can do for you," said a smiling Chip, handing Mark an envelope. Opening it and taking a quick look inside Mark was unable to hide his surprise at the amount. Shauna wasn't sure if his reaction was one of embarrassment or guilt or a bit of both. "Thanks, Mark. We'll leave you to see to the caterers. We're going to bed. See you in the morning." Mark watched them go, still speechless.

CHAPTER 14 HIGH AND LOW

Already high, Shauna poured herself another Baileys from the bar in the master lounge. Joining Chip, sprawled on the bed, she raised her glass and took a big gulp before setting it on the nightstand. She straddled him, squeezing his hips with her knees and rubbed her swollen sex against his rapidly growing prick. She stared down as it grew longer, harder, bigger and changed color. Her juices flowed making their collision smooth and slick. Aroused beyond measure with the alcohol beginning to rule, she was tripping, Chip enjoying her antics. Waving a finger in front of his face she slurred, "I am no longer responsible for what happens or doesn't happen," and giggled, nearly toppling, only an alert Chip keeping her upright.

Drunk as she was, she instinctively knew he was ready and rising to her knees slid him gently inside her. Slowly sitting, impaled, pumping up and down, she watched him slide in and out, becoming darker with her juices. As their urgency took over, coming together fast and furious, they held hands, fingers interlocked, shaking uncontrollably, scared and exhilarated, full of possibilities, a low humming, rising in pitch, vibrating through them, to the room, to the whole house. ZZZZZOOOOOOOOOM . . . A different life form at twice the speed of light they pierced the cosmos, a new paradigm for human interaction, transmuting every new unknown of themselves to merge sequentially with the worlds they flashed through, towards a blackness more complete than any they had ever known, ominous, then . . .

Surrounded by a swarm of disks, floating weightless, individually pulsating in graceful waves of iridescent, bluish-white and a sense of profound intelligence seeking communication . . . and failing . . . and gone, the blackness now complete, a different order of universe, alive . . . An everyday occurrence of sub-atomic particles. A parallel blackness amplifying the visible - no bottom no top no limits no answers. At least not yet.

Two naked bodies. Breathing, the only proof of life. Time rushing to catch up.

"What if all that took place was right here within us? What if that was a spectacular journey through the great cosmos of ourselves? Not just through our conscious minds but through every cell?" Lying in his arms, both of them having resurfaced, showered and gone back to bed, she replied thoughtfully. "Right now, Baby, I just don't know. It's possible but there are so many more questions than there are answers. I do think we're unlocking the universe and beyond. And that could be inside ourselves, or outside, or both. We'll eventually get some answers, but there will always be questions." Lost in their own thoughts and the feel of each other they were soon asleep.

Waking to early morning light, five-forty-five, he stealthily slipped out of bed, padded to the windows and closed the blinds to darken the room. Returning to bed he resisted the temptation to hold her close, sensitive of her need to sleep.

A faint beeping stirred him again. Silencing his watch alarm, seven o'clock, he had a couple of hours before the scheduled meeting. Leaving Shauna sleeping deeply he slipped into the shower to quickly revive himself, dressed and headed for the kitchen, forgoing his workout to make sure he was ready for his people from L.A. Maybe he'd have time later.

As he passed through the master lounge, Troy, who was sitting on the sofa where he'd slept, rubbing night-goo from his eyes, looking more like a teenager than a grown man, inquired, "Have a good rest?" "Such as it was, yes," he replied cheerfully. "And thanks for staying here last night. Given the events of the last couple of days, having you close felt reassuring. Which reminds me, did you manage to organize those security guards we spoke about last night?" "Sure did. Fortunately my buddy was on a job and was able to get hold of a crew for this morning. In fact, I'm surprised I haven't heard from them yet. I'll give him a call and check." "Thanks. In the meantime, I'd like you to stay here till Shauna's ready to leave. You can ask Mark to bring you breakfast when you're ready. Also, when she wakes up, please remind her I have a meeting in my office but will come up to see her as soon as I can. She also might need one of Mark's famous hangover concoctions." "Consider it done." "Thanks. And make sure she gets to her voice lesson at twelve-thirty too, please. You can also pick up some things for me while you're out. I'll give you directions later." And Chip left.

Mark was talking on the kitchen telephone when Chip entered unannounced. Noticeably surprised, Mark quickly disconnected and composed himself. Curious, Chip, after saying, "Hi," asked who he'd been calling so early. "I was calling the food market to see what they had fresh today." "Come on, Mark. The food market doesn't open till eight on Friday mornings. What's going on?" Mark rubbed his hands against his pants nervously. "Look, Mark, if you can't be straight with me, I'll have to let you go." *Bastard,* Mark thought to himself. *You just wait. You'll get yours.* "Okay, Mister Jefferson. I was talking with my girl, Peggy. You know, the one that shared a condo with Ms. Sheffield before she moved in with you? We've been seeing each other for a little while now. I promise it won't happen again and I'm sorry I lied. I was embarrassed about being caught on a personal call." "Look, Mark, you're the best chef I've had so I certainly don't want to lose you and I don't have a problem with you making personal calls, within reason of course, but lying is not acceptable, OK?" asked Chip. Mark nodded and they shook.

Ordering breakfast in the dining area he didn't hear Mark murmur as he left the kitchen, "Better live it up today, buddy, 'cause tomorrow will be your last." Climbing the stairs to the dining area he continued out to the pool deck, wondering if Troy had gotten hold of the guards yet. A stranger he could only assume to be one of them came around a corner towards him. "Good morning. Are you one of the guards?" he asked. "Yes sir." "How does everything look?" "Not a hair out of place," replied the guard, Chip detecting a slight accent, maybe Russian-East European. "Well, that's good to hear," said Chip. "What's the schedule?" "There should be three crews of four so we'll be here till about two. It may be a little longer as we only found out about the job late last night and are still organizing the other two crews." "OK. Thanks. Let Troy know if there's a problem." "Will do."

Nodding his thanks, Chip went back to the dining room where breakfast now awaited him. A fresh vase of flowers from the garden was a nice touch. He hadn't realized how hungry he was and was soon ordering seconds, conscious his L.A. colleagues would be arriving soon.

Shauna opened one eye, peeked at her surroundings. Her other eye joined in. She quickly closed both again as the memories of yesterday came flooding back. Unable to stop herself, she ran through each clip: every detail, every aspect in perfect focus. Conjuring up every thought, every feeling, every emotion, it was like reliving the whole day all over again - in a flash. As the last scene faded a low grade throb in her head established its presence. *Must be a hangover*, she moaned. *My first, and may it be my last.* She shuffled to a sitting position, knees bent, rubbing her eyes and then, leaning forward to rest her head on her knees, groaned again.

A light tapping at the door added to the dull thudding in her head. "Who is it?" she called. "Troy, ma'am. I have something that Gifford thought might help with your hangover." Making herself decent, pulling her nightie down and pulling the sheet up, she asked him to come in, adding, "I need all the help I can get."

Entering, he timidly approached the bed, leaning forward to hand her the tumbler at arm's length, as if afraid she might bite. "This is a Mark special. I can't speak for the taste, but I hear the results are awesome," he said as he backed away, nervous at being alone with her. "That's right. I remember. You don't drink. I admire that, Troy." Blushing bright red, he turned his face away.

Studying the concoction briefly, remnants of raw egg floating on the frothy surface of a pale green liquid, *totally disgusting*, she held her nose and took a swig. "Wow, this, whatever it is, can make you forget you even have a hangover. Maybe that's the secret. Either that, or it's burning a hole in my stomach," she spluttered through puckered lips, grimacing and shaking her head wildly. Troy laughed, completely disarmed. Shauna bravely drank every drop. Thanking Troy for his attentiveness and for staying close, she sank back into the bed, needing to recover from the effects of the cure. Troy went back to his vigil.

CHAPTER 15 ATTACK

Shauna slept late, and later, and later still. A sleep of healing. A sleep only disturbed by the stirrings of hunger which brought her awake. Slowly sitting, expecting to feel the yuckiness of the hangover, she was delighted to be pain-free and alert, chipper even. *You're a genius Mark, thank you.* She stretched, cat-like, deciding that she needed to move her body more than she needed to eat right now. Rising, she skipped to the closet and squeezed herself into a skimpy white bikini, checking herself in the mirror, thinking; *Pretty darn good.* Back in the bedroom she drew the blinds, squinting against the sunlight. Gazing at the half pool outside she decided it wasn't big enough and ran down to the lower pool to dive in gracefully and begin swimming laps.

Troy had followed her down to play lifeguard then remembered Chip had asked to be notified when she was up and around, so went to get him. Shauna sliced through the pool, hardly disturbing the water, effortlessly propelling herself end to end. Chip stood admiring: her style certainly, but more than anything, her. She caught sight of him and called, "Come in Babe. It feels so good."

How could he refuse? Stripping to his briefs he dove in. Sliding against her all the way up, he surfaced, licked her breasts like they were popsicles as she trod water, then kissed her on the lips. Wriggling in response she slid her hands between their bodies and palmed his nipples. "How are you feeling, Love? Did you sleep well?" "I slept great and feel wonderful, thanks to Mark and his remedy. It was gross but it worked." "I'm so glad. But now I have to get back. I just wanted to see you before carrying on." And he climbed out of the pool, grabbed a towel and headed off to change for his next session, sending Troy back out to keep an eye on her. Her swimming interrupted, her stomach reminded her it was empty and she asked Troy if he would get Mark to provide something light she could eat poolside. Thinking to kill two birds with one stone, so to speak, he went to check on the guards. Taking off across the terrace towards the garage he met the first guard patrolling along the driveway. Continuing around to the front, he met two more. Looking for the fourth took him past the kitchen entrance so he popped in to place Shauna's food request. Exiting to continue his round he turned the next corner to a gun barrel smacking his left temple. The fourth guard watched him crumple, unconscious, satisfied he'd be out for long enough.

Shauna was day-dreaming, back against the side of the pool her arms outstretched resting along the edge, bent at the elbows so her hands dangled in the water. She had her head tilted back to catch the sun and her eyes closed . . . relaxed and content. *What a life*, she thought happily.

Excruciating pain! Being bodily lifted out of the water by her hair, she screamed, long and loud. Deep in the recesses of Troy's brain the sound registered but he was in no condition to respond.

Over her shock, Shauna fought against the iron grip tugging the hair from her head, or so it felt, incensed further by her assailants laughter. Unable to turn her head to see who it was, she kicked frantically before reacting to a new source of pain as she bruised and bloodied her heels against the rough side of the pool. One more strong yank and she felt a hand under one armpit and then one under the other and she was dragged out of the pool, her back and legs being scraped raw. A wet, bloody, struggling Shauna, now beached - a dolphin out of water locked in a vice - thought, *I would have had a much better chance if we were in the water*. Not that she was about to surrender. She was mad.

The guard had had no idea he'd be hooking a wildcat. No holds barred. Scratching, biting, head butting, fist pounding, leg squeezing like a python, she was relentless. Which only made him more determined and crazy to tame her, beat her, slice her, rape her – repeatedly.

Dragging her across the deck he was seeking cover, not far from where she'd seen the threesome huddled the night before, she realized. *Was it really just last night?* Seeing a partially opened window she thought might be close to Chips' office, although she wasn't certain, disoriented as she was, she just went for it. Throwing herself from side to side, ignoring the pain now, determined to find help, she kicked and screamed until, with every fiber of her being, she mustered the strength to strike out with her feet and kick herself close enough to the window and screamed: "CHIP! HELP ME!" "CHIP! HELP! CHIP!"

Enraged beyond caution, with one burning desire - no bitch was ever going to get the upper hand with him – her attacker mercilessly twisted her until he had her arms cuffed behind her back: a struggle that seemed to take forever. And he dragged her away from the house.

As if in a dream, Troy heard her frantic cries to Chip. His head dull with pain, he tested his legs. Wobbly. He managed to stand up and, hearing the ongoing sounds of struggle, Shauna's persistent cries, realized it was no dream: beloved Shauna was in trouble. Slowly, putting one foot ahead of the other, bracing himself with one hand against the wall, he staggered towards the sounds of violence.

What Troy saw filled him with revulsion. The guard had Shauna bent forward on her knees, stripped of her bikini. Holding her down with one hand on her back, his other hand holding a gun, the barrel inserted part way into her anus, he was shouting at her. Troy couldn't make out what he was saying and was kind of relieved, expecting it was likely as disgusting as what he was doing.

With her hands cuffed behind her back it was almost impossible for Shauna to defend herself. And it was that as much as the physical abuse that was really pissing her off. Turning her head as far as possible, she could see the huge bulge in his crotch, and the thought of him plunging inside her – never mind any diseases he might be carrying - made her want to throw up. Seeing her looking, he ordered her to not move a hair or he'd blast her ass till bullets spit from her mouth. Fearing for her life and of being forever gone from Chip, although knowing she couldn't give in to the fear of separation, she watched as he removed his hand from her back, unzipped his pants and pulled out his erection. So distracted, watching her watching him as he worked his pecker free, obsessed with the pleasure of power, he was blind to Troy's halting but stealthy approach.

Chip, had been pondering the progress of his meeting. His associates had split into two groups and were in the adjacent rooms working on two different issues that needed to be resolved before getting together again. About ready to go find out where they were at, he thought he heard Shauna frantically calling for help. Running out of his office and down the hall he checked through the open window, almost crying out with horror at the scene confronting him, hardly believing his eyes.

The guard had managed to roughly pull out his prick and was pumping it fast to get it bigger and harder. Shauna was bent over on her bloody knees which had been scraped and torn open while being dragged on the pavement. Her hands were still cuffed behind her back and she was almost toppling forwards. It was all she could do to keep from crashing forehead first onto the cement deck. The guard bent over behind her, had a gun jammed in her anus and was apparently so focused on arousing himself he was either unaware of or ignoring Troy sneaking up behind him. Chip, hoping Troy had seen him in his peripheral vision, rushed to give his support. Arriving close to the action, he stayed hidden by a corner of the house, planning to rely on his instincts and hearing to judge when to move.

Having glimpsed Chip, Troy, wasn't quite sure where he was now but knew they'd only have one chance to disarm the A-hole without Shauna getting hurt and hoped Chip would be ready. A fresh rush of adrenalin coursed through his body helping to further unmuddy his brain and revive the fighting machine he'd been trained to be. Managing to blank out the pain from the brutal blow to his head, his one thought was to strike fast and hard as he moved closer behind the would-be-rapist.

With her head turned watching her assailant, Shauna was well aware of Troy's movements. Flicking him a look they instantly communicated, an intuitive precognition of what they should do and when, and Shauna spun onto her back squeezing her legs tightly around the guards bent legs taking him with her as Troy lunged forward and grabbed him around the throat shouting, "Chip!" Surprised and off balance, the guard instinctively raised both hands to grab Troy's arm to avert being throttled, dropping his gun in the process. Shauna squirmed to reach it, kicking it towards Chip who had barreled around the corner at Troy's shout.

With Troy clinging to his neck, the guard was desperately trying to reach the gun when Chip picked it up. Pointing it at the guard's head he growled, "You so much as twitch and I'll turn you into a sieve . . . Now, where's the key to the fucking handcuffs?" The guard just continued his weakening struggle to pry Troy's arm from his throat. Chip, enraged, fired the gun in the air, stamped on the guard's foot, breaking at least a couple of metatarsals, and kicked him in the crotch. The guard, screamed and doubled over, struggling for the breath to voice his pain again. "The key, Asshole!" Troy released his grip just enough to allow the guard to whimper and croak, "In my back pocket, you fucker," with a pitiful attempt at a snarl. Chip stamped on his other foot, breaking that one too, snapping, "Keep this up and I'll break every fucking bone in your body."

The three other guards appeared, running from either side of the house. "Someone get the fucking key from his back pocket and get those handcuffs off right now! Then cuff this motherfucker with them," bellowed Chip.

Finally free, Shauna lay moaning as Chip examined her. There didn't appear to be any broken bones but much of her back, stomach, legs and feet were bruised and scraped and bloody. There was a noticeable bruise on the side of her face, a bloody wound on her breast - perhaps a bite mark - and her anus was sore and inflamed from the gun. Troy, having finally let go of the guard, had limped to the stack of bath towels and now handed one to Chip to tenderly wrap around her nakedness. She winced as the soft piled cloth embraced her bruised and bleeding flesh.

Noticing his business associates lined up along the glass walls of the living room, horrified but fascinated by the scene, Chip quickly went over, put their minds at rest about Shauna's condition, and asked them to carry on without him, saying he'd catch up with them later. Then he and Troy, as carefully as they could, picked Shauna up and carried her to the master bed. As she lay whimpering, trying to get comfortable, Chip sent Troy to check on the guards and call nine-one-one if they'd not already done so. Following up with a call to Garcia to come help attend to Shauna, he then did his best to comfort her until Garcia arrived.

After what seemed like an interminably long time to a distraught Chip, Garcia hurried into the room. Slowly approaching the bed she looked down at the so naked, so vulnerable, so scraped, bruised, raw and bloody Shauna and turned away, a sob catching in her throat. "It looks a lot worse than it is," said Shauna, trying to soften the blow – unsuccessfully. "How could anyone ever think of doing something like this, especially to you?" gasped Garcia, before becoming all business. "We'll get you cleaned up before you go to the hospital." "No, No, No, I won't go! Never! I detest such places," cried Shauna, almost frantic. Soothing her, Chip called Doc, his team's medic, who said he'd be right over. Relieved, Shauna relaxed and the three of them waited, Chip soothing and whispering, saying how proud he was of the way she'd acted and how she would soon be taken care of. Garcia gently stroked her hair.

When Doc strode briskly into the room he was armed with his regular doctor's bag plus a couple of other larger satchels which he hastily put down on the floor near the bed. After a cursory examination he delivered instructions to Garcia and she scurried off to carry them out.

While Doc was making an in depth assessment of Shauna's injuries, Troy knocked on the bedroom door and advised Chip that a detective Richardson was waiting in the master lounge. Going to meet him, Chip explained what had happened. Richardson, also in charge of the investigation into the murder of Shauna's father the previous evening, handed Chip his card and asked to see the victim. Chip led him to the bedside where they paused to watch as Doc worked. Doc talked them through his conclusions, pointing out where Shauna would need stiches, where less intrusive treatment, adding that although there were no serious fractures, he had a portable x-ray machine on its way to check for hairline cracks.

Chip had never experienced Doc as soft and tender as he was being with Shauna. Previously he'd only known him to be domineering and loud, short-tempered, doing just enough to get a player back on the court as quickly as possible, no matter what the injury. He had to admit that he liked this new man with a stethoscope tending to his Love a whole lot better.

Garcia returned with the items Doc had requested. Chip asked Troy to show Richardson the crime scene and take him to the security center where the two guards were holding the attacker and, on his way back, to ask Mark to make up some chicken broth. "Shauna hasn't eaten anything today and I'm hoping she'll have the stomach for something." Then Chip and Garcia under Doc's supervision and with his help when necessary proceeded to clean a Shauna groggy from pain-killers. Carefully dabbing and swabbing as needed, covering the more heavily congealed areas with wet cloths to help soften the mess first, it was a painstaking labor of love that took their total concentration to make sure they didn't exacerbate her injuries, tear the skin or peel it and cause further bleeding. But working together, sensitive to the body they were ministering to, they efficiently prepared her for Doc to sew and patch.

They could hear Troy a mile off yelling with frustration and anger, "THE GUARDS ARE GONE! WOULD YOU BELIEVE IT! ALL THE GUARDS ARE GONE!" He stormed into the bedroom black with anger, red with exertion. Motioning him to settle down Chip asked what was going on. "All four of them have disappeared. I showed Richardson the scene and took him to the security center and the guards weren't there, none of them! I checked with Mark and the three of us searched every room, but no joy. The A-holes took off at some point. Richardson put out an alert and has gone chasing but he only has a basic description of what they're driving so I'm not holding my breath."

"Fuck, fuck, fuck!" raged Chip. "You've got to be fucking kidding me! You're telling me this was a conspiracy; with Shauna as the target? I don't believe it. Why? What possible reason would they have? There's got to be something else going on . . . or someone else . . . Someone with a motive or a plan orchestrating it, directing them. There just has to be." "Maybe," responded Troy. "Richardson said he thinks the murder of Shauna's Father and this attack could be linked. He also said he'll be back to question you, me and Shauna later, when she's been fixed up." Chip nodded thoughtfully. "OK . . . Now, can you get me four more guards to interview, ASAP? And this time let's make sure they have a least three references, please? When you've organized that would you then look in on the guests in my office, make sure they're OK, see if they need anything. Thanks." Troy left, flipping through his mental files for names to call. Chip called after him, "TROY! Make it quick would you. I still want Doc to check your head, make sure you're okay."

Doc, who with Garcia's help had been treating Shauna throughout the interaction with Troy, was almost finished. Putting a last delicate stitch in her breast, he whispered, "This has been very rough on her," and gave her another pain-killer. "Now," he said, "let's take a break and let her rest. I could sure use some coffee, how about you two?" Collapsing into one of the loungers by the bed he spread his legs, rested his head against the back and closed his eyes. Garcia took the other chair while Chip went into the lounge to make the coffee.

As it was brewing, Troy came in with the soup and told Chip that his business buddies were doing just fine and had wished Shauna a quick and speedy recovery. Thanking him, Chip took the large cup of lukewarm soup and took it to Shauna, asking Troy to finish making the coffee and pass it round.

Speaking softly, Chip gently raised Shauna's head, and brought the cup to her lips. "Please Love, just sip a little. It will help you heal and counteract the medications." She struggled to oblige. "That's my Love. OK, now, a little bit more." She complied. Chip smiled, kissed her soupy lips and attempted to carefully cajole another spoonful into her mouth. She shook her head in protest. "All right, that's enough for now. Well done." Kissing her again, he set the cup on the nightstand, picked up the coffee Troy had thoughtfully left there and slid down to sit on the floor. Gently placing his hand on Shauna's stomach, he took a swallow and tried to relax.

The four acolytes were content to sit, sip and think, but Shauna wasn't. She wanted to tell Chip about the night before but the pain-killers had her wooly-headed and confused, the words mere incoherent mumbles. Frustrated she became agitated and Doc roused himself to go to her side. "Sweet Lady, you need to calm down. Whatever it is can wait until later," he soothed.

Shauna's eyes filled with tears as she nodded OK. At that moment Chip loved Doc for his kindness and compassion.

Doc checked her over. Everything seemed to be fine. The others had joined him by the bed and the four of them took hands and closed their eyes, giving a silent prayer to Shauna for her healing.

The x-ray technician arrived and he and Doc, as quickly and carefully as they could, rattled off ten shots of Shauna's injuries that Doc wanted to check. Plugging the x-ray drive into his laptop set up in the master lounge, the technician and Doc scrutinized the results. "She must be made of rubber, or unusually flexible," observed the technician. "The only problems I see here are a couple of possible tiny hairline fractures in her upper left shoulder - right here." And he pointed to the location. "Even her ribs are unscathed. Her knees are fine too, although they were scraped nearly down to the bone in a couple of places. You did an excellent job there, along with sewing up her breast and shoulder blades. I would say she is a very lucky woman." "Amen to that," said an exhausted but satisfied Doc.

Returning to the bedroom Doc told the others their findings. They each thanked, praised and hugged him, and he willingly received it all, thankful to have been able to help such a beautiful person whose presence had bewitched him. No ordinary female - brave and vulnerable and so very different from most, if not all, the women he was used to seeing hanging around his players.

Taking his time, Doc then checked Troy. Reporting there was no serious damage and that he'd be fine, he went on. "Give yourselves a hand too, for what each of you has done today in helping Shauna." They smiled, grateful to Doc and each other. Doc continued. "I'm going to rig up a saline and water drip to keep her hydrated, so watch her. She might want to pull it out. And Chip, try and give her a little broth every hour - maybe you and Troy could share the task. You've got a good lad here and he has a head as hard as stone, which is a good thing." He thumped Troy on the back. Troy blushed.

Carefully manipulating Shauna they replaced the bed linen and left Chip alone with her, sitting by her side holding her hand as she rested in fresh laundered bliss.

CHAPTER 16 INTERVENTION

Having vetted the new guards and sent Troy and Garcia to eat, Chip was sat beside Shauna. "Please, Baby, call Ivan and R Jay to come over and keep me company if they can." She pleaded. "You get out of here with your colleagues. I'll be fine." Seeing him ready to protest, she held up a bandaged hand and softly said, "Please, if for no other reason, do it for me. I need to rest" He got on the phone and made the calls. "Now, how about some more broth?" she asked.

Although things seemed to have quieted down, Troy brought his food back to the master lounge to keep guard while he ate. Chip, finished plying Shauna with broth, headed downstairs to tie up loose ends with his colleagues and Shauna settled back on the bed, eyes closing. Startled awake to Ivan and R Jay standing by the bedside, wide-eyed, listening to Troy fill them in on what had happened, riveted to his every word, she said, "Hi." "Wow, wonder what the other guy looks like?" laughed R Jay. She started laughing too before grimacing with pain. "Did you come just to torment me or what? No, don't answer that! Look, thanks for coming, I really appreciate it, I appreciate you and I love you both. I really am so glad you're here." the four chatted for a while until, once again, Shauna fell back to sleep.

It was just after eight when Troy let Chip and his associates out at Charleston's to the sound of distant thunder. They'd left Shauna asleep, looked after by Ivan and R Jay who'd been playing cards at a table they'd set up just inside the bedroom door, and the four new guards patrolling the grounds.

Seeing his passengers into the restaurant, Troy went for a spin. He liked this part of town and had at least an hour and a half before he had to pick them up, so he relaxed behind the wheel and did what he enjoyed - driving the limo and exploring.

As he drove, he pondered the recent events, wondering if Richardson was making any progress that would lead to the arrest of the would-be rapist and his co-conspirators or Shauna's father's killer. Grateful Shauna had made it through alive, without being raped, he prayed for her to heal quickly as he cruised aimlessly.

Inside the restaurant Chip was restless and bored. Finding it difficult to concentrate on the conversation, he wanted to be curled up next to Shauna. He and his associates had originally planned to get another early start in the morning and hopefully wrap up their business before noon so they could all take it easy and get ready to attend Shauna's performance. Now, with what had happened, tomorrow was up in the air and he was going to let them know how Shauna was before making any other plans.

Back at the house, all was pretty uneventful, which was a welcome change. Ivan and R Jay were watching a low-scoring baseball game on the television and Shauna was sleeping. The only excitement was Shauna's antics as she used the bedpan Doc had left for her. She wished she had a penis to make the job easier and even wondered about a catheter before catching herself, thinking, *why would I wish that on myself?* But with a tube feeding her hydration, the idea of having one facilitating liquid disposal didn't seem like such a bad idea.

In the kitchen, Mark was almost finished making sure the place was spotless. A slob at home, he was a different personality on the job - obsessively neat and clean and apparently out to impress. He left food for Garcia, Shauna and Troy, muttering quietly under his breath, "I can hardly wait to get out of here and head over to Peggy's." It seemed like he was talking to himself more and more these days. *I better watch that. Trouble I don't fucking need.* He hung up his hat and jacket and whistling a merry tune went to get his car. On his way to the garage, he thought of Shauna in the master suite and chuckled. *What a day!* What could have been better than to witness the bitch all beaten and bloody. *To think that the Russian mafia was responsible, had managed to pass themselves off as guards even though they could hardly string together a sentence in English between them. Pity they didn't get to rape her though.* And his thoughts turned to what was supposed to now be planned for tomorrow, *Assuming the bitch turns up of course. But what the hell, whatever happens, I won't have to be here any longer, spying on Mr. High and Mighty and his oh-so-perfect lover. I've had enough of this gig and reporting to that asshole of a brother who thinks he's so smart and untouchable and tough. It's my ass that's been on the line this whole time, not that there was any danger I'd be discovered. I'm the one who's too smart for that!* As he drove off, he waved to the guard checking his departure. "Good riddance asshole," he hissed as distant thunder rolled.

Troy drove the inner city streets, feeling the limo respond to his touch, wandering wherever he wanted, enjoying the sounds filtering through the open moon roof. Taking a sharp left turn he was startled by the spectacle confronting him. Hovering above the suburbs to the west was what looked like a spaceship at the center of roiling thunderclouds. A second thought: the craft was the source of the clouds and jagged lightning surrounding it – the rest of the sky clear and cloudless in the dusk. Troy blinked and knuckled his eyes not believing what he was seeing. "Holy Mother in Heaven!" he exclaimed. "What the heck is that about?"

He looked around to see drivers and pedestrians seemingly going about their own business oblivious to the phenomena ahead of him. He drove carefully, one eye on the traffic, the other keeping a close watch on the hovering craft. And then it was gone! One second there, the next not.

Darn, where'd it go? Come on. Show yourself, he urged, wanting to track the apparition or whatever it was and Bang! It was back. Closer - although difficult to be sure of distance or size - he sensed it was both drawing him towards Chip's home and waiting for him. As if wanting him to follow and compelling him to at the same time. *Am I dreaming this, or am I awake?* He wondered, pinching himself, registering pain. *I guess I'm awake.*

The thunderheads, lighting and rumblings dissipated as the spacecraft descended, touching down lightly behind the terrace. Troy could see the craft pretty clearly as he pulled up the driveway and parked in front of the garage, thinking of all the spaceships he'd seen in magazines, comic books and movies.

Two spheres connected by a tube, hovering vertically. Eight evenly spaced rods slowly emerged from the lower sphere to bend in the middle like knees and become legs that developed what looked like suction cups as they made contact with the ground. Apparently stabilized, the spheres took on surface texture and he realized that they had been spinning so fast they'd appeared smooth. Not having seen such an oddity before Troy was at a loss as to what it was even made of, let alone how it worked, why it was there or where it had come from.

He thought to get out of the car and go and introduce himself, so mesmerized he didn't think of warning Shauna and the guys. *What if they don't understand me? What if they think I'm an enemy? What if they're hostile?* And he closed the windows and moon roof and turned on the air, keeping the engine running for a quick getaway should it be necessary. Checking to make sure he had time before he needed to be back at the restaurant, he waited and watched.

A light appeared from under the ship, becoming brighter until it was almost blinding as a screeching reached his ears. An amorphous blur of pure light energy, crackling, sparking and pulsing, emerged and floated toward him.

He shielded his eyes with his hand before fumbling on his sunglasses. Coalescing into a fuzzy-edged oval, the light pierced the garage wall to hover in front of the limo and send a laser-like beam that visually pulsed around his head before rendering him unconscious.

Making its way straight through the house to hover outside the glass wall of the master suite, it aimed a second beam to knock out Ivan and R Jay before dimming and floating through the glass to hover at the foot of Shauna's bed. A multitude of blue-white light-disks – the same Chip and Shauna had encountered on their last space-time journey – poured out. Their thin outer edges undulating gracefully in waves, they darted and floated in seemingly random patterns around, over, under and through the sleeping Shauna. Though it appeared they had intention, it wasn't revealed until Shauna, having felt nothing, slowly awakened to a strange, delicious feeling of blissful peace. Gradually becoming aware of the glowing disks, she noticed her pain fading away until, blessings of blessings, there was no pain at all.

She lay perfectly still. *Was this real? Could this be a dream?* She dared not move. In the quiet, as she lay there, she heard the disks communicating using quiet chirps, and clicks and wondered what they were saying, longing to be able to understand them, having so many unanswered questions. Hungry to know them, sensing they could feel her longing and passion to be one with them. They seemed warm but she wondered why they had come, other than to help her. Maybe that was enough of a reason. *Can I expand within my own person to accept that they've come because of who I am? Can I step up to live the larger person I have always longed to become and now realize was always meant to be?* As she reflected, she knew in her heart that Chip would be in sync with her in this revelation. *It will be so much easier, and much more fun to make this quantum leap together. And that's just how it's going to be because I claim this new life! I will not resist!*

Emerging from her reverie to an increased chatter between the disks, their clicks louder and more rapid, their previously graceful movements now abrupt and agitated, she watched as they paired off. Working in concert they trapped the ends of the different bandages and unwound them to expose, much to Shauna's astonishment, beautiful radiant skin. She gingerly moved her fingers, to find them flexible and totally without pain. Crying with joy and appreciation, she gently stroked the few disks in range. They glowed brighter and quivered as if with pleasure at the contact. Examining herself, both visually and by touch, unblemished, healed, fresher than ever, she almost missed the discs retreating through the glass. Leaping from the bed she rushed after them, sliding open a glass panel to the deck outside just in time to witness the flash of their departure, knowing she would meet them again.

Overjoyed, she hurried back inside, eager to show the guys and Garcia her renewed flesh and to prepare for Chip's return. *This will really flip him out,* she thought, excited, skipping into the closet to grab a robe.

"Hi boys, how's it going?" She asked, as she joyfully pranced around in front of R Jay and Ivan sprawled on the couch in front of the television. Still befuddled, their eyes barely slits, their mouths dropped open in shock. Shaking their heads and rubbing their eyes to clear them, they did a double-take. Shauna, whole, healthy, and full of life. How? Leaving them gaping, she called Garcia, asked her to come help, and waltzed into the bathroom to shower.

When Garcia arrived she could hear Shauna singing in the bathroom and found Ivan and R Jay arguing where they still sat on the couch. Interrupting them, she asked what was going on. They explained and Garcia crossed herself, thanking God for a miracle. Ivan and R Jay were tending to agree with her. Neither of them had had much time for religion but what they'd seen so far certainly seemed to suggest a miracle was the most likely possibility. And they were all correct, except the miracle had not been the work of a mysterious deity.

Shauna was singing in the shower feeling better than she'd ever felt. Realizing the disks had not just healed her but had left her rejuvenated, she felt ready to give the performance of her life the following evening. For now, she was thinking of Chip, the look on his face. Wanting to look her best she called out for Garcia, hoping she was in earshot.

Garcia, who'd been waiting uncertainly in the bedroom, responded immediately. Seeing Shauna she threw her hands to her face, gasping, sobbing and finally laughing. She rushed to Shauna and they embraced.

Sparkling with life, scrubbed, primped and pampered, Shauna entered the master lounge and went to Ivan and R Jay who stood up so she could hug them and kiss their cheeks. They marveled at the spontaneous, totally recovered Shauna as she pranced to the mirror and slowly turned to admire her new self.

Peggy and Mark were at her apartment, untangling after sex. Hot and sweaty from Mark's near rape of her, Peggy watched him scramble out of bed to the shower leaving her to pull herself together. *Well, that wasn't love making as far as I'm concerned. There was certainly no damned pleasure in it for me.* Peggy was disgruntled. *Let him hide his own darned packages from now on!* She got out of the messed up bed, sketchily made it presentable, put on her robe and fussed a little with her hair. Mark exited the bathroom and slipped into his clothes. Announcing he had an early start tomorrow he congratulated her for hiding his package so well, saying with a chuckle that he had a mind to look for it each time he came. And then he was gone, slamming the front door behind him. Peggy punched a pillow mercilessly.

Inspector Richardson was following his nose. He prided himself on being a hunch kind of person – 'go with your gut' was one of his mantras.

Intuitively weaving a route in pursuit of the absconded guards, he was being shadowed by his backup, two of his favored detectives, a young man and woman, who he'd called to help.

Richardson knew back street Austin well and his nose had led him to an older part of town, not that far from the crime scenes at Chip's mansion. The lots here were surprisingly large and most of the ranch style houses – long, single story, rather plain, built of brick and wood - sat well back from the road. Now his nose and gut had stopped twitching. Parking against the curb he got out to look around. The detectives following joined him, observing the property he had stopped in front of. A long driveway with a swimming pool on the left backed by some shade trees led to a house they could hardly see at the back of the lot.

"OK, guys. I have a strong hunch that this is where we need to be looking. Pull further down the street and see if you can make your car less conspicuous. Scout the neighborhood, see if you come across anything that might be useful, but I have a feeling this is the house. We're looking for a white 2001 Taurus, license plate unknown, and four Caucasian men, possibly Russians. Have Greg back at the precinct check property records for this place and the houses on either side. Be careful, these guys are dangerous so don't take unnecessary chances. If anything seems off, let me know, and check in with me every half hour anyway. Just as well there's very little moonlight." Leaving them to carry on, Richardson then set off to do some snooping of his own.

CHAPTER 17 TELEPATHY

An unsettled Troy parked in front of the restaurant. He had a feeling something important had just happened but didn't know what. He'd woken in the limo back at the house, and remembered driving the streets but had no recollection of why he'd ended up there. Chip came out of the restaurant with his colleagues. "Great timing," he said, smiling as they all reached the limo and climbed in the back.

Having missed Shauna since he'd left her at home, Chip was eager to get back and be with her and willed Troy to go faster, feeling like they were crawling along. Reaching the driveway gates they let the Californians out to pick up their rental sedan and drove on through under the watchful eye of a guard.

Chip leapt from the car as soon as it reached the side entrance, barely landing on his feet, too impatient to wait for the vehicle to stop. Pushing the house door open, poised to rush to Shauna, he slowed then stopped as he heard what he thought was her singing. *How could that be? Maybe it's a recording.* Not that he knew where it could have come from. As the sound grew louder, the words became distinct, Shauna appeared at the top of the stairs – at least he would have sworn it was Shauna if he hadn't known she was heavily bandaged and sedated, lying in bed.

The Shauna apparition, poised to descend, continued her song. Dressed in a long sheer nightgown that swayed to her movement, tantalizingly hinting at the magnificent body it adorned, she slowly stepped her way down towards him. His faculties shut down. He collapsed to the landing, shaking, lowering his head to his knees covering it with his arms he moaned and babbled in disbelief and shock, that became denial and anger. "This can't be! It's not possible. Why would you do this? Where is my real Shauna? I WANT SOME ANSWERS HERE AND NOW. Damn it!" She reached him in an instant, stunned she could move so fast, and sank down beside him, caressing him with words and touch.

Gently taking his head in her hands, turning it so he was facing her, she gazed into his eyes, pierced his turmoil within and led him out of the deep crevasse he'd plunged into when his old limiting beliefs had crashed on seeing her, inexplicably healed. Covering her hands with his own, he kissed her with gentle passion. Lifting her gown, he then scanned her whole, healthy body, head to toe. He touched her breast where the stitches had been. He saw nothing but a shining Shauna - a bright and relieved Shauna. Overwhelmed with joy at her miraculous recovery he apologized for his momentary breakdown, eager to hear the full story behind it. And then Troy came in after parking the limo.

Shocked to see her Troy sat to steady himself. "What happened?" he exclaimed. "You look completely healed and beautiful!" "Thank you Troy. I'll tell you everything, just not tonight." Troy nodded and excused himself, having no idea what had happened to Shauna or any thought that it might be connected to his earlier unsettled feeling.

Satisfying himself that Shauna was one hundred percent, Chip watched her up to the master suite before going to brief the new shift of guards. Garcia and the guys were now watching basketball, an overtime game that had Ivan and R Jay on the edge of their seats, totally immersed. Shauna shooed a tired looking Garcia to bed before sitting to watch the end of the game with them.

At the final buzzer, R Jay asked, "So, Oh Miraculous One, did Giff go ballistic when he saw you?" "Oh yes. He went ballistic all right. Not content to just see everything with his own eyes, he had touch with his hands too to be a believer." Shauna chuckled. Ivan mentioned they'd been talking about taking her to the Caribbean, thinking the salt water would help her heal. Now she was healed they could still go but she'd be able to have fun instead, he suggested. "My vote's for Jamaica!" said R Jay. Clapping her hands, excited, Shauna jumped up and danced around the room chanting, "We're going to Jamaica! We're going to Jamaica!" Ivan and R Jay leapt up to join her and, arms around each other's shoulders, the three of them pranced in a circle, chanting in unison. Finished with the guards, Chip arrived to make the circle bigger before they all collapsed onto the couch, laughing.

As they sprawled, Shauna marveled at how different Chip was becoming alongside her, had already become with his openness to forever changing and their evolving oneness. In contrast, R Jay and Ivan, much as she loved them, seemed predictable and one-dimensional, as if content with life as they'd always known it, apparently blind to how Chip was evolving. *We don't really grow old*, she thought, *we get stuck, stiff and tight. If we don't open up to the new or even acknowledge it when it smacks us in the face and allow it to propel us to keep moving forward, the body shrivels. Gravity takes over and we succumb, not to what we think or feel, but to the weight of those around us, prevailing opinions and beliefs. We divert from being who we are to being what's acceptable and comfortable. We unwittingly suppress our natural propensity for living abandoned.*

Saying their goodbyes, Ivan and R Jay went to shoot a few hoops downstairs before leaving. Chip and Shauna slipped into swimsuits and headed to the larger pool where Shauna dove in, surfacing on the far side. Opening her arms wide she silently invited Chip to join her. Needing no further encouragement, enticed by her smile, her very presence, he followed her in. Coming up beside her he turned her to face the shallow end and plunging under the surface grabbed her ankles to lift her legs so she was lying on the surface and towed her till he could stand crotch deep.

"Do you have a place for me?" he asked, holding up his huge glistening prick and slowly parting her legs. He licked all the way to her well-trimmed sex as she wiggled and squirmed under his spell. "I thought we were coming out here for a quick dip and a long chat?" she said. "I know," he replied, aroused. "Well, I want you in me where you belong. So, now what?" "Now this," he replied, sliding her scant bikini off. "And now this," he continued, moving between her legs flaunting his gorgeous erection. "And finally this," he finished, slowly teasing her with his cockhead.

"Quit knocking at the door Baby and come on in. Fuck! I'm not afraid to beg! Now! Please!" "You know, I love you more than ever when you beg." "You do, do you?" she said, closing her eyes, enraptured with the enormous prick fully entering her. Holding her impaled, he walked her round so she could lean against the pool edge, buoyed by the water, before he began his rhythm. Shauna went berserk, doing her best to match him before exploding to the feel of his cum streams. Clinging sex to sex, anticipating their next trip, they felt themselves enveloped by a swirling stream of hot air. Wondering where it had come from, they opened their eyes to see it alive with rapidly flickering pinpricks of light, like fireflies on steroids that began changing colors randomly. Pulsing between a faint yellow through orange to a stronger red and back, the glow was soon accompanied by what sounded like soft breathing as the lights coalesced into a glowing swirl inside their minds and a message interrupted their thought-stream:

You not travel in cosmos tonight. We happy find you. Rest now. You need rest.

Soon we meet again. Easy you find us. Bye Bye Bye Bye Bye

Alone again, waist deep, they were astounded. Had an alien life found a way to communicate? Mind spinning a-mile-a-minute, Chip observed, "I can see smoke coming out of your ears." Mind churning equally, Shauna replied. "Well, look who's calling the kettle black." Laughing, accepting that all would be made clear when they needed for it to be, they relaxed, allowing their minds and bodies to slow down and just feel. Certain that when whoever or whatever was ready for them and they, and whatever else might be necessary, were also in alignment, a cosmic transformation that had never dared happen would manifest,.

Donning a couple of white robes, they picked up their wet swimsuits and settled on loungers, feeling their exhaustion as everything around them stilled. There seemed to be a trillion stars lighting the sky. *How many telescopes all over the world are trained, right this minute, on some small segment of the many universes?* wondered Shauna. *Was there someone brilliant enough to offer a theory so revolutionary it would turn everything we think we know upside-down, inside-out, back-to-front? Demanding a rethink of how everything has happened, is happening, and will happen – how, where and why humans fit. Maybe, just maybe, there'll be a true coming together. At least,* Shauna thought, *we now know we're not alone.*

And she went on to consider just how human knowledge had been suppressed: whether from fear, greed or the pursuit of power and control, and how that had retarded the evolution of man's understanding of everything. How the few persisted in dominating the many and the many continued to allow it. Thankful for individuals who dared to step out, to not stop until they found new answers, unwilling to be shackled by entrenched beliefs and stagnant thinking that kept populations ignorant and controllable; grateful for visionaries willing to risk failure and ridicule. *What is it that makes so many willingly accept suppression and what is it in the few that makes them willing to sacrifice anything and anyone to gain and keep control? It's not so much divide and conquer as divide and kill,* squirmed Shauna. *It's division and separation in all its guises that leads to death and it's the division within oneself that's the most lethal.* And, "SEPARATE THEM!" rang loudly in her memory.

Turning to Chip, signaling him to wait, not quite sure how to start, feeling unsettled at a gut level, she quickly adjusted to focus in on what she really had to say. Allowing her subconscious free reign, she concentrated on understanding her feelings and how to communicate them.

She had heard of telepathy, but had never given it much thought. Now, as she intentionally explored her depths, she realized that tonight she'd experienced it with Chip and the Presence earlier. *Is it possible*, she wondered, *that the ability has already been activated in us.* And she started to focus on transferring her feelings and experiences without speech. Chip, who had been watching her intently, sensing a deeper working, had intuitively relaxed and opened his mind to receive whatever she had to say, content for her to organize her feelings before speaking. And then she did. But she didn't. He knew he heard her, yet knew she wasn't speaking, as her words flowed into him. And he knew she heard him too, because she responded to his spontaneous reaction without him opening his mouth. They flowed their thoughts together, reveling in the direct access, unfiltered, raw, vulnerable, phenomenal.

She took Chip through her discovery of the conspirators, the words she'd overheard, sending a disturbance through their transfer concentration; her father's murder; the attempted kidnap and rape, her feeling that there was a connection between the three events; her healing, everyone else rendered unconscious and without the memory. How she'd allowed them to believe in a miracle until he'd come home and been so shocked. His clouded response flowed into her as he released everything the experiences had stirred. And they marveled at the immediacy, the ease, the detail and the power of this thought-speak.

Disengaging, sensing him carefully mulling everything over at a deep level, Shauna stretched out on the lounger and patiently waited. "Well, my Love, that was amazing and so much more intimate than talking. It felt like I was feeling what you were feeling only somehow translated into words and when you told your experience at the pool I felt such rage and fear of loss but then your aliens left me peaceful and exhilarated. I'm so thankful yet blown away. I'm excited by them, worried by the threesome, fearful for your mother and talking seems so antiquated." He finished, laughing at his verbal dump.

Shauna lay cradled beside him, tears flowing down her cheeks. Squeezing her closer, he kissed her lips and then all over her face. Rearranging himself, he took a corner of his robe and wiped away her tears before offering his hand to pull her up and off to bed.

The two detectives had been poking around for a while now, careful not to be seen, getting their bearings and assessing the nature of the neighborhood. They were now ready to more closely examine the property Richardson had thought could be the most likely candidate. Their first observations suggested it probably belonged to an older couple - no signs of kids and neglected landscaping. In fact, everything looked somewhat dilapidated. Maybe any relatives lived too far away to lend a hand.

As they started down the side of the winding driveway toward the house, headlights appeared along the street behind them. Not wanting to take any chances they scrambled for cover and flattened themselves against the ground behind a thirsty looking, scraggly chunk of shrubbery. Just as well. The car slowed and paused at the front gate before swinging into the driveway and stopping almost in line with them. A hulk of a man got out to close the gate. The detectives identified the car as a new Buick sedan. The exact color was hard to tell in the dark - light tan perhaps. The man, surprisingly agile considering his size, got back in and drove to the house and around the side. They strained to read the license plate but could only pick out a sticker on the rear bumper with an ACERS logo. Listening for the garage door they heard the engine stop and the sound of a car door close instead.

The four Russian pseudo-guards were in a windowless brick structure behind Coach's house, weak light from low-wattage bulbs adding to the dismal atmosphere. They were hungry, impatient for food and nervous, feeling shabbily treated and distrustful of their host. But then who did they trust? Not even each other. They heard a car stop close by and its door open and close. Moments later the building door opened and in came a hulk, juggling pizza boxes and a couple of six packs of soda. Tossing them on the table, he said in Russian, "Here's your chow, guys. You need to it eat fast because we think you may have been spotted and we're going to have to move you soon."

In the relative silence of their hurried meal they heard another car arrive right outside, its engine idling, waiting. Finished eating, the four Russians exited, two stopping to take a leak against the building before climbing in the back with a third climbing in the front. The fourth hobbled painfully behind, getting in the back with the other two, and the fully-loaded, sagging, beat up, two-tone jalopy - green and rust - drove off. The hulk surveyed the mess they had left. Deciding his wife could clean it up in the morning he closed the door and headed for the house.

Mark finally arrived at his luxury town house. Who would have guessed that he could afford anything like this? Or the gleaming black Jaguar he pulled into the garage. Strutting into the sparsely furnished but expensive home he opened a well-stocked refrigerator and grabbed a beer. Slugging it down he grabbed another, plunked into his favorite leather chair and contemplated his day. That latest phone call had been the last thing he'd wanted – playing chauffeur to four jackasses. Well, it was done. Now he could rest until tomorrow, which promised to be very busy and eventful. Convinced it would be a success, he went to bed and a sleep tormented by nightmares. *Mark, you arrogant, ignorant, low-life, what you are about to do sucks big time!*

CHAPTER 18 ENOUGH

Waking, Chip could feel Shauna piled partly on top of him, adoring the feel of her body so close as she breathed softly through slightly parted lips. He gazed at her for some time, feeling so thankful and grateful they had found one another, that he was sharing his life with someone so spectacular. He felt completely surrendered to her as he surveyed her slumbering presence. Her long curled lashes lay delicately against her upper cheeks in such perfection that he edged her closer to study them better. He was spellbound for what seemed like a long time.

Getting out of bed, careful to disturb her as little as possible, he strode buck-naked to the window wall, opened a panel and went out to the pool. The water invigorated him as he swam, getting the endorphins going, churning up the water with his legs and feeling the tension leaving every muscle as he stretched his arms out in front of him with each powerful stroke. The early morning sun on his back stimulated his sensuality and he gave thanks for his handsomely functioning body and the strikingly beautiful woman who'd so quickly become such a part of his life. He was happy and stirred about the choices he made every day beginning to clearly understand how getting what he wanted was now inextricably connected to how vulnerable he was with Shauna. Yes, he was releasing old patterns and beliefs, but in so doing he was becoming more and more the Chip he had never felt he could actually become. He turned on his back and quietly floated, allowing himself to enjoy at the deepest microscopic level the infinitesimal pleasures and sensations of the now.

Eventually the gym called as he felt the need for more vigorous exercise. Something that would quiet his sensual arousal, over-riding it with the heart-pumping, muscle-moving routines he was used to.

Mark made his way into the kitchen to get an early jump on what was needed for the day. He wanted to make sure he could leave early enough to accomplish his latest assignment and still arrive at the nightclub on time.

He busied himself with breakfast for Chip and light snacks for later for Chip's business associates. Anticipating that Shauna would probably want something light on performance day and Garcia her usual - he'd have to check with Troy - he was happy at the thought that this would be his last day on the job. He hadn't given notice; he was simply going to disappear.

Coming awake, Shauna stretched, taking the time to enjoy the response and flexibility of her toned body. Nothing to do; nothing to think about - for right now. What a luxury. She was going to take advantage. And she did, starting that very moment, allowing her mind to wander wherever it chose until she remembered with a jolt that she'd missed her session with Richard the day before. Rolling over to the nightstand, grabbing her phone, she left a contrite voicemail, apologizing and explaining there'd been an emergency, promising to fill him in when they actually got to speak.

Chip came in from his workout and gave her a lingering kiss. Before heading to shower and dress he detailed his plans for the morning, saying, "If you need me for anything, save your voice for tonight and just text me." She watched him enter the bathroom and listened to his movements as he got ready, but was asleep again before he passed back through the bedroom on his way out, unable to resist a last kiss on her forehead.

Not long afterwards, Shauna rose and took a light breakfast down by the main pool. As she relaxed with coffee afterwards, she felt almost jet-lagged by the previous day's events and went right back to bed, the caffeine no competition for her fatigue.

Roused by Chip's gentle yet persistent shaking, Shauna sat with alarm. Explaining that something had come up and Isabella, one of his associates, had been insistent on meeting with them both, he handed her a loose t-shirt and she quickly slipped it on and they went into the master lounge. There stood an attractive brunette of medium height, somewhere in her mid-thirties, a toned body in casual but expensive business wear and low-heeled shoes. Calm and collected, her blue eyes concentrated on Shauna as she introduced herself. "Hi, Shauna, I'm Isabella. I apologize for disturbing you but it has become imperative that I speak to you both." Shauna, still not fully

1 B

composed, ushered her to the couch in front of the television saying, "I don't know if I want to hear what you have to tell me."

"Look," said Isabella, as they sat, "This is going to come as a shock to both of you but I've been informed of a plan that endangers you both." Raising her hand for them to remain quiet, she continued. "I must apologize to you both, but particularly you Gifford. As you've likely surmised from my previous statement, I am not just a bean-counter. I work for a government intelligence agency, operating undercover while supervising the local efforts of a Special Task Force, set up to independently monitor the two of you and a ruthless oligarch who seems to be as interested in you both as we are." Handing them her credentials to check, she continued. "Up till now we thought he was in Russia, but information I received this morning identifies the person we've been watching as a surrogate and puts the man himself right here in Austin with the intention of abducting you, Shauna, and if he doesn't get what he wants, killing you. We gather he considers you, Gifford, an irritation to be made an example of and disposed of if necessary."

Observing their reactions, Isabella took note of their darkened faces and tightly clasped hands, knuckles showing white. Leaning toward them she gently placed her hands over theirs, blinking back tears. Her obvious concern and warm touch doing more than anything else could to help calm their fears as she waited patiently for them to regain a measure of composure.

"You will undoubtable be further upset by the fact that, as part of our protection protocol, we've been monitoring you, Shauna." She paused for a reaction, but seeing Shauna still catching up, went on. "When you reached puberty, your energy signature started showing up as an anomaly on various seismic monitors. Once you were identified as the source, it was determined prudent to track you through passive surveillance. That was until last Saturday when your energy started spiking off the charts and active monitoring of your physical connection was initiated and . . ." "You mean you've been monitoring our private activity? Who the fuck do you think you are?" exploded Chip, interrupting Isabella mid-sentence. "Believe me, it was the only way we could be sure the energy surges weren't caused by hostile action." "What do you mean, 'hostile action'?" asked Chip with somewhat less force, glancing at a wide-eyed Shauna. "That's why I needed to talk to you so urgently, to explain the situation and prepare you for what could prove to be an extremely dangerous confrontation." "You'd better get on with it then," said a slightly mollified Chip as Shauna nodded in silent agreement.

"We've been tracking the oligarch I mentioned before for a long time. With a few others he has managed to somehow insinuate himself into control of a major chunk of world commerce. Now, we have no doubt he has achieved this illegally, but as yet have been unable to find the evidence to prove it. He's a master manipulator, totally devoid of any morality or restraint, a master of disguise and . . . I've called him ruthless – but that really doesn't describe the level of depravity he is believed capable of: death by torture and dismemberment of opponents and competitors, the slaughter of innocents on nothing but a whim. He apparently operates like a modern-day Genghis Khan, spreading fear and evil wherever he pleases, using the billions he's amassed to maximize his influence where violence would leave him too vulnerable.

"Once head of the Russian Mob, we were led to believe he was Russian. Turns out he's from Scotland and the Russian Mob wasn't big enough or gross enough for him. He's moved on to richer pastures, bigger, uglier, less competitive and more lucrative. Adept at recruiting, his charismatic personality attracts both the super-smart and mindless scum. So he's surrounded himself with an, as yet, impenetrable legal infrastructure that has kept him insulated from the villainy he's suspected of and, as a last resort, sometimes probably a first strike, a network of enforcers who implement his need for death, destruction and mayhem and protect him from retaliation. He despises anyone with power and loathes competition and, we believe, eliminates any rivals or those he deems a threat. His organization has become so vast, widespread and insidious that, while it's been possible track him - although this morning's news has me wondering about that - it's been impossible to take him down: which is where it becomes personal and pertinent for the two of you.

"Another shock is that not only is he in Austin but he's impersonating the head coach of the Acers basketball team." Shauna gasped, looking wildly at Chip and gripping his hand tighter. Just as devastated, if not more so, he just stared disbelievingly at Isabella, not really trusting himself to speak. All too aware of the bomb she'd just dropped, Isabella continued. "At this point our best guess is that he had the real Coach disposed of, how long ago we don't know. Anyway, having found him, we intend to make sure he stays found. A few other pieces of the puzzle that have also come to light are, first: he was not born Igor Vronsky as originally documented, but Sean Cameron, whose brother is also heavily involved, and second: his underlying affiliation is to a Scottish power cult with the objective of controlling world commerce - as the cult master, he is well on the way to ensuring they achieve that objective.

"In relation to that, it's too bad your father got side tracked with your beauty and aliveness when you were so young because at the time he was in contention with Cameron to be the next Master. How different it would have been had your father taken over. Instead, he practically buried himself alive with guilt and remorse."

Chip glanced at Shauna, who'd squeezed his hand again, but that seemed to be her only reaction and Isabella continued.

"Anyway, third: It seems that he too has been monitoring your development and is aware of the significance of your energy spikes." Misreading Shauna's confusion, she commented. "By the look on your face, I'm guessing you have no idea what I'm talking about."

"It's not that. I just don't see how he or you can possibly know what Chip and I have been experiencing."

"I'm not sure that we do. I'm talking about the energy itself and the form you take, not your personal experiences. What we have observed is that when you bond sexually, you become one indivisible body. This has never happened before . . . ever. You are triggering a quantum leap for humanity. Just as your biology is changing so is your physical structure starting with a trend towards androgyny, not as a throw-back to the time of the Pharaohs and their lineage but a completely different metamorphosis that could change everything, including your personalities.

"Right now, when you return from your travels you're still recognizably Shauna and Gifford. But we don't know if that will always be the case. Precisely how any changes will play out, how quickly, what form you'll become or how it will impact life in general, we can't be certain but we do know the outcome will set a new standard for this planet at least. In the process, Gifford appears to have metamorphosed not just to a new man but to a true manifestation of male. In abandoning himself in surrender and vulnerability to you, Shauna, and in both of you treasuring and honoring your own bodies and, more importantly, each other's, we suspect you have eliminated the need for the usual distractions of intimacy. And, in truly becoming one body, albeit at the moment fleetingly, you each now hold the other's life in the atoms and cells of your own body.

"It would appear that you've transcended the familiarity that kills innovation and freshness and leads to boredom and infidelity, expanding yourselves instead to nourish, support and thrill each other, clean out your pasts to be the new, fresh, ever-changing individuals you each need to be for the future. Everything suggests that this is true intimacy. You've each made the other more important than yourself, discarding the path of self-discovery that would have ended in boredom, an endless loop of egocentricity - separate, isolated and marginalized. Choosing a life without ego - the ultimate survivor, even at the expense of its host – you have made it possible to pursue a total freedom, both unlimited and indivisible.

"What we, and we assume Cameron, have identified as a result of your coming together, is a previously unknown transformative energy which by any measure available looks as if it will totally change existence as we've known it and bring an end to everything negative and destructive. Which means Cameron and his ilk and everything they've strived for will no longer be sustainable. That's the power he wants to corrupt for his own evil purposes or, if that proves impossible, to destroy to save himself and everything he's worked for.

Seeing that Shauna and Gifford still didn't totally get the how or why of what was being said – she wasn't sure that it would be okay to think of him as Chip, not knowing if it was a pet name that only Shauna used - Isabella decided to provide some background. She needed both of them on board when she got to what she and her superiors were going to be asking of them. "Look, let me explain. If you know what to look for you'll find that this energy that you're the manifestation of has been spoken about for centuries, the subject of numerous legends and folk tales, written about in ancient manuscripts that only a privileged few have ever had access to. The ruling classes have known of you from the beginning of time and many prophecies have been fulfilled by loyal followers and admirers throughout history and across the world."

Although surprised by the revelation, Shauna could see how it would tie in with the strong feelings she sometimes had when she sang and spoke; that a unique sound and vibration flowed from her body to ignite those who were hungry to live a different way.

Isabella resumed. "While I can see that you're now beginning to understand what I'm saying, I don't know that you fully appreciate the magnitude of the ramifications. You are the catalyst for the integration of every universe as one organic energy, creating a united cosmos." Seeing Shauna struggling with that concept, Isabella expanded. "Look at it this way. Human evolution has been exceedingly slow. Change has been resisted and incremental. And through all that you have been essentially dormant, biding your time; an integral part of biological life. Even when a simple one-celled organism you were the extraordinary intelligence and alertness, gradually evolving yourself, choosing the strongest, healthiest and most intelligent life to carry you forward; crawling out of the soup to dry land, constantly vigilant, making sure your precious carriers survived, always searching for a better carrier to move onward; rising to walk on two legs, through the primitive and animalistic to larger brains, more coordination, more adventurous, more skilled. Couples became families became tribes became societies. From every source, life spread, expanding to meet the individual and collective needs. The advent of tools and weapons for killing and the concepts of territory and protection made your choices more complex. But you knew to remain unseen.

"Fire heralded the first extraterrestrials and their knowledge and abilities both intrigued and mystified you. They used their advanced technology and powers to help us humans along our evolutionary path, some becoming entangled with us sexually in the process. You saw the opportunity and expanded your potential through one such interaction between alien and human and your power and influence leapt forward as a result.

"So, at every step you have made wise choices. When you chose to be born, you manifested a breakaway from evolution. You became a revolution. You have the best human characteristics, modified by the legacy of your extraterrestrial father- and not just physically. Your ever-increasing hunger and drive to soar above the squalor, fighting, struggle, greed and wrong use of power rife among humanity plus your desire to always be in charge of your destiny, have molded and tempered you into a new and fresh human expression. You have been stealthily creating a world within our world. After all, when you think about it, there really is nothing new under the sun. Nothing, that is, except you."

Although both Shauna and Chip had been sitting transfixed, Isabella suggested a break to give them time to absorb what they'd heard, and her time to refocus her priorities. Both Shauna and Chip took the opportunity to stretch, Shauna thinking back to when she was a teenager and her mother had told her numerous stories about aliens.

One that immediately came to mind was the disaster of Atlantis where the aliens, fascinated by sex with humans - who at the time were not far removed from animals - compromised their metabolisms to became unbalanced, changing from benign and supportive to aggressive and controlling, leading them to divert the atomic power of their cells from the service of others to a force for domination, triggering a nuclear fission from within that ripped right out of their bodies, eventually destroying the civilization.

She also wondered about their superior intelligence and technology. She'd certainly heard speculation about the alien origins of so many of man's supposed innovations from the pre-historic to the present: from Machu Picchu and Stonehenge to immunization and space flight. *How often,* she wondered, *has Mankind's self-centered arrogance had to yield, bend and sometimes even shatter in order to forge ahead towards its goals?* She was interrupted by Chip handing her a bottle of water, having grabbed himself several from the refrigerator. Isabella accepted a bottle too, downing almost half before continuing.

"Your most brilliant achievement, Shauna, for yourself and humanity has been to attract Gifford into you. Out of the billions on this planet, he was your choice. You always knew you couldn't do what you have to do on your own, which is why you chose to be carried until now. But at some level you must have sensed that the time was right to become physical, that the connections and support you would require were coming into being around you. That those you would need in order to be free from the limitations of an old life, an old history and the dangers of a dark future, to continually live fresh and new, were emerging.

"Given the news about Cameron, we believe you, Gifford, are the reason he moved here. Unlike Shauna your energy signature is much less developed, being unobserved until a few years ago when you started registering intermittently. It seems that without your awareness your energy started spiking when you had sex. This, we believe, is what drew Cameron's interest. He couldn't get close to Shauna because she was still too transient, but you were locked into a contract here. So he moved to be ready should you blossom like Shauna and has had you closely monitored ever since. Of course, he couldn't have anticipated, any more than any of us could, that the two of you would come together and be creating what you are.

"Together you are forging a connection, a fusion of power that is constantly leading you to transformations. You become one united body as you link and couple, and your orgasms are so synchronized and the power you generate so intense you're creating a new physics. Most people only use a small percentage of the brain in their skull and most never consciously use the brain in their gut or the intelligence in every cell. But when you two launch at orgasm, you are drawing on more and more of this untapped capacity to eliminate the limitations of space, time and an old reality. This is the source of your infinite power. You have ended the separation between mind, body and soul to be the complete individuals you each are, and have ended the separation between each other to become one body moving with the same focus, the same intent and the same passion for humanity and all life. The two of you have connected so quickly, precipitating our greatest challenge as a species, this imminent confrontation with Cameron and his network, while at the same time providing the means to finally bring an end to the forces he represents. However, before I get into that, let's take another minute to stretch."

They stood stiffly and shook their limbs. It felt good to move. Shauna again running with the thoughts Isabella had stirred, particularly about Chip. As she eased out the kinks she thought back to their first interaction when theirs eyes had met and they'd probed each other. She'd known he was unformed but sensed he was ready. *And how he had responded! Awakening literally overnight to receive the electro-magnetic fire from within my biological structure he's allowed his nervous system to be rebuilt and his DNA to be re-arranged – taking the short cut to being who he was born to be and now is, open to grow and expand as a higher life. Changing for me, whatever it takes, and becoming lighter and brighter and more him in the process.* And she was so grateful for the joy and excitement he brought her. The consistent caring, abundant love, nourishment and support of their combined wellbeing she felt from him, so rare, perhaps even non-existent in anyone else. *Right now it feels as if the majority of people sleepwalk through life, living from the neck up, functioning as isolated units, thoughts controlled by mind chatter that continuously analyzes and repeats senseless beliefs, archaic genetic programs and traumatic life experiences that are so deeply embedded in the human structure. Living in a separation that kills, not time or age but the continuous accumulation of baggage each body carries until it becomes so fossilized inside that it wears out and stops. People darken, fall, settle for alone. They wither. And they let gravity take over.*

The break over, the three sat again. Chip and Shauna opening themselves further to take in what Isabella would have to say, unsure if they were nervous or excited.

CHAPTER 19 PLAN

"Now that you have a better understanding of why you've been targeted, let me explain what we've learned about Cameron's plans and how we would like your help to not just thwart him but to dismantle his entire network.

"While we were caught by surprise by how fast Cameron and his global network organized in response to the immense power you've been generating, we've been able to activate various Federal Agencies and both local and international law enforcement. Led by the Special Task Force and its director in Washington D.C., an operation has been devised to ensure the safety of you both while providing a framework for collecting the hard evidence necessary to ensnare Cameron and his key associates and engineer the destruction of his operations worldwide. As I said before, now that we really know where he is, we need to take advantage of it.

"His plan, which we have received from an impeccable source, is as follows. After your performance tonight, Shauna, you will be approached by Mark, your chef, and Harvey Sexton who'll offer to buy you a drink. What they'll give you will be spiked with the drug Ecstasy. Once you're under its influence, they will spirit you away through the rear entrance to either a truck loaded with several other women or to an SUV. Either way, you'll then be driven to Houston docks. Next you'll be transferred to a freighter where you'll be joined by the current head of the Russian Mafia, Josef Karpov, who goes by just Josef, for passage to Russia together. Apparently, in exchange for Josef's help, Cameron will gift you to him until the furor dies down when he will retrieve you for 'debriefing' - I believe that's how he's said to have put it.

"Now, you may be wondering where Gifford fits in all this. As I said initially, Cameron sees you as an irritation to be used as an example and has arranged for you to be assaulted and your penis cut off as a trophy for him if you try to interfere with his plan. He obviously expects you try because he's arranged for three of Josef's thugs to take care of you when you follow Shauna out of the club."

Seeing Chip and Shauna freezing into each other, obviously tuning her out, Isabella addressed them forcefully. "YOU NEED TO LISTEN! Just in case I didn't make it clear enough, Cameron wants you for himself, Shauna.

He needs to have everything you have. He doesn't just have a multi-trillion fortune riding on this, he knows that if he can't possess you, his goals and lifelong ambitions will never materialize and it will be impossible for him and his kind to survive. HE KNOWS THIS! Just like we do. To get what he wants he will do whatever it takes; the more gruesome the better. And if he can't get what he wants out of you he'll tear you apart so everything you already are and will eventually become will cease to exist and humanity will spiral into oblivion taking with it not just our universe, but everything! THIS IS WHAT'S AT STAKE!

"Do you think if we could see any other way we'd even be considering your involvement? It's not unprecedented to ask civilians to put themselves at risk but it's always a last resort, ALWAYS! I'll also point out that we know your power and your value and will have our best people supporting you every step of the way. At no point will you be on your own. So, please, hear me out." As neither of them responded, she carried on after taking a mouthful of water.

"It may seem that the obvious strategy would be to simply kill Cameron. Unfortunately, if all we were to do was kill him, he would immediately be replaced by who knows who. And then we'd be back to square one. Unless we dismantle his network we will always be in danger from it, and you will be constantly looking over your shoulders, wondering when. Much as we'd like to, we can't possibly protect you forever, in fact it's not really possible to provide one hundred percent protection to anyone, ever, let alone for forever. What we can do, though, is make sure you are never alone or unprotected while this operation unfolds. And that is what we've based our counter-plan on."

Having got the worst of what they were facing out of the way, a sympathetic Isabella suggested another break. This time Shauna and Gifford simply held each other while Isabella sat with her head in her hands, trembling from the effort of staying clear and assertive, even though she was feeling every inch of their bewilderment, anger and fear. Head still in her hands, she quietly said, "You two are civilization's next step. And those who hear you, who feel the penetration no matter where they are, will come. I am one of those people, Shauna, Gifford. I've heard your call and I'm with you, totally." Without raising his head from where it was resting against Shauna's, Gifford said: "Maybe you should start calling me Chip then." Thanking him, Isabella proceeded to outline the counter-plan, detailing how they intended to minimize the effect of each step before dropping her second bomb.

"No matter what happens from tonight onwards, we don't think you should expect to ever return here. Not to this house, this city, or even this country." Chip exploded with a rage he had never before experienced, springing from the couch roaring incoherently, pummeling the air, unable to articulate his anger and frustration. Shauna immediately rose to tightly embrace him, holding him until he calmed enough to spit out, "You expect us to play along with this fucking asshole scheme? Without any guarantees! And now this?" and he slowly slid back onto the couch as if defeated, Shauna holding him all the way down.

Shaken by his outburst, Isabella did her best to reassure him, and Shauna, even herself, she was so upset. "We've had top people on this and in place for a long time waiting for the right moment. Now we're being forced to react and it's certainly nowhere near the right moment, but Shauna's wellbeing is our primary focus and has been all along. If anything and I do mean anything, looks too risky or remotely uncontainable, we will immediately whisk her to safety and, if necessary, abort the operation."

After a few moments, Shauna quietly said, "I always wanted a Guardian Angel . . . I understand how important what you've told us is, not just for me and Chip, and I appreciate everything that's been done so far and the effort this is taking from so many. I'm especially touched by the feeling you have for us and can only imagine how difficult this must be for you too . . . I think we should let her finish, Love. I really don't know that we have any other option than to do what we can to stop the madness."

Mouthing a silent thank you to Shauna, Isabella softly continued.

"We believe the best course of action is for you to proceed as if you are ignorant of everything I've told you; to act as normal as you can until Mark and Harvey make their move. Just follow your usual routine Shauna, although I do suggest, you take a change of clothes for after the performance so you'll be more comfortable for whatever happens. As for you Chip, go with Ivan and R Jay as if it's just a regular night out, but wear a pair of sports shoes or similar that would be good for running if necessary."

Interrupted by a soft tapping at the door, Isabella signaled Shauna and Gifford to stay put and, hand gripping the gun in her handbag, went to the door. Cautiously opening it a crack, she peeked out before flinging it wide and opening her arms to hug an extremely good looking, copper-brown hunk of a man.

Large dark eyes radiated warmth and confidence, inviting trust. And his chiseled features with voluptuous lips and a prominent nose held a tantalizing smile. Dreadlocks fell to the broad shoulders of a body to live for: ripped arms, beautifully defined and muscular, his waist small and firm. *I bet he has great abs*, thought Shauna from where she sat staring. Immediately attracted to his presence Chip rose to give him a strong, welcoming handshake. "I'm Chenaugh. You must be Gifford." "Call me Chip." And they were hugging each other like brothers. Although Chip had two or three inches on Chenaugh, they clearly met as equals. Breaking contact, Chenaugh then turned his gaze to Shauna, saying, "So, you're the culprit who needs all this attention," sending a shock of electricity up and down her spine. She nodded yes. "Well, you certainly are the most beautiful creature I've ever had the pleasure to meet," he observed, holding her gaze a little longer before address them all to apologize for being late, explaining the delayed flight from L.A.

"A few things you should know about Chenaugh," said Isabella, "He was born into poverty in a country of perpetual wars and civil strife, the Sudan, and lost both his parents at an early age. He understood that he'd have to get out if he was to survive and so he and a couple of his friends started running and never looked back. They ran for three days straight and by dumb luck ended up in a refugee camp in Kenya. Within six months he'd been adopted by an American couple and was living in the States. He carried on running, became an excellent student, attended Harvard, and was snapped up by the FBI on graduation." "I started off running for my life and have been running ever since. A day without running is like a day without joy," added a smiling Chenaugh.

Pleased that the three of them had hit it off so well, Isabella went on. "Chenaugh, is one of our best agents. Fluent in Russian he has been undercover in the American branch of the Russian Mafia for years and has become a trusted security advisor to their leadership. He will be in place to keep an eye on Shauna throughout the operation. There will also be a second Russian-speaking agent riding as a guard in the truck with the women. So at all times, Shauna, you will have at least one and maybe two personal protectors.

"Chenaugh will wait here till this evening when he'll make his own arrangements to get to the club and keep you safe from there until the operation is over." Pausing to make sure she'd covered everything, she remembered and said: "While I've been with you, colleagues of mine will have spoken with our business associates, Chip, and they should be finished and on their way back to L.A. by now. Shauna, Richard has been informed that you're resting up till the performance and sends his regrets that he can't attend, which is just as well under the circumstances. We've also arranged for Troy and Garcia to enter witness protection, possibly with some of Garcia's family who want to be with her. I'm sure they'll miss you a lot, but we can't leave them vulnerable to anyone seeking information or reprisals." She then asked if they had any comments or questions.

Shauna and Chip sat mute: swamped with information, logistics and details and overwhelmed by a mix of emotions. "Look, I know I've given you both a lot to process, hopefully enough for you to fully appreciate not only how serious this is but how incredibly potent you are. Soak everything in and remember it. My sound might be greater than your own in moments of doubt or uncertainty. Now, one final thought. Don't have sex until this is over. We don't want you transmitting any vibrations that may trigger the enemy to act prematurely or in any way change the plans we know about. Now, I suggest the three of you get some rest. It's vital that you be as relaxed as possible tonight." She stood and left to make sure the counter-plan was progressing on schedule.

"Whew, that was a head full!" exhaled Shauna, furrowing her forehead and rubbing her eyes as she vigorously shook her head as if to clear it. "Yeah, and we better make sure it works out as planned, Love," said Chip. "I guess we're being monitored right now, so we might as well get some rest as suggested," he added, taking off his shirt and flopping on the bed. Offering Chenaugh a choice between sleeping beside her and Chip or taking a guest room, a weary Shauna called Troy to keep watch outside the bedroom and snuggled up with Chip. Chenaugh chose to take a shower in the master bathroom and then joined Chip and Shauna. Soon there were three people sleeping in the big bed.

Startled awake, Chenaugh quickly silenced his watch alarm, noticing neither of the intertwined Chip and Shauna had stirred. As he gazed at them he enjoyed a sense of them reciprocating each other's lives even as they slept. He was hungry for such a deep connection too. Rising to get ready he thought of a sexual intimacy with Shauna and left a thank you note on his way out. If only he could read the future!

A little later the slumbering duo was rudely awakened by icy-cold washcloths covering their faces. Garcia, unable to rouse them in the normal way, had resorted to a technique she had learnt as a mother of eight. Their resulting dour mood needed some work though. Begrudgingly they slowly headed for the showers for a water-blast wakeup. It worked. They came out refreshed with glistening, lotioned skin, ready for whatever was going to come their way.

Leaving what was left in her wardrobe to Garcia and her daughters, Shauna dressed simply: a short-sleeved lightweight top; hip-hugging slim-line jeans, colorful sports shoes and a waist-length leather jacket to carry.

Chip wore black, slacks, a glittery tee shirt, loose jacket, sports shoes and, of course, his bowler. Oh yes, and two pairs of briefs, one over the other to provide a little bit of crotch protection, wishing he had boxers made of metal, mindful of Isabella's warning of what Cameron had in store for him. He was as ready as he'd ever be.

As they had woven the dance of dressing it was almost as if Chip and Shauna had purposely avoided one another. But quite to the contrary, they had been aware of each other every second, attuned to each other's every gesture and expression. Before leaving the master suite for the last time they each embraced a Garcia weeping with sadness at having these two special people leave her life forever.

As his own final act, Mark had laid out a light snack for them in the dining room before leaving without saying goodbye. The two sat to pick at their plates in silence. Shauna ate very little before a performance anyway but Chip had no appetite, barely able to accept how soon she would have to go. They could almost feel the tick, tick, tick of what little time they had left together going by so fast.

Troy arrived to drive Shauna to the club. "You stay here, my ever-so-precious Baby," trembled Shauna. "Troy will take good care of me." A long drawn out kiss and Shauna turned briskly to head for the limo before she cracked apart with sobs. Leaving a life she had known for such a short time yet one that seemed like she had lived forever, in exchange for risks, dangers, and the unknown and the unthinkable - separation from Chip for she knew not how long. It all seemed too much.

CHAPTER 20   PERFORMANCE

In questioning Chip's neighbors, Richardson had discovered that one of them on an impromptu tour of Gifford's house on the night of the party had seen Mark scurrying through the kitchen entrance just before she'd heard about the murder.

His follow up investigation of Mark not only uncovered the town house and Jaguar purchases but several aliases he'd been using. None of them had meant much until he'd come across the name Mark Cameron, younger brother of Sean Cameron. *Jackpot* he'd thought. It turned out that Mark was suspected of being a professional killer who hired out to his brother and anyone else who wanted his services. Having studied for a time as a gourmet chef, he'd also been the obvious choice for Cameron to insert into Chip's household as a spy.

It also hadn't taken Richardson long to find out about Mark's connection with Peggy and where she lived. He was soon knocking at her door. Disenchanted with Mark, especially after Richardson told her about the secret life of luxury she'd been excluded from, it hadn't taken much probing for her to lead him directly to the outdoor potted plant and unearth the package Mark had given her to hide. "I put it here when wondering where I should 'plant the package', so I literally did plant it." She grinned. *A female with revenge in mind* thought Richardson, now having the gun that would prove Mark was a murderer.

Richardson would also like to drain Coach's pool to see if what R Jay had reported as happening during the basketball picnic was true - an attempt on Shauna's life. *So*, ruminated the Detective, *was this plan set up months ago or simply an attempt to take advantage of happenstance?*

Mark pulled into the long driveway of a single story brick and wood house on a large neglected yard to the left of Coach's house. Mark had thought it a stroke of genius to take the four Russians on a seemingly endless winding tour all over the back streets of Austin only to deposit them right next door to where they had previously been hiding. The elderly couple who owned the house had been paid handsomely to go find a hotel for a few days and ask no questions. Mark of course didn't know that Richardson's two detectives were now following his every move - already aware of his now-not-so-secret town house and luxury sedan.

Picking up three Russians – the fourth with broken feet having been discretely 'disappeared' for incompetence and endangering the whole scheme - he drove to the club and dropped them off. Entering the club the three casually meandered about, blending in like they'd been told to. They noticed their target, Chip, had not shown yet. Mark drove the car around to the back and parked close to where he knew the kidnap truck would wait when it showed up. He went in the club searching for Harvey, pumped with adrenalin and eagerly anticipating the next moves.

Sean Cameron was in no hurry. As far as he was concerned the plans were sufficiently flexible to cover any eventuality and he could slip into the club and leave whenever he felt like it, probably towards the end of the performance. He'd see how the mood took him. *I'm mainly going to see the 'song bird' in all her splendor one last time before she turns into a sparrow. What a worthy adversary.* Cameron chuckled to himself, deciding to lounge a little longer before getting dressed, just because he deserved to. His wife and two boys were keeping their distance. They knew the consequences if they didn't when he was in a mood like this.

Waiting for Ivan and R Jay to pick him up was almost unbearable for Chip, consumed with Shauna and what was to come. *I can't start out like this. I feel miserable and in so much pain. I've got to feel my power with Shauna and stop this self-pity.* He began to visualize playing with her in the blue waters of a sunny, bright Jamaica. He thought of all the people who were helping them, many of whom he'd never met and probably never would, and began to feel a strong gratitude for what he had. A lightness rippled through him and the flicker of a smile spread from his fine-looking lips across his face and his spirit lifted until he felt more than himself, empowered to be whatever would be necessary to see Shauna safe beside him and Cameron in Hell.

Finally, the entrance buzzer! Recognizing R Jay's voice over the intercom he hurried out to the car, not bothering to lock up. *Don't need to, having the guards on site and I'm not coming back anyway,* Chip thought to himself. Ivan and R Jay looked somber. "Hey bros, why the long faces?" asked Chip. "Just makes you look uglier." He chuckled. "Geez man, what kind of a fairy godmother turned you into such a Disney delight?" replied R Jay who along with Ivan had been in a funk since they'd been filled in on Chip's and Shauna's situations. "Hey Man, what's turned you into 'The Grinch'?" retorted Chip. "Let's all be Spiderman and dedicate ourselves to bringing the bad guys to justice - and have some excitement doing it," chimed in Ivan." "Hey, bro, you've got some big cajones man," R Jay laughed. "All right," said Chip. "This is more like it. "So, we lose a good friend, probably never see him again and we're laughing?" said a mixed up R Jay. "Come on you guys. Let's do this thing, go have some fun afterwards and take it one step at a time. Crap, Ivan you drive like a turtle. Pedal to the metal, man," Chip finished.

Arriving at the club, Ivan arranged the valet parking while Chip, trying to retain an air of normalcy, hastened backstage to find Shauna. He caught up with her in the dressing room, getting her hair done in the long and flowing style he personally loved. She was wearing a dazzling gown he'd never seen before and he rushed to kiss her cheeks, nose and lips without smudging her lipstick. He whispered in her ear, trying hard not to choke up, "I love you so completely, my Precious." Their eyes met, sealing their togetherness even deeper, and he left to claim his seat at the table where Ivan and R Jay already sprawled.

Shauna finished the final preparations for her last performance in Austin. Composing herself, she let go of the torment, fears, and what-ifs, sick and tired of her monkey mind running wild, dominating every thought, emotion and feeling. *LET GO, LET GO, LET GO,* she screamed inwardly. *That's better,* she thought, reaching the place where she didn't care who was attending her performance, or who wasn't - how evil they were, or how good. She didn't give a damn who liked her or not. All she cared about was giving the performance of her life - especially *for* her life. Chip was silently applauding her, feeling her internal shift from where he sat but right there with her.

As the orchestra played the opening bars of her first song, Shauna stood tall and proud, squared her shoulders and walked on stage to stand at the microphone, Stunning in the first of the four gowns she would wear that night, she looked around radiating confidence and credibility. As a hush fell she burst forth with the first words, a revolutionary sound . . . Holy.

Everyone listened, transfixed. Isabella, roaming the room, stopped, covered in goose bumps from head to foot. Even those who were against anything Shauna stood for were intimidated by the reverence she was being accorded. Cameron, who had slipped in early and was hiding in the back, cringed at the magnificence of his number one obsession. Being serenaded by such purity was disgusting him. It was so unworthy of his presence. Yet under it all he could feel the power he craved, and the desire to rip out her throat to get to it became almost overpowering. Quickly, before his rage betrayed him, he scanned the room, locating his top two lieutenants. Signaling them a slight change in plans he slipped away, overcome by his malevolent bile but confident that all would be taken care of.

Shauna felt a dark energy leave the hall. Richardson, who was lurking in the shadows, experienced a similar gut response and discretely shadowed Coach when he saw him leaving, having been briefed on his true identity. *I might as well track the maniac and see where he takes me*, thought Richardson.

Shauna and her companions, seemingly blending as one biological organism, one inseparable unit together, soared higher and higher with each number – each player adding their own flavor to a unique confluence that transcended anything any of them or their audience had ever experienced before. They were all-out - unwilling to be bound by anyone or anything. Not rebellious, just free.

Flowing equally smoothly through her costume changes, now in a gown Chip adored, Shauna sang not just to the audience or the planet but specifically to Chip. Pouring her love out through every song she recharged their connection. And every person who had an open heart could feel the power, experiencing themselves as the object of her passion, yet knowing they weren't. It was a sensation that continued through a varied program linked by tender conversation that including mentioning a two week vacation, but not that this would be her last Austin performance.

In her final gown - a figure-hugging white, showing every swell and ripple, the jeweled straps emphasizing the glow of her skin - long jeweled earrings and strapped silver stilettoes, she was a smoldering presence, inspiring a mix of awe and applause, interspersed with envy from judgmental tight-asses.

Shauna could feel it all and couldn't have cared less. She was high on being the full-out Shauna she wanted to be. Just seeing her move was a show in itself and she looked to Chip and saw he was grinning ear to ear with that irresistible mouth of his.

The finale capped what Shauna had set out to do - to far exceed anything before. In fact exceeding even her own highest expectations, changing the environment both within bodies and beyond any boundaries. She stood proudly before the audience and her team of performers, shining with how honored and cherished she felt.

The standing ovation went on and on until Shauna, after gracefully curtsying one final time, left the stage carrying a huge bouquet she'd received. The applause went on until she reappeared for an encore – which became three. Afterwards she waved good-bye and left for backstage. She sat down in the makeup area, trembling yet fulfilled - a wonderful feeling that fueled her for what was to come. She thought of Chip whom she was longing to touch - soon!

CHAPTER 21 HAYWIRE

Shauna knew it was important to be working the room outside, especially her loyal patrons, but was impatient for Chip, wondering if what she was feeling was similar to how an addict felt when they didn't get their fix the moment they needed it. Overriding her addiction she rose, preparing to leave, when he came in. Rapidly coming together, Shauna wrapped herself around him. Holding him even tighter in response to his whispered, "It's so good to hold you, my Love."

Disengaging he held her at arm's length. "I doubt you've ever sung so superbly. Your voice, your sound, was so rich and powerful, I sense you're drawing more and more people to your flame, Love; preparing them with motivation and purpose to cast their own log on the growing blaze. They'll create a heat for their own bodies that will never dim but trigger their innate body electric to shine like a beacon to, in turn, wake others to a new life of freedom. I see everything from yesterday backwards being burned away and a new level of bio-intelligence directing each person who responds. They'll be free of all history, beliefs or obsolete habits. Wow! Listen to me! You've got me going in such a joy I'm outgrowing this skin again. I love you, Shauna, but come, we have work to do." Shauna could feel Chip's body thrumming and followed him with a grateful, inspired heart.

As she visited with the fans she noticed, through a gap in the crowd, a short, plain-looking woman with light brown hair worn in a nondescript, rather unattractive style. For anyone else she might have been lost in the crowd, but for Shauna she would stand out anywhere. Excusing herself from those around her she almost started running toward the woman but remembering Isabella's admonishment just in time, glided over, reached out and hugged her, drawing her close to whisper, "Mummy, I am so happy to see you! I was wondering when you would show up." Her mother responded equally quietly, "My dear daughter, I was told by The Sisterhood of Protectors to come immediately and I would find answers to my many questions. Although I already have an inkling of the complex dangers and conspiracy you're facing.

"I've always known you were conceived for a purpose, to make a huge difference on this planet, but I've also felt there are those who would strongly oppose who you are. Fortunately, as you've grown, so have the numbers who want you to succeed and are ready to support you however they can. I'll be watching tonight and the many who've come with me from Scotland will be standing by too. Beyond that we will have plenty of time to talk later." "That makes me so happy," responded Shauna, who was once again drawn to the depth and alertness in her mother's eyes that lent her a magnetism not immediately apparent, saying, "You've always been here for me and I love you so." "Now be off, Shauna, and do what you were instructed to do." They kissed and Shauna reluctantly left to go backstage again and prepare for another kind of performance of her life.

Wearing her kidnap clothes, wishing she'd chosen a less revealing top, hair pinned in a pony-tail, Shauna thanked her assistant saying, "If you want anything of mine, it's yours, and that includes the gowns." The assistant thanked her, overwhelmed by her generosity, wondering why, not realizing it would be the last she'd see of Shauna unless she took on the new life Shauna had poured out every time she'd sung.

Chip was ready but becoming more nervous by the second. Shauna rubbed his back and when he whispered, "I'm more worried about you than I am about me," replied. "Please don't be. I need you totally focused on what you need to do. That's the greatest help you can give me, Babe. I'm well covered. Remember that." Shauna was still trying to put her performance behind her. *Shit it feels like it only lasted for a moment. I wish we had more time. Although it isn't more time we need.* And a brief smile flirted with her firm lips. Chip brightened up for an instant and thanked her with a kiss. "Damn it," said a tearful Chip. "I wish this were simply a bad dream and we were heading home where we belong for some Baileys and a swim and a wonderful fuck in bed." Shauna pressed her body into his, wrapped her arms around him and held him close. She let the undying passion she felt for him do the talking.

The club maintenance crew was almost finished with setting up the club for the after-performance clientele. Bar tenders were still stocking the four bars, one on each wall, while customers lined up outside, waiting. It looked like they were going to be mobbed.

Isabella was hanging out at the corner of the bar nearest the rear exit, keeping a vigilant eye on all that was going on and who was where. It seemed like she had eyes in the back of her head. She was amused by Harvey at this moment. He was fidgety and beads of sweat were running down his face. Mark had just left, presumably to fix the drugged drink and she expected Harvey would soon join him so she made her way over to him.

Immediately extending her hand for a shake she said as pretentiously as she could, "Hi there. Are you *The* Harvey Sexton, creator of the Sexual Work Shops?" This made him pause and take notice. Although she could tell he was distracted, she could also see he was flattered and enjoyed the ego stroking. "Why yes. And who wants to know?" he asked as he ran a hand through his well-groomed and greased hair. "I'm Isabella Lopez from Los Angeles visiting friends for a few days. We met briefly a while back but you've probably forgotten. I'm head of a well-known clothing line." "Oh yes, of course," stammered Harvey who really had no idea. "Anyway, I belong to several groups - you know, in my line of business - and we came across an article in the L.A. Times about you and what you do." She said, making it up as she went along. "Oh, you mean recently in the Reporter?" Harvey responded. "Of course. My mistake. Anyway, we wondered if we could get together with you to talk about holding a series of workshops with us. Would you be interested?"

Becoming more and more agitated, Harvey kept looking at his watch. "Er, I'm so sorry, but I have to be someplace right now. Why don't you give me a card and I'll get back to you?" "Sounds good, but I've left them in the car. Why don't I walk you out and I can get you one. It will give us more time to talk on the way too." And she took him firmly by the arm and nearly dragged him with her. *He doesn't weigh much. Either that or I'm particularly pumped up for tonight*, noted Isabella. They got to the front lobby where Harvey collapsed into a nearby chair. He bent over and started babbling. "I can't do it. I just can't do it. I can't do it." He looked up at her. Snot was running from his nose and his eyes were red and watery. He bowed his head, wiping his nose with his hand and rooted in his pockets, presumably for a handkerchief. Isabella took out a tissue and dabbed at his face, whispering soothing words to him. She even felt sorry for the man. At least he had a conscience. "Now, tell me what it is you can't do? Believe me, you can trust me."

Harvey looked around nervously and suspiciously. "An awful crime is about to be committed. A plan is underway as we speak to have a wonderful and beautiful woman - the one who sang here tonight - kidnapped and sent to the head of the Russian Mafia to become his mistress and I can't stand to think about it. I so desired her for myself that when she rebuffed my advances

I became so angry and jealous that I agreed to play a part in this disgusting scheme and it's tormented me ever since. But NO MORE!"

Quietening him, quickly scanning the area to make sure no one was paying them undue attention, Isabella asked that he quickly share the plan with her in as much detail as he could remember. "Well, I was supposed to help Mark drug her, and escort her to a truck parked in the alley with other similarly drugged women. They were then to be transferred to a shipping container for onward transportation by ship to Russia. But I have just discovered that she will be taken to a waiting SUV instead and be driven directly to the ship docked in the gulf near Houston where she will be kept in a maintenance room below deck. The Mafia chief, Josef I think his name is, is supposed to arrive by helicopter to pick her up and take her to a private airfield near Houston International where they'll take a private plane to Moscow." "How do you know all this Harvey?" asked Isabella. "Woman, I have ears to hear and some smarts to figure things out.

"They had to work hard to convince Josef to go along because he wanted to have a nice leisurely cruise getting to know Shauna, if you get my drift. But they explained she would be sleeping the drug off and he had no interest in having sex with a corpse-like woman, thank goodness. But then, I shudder to think what will happen to her once they are in Moscow. A sex slave, a drug addict? My mind keeps playing one terrible scenario after another. And I just can't let any of them happen." Harvey started sobbing again. "You're absolutely right," responded Isabella, patting his shaking arm.

"Now listen to me, Harvey. Do exactly as you've been asked. I'll make sure Shauna is safe and that you're protected, but you better get a move on and link up with Mark who must be wondering where you are. And it's imperative you talk to no one about this conversation, absolutely no one! Now, get going!" She gave him a reassuring smile and kissed his sweaty cheek. "And thanks."

With not a second to lose, Isabella sprang into action relaying this latest information and her instructions to her local crew via her wrist mic. She thought how miraculous it would be if they were to nail Josef when he landed in Moscow with Shauna. And then intervene to rescue the other incoming women. The evidence would be indisputable. Now all they had to do was link Cameron to the proceedings.

The change in plan made protecting Shauna even more precarious. Now they had to get Chenaugh on the plane with her and Josef and make sure she was kept safe until Josef was arrested. Not easy but also not impossible given Chenaugh's established position with the Russian Mafia in the States. They'd also need to move their crew on the ground in Odessa to cover Moscow which would require some rapid transportation arrangements. Although probably easier on Shauna, this new development was going to cause some real operational headaches.

Isabella immediately contacted her Operations Chief, Comstock, who'd already heard the updated information. "I need to know that we can get our agents in Odessa to Moscow in time to monitor Shauna's arrival," said Isabella. "You've got it," Comstock replied.

Having set the revised plan in motion, Isabella rapidly headed backstage to where Shauna and Chip were waiting for their cue to begin the nightmare. They were both pacing to release nervous energy. Isabella advised them that the operation had changed for the better and to follow the lead of their operatives as there wasn't time to fill them in. Suffice it to say that it would be easier on Shauna and Chip and would guarantee they would have Josef in the bag. And in the process, she was confident Cameron would come out of the shadows long enough to be grabbed. Isabella reminded them again to act normal, relax as much as possible, and most importantly, to remember they would be in the best of hands. Their safety was the top priority of everyone involved in the operation - even if at times it might not seem that way. She gave them both big hugs. "I'll be seeing you soon." Her hugs and words reassured Shauna and Chip and they needed every bit of reassurance they could get.

Isabella then contacted Chenaugh to make sure he was up to speed. He had very few questions - mainly listening to her run-down of the revised plan and his participation. That's what Isabella treasured about him. He was the consummate professional, supremely confident in his abilities without being arrogant, extraordinarily capable and with the rare ability to operate spontaneously and intuitively should the need arise. Yes, he was the best. *I wish I had a few more like him,* mused Isabella.

Richardson had tracked Coach right back to his house. "Damn it," sputtered Richardson. *This guy is unreal. He must have balls as big as boulders. I can't believe he's lived and worked here for as long as he has and not given himself away or been arrested. The authorities, all of them - FBI, local and international law enforcement – have all been watching him and none of us have been able to pin anything on him. Hell, even proving he knowingly harbored the four apparent mobsters wouldn't be worth the effort. And, I'm betting we won't be able to prove he had anything to do with the death of the one who assaulted Shauna either. Not enough evidence and too many friends in high places. I might as well go back to the club and make myself inconspicuous and useful.*

He turned on the car radio, found some soothing music and pressed the 'pause' button in his computer brain. "That's more like it." He let out a well-deserved sigh and drone-like headed for the club. On arrival he parked near the rear where he could observe an SUV and truck crouched in the shadows between the lot lights and partially hidden by dumpsters. He hunched down in his seat. Behind the darkened car windows, Richardson became the invisible man.

An unfamiliar man entered the make-up room, flashed credentials identifying him as FBI agent Tom Carlyle, and notified Chip and Shauna that they could make their appearance as soon as they felt ready. After he stepped back out, Chip took Shauna's hand and put it against his chest saying, "Think on this. When this is over we'll be together in a way you've never experienced before. This is my promise!" They kissed, entwining their tongues in the process - their last kiss alone for who knew how long - before heading out the door,.

As soon as they stepped out from the cloistered back room, they were confronted by a seemingly impenetrable crowd of the young, old, fat, thin, happy, suppressed, rhythmic, clunkers, present, detached, short, tall, attractive, plain, bored, high. Chip suggested they have a dance first before going to the bar. They elbowed their way along, being bumped and jostled, until they could feel some relief from bodies pressing against them. Chip put his large hands on Shauna's butt, as she wrapped her arms around his neck. Every time they were rammed into by careless dancers, Shauna's breasts would flatten against Chip's chest and they would smile at each other, enjoying the additional sudden and unexpected closeness. The music ended.

The next selection was not to their liking - besides, they had to begin a dangerous life-saving performance now, so hand in hand, they bumped and shoved their way towards the crowded bar. Shauna whispered in Chip's ear, "I wonder how many people are for us and how many against?" "Me too. There's certainly enough who look like they'd be wise to avoid and stay alert around," he whispered back. This was surely a night with an unusually high number of people in attendance.

They aimed for Ivan and R Jay propping up the middle of the bar. Chip had to bully his way in, making a small space beside them, his back against the bar with Shauna facing him. "Remember, Love, keep your right arm free from your jacket. In fact, let's throw the whole thing over your back or, better still, tie it around your waist."

Facing the bar, it didn't take long for Shauna to get the attention of one of the bartender's. After asking Chip what he wanted to drink, she ordered him a draft beer and herself a vodka-martini. As she waited, she was sure someone was taking advantage of the crush and feeling her up from behind. Whirling around, clenched fists at what she estimated would be groin level, she connected. The young stud who'd been pressing against her turned away, doing his best to jack-knife, clutching his pounded genitals with an agonized groan. "Well done, Love. Keep 'em cocked and ready," admired Chip. Thanking him she blew on the tip of her finger and holstered her hand.

Their drinks came. Chip turned and reaching over several heads took them and paid. "Crap, I could get a six pack for this price," complained Chip. It wasn't easy to hang at the bar, but Shauna, Chip, Ivan and R Jay held their ground.

Here it was. The plan had begun. There was turmoil behind them as Mark forced his way through the crowd towards them. Peggy was not in sight. Reaching them, Mark unceremoniously shoved himself between Shauna and Chip who was apparently deep in conversation with the guys. Mark's face, just inches from hers, sported a huge leer. She could smell alcohol on his breath and cigarette smoke on his clothes - an obnoxious combination. She willed herself not to turn away or flee. "Hi there star of the evening." Shauna heard a familiar voice coming from behind. Turning she bumped into Harvey. The two conspirators had managed to sandwich her. Mark leaned in closer so she could feel his breath, "I see you're drinking vodka, my dear. Well, for such a commanding performance, I have asked the bartender to make you a very special variation on a vodka tonic with a unique additional ingredient - chocolate coconut water." Chip, who was listening intently while appearing to be otherwise engaged, had half expected Mark, drunk as he was, to say the unique ingredient was Ecstasy.

Turning to lean across the bar Mark shouted, "Yo Marco!" Receiving no response he yelled the name again, this time at the top of his lungs. A tall bartender swiveled his head and seeing Mark, set down the drink he was mixing and reached under the counter. Coming up with an already prepared cocktail, he stepped along the bar, pissing off the customers he'd deserted, and stirred the drink a couple of times before handing it over, his movements almost robotic. The cocktail glass contained a swirling amber liquid in which Chip, who knew to look, could see the minutest of granules as it passed from Marco to Mark and then to Shauna, with Mark's toast: "To your health you lovely thing." By that point the granules had begun to settle at the bottom of the glass, but only someone really looking for them would notice. Chip and Shauna were instantly on the same page, knowing that Mark, for whatever reason, had not ground the Ecstasy to as fine a powder as it could and should have been. The added chocolate coconut water helped disguise the sloppy job of pulverizing the drug, but not the fact that Mark had chickened out of dumping the drug directly into the drink, getting the bartender to do the dirty deed instead.

Certain Marco had been paid handsomely for his assistance, Chip kept an eye on him and was rewarded with a view of a bulging left hand pocket in Marco's slacks; a bulge that indicated a substantial roll of bills. So Mark was not a complete dummy. He'd been sharp enough to know that adding the drug to Shauna's glass unnoticed and without mishap in this environment would have been next to impossible, and that in his impaired condition it would have been beyond impossible.

Although the press of the crowd had eased as more people took to the dance floor, Shauna continued to hold the drink firmly – wanting to retain as much of the concoction as possible for later evidence. Peggy arrived at the bar all excited and glowing with sweat. She leaned into Shauna giving her a moist peck on the cheek. "We're all here. What fun!" she blathered. Ignoring Mark, she grinned at Shauna and Chip, who was still pretending to be distracted with Ivan and R Jay, and then yelled at Marco to bring her whatever Shauna was drinking. "'Okole Maluna', as they say in Hawaii. Or, 'Bottoms Up'!" slurred Mark, before taking a gulp of his Jim Beam over ice.

"I'm not drinking tonight," said a nervous Harvey, "Maybe later." The truth was that the more Mark drank, the less Harvey was inclined to. Shauna courageously took her first sip of the doctored drink. Actually, it tasted pretty good. Chip was nursing his beer while trying to keep Shauna in view over Mark's shoulder. Shauna was still aware enough to not shake up the drug sediment towards the bottom of the glass. She decided not to prolong the inevitable and took another sip, this time, a big one. Then another, and another, pretending to like it. Peggy, watching Shauna, sipped her own cocktail. "Wow, these are tasty. What are they called?" "Ohhh, I doan haff . . . a cloo," said a giggly Shauna. She could feel herself slipping away, being replaced by a loose, out-of-control, cat on a hot tin roof, surprised at how quickly she'd been affected.

She staggered around as Mark steadied her. "Here you go, doll," said Mark as he lifted the glass to her lips again. She shook her head and then with an uncoordinated wave of her hands, knocked the glass out of Mark's hand, sending it to the floor with a tinkling splash. *A least she finished almost all of it,* thought Mark.

Just then, as part Isabella's prearranged plan to inject Shauna with an antidote as quickly as possible, a man approached to Shauna's right, covertly whipped out a syringe and plunged it into her arm just as she suddenly jerked away. The ultra-thin needle broke off in leaving the doctor in mufti befuddled and unsure what to do without ruining the whole game plan. Unfortunately, Shauna was already in no state to remember what was supposed to have happened or what she was supposed to do.

Chenaugh materialized from nowhere, forcing his way through the crowd and sending the doctor packing, after slapping him several times on the face to thaw him out and get him moving. As he turned Shauna away from Mark to check the damage, Chenaugh made like he was flirting with her, knowing she was probably close to hyper-sexual, one of the effects of the drug. Proving him correct, Shauna was all over him, trying to get her clothes off in jerky ineffective gyrations. Whatever he decided, he knew he must be quick. One glance at Mark and Harvey told him that Mark's ego would not tolerate rejection.

Shielding his actions from Mark, Chenaugh pulled a compact tool and small atomizer from the small survival kit strapped to his waist. Grabbing Shauna's arm he used the tool to burrow into Shauna's flesh where the broken end of the needle could barely be seen. This was no time for sentimentality. Out came the broken piece of needle as his lips on hers stifled a bloody murder scream. A relieved Shauna renewed her sexual antics. "Well endured," murmured Chenaugh as he smiled down at her briefly and applied the antiseptic wound sealer, squeezed her face to pucker her lips and gave her another disrespectful kiss. He then stood tall and menacing and swaggered off, shouldering aside anyone in his path.

Bemused by the brazen flirtation that had finally penetrated his alcoholic stupor, Mark nudged Harvey to get a move on. Clumsily working his hand under Shauna's blouse, Mark rubbed her back sending her into paroxysms of sexually charged shivers. She was more than amorous she was a walking sexual time-bomb. He could do anything he wanted with her and she would be turned on by anything.

"Ooooooohh, the liiiiights aaare sooooo preeety," said the doped Shauna. She seemed to be transfixed by any type of light and had crammed her hand down her pants to rub herself. Untying Shauna's jacket from around her waist, Mark draped it over her shoulders. She tried shrugging it off but the press of people kept it in position. Mark hissed at Harvey, "Come on get with it. Wake up man!" Mark and Harvey each took one of Shauna's elbows to guide her away. Although she fought with them they gradually made their way through the crowd, rubbing her back to distract her with sexual cravings. "Come on pet. You'll love where we are taking you." Half escorting and half dragging Shauna, Mark and Harvey finally made it to the rear exit. Not seeing anyone following, Mark figured everyone was too busy drinking and dancing. But he was wrong. There were hidden eyes and ears watching and listening.

Sticking to the plan, Chip had watched their progress through the throng, seething inside. Furious that he hadn't just stepped in and beat the hell out of them, as soon as Shauna disappeared outside, he shook himself free from Ivan and R Jay who'd been restraining him, and signaling them to follow, forcefully barged his way across the room in pursuit.

By the time Mark and Harvey had Shauna in the alley heading towards the truck, she had managed to ditch her jacket and blouse and then ripped off her bra, waving the flimsy material in Harvey's face. What could he do but fondle and lick her breasts which drove Shauna insane.

Mark, wanting his share, spun her to face him and unzipped her jeans, ramming his hand into her crotch and shoving her panties aside. He plowed his fingers into her pussy after a few misses. She didn't seem to mind. Quite the opposite. She stuck her tongue out and gave him a long lick from the chin up to his forehead. Her hips were gyrating and she began to fumble with the buckle on Mark's jeans to get at his obvious bulge, all thumbs and struggling.

Harvey reminded him, "Hey man, you know the instructions. This is Josef's woman. Your brother paid big bucks to make sure she is. Don't mess up. He'll find out one way or another. And even if your brother doesn't find out, which I'm sure he will, Josef will, and you'll end up in a meat grinder." "OK, OK, OK!" roared an increasingly desperate Mark.

"You watch the bitch here while I go relieve myself." And off went Mark, but not too far. He looked carefully around first, and then with his back to Harvey and the hyper-sexed Shauna, opened his jeans and reached into his boxers.

Knowing Shauna was more than a handful for Harvey and he'd need to be quick, Mark immediately started masturbating like there was no tomorrow. Pretty soon he was moaning and shooting his load. His shoulders slumped, the tension gone. Life could go on now. He dug a used handkerchief from his pocket and cleaned himself. Throwing the twice dirty rag on the ground, he hastily put himself back together. "Well that's a hell of a lot better!" exclaimed a returning Mark, grinning. Harvey was disgusted, but hid it well. Within lay a coward.

They set off again, enticing, cajoling, and dragging a rambunctious Shauna toward the parked truck loaded with pussy and a few guards. Passing the truck they finally spotted the dark SUV parked against the alley wall, snuggled in between two large dumpsters - not a great hiding place, but better than nothing. "Come on doll, only a little further before you get your big surprise treat. Yes, I know, you want some sexy action. Here we go. Kissy, kissy." Mark gave in to Shauna's relentless need, kissing her roughly a bunch of times. Shauna, feeling such disgust with her role-playing, despite her partially drugged state, wanted to purge herself of his touch and kick him in the crotch.

Sudden chaos ensued. Unexpectedly, twenty or so men and women came running full speed towards them. Hidden in the group was Chenaugh. The group swarmed the threesome making it difficult for them to advance towards the SUV, or to do anything for that matter. The two occupants of the SUV's front seats were slow to react. Drawing their guns they exited the SUV just as the high energy crowd surrounded them. They were immediately disarmed and roughly pushed to assume the position against the vehicle and patted down for other weapons.

Chenaugh, emerging from the crowd confident and unshakable took charge. Speaking in Russian he ordered the surrounded SUV occupants to stand up and turn around with their hands clearly visible. They reluctantly did so. Pointing to a shaken Mark and Harvey, Chenaugh ordered for them to be cuffed. Grabbing Shauna's hand he continued, "I'll take her and join these two gentlemen in the SUV." Then, speaking in Russian again, he addressed the two thugs and flashed them his Russian diplomatic ID and an authorization signed by Josef Karpov to be Shauna's escort. His brisk, sure movements and tone of command left no space for questions as he turned to see who was distracting him. It was a flushed-faced, fully animated Shauna, pawing him for some attention.

Chenaugh got ahold of Shauna and held her to him in a tight grip while barking out his final orders. "Get those two," indicating Mark and Harvey, "to the local precinct and take this with you," he said, addressing two men from the crowd, handing one a plastic bag with Mark's handkerchief inside. "Make sure you get this to the lab. See if we get some evidence out of it." Mark felt defeated and dumb. Addressing the crowd, Chenaugh thanked them for their participation and they dispersed, fading into the night.

The two Russians were relieved to have not been taken away, but ordered back to the car instead. Little did they know that Chenaugh had already called for backup at both the ship yard and the private airport. He got in the backseat of the SUV and pulled Shauna in after him. She affectionately cuddled up to him, rubbing her breasts against his arm. He was so handsome and she wanted some loving bad. He rubbed her breasts and then harshly told her to settle down. His rough manner startled her until he flashed a quick smile at her which started her needing and wanting all over again. "Hurry up. Let's go!" said an impatient Chenaugh in Russian. Shauna giggled. The car started moving.

CHAPTER 22 HOSPITAL

Chip reached the rear entrance of the club and waited for Ivan and R Jay to catch up with him. Thinking of what might be happening to Shauna, his mind raced a mile a minute until he spoke forcefully to himself: "Shut the fuck up!" more than once. He knew he couldn't let negativity dominate or he'd be lost in a loop of darkness. With still no sign of his friends, Chip impatiently pushed though the exit door into the alley. Carefully looking around and seeing no one he started walking fast towards the parking lot, looking for the SUV. Hearing footsteps behind him and expecting to see Ivan and R Jay, he looked over his shoulder, shouting, "About time!"

Three dark figures were rapidly approaching, spreading out to surround him. Just then he remembered Isabella explaining that the three pseudo-guards would be coming for him and he turned around to face them. Here were the assholes who had almost stolen Shauna, minus the one he'd disabled and who he suspected was now rotting somewhere deeply dead.

Chip took a defensive stance with his legs spread apart, bent at the knees. Eyeballing all three, registering their relative positions, he stared straight ahead, allowing his peripheral vision to follow their constant re-positioning. He kept moving to disrupt their advance until one of them lunged, rushing out of the night, intense hatred disfiguring his face as he came. Chip took a couple of quick steps forward and crunched his assailant's nose with an elbow, sending him to the blacktop. The other two thugs immediately took out knives and began to circle him, swinging their wickedly sharp blades back and forth before them. The two of them moved in on Chip, leading with their sharp steel weapons. One split second of indecisiveness and Chip's upper arm was oozing blood.

But it wasn't the cut that enraged Chip it was the intolerable smirk on the bastard's face. Not wasting a second of his adrenalin-pumped, vengeful anger, Chip rushed him and using his height and reach advantage kicked the assailant's crotch out of the park. *Two down, one to go.* Too late Chip sensed the third behind him and felt a sharp searing pain in the right upper side of his inner thigh where the attacker's knife had deeply penetrated. Good thing it was a short blade - and hadn't been any higher - or cut any veins or arteries.

He wanted to end this fast and get a tourniquet on his leg. *Where the FUCK were Ivan and R Jay?* His chances were better with two of the guys disabled rather than having all three of them dancing around him but he'd feel a lot happier with some help. He needed his buddies!

A shadow stealthily exited a nearby car parked against a wall just outside the alley. The shadow had been carefully watching this unfair fight, expecting backup to arrive any second. Realizing that any backup may be too late he'd made his move. "Hey asshole, come get me! Gifford, I have your back," shouted Richardson as he aimed his gun towards the third attacker. The thug with the busted nose was still lying on the pavement out cold. The kicked-balls guy was struggling to his knees getting ready to try again. "Makes the odds more even now, huh?" grinned the Inspector. "Sure does. Thanks for the intervention," said a relieved but hurting Chip.

The Russian thug still standing, not seeing Richardson's gun or too dumb to make the connection, rushed Chip knife first, receiving a bullet to the knee for his trouble. Stopped cold, he collapsed, screaming in agony, and passed out with the pain. The incident including the preamble had lasted maybe forty-five seconds. "I've already called for backup." said Richardson. "My two detectives should be arriving any minute. I'll take care of the last one and you can do the honors with the first two. Here take these," he said, handing Gifford a couple of plastic ties. "Better get the one over there coming up for more pummeling first." Chip limped over to sore-balls and got him restrained, resisting the temptation to kick him again. He then struggled over to broken-nose and cuffed him. Chip heard the ambulance coming. It seemed ages before it got there. "Thanks again, man," said an appreciative Chip.

He looked down at his leg and didn't like what he saw. He didn't want a blood transfusion, with all the stories he'd heard about contaminated needles.

Having cuffed the shot attacker, Richardson walked over to check on an anomalous shadow he'd seen on getting out his car. Squatting down beside a dumpster to get a closer look he muttered bitterly, "Just what I suspected." He rose up and pointing toward the ground, yelled over to Chip, "Here are the two backup agents – garroted - probably didn't know what hit them. No doubt Josef's thugs are responsible."

The kneecapped assailant and his broken-nosed associate had been taken to hospital by the first ambulance on the scene. Richardson's two detectives were now shepherding the sore-balled attacker into a police car that had rolled up right behind a second ambulance. Gifford was sitting on the back steps of the ambulance receiving treatment from two paramedics who were insisting he needed to go the hospital. Gifford was arguing and protesting that he didn't have time and he didn't want to be in a hospital. "Look! Both wounds could easily get infected and if you lose much more blood, you'll be dead," said one of the paramedics, "so shut up and let us do our jobs and take care of you."

Chip let them take over and they lifted him into the ambulance, strapping him to a gurney and starting an IV in his left arm which hurt more than anything he'd endured in the fight. An oxygen tube was stuck in his nose, which he had to admit felt good. The more Chip focused on relaxing, the more his inner thigh throbbed. "We'll give you a stronger painkiller at the hospital once you've been thoroughly checked out," said the medic. "In the meantime, take deep breaths and relax. You've been through a lot."

The medic up front radioed the hospital with their ETA and the status of their patient, advising that he'd likely need a blood transfusion. "How long do you think I'll be in the hospital?" inquired Chip of the medic sitting with him. "Don't make any plans for a few days," was the reply. "Now try and relax and think about your own recovery." Richardson banged on the ambulance doors and stuck his head inside saying, "Hey buddy, you'll be OK. I won't be following you to the hospital, but will check in on you later. I need to track the SUV with Shauna and Chenaugh and see what's next." The piercing ambulance siren reverberated through Chip's head as they sped away from the already cordoned off crime scene.

Chip, far from relaxing, was battling non-stop mind chatter. First of all he felt guilty that he'd not once thought of Shauna and her situation in the heat of his own battle. He spun this around and around in his head like a mouse on a treadmill. *What the hell good is this? Enough! STOP!* He began to think of Shauna in a different way - that wherever she was, she was all right - that there was someone, hopefully Chenaugh, watching over her. No harm would come to her. And he would keep his promise when they reached Jamaica together. Dwelling on these thoughts he felt better but then suddenly plunged back into the pit on wondering what had happened to his buddies, Ivan and R Jay.

The room was dark. They could tell there was a curtain in front of them and that the backs of their chairs were close to a wall. They could also tell that they were still at the club in some back room because the music and sounds of a large crowd could be heard. But what they wished was that they could call for help. They desperately needed to get out of wherever they were. Duct tape had been generously used, not only over their mouths, but also around their ankles, their wrists, which were behind their backs, and around their bodies, strapping them firmly to the chairs they were sat on. Ivan and R Jay turned their heads to look at each other. What they saw in one another's eyes was a mixture of fear, frustration and anger. R Jay desperately tried to speak, communicating a jumble of unintelligible muffled grunts. If only they knew Morse code they could blink!

The last thing either of them remembered was being attacked from behind as they were exiting through the rear of the club and entering the alley to help Chip. In fact, a group of Cameron's men, planted early on at the club, had encircled them, knocked them out and swiftly carried them backstage to the makeup room, and taped them immobile before taking up strategic positions throughout the club. So far, they had followed their boss's orders to a 'T'. Right down to their clothes and how they blended in like chameleons - even engaging in a dance or two.

The two hostage basketball players heard footsteps coming their way. They tried to brace themselves for what was to come. The curtain was flung aside and two beefy thugs carrying machine pistols entered, standing directly in front of the apprehensive prisoners. "Give us the truth and you'll be fine," said the slightly larger one with a heavy Russian accent. Taking in the unkempt brown hair and lumbering gait R Jay was immediately reminded of Yogi Bear. "If you don't we'll just hurt you and then kill you," he said nonchalantly - an emotionless grin on his otherwise expressionless face. "So whatsit gonna be?" asked thug two who, of course, R Jay mentally dubbed Boo-Boo. Both hostages nodded yes. Yogi walked right up to R Jay and prodded him with his gun, saying, "Let's start with the little guy who looks like he'd rat out his mother to live." R Jay didn't move - didn't even blink. The thug squatted down level with his face and yelled: "ISN'T THAT RIGHT?" R Jay moved his head up and down vigorously.

The tape was removed from R Jay's mouth the fast way. One corner lifted for grip and the rest violently ripped from his mouth. A piece was left dangling from his cheek. His face was red and some hair stubble could be seen attached to the sticky side of the tape. Yogi laughed and said to his partner, "Hey, could be a real cheap alternative to waxing. Let's get on that TV show where guys with lots of money look for ideas to make them more rich." They both laughed and wished they had more time and a less public place to try the tape on the rest of the two athletes' bodies.

R Jay took advantage of this time to recover from the pain. Boo-Boo stepped over to Ivan and said: "I bet plenty you got a lot a body hair, huh?" He grabbed Ivan by his hair and yanked, ripping out strands and small clumps which he dropped on the floor before wiping his hands against his pants.

They got down to business. Boo-Boo moved around behind them out of view as Yogi began with the questions. He wanted to know what the authorities' plans were. Rumors were circulating that once everyone was rounded up and put on a plane, Shauna, Chip and their rescuers would be headed for Costa Rica. He wanted to know if it was true "Yes," squealed R Jay. "Well, we're not convinced about that," said Boo-Boo from behind, tapping R Jay on the side of the head with his gun butt. Not waiting for R Jay to recover, Yogi continued, "We've also heard that you're headed somewhere else after Costa Rica. Is this true too?" "No. Oh no. That's not true," replied a shaky R Jay. *Why the fuck can't you lie like you mean it, R Jay,* thought Ivan. *We have to convince them. Our lives are on the line, or do you think this is all a joke!*

The impatient and irritated Boo-Boo slugged R Jay again as Yogi repeated, "Are you assholes heading out for another location after Costa Rica?" This time a woozy R Jay replied with more conviction and volume, "Not that I've heard. No, definitely not. We have reservations on hold at a seaside resort and appointments for various activities there." "Why on hold?" "I don't know. That's not my department."

R Jay was relieved that he hadn't been let in on all the plans. It was obvious these guys were just warming up and he had no doubt they'd not stop till they got what they wanted or he was dead. Not wanting to wait for that inevitability, R Jay, despite being a little disoriented, decided to act. Watching the pacing Yogi slowly think his way through his options, R Jay waited. Finally coming to a decision Yogi approached R Jay who coiled himself, giving thanks they'd not thought to bind his legs to the chair, and launched himself, chair attached, across the intervening three feet. Although R Jay had not been able to muster much force it was enough to startle Yogi who reflexively fired as he fell backwards off balance. A string of bullets passed to the side of R Jay who heard them ricocheting left, right and center and scrunched his eyes, flinching.

A dazed R Jay, lying on his side strapped to his chair, took a look around as far as his restraints would allow. Ivan's head was flopped down to where his chin was resting on his chest. R Jay hysterically yelled out to him as an uncontrolled sob shook his body. "No. No. No. Come on Bro. Come on. You can't leave me like this. Not you." Blood was trickling out of Ivan's mouth. He had been hit in the neck - a fatal shot. R Jay passed out.

The makeup room was rapidly filling with people who'd heard the shots and traced their location. Isabella joined them, especially impatient to see what had happened. She pushed her way to the front of the crowd where she saw four dead people. Going to each one she checked for a pulse. Dead, dead, dead. She came around to R Jay, leaned over him and placed her fingertips on his neck. Her whole demeanor changed. Without thinking she blurted out loudly, "This one is still alive! Sam, call an ambulance. Bruce, get the tape off of him. Joe, get in here and help. And be real careful, I don't know how bad he's hurt. Let's get on it!" At that instant Isabella realized she'd blown her cover and that of the three FBI agents she'd just named. Not dwelling on the mistake, she asked everyone else to leave.

As the onlookers filed away from the gruesome scene, two burly men shoved their way inside, angrily shouting at each other in what to Isabella sounded like Russian. Guessing they were probably arguing about how to handle the situation, she was about to confront them when the thinner of the two produced a pistol and aimed it at R Jay. Instinctively, Isabella drew her own pistol nestled at the small of her back and fired from the hip, hitting the gunman in the side of his head and sending him to the floor where he lay silent. The FBI agents looked at her in amazement, one of them alert enough to rapidly cuff the stunned remaining Russian.

A cool Isabella wanted to be in charge of the interrogation, expecting the captured man could give them another piece of the puzzle. But just as she was relishing the prospect, her earpiece came to life. It was her boss, Comstock, interrupting her thoughts. "I'm pulling you out of there as of this minute. You're not safe. Turn your gun over to Joe and have two agents go with you around back where there's a car waiting and a replacement gun. Wait till you see its headlights flash three times then get in alone. I need the other agents back at the scene of the shooting." *Damn*, thought Isabella. To Comstock she said, "I obviously have mixed feelings but you're absolutely right," while thinking, *Just remember, if it hadn't been for me, there might be more than three dead.*

The two agents were ready to take Isabella around to the back, having already checked the immediate area themselves and got the all clear from the other agents in the club and outside. Everyone involved in the operation had already got the message from Comstock that Tom would be taking Isabella's place on site.

Following the plan, Isabella climbed into the backseat of the car, immediately becoming aware of another person sitting on the far side. In the dark it wasn't easy to make out who it was, until Isabella's eyes adjusted. "I don't know your name. We haven't formally met, but I know you're Shauna's mother," said Isabella, offering her hand. In an unsteady voice, the woman replied, "I'm Janet," and she shook hands. Sensing Janet's fear and concern and seeing the aftermath of tears, Isabella quickly scooted over to her and wrapping her arms around the distraught woman gave her a reassuring and warm embrace. "Thank you so much," said Janet. "I needed that. I'm so worried about Shauna. And now I'm being spirited away somewhere protected and secluded." Her Scottish accent was thick. Isabella had to concentrate to understand her, which was good in a way. It kept her mind off her own dilemma.

At first glance, Isabella thought that this woman she was sitting with would blend into any crowd, anyplace. She was of average height, plain featured, with hair that could at best be described as 'mousey' and she was dressed in off-the-rack anonymity. But then, as Isabella kept peering at her, she noticed that her pale blue eyes had a sparkle and aliveness few people displayed. Those awake enough would detect this brightness of her and pause, wanting to find out more about her. After all, there had to be something special about her to have a daughter like Shauna.

Isabella was familiar with the two agents in front who had identified themselves when she'd boarded. Knowing Comstock kept his best men for important assignments Isabella felt honored and was appreciative to be in such seasoned hands. "Where are they taking us? Do you know?" asked Janet in a timid voice. "Honey, all I know is we're in very capable hands. These men will keep us safe and out of harm's way. So try to relax and let me hold you, OK?" responded Isabella tenderly, although she too was wondering where they were going.

Richardson stealthily navigated Coach's property until he was safely behind the main house. He couldn't believe he was here again and that Cameron in his guise as Coach was, in all likelihood, holed up here too. At least that's what he was thinking. He didn't see a car, which in itself didn't mean much, but he was hoping that the wife and two boys were out, maybe even escaped, keeping clear of Coach for whom not much seemed to be going his way. Slowly, Richardson edged closer to the out-building when he heard shouting and banging coming from inside. Coach's powerfully loud voice was clearly audible, cursing, ranting and raving. *Whew. Thank goodness I'm not at the other end of that tornado*, thought a sweating Richardson. *Coach must have gotten news not only about the Gifford debacle, but also the shootout inside the club. I'm sure that's not what he had in mind when he hired a bunch of Russian Mafia enforcers*, was the detective's take. Coach finally settled down enough to start giving orders to what Richardson assumed were other members of the mobsters team.

Coach went on speaking for a long time as Richardson, hunching in the bushes lining the back end of the building, listened hard, straining to make out what was being said without success. "What a damned shame!," muttered a frustrated and temporarily defeated Richardson, before he backed out of the bushes and retraced his steps back to his parked car. *We sure as hell fucked up by not bugging that building.*

Chip lay heavily sedated in a hospital bed. He was unaware that there were two FBI agents inside the room and two other guards right outside the door. It looked like they were expecting trouble. Chip was also unaware that a heavily sedated, traumatized R Jay, protected by two additional agents, was in a deep dreamless sleep in the next room. The doctors attending Chip had thought it best for him to get some strength back before letting him know what had happened to his pals.

Chip stirred, moving his head on the pillow and lifting his arm onto his stomach. The agents were immediately alert, glancing from Chip to each other and then one checked the door was still locked and the other peeked through the closed blinds to see the immediate vicinity was clear. They both relaxed and remained in position - one by the window, the other, by the door.

Chip fought to come out of the stupor he was in. Slowly opening his eyes he stared straight ahead, trying to get his bearings with no idea where he was, how much time had passed, whether it was night or day or even if this was another nightmare he was having. He felt a faint throbbing in his groin and turned his head to see the bandaging on his shoulder and arm. The guards approached him, hovering and he could see their lips moving. Slowly, Chip began to distinguish the words. ". . . all right there, Buddy. You're in the hospital, safe, and soon to be sound. You've sustained a bad knife wound to your leg and a surface slashing right here," he said pointing to Chip's bandaged arm. Chip just wanted to go back to sleep and hide. He didn't want to recall the attack, even as memories of the incident came rushing back to him. Chip haltingly asked, "How long have I been here? What day is it?" "It's Monday, Sir. You were brought here Saturday night. And lucky for you, just in time. You've been patched up and were given two units of blood, so it shouldn't be too long before you're good as new and out of here." "What are you doing here?" asked Chip, fading again. "We're here to protect you. There are two more guards outside the door - just to be on the safe side. So you just rest now. And know that you're safe."

"I'm glad he's still out of it." "Yeah," said the other agent. I thought any moment he was going to ask about his friends." "Me too. No telling how he's going to react when he finds out one of his best friends is dead and the other so traumatized he's had to be sedated. You know they've all played basketball for the Acers for I don't know how long?" "Yeah, I've been to a lot of their games. I'm going to go check on the other guards." He turned to leave.

As the agent opened the hospital room door, he felt a bullet burn through his upper arm and tumbled backwards with the impact, allowing the door to swing wide. The guard by the window unhesitatingly drew his gun and returned fire through the door opening, hitting an unfamiliar nurse in the chest. Reaching the door he knelt by his now ghostly-white-faced partner before checking the nurse for a pulse. Not finding one, he turned to survey the carnage in the corridor. Both of the guards lay on the hallway floor face up with looks of surprise and horror etched on their dead faces. Pools of blood were still expanding around their heads, coloring the floor. Feeling nauseous, the agent who'd been shot in the arm, thanked his partner. "That was a mighty fine save, Jim. If you hadn't been on the ball the rest of us would be dead too, including the guys we're protecting. Really man, I owe you big time." "You would have done the same thing, Ed." They roughly hugged each other as the adrenaline subsided, Ed wincing as Jim caught his arm wound in the embrace.

Contacting Comstock they reported the incident. "Fuck!" exclaimed Comstock. "Somehow Cameron's people seem to know our every move. Either they're a helluva lot smarter than we've been giving them credit for, or we have a leak. I'll send additional backup. You sit tight and stay sharp. I'll let you know when we've made fresh arrangements. And I'm sorry about the two dead guards."

Turning their attention to the dead nurse they slipped on latex gloves and checked the body. Finding a full syringe in one outside jacket pocket and a cellphone in the other, they bagged them as evidence for immediate delivery to Comstock. They then arranged for the hospital staff to move the bodies ready for transportation to the city morgue and to clean up the mess before Chip woke up.

Closing the door of Chip's room to block out the gruesome aftermath of the attack, Jim and Ed were faced with a half awake Chip who was trying to sit up without much success. He had a painful look on his face as he put his hand on his wounded thigh. "I wouldn't do that if I were you. We don't want any stitches coming loose. You've been through enough. Here, let us help you," said Jim, pressing a button at the end of the bed that slowly tilted the headboard end to raise Chip to an almost sitting position. Chip thanked them and announced he was hungry and thirsty. "Great", said Ed. "That's a good sign. What would you like?" Ed took his order and buzzed the kitchen. "It'll be here soon."

Chip lay back on the pillows with his eyes shut, holding back tears. He was afraid to ask what was happening. He had a gut wrenching feeling that he already knew. He was missing Ivan and R Jay. After all, his long-time buddies hadn't shown up to help him when he left the club, and they wouldn't have not just shown up unless something really bad had happened to them.

Finally the agony of not knowing outweighed his fear and he asked, "I want to know what happened to my two bros?" The two agents gently and briefly told Chip what they knew, which wasn't much, and how sorry they were about Ivan. "R Jay is heavily sedated in the next room but we should learn more when he's able and ready to talk. We hope it will be soon because we're pretty sure he can provide some answers we all need," added Jim.

"And what about Shauna?" asked an unraveling Chip. He had so many emotions stirring he was close to shutting down again. The agents, aware of this, attempted to distract him with the food he'd requested. "Why don't you eat, get some rest, and then we'll continue," said an empathetic Ed.

Chip insisted they tell him now. "I don't feel like eating right now. I want to know!" "Easy. Easy there," interjected a soothing Ed.

"The last we heard was that she's been taken by SUV to the docks in Houston and transferred with Chenaugh to a ship bound for Russia. We believe that once Josef arrives she'll then be taken by helicopter to a private airport for a direct flight to Moscow by private plane. We're not sure, whether at that stage, Chenaugh will still be accompanying her. He's considered a valuable asset by both sides so we'll have to see." "I want Chenaugh staying with Shauna," asserted a determined Chip before emptying his glass. Ignoring his food, he lay back and closed his eyes and gave to his Beloved. The pain he felt in being separated from Shauna was more than his throbbing thigh. Distraught and weary he was having a difficult time taking everything in but wanted to be out of the hospital and doing something, anything, to help - to be involved.

There were many aspects of his job that Williams, the Austin Police Lieutenant who was liaising with the Special Task Force, didn't like. And right now he was mulling over a task he absolutely detested – having told Richardson that his two favorite detectives, the ones he'd assigned to help guard Chip, had been killed, he had to notify their next of kin and have them come to identify the bodies.

Meanwhile, Dave Comstock, head of the Special Task Force who'd flown down from Washington D.C. to take control on the ground, was contemplating the mountain of data that had been accumulated from the microcams, each the size of a button, his agents had been wearing during the night's operation. He was hoping that if he and a few of his staff worked through the night they'd have some answers before morning of what had gone down and when. And possibly some indication of what might be in store as the operation continued.

He was also anticipating a fresh influx of data within the next hour from the listening devices his agents had planted at Coach's house and in Chip's and R Jay's hospital rooms. He was also expecting to hear from his agents, Fin and Jones, who were keeping an eye on the truck of women which, as far as he knew, was still parked behind the club.

Reviewing events as he knew them so far he was particularly discouraged by how many agents they'd lost so quickly. Considering how long he'd spent setting up the operation - all the planning, the moves they'd anticipated, the key players they'd identified, the contingencies they'd allowed for - they'd still been caught off guard. His body sagged from the responsibilities that came with his position, and the ones he assumed to support his team and their mission. He was extremely thankful for the way Chenaugh had stepped up to take such a key role but missed Isabella's participation. He wondered how risky it would be to get her actively involved in the field operation again, now that she'd exposed her FBI affiliation. He wanted no more deaths. But he was going to be disappointed yet again.

CHAPTER 23 CHAOS

After Shauna had been whisked away, the truck full of women was delayed, waiting for additional guards to escort them to Houston. In the back of the waiting truck, most of the women were still wide awake, very hot and very sweaty. They were becoming disgruntled. One woman tugged at the back door of the truck, repeating in a muzzy voice something that sounded like she wanted out of there. A chorus of other women joined in. The guards became riled, slapping a few of the louder females, telling them in broken English to shut up or they would be slammed around harder. The women quieted down, although a few whimpered to themselves.

The majority were trying to remember just what they had been offered that would entice them into a hell hole like this. The truck interior was beginning to stink - a combination of sweat, vomit, fear and poor ventilation. The women wanted to be let out or at least to get going. A guard piped up saying, "Yo babes. Yo no haf anytink to says bout yo sitooation, so shot up." He took out a short-bladed knife, wielding it menacingly, emphasizing his meaning.

The truck driver and guards were impatiently waiting for re-enforcements to show, glad they'd parked at the back of the lot, well away from the scene of the attack on Chip that was now swarming with police. Eventually, three non-descript cars quietly drove up. One swung in front of the truck to take point position while the others pulled up behind it. A few words were exchanged between the truck driver and driver of the lead car before the convoy started off and slowly moved through the alley and onto the street that would take them towards Houston.

None of them noticed a plain tan sedan easing out of the shadows to follow. Comstock's agents, Fin and Jones, had already put a tracking device on the truck but had been ordered to keep as close as they could.

Soon realizing that the convoy was staying off the main routes to wind its way through narrow, poorly lit back roads, the agents wondered if it was to minimize exposure or because the truck wasn't safe at high speeds. "Wonder why they're not using a more up-to-date vehicle," mused Fin, the driver. "Sure would have made more sense but I guess there's a reason," said

Jones. "Anyway, what I'm really wondering is why there's so many of them."
"Yeah, and they look like the worst possible kind too."

The truck trip proved to be boring and uneventful and very slow. The women had been told to each claim a pallet on the floor and stay put with the bag of clothes and personal items they'd each been allowed to bring. Some of the women, discomforted by their clammy, sweat-stained clothes decided to change. Two of the guards waited until the women were mostly naked before ordering them to go to the front of the truck and lean facing the wall, legs spread. Protesters were quickly silenced by the flash of a knife.

Claiming four women each, the two guards roughly pushed them into separate huddles. The men, horny as hell from just watching them, couldn't wait to get their pants unzipped, not even bothering to drop them. Pulling out their peckers, wanting each woman to suck on them, and not just one by one, they forced an orgy: humiliating, disgusting and degrading. The other women, frozen to their pallets, closed their eyes and covered their ears, praying they wouldn't be next. The men were brutal and relentless in their pursuit of pleasure, ravaging the women's pussies, and anuses with both fingers and pricks until they each finally came, waving their pricks to fling semen at the women, cursing and taunting them, jeering and laughing. Satiated, the men collapsed to the floor exhausted and pleased, demented smiles disfiguring their already ugly faces. The raped and ravaged women just cowered, crying and holding their bruised and torn bodies.

The spared women, hesitant at first, anticipating reprisals, helped the abused women, several of whom couldn't walk unsupported. Leading them back to their individual pallets on the floor, they cleaned their violated bodies with whatever they could find and helped the worst off get dressed and comb their hair. A moment of solidarity after all the brutality. "Oh, if menshon thiz to Boz, yoos dead woomens." Said one of the guards who'd stood by and watched, flashing a mouthful of bad dentistry as he grinned.

The attackers by now were snoring on the floor where they had collapsed. It was rather amazing that at the same moment, every woman had the same thought: *Let's kill them while they sleep. It's all of us against the remaining guards.* The spark of a great idea quickly faded as the women took thought, not quite trusting each other. You could see it in their posture - hunching into themselves, withdrawing from action to get comfortable or distracting themselves by helping another. To help block out the nightmare they began to sing softly, the song being taken up woman by woman after the initial line. The guards' first reaction was to get them to stop, but listening decided it was better than silence and might help to make the journey less boring.

After what seemed like hours of travel, the convoy approached a gravel and dirt road off to the right that pointed toward a low hill silhouetted in the distance. The point car pulled over and parked on the shoulder on the far side of the turnoff while the driver waved the truck and the rear escorts to take the track. Following directions, the truck driver swerved onto the track, sending the truck swaying back and forth so everyone in the back slid back and forth on the floor with it. Limping along on the dirt and gravel road, bumping about on the washboard surface, the truck was just barely able to make it to the top of the hill before slowly descending as the brakes squealed and ground, metal against metal. Finally, out of sight of the road behind them and the intersection where they'd turned off, the driver stopped the truck, opened the back and announcing he was taking a break, strolled off lighting a cigarette. Making it clear that the women were to stay in the truck, the guards in back climbed down to stretch their legs, urinate and have a smoke.

The two escort vehicles had followed the truck over the hill and stopped just behind it. The occupants climbed out of the vehicles, did a little stretching and exchanged a few words with their fellow countrymen, but kept their distance. Jones and Fin in the tailing car, stopped well back from the turnoff so they wouldn't be seen, and waited. Watching their tracker screen, they knew the truck had gone off road, and had stopped behind a hill. There was no way of telling what the Russians were up to, but they were being closely monitored and their route had been videoed and reported into headquarters.

When they climbed out of the truck, the guards had instinctively kept together, enjoying their break, talking quietly amongst themselves. The men from the escort cars, taking notice of this, silently and unobtrusively signaled each other.

The truck driver, who was leaning against the side of the cab, caught some of the signals out of the corner of his eye and nervously edged his way to open the cab door, unfortunately too late. The men from the cars raised the small submachine guns they'd concealed in the darkness and killed the guards and driver, their supposed colleagues, within seconds. A lone figure emerged from the darkness and watched as the three occupants of the rear car also gunned down the four occupants of the first car.

Having executed their betrayal with alacrity the remaining three shooters made a quick inspection of the bodies, making sure none of them was alive before getting to work. Removing their jackets they proceeded to haul all the bodies into the truck alongside the cowering and whimpering women and closed the back doors. Putting their jackets back on, in spite of the stifling humidity, they left the truck and walked back to the cars. Startled by the lone figure now leaning against the driver's door of the first car they moved to raise their weapons. Vladimir, Cameron's chief enforcer, who had been inserted by helicopter to await their arrival, commanded them to stand down. Recognizing his voice and knowing his reputation, they immediately complied. Ordering them to take the other car while he got in the one he was leaning against, they drove both cars back to the turnoff where they disembarked and clustered around the front passenger side window of the waiting third car.

After a brief discussion, Vladimir and the three shooters got back into one of the empty cars, turned it around and drove back to the truck. When they arrived, Vladimir waited for the others to move toward the truck in front of him before opening up with his machine gun, killing two of them instantly. Motioning the remaining shooter to lay down his weapon and reopen the truck doors, he used a burst of bullets through the truck ceiling to encourage the women to exit the vehicle. That's when the women discovered one of them had been killed, either by a stray bullet or ricochet. Vladimir watched as the women climbed out and dragged the dead woman's body after them, avoiding the thugs' bodies as best they could. Keeping an eye on the women as they huddled together around their dead sister, he forced the shooter to dump his two dead associates in the back of the truck and after taking away the shooter's cellphone, motioned him into the truck cab. Tossing the cellphone to one of the women Vladimir suggested they dial nine-one-one and ordered the driver to turn the truck around and get moving towards Houston without stopping. Climbing into the car, he followed the truck. When the driver of the vehicle waiting at the turnoff saw the truck and tail car headlights approaching he pulled out and took the lead to continue towards the Houston harbor.

"Well, what do you think?" "I'll be damned if I know," exchanged the two FBI agents. They'd heard the faint sounds of gunfire carried through the still night air but were confused by the coming and going of the vehicles and now the abandoned car. They surmised it was probably a lack of trust, or simple miscommunication. Whatever, they needed to keep track of their quarry and cautiously edged their way back onto the road to continue their surveillance.

Coming abreast of the abandoned car they decided to quickly check it for evidence before driving on. Not much of a risk of losing contact given the slowly moving blip on their tracker screen.

In all the back and forth it was obvious the mobsters had been distracted and careless. "It doesn't make sense them leaving a car behind, particularly with all this crap in it. They're either stupid, or were in a bigger hurry than we thought," said Fin. "Sure looks like it," responded Jones as he rummaged around in the back seat. "Hey! This looks interesting," he called, pulling out what looked like a small cellphone that had been wedged down the side of the seat.

Closer examination revealed it to be a remote detonator which seriously puzzled them. If they needed something this sophisticated how would they forget it? "Maybe a simple oversight or there's something going on we don't know about," said Jones - more to himself than his partner.

"Hey, Bud, we better get moving before they remember and come back for it," said Fin as he scanned the interior with his microcam, including a close-up of the device before Jones stuffed it back where he'd found it. "You don't imagine that . . ." He didn't need to finish what he was going to say. A quick glance had told him they were both on the same page. Gathering some of the trash for forensics to work on, redistributing the rest to obscure their intrusion, they stepped back to their own vehicle.

Throwing the bagged evidence in the backseat they drove back the way they'd come. Thinking it was entirely possible that one of the mobsters would come back to retrieve the detonator, they didn't want to bump into them on the road or be sandwiched between the convoy in front and an enemy vehicle behind. Seeing a bush on the opposite verge they quickly turned round again and parked up, facing the abandoned car, to wait some more. They were just settling in when a pair of headlights appeared, racing toward them from the direction of the convoy. Slowing, the vehicle u-turned and came to a halt beside the abandoned car.

The driver got out, opened the rear door of the abandoned car and leant in. Seconds later he eased back out, holding something in his raised and waving hand - something that had so carelessly been left behind. Or had it? Returning to the idling car he climbed in and it zoomed away, the tail lights eventually disappearing in the dark. The agents set off to follow, assuming the car would rendezvous with the truck. But then, what?

"These guys are real characters. They act more like kids than anything else at times," observed Jones. "Yeah, but stay alert. They may not be bright but they can be really mean fuckers," warned Fin as Jones drove after 'the kids' as he'd now dubbed them.

As the convoy crawled on its way, dawn broke through the night. The faint pastel strokes of a new day blossomed before they too were washed away by an increasingly bright and burning sun. Instead of whittling away the miles, the slow monotonous trip seemed to push Houston ever farther away, and the driver of the truck was becoming increasingly enervated. Almost hypnotized by the rising heat waves and undulating engine roar as the truck strained its way forward, he half-heartedly pondered his fate.

The terrain ahead looked barren and lifeless and flat. If it weren't for the heat mirages shimmering intermittently across the road in front, the monotony of this stretch would have been unbearable. The driver and his escorts hadn't seen any other vehicle for miles. The agents following were forced to stay well out of visual contact with the target convoy and were hoping that both cars were still with it.

After crossing the stretch of flat nothingness, they topped a hill that seemed to swell out of nowhere. Pausing to take in the tremendous view that stretched to the horizon, they were suddenly confronted with a brilliant flash spreading in all directions. Centered several miles ahead it was as if a magnifying glass had focused the rays of the sun and set the earth on fire. The two agents were immediately ripped out of their monotony-induced torpor.

Jones, who was driving, instinctively reached over and turned the air conditioner to max and then accelerated hard. Fin, who was rocking in his seat bug eyed, sent a charged look Jones's way. They didn't need to speak to know what had just happened. As they sped over the hill and down, Fin rummaged for a pair of binoculars, finally pulling them out from a heap of gear in the backseat and focusing them on the still raging fire. He was searching for any human movement, but saw none. He also realized there were only two vehicle skeletons. The remains of the truck were obvious but the other ruin could be either of the cars they'd followed. The fact that it was at the front of the truck suggested that the car that had brought up the convoy rear was the one missing. All of a sudden, a car flew over the rise in front of them where the road had taken a dive into the plain below. Jones had a split second to see who was inside, making out just one person – the driver. "I'd bet that was the guy who picked up the detonator," said Fin as the car flashed by. "You'll get no argument from me." said Jones.

Jones and Fin had been in communication with Comstock throughout their surveillance but when they told him about the bombing he was impacted more than he would have expected. His heart racing, he popped a pill and assessed the situation. He wondered how many were dead and who they were.

Jones and Fin stood silently at the scene of the smoldering vehicles. They were thinking similar things. What was the purpose of all this killing? What kind of maniac were they dealing with? They were gagging, not just on the smoke, but the stench of burnt flesh. They could see the still smoking, charred remains of the men in the lead car and the driver of the truck, the missing car undoubtedly the one that had passed them. "Fuck," said Fin, "What are the odds that he's the mastermind."

They tracked the forensics helicopter coming in to land and watched as four men got out carrying protective suits along with the tools of their trade. After trading the obligatory black humor the four got down to work. Suiting up, looking like astronauts, they waddled about their business. Fin and Jones didn't envy them their task of sifting through the remains. The odds were they'd be at it for some time. "This is one hell of a mess," sighed a disgusted Jones. "It's at times like this that I hate my job!"

Jones and Fin left the scene. The order from Comstock had been to get back to Austin. They really wanted to go to the harbor and help out with Shauna, but orders were orders. There were no goodbyes, only cursory waves as the specialists combed through the wreckage. The two agents got back in their car and drove pedal-to-the-metal back toward Austin. "Wonder who the one man left standing is," mused Jones as he drove. Fin just shrugged.

Their return to Austin, though quick, remained mostly silent. Even a stop for fast food to appease their growling stomachs and quench their thirst passed with little more than an occasional mumbled complaint. Arriving in Austin, they entered a heavily guarded headquarters to become part of a loud, buzzing, chaotic scene. People were racing around from one station to another - like a giant game of whispers. From the doorway it looked like a movie on fast forward. Jones and Fin, trying to avoid getting in the way, weaved their way through the maze of people, desks and equipment to get to Comstock's office.

They found a weary, but ever-alert Comstock holding two phones while scanning a printout as it came off the fax. Immediately aware of their presence he nodded them to the visitor chairs facing his desk. They sat down and waited . . . and waited, ignoring the wild activity outside and Comstock's continuing juggling act. They were still impacted by what they'd witnessed. In all their years of working for the FBI, they'd never experienced such a combination of senseless slaughter and disregard for innocent lives.

"Thanks guys for all your good work," said a momentarily freed up Comstock. We'll add the info you've provided to everything else we've got and hopefully our analysts will come up with some useful leads. For now, go home and get some rest. Your next assignment will be as part of the team, already in place, guarding Gifford and his friend in nearby Waco, Texas. I'll fill you in in the morning." He turned to his desk, once again getting immersed in the never-ending details. Jones and Fin were glad to get out of there.

Comstock had divided his re-enforcements: half were guarding Gifford and R Jay's hide-out and the other half were guarding headquarters. His elite team had the two buddies sequestered at a large sprawling ranch on the outskirts of Waco. They had used the place before with success and the wealthy owner, an aging widower, had proved both co-operative and friendly. The team had the place well-guarded. Apart from the agents on site, there was a security system inside the main house which would detect a fly on the wall, and the nearby air force base had been alerted just in case there was any kind of threat from the air.

The team was still pondering the next steps for their well-guarded charges. Gifford, who was physically able to move around on his own, was becoming increasingly restless, being separated from Shauna for so long. She was on his mind and in his heart continually. R Jay was in a state of severe depression, talking all the time about wanting to go home to his family. The only person he would talk to was Gifford and he had unloaded on him, the whole gory story about what had happened in the make-up room, not once but many times. Gifford finally had to tell him he couldn't listen to it again. R Jay had to be kept sedated and Gifford looked after his buddy - taking his turn as part of a suicide watch. Sometime in the near future, and Gifford hoped that would be real soon, R Jay would be moved to a secure rehabilitation center for counseling.

Richardson, who had initially started following the agents as they followed the truck convoy, realized that there might be better ways to use his time and talents. Knowing the truck had a tracker attached and Jones and Fin were experienced agents, he whipped his car around and headed for the nearest access road for the highway to Houston. Driving fast to beat the slow moving truck to the docks, he was intent on making sure Shauna was safe. His heart went out to her. *Crap. Do you suppose I'm falling in love?* thought a cheerful Richardson until a rasping filled his ear and Williams' voice commanded him, "Richardson, get your butt back here, ASAP. Cameron has given us the slip. We need you here. Comstock has called Isabella back in and you'll partner together. She should be safe here at headquarters and the two of you should make an excellent team." "Copy that. I'm heading back," replied Richardson. And he took the next exit to return to Austin at full speed.

"OK, OK. Tell me again what happened right before the bomb blast and be more precise," yelled an impatient Sean Cameron. Vladimir repeated again, detail for detail, what had taken place. He was getting exasperated and trying not to show it. The two were seated in a large, well furnished, dental office in downtown Austin. Cameron, not wanting any snafus and wanting somewhere neutral and unknown to the authorities for this top priority meeting, had contacted the office owner who he'd had dealings with in the past, and paid him well for its use. The front door was locked with a 'closed' sign on it. The blinds were fully shut and two of Cameron's men loitered in the hallway outside ready to respond instantly should their beloved boss need them or an unwanted passerby get too close. Cameron listened intently as Vladimir repeated his account of events. "Yeah, Yeah, Yeah," said Cameron, slapping his knee and chuckling. "Good work. Good work. You'll be rewarded handsomely, Vlad. This is one hell of a message for Josef. He'll know someone is after his ass – wiping out his men and assets. He'll be a beggar on the streets by the time I'm finished. But he'll never suspect me. Why would I destroy one of the gifts I was giving him? Ah, indeed, but what a gift I really am giving him." He thought of Shauna as he slapped Vlad on the knee and rose, indicating the meeting was over. Vlad, wanting a little more information, asked, "So Josef will still fly out with his prize, Shauna, and won't know about what happened to the women or his men till later?" "That's it, smart one." Cameron slapped Vlad on the back then punched in the appropriate code on a keypad unlocking the front door. Hearing the lock release, one of the guards graciously pushed the door open allowing Cameron to walk through with a relieved Vlad following.

Vlad had one more meeting - the most important one - before being helicoptered to Houston where a different kind of transport awaited him.

CHAPTER 24   EXPLANATION

Shauna was dozing fitfully on a mattress with just a sheet - a luxury given the accommodations. She had been vacillating between acting ditzy and being dopey and sluggish from heavy sleep. The mattress lay in a corner of a large maintenance room in the bowels of the cargo ship she'd been imprisoned on. She had yet to become accustomed to the stench, a strong mixture of oil, grease and creosote that assaulted her senses whenever she emerged into consciousness. Half the room was filled with rope, barrels, an assortment of tanks, buckets, dirty sponges and a whole mess of stuff she didn't even try to identify. All-in-all, on the rare occasions she'd been awake and clear-headed, it was a grim reminder of her hazardous situation.

At those moments she would have no doubt experienced a measure of comfort had she known that a team of Navy SEALs had the ship under surveillance. In place mainly to intercede on Shauna's behalf if needed, they were also there to keep an eye on crew activities and report back anything suspicious. So far the SEALs hadn't seen anything of note, just the usual preparations for a long voyage. They were however considering how best to find out what was actually in the cargo containers they'd watched being loaded all morning.

A clanging on the bulkhead door had the still sluggish Shauna shrinking back into her corner. Although trusting and open by nature, she had been given no reason to welcome any of the Russian thugs she'd experienced so far. A sailor she didn't recognize entered and placed a tray of food on the floor near the door. Although he made no move to approach, she could see the lust in his eyes as he looked her up and down. They all seemed to do that and it scared her. She still had a fear of being brutally raped. *I guess they can get past the messy hair, grimy face, dirty clothes and rank smell*, she reflected.

The ship's crew had been told in no uncertain terms that this woman was extremely valuable property and anyone so much as touching her would regret it. Clear enough. Before her guard turned to leave, she indicated that she needed a drink. Understanding her simple signing, he mimed that he would be right back. She was almost crazy with thirst from the after effects of the drug and wanted to do nothing but sleep - a good thing. What better way to pass the time and be inconspicuous as well. The sailor returned with a big pitcher of water and a tin mug. Shauna didn't waste time messing with the mug. She reached for the pitcher with shaking hands, unsteadily raising it to her mouth before guzzling down the much needed liquid. She hadn't realized just how weak she was and gestured for more water to combat her dehydration as she continued drinking.

The sailor churlishly yanked the pitcher from her hands and left. She prayed he'd return soon with the additional water her body was craving. She was sick to her stomach anyway - a result of coming down from the Ecstasy. She felt like retching but dare not - nothing to rinse her mouth out with and nowhere to throw up without having to live with the stink of vomit afterwards. She went back to the mattress and curled up, pulling part of the sheet over her. She remembered that she'd been stripped of her favorite belt and her shoe laces - as if she would want to strangle or do harm to herself. She sat up and removed her floppy shoes then lay back down, quickly falling into a half- sleep state - so longing for her beloved Chip. Her real pain was the separation.

The first thing she saw when she opened her eyes was the pitcher of water standing a few feet from her. All she could do was focus on that. In her still partially drugged state, she crawled to the water and once again greedily gulped it down. It was then that she became aware of someone standing near the door on the inside of her prison. She sat back, her fear clearly visible.

As he slowly advanced, her fear increased, fueled by the uncertainty of his intentions. He definitely looked and carried himself like a mobster. With rough unshaven facial features, dirty, copper-colored skin and long, unkempt black hair, his eyes piercing hers. His bedraggled, wrinkled suit needed attention and his shoes were dusty and scuffed. He spoke something to her in English with a deep voice and thick Russian accent. She shook her head from side to side to indicate she didn't understand. He repeated, more distinctly and slower this time: "I am your friend. I am here to help you." Shauna's reaction was to remain cowered in the corner she'd instinctively backed into. "Here, my dear friend. Let me prove myself to you," he added.

Shauna finally spoke up defiantly, "Who are you and what are you doing here?" The man could sense she was gaining confidence. "I'm here for you," he said. "And what does that mean?" asked an unconvinced Shauna.

"This," said the Russian stepping back and bending forward slightly while clawing the nape of his neck one handed. Shauna watched with concern. "It's OK, dear Shauna. Please, you need not fear me." Shauna felt, for the first time, a sound of sincerity in the man's voice. "Please, I'm not going to harm you." And he began to pull hard at the back of his neck, his fingers scrabbling for purchase. His left arm across his face, he slowly pulled his hand forward and a thin veneer of what appeared to be skin, peeled away from his neck and along the side of his face, revealing misshapen and hard to recognize features. The man kept adjusting his grasp, continuing to pull the second 'skin' across his face, further distorting his features with the pressure. The top of his head started moving up as he continued to pull. Shauna had to remind herself to breathe. She was transfixed, wide eyed as dread-locks came into view. She saw them, but didn't make the connection until continuing the obviously painful pulling process his whole face was exposed.

Not believing her eyes at first, she finally got up and rushed to hug Chenaugh, her protector. The mask was still dangling from one side of his face and, feeling a sense of urgency in case one of the sailors decided to check in on him and Shauna, they removed it completely. Shauna found it tricky working it free even though his hair had been heavily greased to facilitate removal.

A tired and bruised-faced Chenaugh stood before Shauna. He took some of the grease from his hair and smeared it on his damaged face. He winced. It smarted. Taking off his suit jacket he now wrapped his arms around Shauna and held her for a long time. Then he kissed her on both cheeks. "I know you must have a lot of questions, but first let me complete the transition before we're intruded on." So thankful for his presence, she took his face in her hands and, looking into his big brown eyes, kissed him on the mouth. His face became even darker and he turned to cross the room to where another mattress lay.

Shauna had totally forgotten it was there - hardly surprising since she'd been so out of it. And it looked different. A big hump under the sheet made it look as if someone was sleeping.

Bits and pieces of a long conversation with Chenaugh came back to her: Have to leave------not to worry-----remember-----coming back to you------Navy SEAL-----help me-----Love you . . . Her mind went blank.

She was hungry. As if Chenaugh knew this, he dug a couple of worse-for-wear bananas out of his pocket, handing them to Shauna. She couldn't get the outer skin off fast enough. Brown spots, mushed areas and all, it didn't matter. She gobbled them up and licked her fingers. "Oh that was great. Thank you so much." "Damn, if I had known what a treat those would be for you, I would have brought some more, even though I found them hard to come by - not like in Jamaica. I want all of us there together and soon!" "Oh, me too, ME TOO!" enthused Shauna.

The bananas with their potassium fix did wonders. Shauna could have just slumped to the floor and gone to sleep. She forced herself to stay awake. She wanted to know what Chenaugh had been doing - and if he had any news about Chip.

Chenaugh sat on Shauna's mattress leaning against the wall with his legs straight out. Patting his thigh he beckoned Shauna to come lie with her head in his lap. Shauna had been craving a friendly human touch and was stretched out on Chenaugh's lap in no time, looking up at him expectantly. Just as they got comfortable, they heard a soft sequence of taps followed by the sound of a key twisting in the door lock. Chenaugh immediately excused himself. Gently easing out from under Shauna he quickly strode to the door and opened it a crack. A short, whispered conversation later he swung the door wide to usher in a figure in a glistening wetsuit carrying an equally shiny, bulging, black plastic bag.

Shauna suddenly realized that Chenaugh had disrobed down to his briefs. *Wow, what a ripped body. Would I ever love to run my hands along his shoulders and arms,* thought an admiring Shauna. *And am I really being so slow or am I unknowingly passing out for spells,* she wondered. *I'll be glad when the drug effects are totally gone, but in the meantime it's nice to hide in sleep when necessary.*

Taking the bag, Chenaugh went to his mattress and set it on the floor. Picking up a similarly bulging and sealed bag he returned to the door and gave it to the figure who had been waiting quietly. The figure slipped out. Chenaugh closed the door behind him and went back to his mattress. Opening the new plastic bag, he took out a pair of cargo pants and a short sleeve shirt and hurriedly dressed, wishing he could have showered first. He'd known that stripping to his briefs had not been the wisest decision but he'd felt so disgusting he'd just had to get out of his 'work' clothes.

Re-positioning himself under Shauna, gently easing her straggly hair away from her face, he asked, "So where do you want me to begin?" "Do you have news about Chip? How he's doing and where he is?" Not wanting to upset this woman he had fallen for instantly, he was somewhat economical with the truth. Giving her an edited blow by blow of Chip's altercation, knowing she would be filled in eventually when she was clear-headed and more like herself, he spoke of a couple of superficial wounds and how Chip was now healing at a secure ranch somewhere in Texas until Comstock, the Special Task Force leader, decided what to do with him next.

Chenaugh paused. Just in case she was ever interrogated by their adversaries, he didn't want any future plans compromised. Shauna was contemplating what he'd told her. "I so wish I could use thought-speak with Chip, but it doesn't seem to work in a drugged state. I'm sure he's figured that out too. I'm also confused about you being disguised as a Mafia mobster - and an excellent one at that. What was that about?" She reached up to touch one of his broad shoulders, running her fingers over the bulging muscles and down his arm.

His skin automatically erupted into goose bumps and she could feel his crotch change temperature under her head which was still lying in his lap. *Oh, you are not only gorgeous but extremely potent*, she thought, able to discern, even in her still partially drugged condition, the minutest variation in physical responses - especially the pulse of sexuality.

Feeling safe for the first time since being drugged, she let her head fall to one side and before Chenaugh could say anything more, she was asleep. He tenderly placed her on the mattress and curled up with his arm around her, ready to rest. They both stank with bad body odor and foul dog breath. Thinking on it before sleeping he decided to do what he could to get them showers and tooth brushes. Maybe they could just throw themselves into the sea with their mouths wide open and gargle.

Chenaugh dialed in to sleep mode one: one eye and ear tuned to what was going on at all times. If he heard anything he would immediately scoot over to his own mattress and feign sleep, not giving anyone a reason to think he was threatening Josef's property. His other sleep mode, deep and uninterrupted was something he'd rarely experienced since he'd been in the field and as he lay there he fantasized about a vacation with lots of it - oh sweet heavenly Jamaica, his favorite destination. At least his communication implants had kept him connected to Comstock. And, the SEALs were a real blessing.

Chenaugh dozed, he wasn't sure for how long but sensed the tide rising. Shauna had not stirred and he watched her adoringly, hoping the operation would soon be over for her and everyone involved - even the enemy. He wasn't the heartless monster he'd acted as for so long and was glad he still had compassion for everyone, including those who had none of their own. Despite everything he'd endured he still had an open and welcoming heart that could embrace even the most despicable individual. He quietly got up and went to his mattress to rummage through the plastic bag for a pair of boots, cargo pants and shirt for Shauna. They'd be a lot more comfortable than the frayed, dirty leather jacket, ripped soiled jeans and stained top she was wearing. The fit would be less than desirable but they were clean. Unsure whether she'd accept clean briefs without a shower first, he added them to the pile anyway before tossing the bag behind a stack of containers to hide it.

Chenaugh surveyed the maintenance room, picking out a lidded canister that looked like it would make a serviceable toilet. Moving it to a more private place and tearing up some rags he found, he got set to relieve himself. As he squatted, he thought about the SEALs. Thankful they would dispose of his Vlad disguise he finally felt free from the stress of being Cameron's main enforcer. Shifting into the persona of Petrov, the security expert he'd established with the Russian Mafia, was a piece of cake by comparison. His talent for impersonation, for becoming the person he was taking on, was legendary and had made him indispensable as an undercover agent, keeping him safe throughout the years. Knowing there was no one else as capable, with this particular skill-set, he was well aware of his value - both as an agent and as a human being.

A banging at the door preceded a sailor entering with a tray of food. Startled at seeing Chenaugh, not knowing who he was, he halted and yelled for backup. A second sailor came running in and rattled off a sentence in rapid Russian. Mollified, the first sailor stepped forward, placed the tray on the floor and turned to leave.

Speaking Russian, Chenaugh, thankful that in the interaction between the sailors his change of clothes had been overlooked, asked for food for himself and water for both him and Shauna. Continuing, he pointed out that Josef would no doubt expect his 'gift' and her bodyguard to be clean and asked when they could take a shower and get presentable. The sailors mulled this over and agreed that it made sense to let them clean up. "We'll be back to get you." "Don't forget the water. She needs to be in tip-top condition for Josef." reminded Chenaugh as they were closing the door.

The exchange had awakened Shauna who sat up looking dazed. Stretching, she remembered where she was, disappointed that her surroundings were the same, that the dream she'd woken from hadn't altered her reality. She looked up at Chenaugh and smiled. "Good morning", she said. "I'm not sure what time it is, but who cares. We'll make it morning." Chenaugh smiled back. He brought her the fresh clothes and said he was hopeful they'd be getting a shower soon, suggesting she might want to wait till afterwards to change. Sniffing her armpit, she wrinkled her nose and nodded.

The first sailor returned, balancing a second tray of food and a jug of water in one hand as he opened the door with the other. Seeing his difficulty, Chenaugh moved to help him. Taking the movement as a threat, the sailor dropped both tray and jug and reached for his gun. Chenaugh stopped dead, motioning the sailor to calm down, explaining that he'd only wanted to help - that he wasn't an enemy, they were on the same side. The sailor, presumably believing him, ignored the new mess on the already dirty floor and simply left.

Shauna needed to pee and Chenaugh pointed her in the direction of the lidded canister he'd used. When she returned he set up the original tray in front of her mattress and beckoned her to sit. Sliding down beside her he dipped the cheap spoon into the mush and offered it up to her lips. She obliged him and ate. It tasted vile but she knew she needed the sustenance and it was nice to be babied after what she'd experienced.

The sailor returned, going through the same balancing act. This time Chenaugh waited for the sailor to set the tray and water down, smiling and thanking him. Actually drawn to the muscular, well-built stranger, the sailor gave him the benefit of the doubt and smiled back - after all, as the stranger had pointed out, they were on the same side, even though he was an American Russian. Taking advantage of the apparent thawing, Chenaugh asked if he could get them toothbrushes and paste. The sailor said he'd look into it, adding that his name was Ilya and asking for Chenaugh's. "I'm Petrov," Chenaugh replied, extending his hand. "Thanks for your help." But Ilya backed up to leave. *I guess we're not ready to be that buddy, buddy yet,* thought Chenaugh. *But I sure could use a sympathetic supporter to help get me on the chopper with Shauna when it comes.*

Finished eating, Chenaugh placed the trays and jugs near the door and they relaxed a little, content to enjoy being together. Shauna lay back on the mattress, her allure shining through the battered clothes and grimy skin, her fabulous cleavage inadvertently exposed as the partially zipped jacket gaped just a little wider. Chenaugh couldn't keep his eyes off her and admonished himself for even thinking what he was in the circumstances, but then thought, *Why the hell not? It's the perfect distraction.* And he pictured sliding his hands under her jacket and exploring - but he didn't. Wondering if she could read his mind, he hoped so.

She interrupted his fantasies by asking what he'd been up to, saying she was particularly interested in his role with the Russian Mafia. "Chenaugh more than ready to unburden himself, pondered where to begin and how much to share. While he didn't expect Shauna to judge him, he was concerned about endangering her unnecessarily before remembering that, given the danger she was already in, nothing he could tell her would make it worse. Making a decision he said, "Shauna, much as I want to confide in you, I don't want to upset you unnecessarily. What I know could turn out to be superseded by events and what I've done has not always been virtuous, but if you promise to stay quiet and stay awake, I'll give you the short version." In response, Shauna put her arms around him and hugged him tightly, whispering, "Please."

Getting comfortable, Chenaugh still questioned his decision to share his burden. Shauna cuddling against him was the reassurance he needed. "Don't forget you've promised not to go to sleep." Shauna nodded yes against his shoulder as she snuggled closer and he began. "After arriving in the SUV I was quartered here with you. Then, while you were still sleeping off the worst of the drug's effects, the SEALs helped me off the ship, taking me to the other side of the harbor from where I was whisked by helicopter to the Task Force Headquarters.

"Comstock briefed me that they'd intercepted a message from Cameron to his field people that he needed his enforcer, Vlad, found and brought back immediately. Hearing this, I knew that whatever the assignment, it would mean unnecessary killing. Yes, the real Vlad was no longer a threat – he was captured in Argentina and is in solitary confinement at Guantanamo, so there was no danger that he'd reappear while I was impersonating him. No, the problem was that Cameron only used Vlad for his most dangerous and brutal operations and, wanting to cut Josef's network out from under him, needed Vlad, the only person he trusted, to start the ball rolling. So I was asked to go undercover as Vlad, knowing that killing and mayhem would be involved.

"Although I was reluctant - I told Comstock I wasn't sure I could successfully complete the assignment - he was adamant that I wasn't just *the* man but was the *only* man. He explained that fresh information suggested

Cameron had become even more dangerous and unpredictable since the capture of his brother Mark, who, along with Vlad, he'd relied on for so much of his dirty work.

"He's become as obsessed with mutilating Chip as he is with possessing you. Apparently enraged by what the two of you have together, he wants to cut off Chip's genitalia and feed them to his dogs and to not only take your power before killing you but to keep you for himself as a kind of concubine. So he's not going to wait for Josef to turn you into a drug-addict-whore but will grab you back as soon as he can. Even so, once he's wrung you dry and tires of your charms he'll turn you over to his most vile and merciless psychopaths for them to cut out your sexual organs one by one and put them in jars so you'll have a permanent reminder if you should survive.

"Just as Comstock expected, after hearing that, sickened by the imagery, I had to do everything I possibly could to prevent such an abomination." Feeling her shaking he wondered if he should have been less detailed and held her tight. As her trembling abated she said, "Thank you for being so honest. I'll be okay now." And she asked him to go on.

"Once I'd agreed, Comstock explained what he understood the assignment would require. Having heard Josef planned to double-cross him, Cameron wanted Vlad to kill all the women and guards Josef had provided with the truck and make the convoy vanish so Josef would have no way of knowing what had happened to his men or his 'gift'. Essentially he wanted Vlad go to any lengths necessary to make sure Josef was undermined and he, Cameron, came out on top." Chenaugh paused again to comfort Shauna while she cried into his shoulder, unable to fathom the complete disregard for life shown by the two adversaries. Eventually stopping her sobbing she looked up at him. "Have you heard enough, or do you want me to continue, my Precious?" he asked. "Please . . . I want to know . . . I need to know," she said, relaxing against him once again.

"The make-up genius I've used in the past was putting the final touches to the Vlad mask when I arrived at his studio. All I had to do was sit down and be transformed. As usual it took a while to get used to the mask and adjust my breathing, but I could already feel myself taking on the character. With a change of clothes and a last close inspection I was ready to rendezvous with Cameron as arranged by Comstock's team. Meeting him in a coffee shop in downtown Austin, I listened to the plan which was almost exactly as Comstock had described it.

177

"From there I was flown by helicopter to a remote hillside where I waited in the dark for the convoy to arrive." Shauna, feeling him nervous and hesitant to continue, soothingly coaxed him on and he relayed detail by detail every bloody act of the plan and how he'd modified it to save the women.

"Oh, Chenaugh, I can feel just how much it's affected you and I'm so touched by your feeling for those women, your courage and dedication. I can't tell you how grateful I am for how you've invested so much of yourself in my safety too. I don't know that there's anyone else who would have gone to such lengths." And she pulled his head towards her to kiss him full on the mouth.

Chenaugh lay still, so full of emotions. Feeling a blessed relief at her response he allowed himself to cry, letting full body sobs wash him clean. His face wet, he drew her closer, saying quietly, "I wish we had more of you in this world." "We will," she whispered back, as the door was pounded on before being unlocked and the spell they were weaving was shattered.

CHAPTER 25 EXTRACTION

The door opened to Ilya with a towel, bars of soap and a tooth brush. Turning down the passageway he barked for them to come, adding that Josef's helicopter should be arriving within the hour and they'd best hurry. Chenaugh, who had already risen to his feet, turned to see Shauna had slumped over feigning sleep. Quickly stooping he picked her up, threw her over his shoulder, grabbed his boots and Shauna's fresh clothes and hurried to follow Ilya through the bowels of the ship. Explaining that Shauna's narcosis was one of the drug's after effects, Chenaugh was thinking to himself, *Shit, we'd better make this quick. I need to get focused and let Comstock know what's going on before Josef arrives.*

Any idea of 'luxury' either Shauna or Chenaugh had entertained at the thought of a shower was soon disabused. There was none. They found themselves in an unbelievably filthy facility that looked like it hadn't been cleaned since the ship had been built. No strangers to deprivation, they still both cringed at the thought of actually stepping foot in the layers of dirt and scum, of allowing their naked flesh to touch any of the surfaces you could almost see rippling with bacteria. But in they went. Ilya had shown them through and stood guard outside with the door open on the sparse communal space. It featured a row of shower heads placed about four feet apart along one wall and a row of benches opposite. Reeking urinals ran along both narrow ends of the room. Chenaugh guided Shauna to the bench furthest from the doorway.

"Well, my Precious One, I didn't promise you a swanky vacation," said Chenaugh stripping off his clothes and laying them on the bench. As Shauna followed suit, Chenaugh tried the row of showers to find there appeared to be no way to regulate the flow. The water just gushed out of the rusty spigots in one huge uneven jet. "We could get a massage from this if we want. Just stand in the right place to pummel the sore spots." Shauna wasn't amused.

Both naked they looked at each other. Shauna's eyes went to Chenaugh's huge, limp penis. She was almost hypnotized by its size - not so much long, but thick. Dragging her eyes away from the magnet of his groin, Shauna allowed them to roam his entire body, admiring every inch. "Dear

Cheanaugh, You certainly are 'big'. And virile. And extremely handsome." Chenaugh having intended to call Comstock under cover of the shower, was totally distracted as he feasted on Shauna's body, head to toe and everywhere in between, as she stood unflinching and proud. "And you are quite beautiful. I've not met anyone who comes close to your magnificence," said her admirer. "Thank you, Sir," she acknowledged, an appealing blush invading her pale cheeks. His rapidly hardening prick was testimony to his own instant arousal. Fascinated by his responsive body, a quick look into his smoldering brown eyes confirmed his desire was way up and rising.

Doing her best to ignore the mutual attraction, Shauna placed her hand in the water stream to test the temperature. Only one. Lukewarm. "Well, at least it's wet," commented Shauna. *Wow! If it weren't for Chip this could get a whole lot more complicated. I can't pretend nothing is happening but hunk and I will have to get over it. We have to make our feelings for Chip and each other more important.*

In the absence of washcloths, they tried scrubbing themselves directly with the soap, a rough experience. To avoid soaping themselves raw they switched to generating whatever lather they could with their hands and using the meager result to hand clean their bodies. "Turn around and I'll scrub your back while you keep your hair out of the way," offered Chenaugh, holding up his ready-lathered hands. Shauna willingly consented. His strong cleaning touch soon began to arouse her even more so she stepped directly under the water jet to rinse off and cool down. Not daring to use the coarse soap on her hair she made do with a thorough rinsing and finished off by hand-scrubbing her crotch and armpits several times. "My entire kingdom for a little deodorant."

Chenaugh rinsed off alongside her, eyes closed and reliving her touch on his back from when she'd scrubbed him in return. He'd wanted to implore her to "Keep going. Keep going. Never stop. Let me live in this bliss forever." Shauna looked at him with her eyes wide and her mouth a perfect 'O' as she released an extra-long inhale in an abrupt burst of longing. Helpless to resist she stared at his erection, the likes of which she would have thought impossible. He was immense! She became self-conscious at her reaction. Fascinated by the color, the pronounced veins and enormous head, the rich purple and dark-red throbbing mast held her total attention. She was suspended in awe wondering how such a colossus would fit.

Gently taking her hand, Chenaugh rubbed her fingers back and forth along his marvelous manhood. Bewitched by the feel of him as he became even larger and harder, Shauna timidly asked to touch his correspondingly massive testicles. He nodded and she slid her hand over them, feeling the fuzzy short hairs as they quivered at her touch and her body flashed with a charge that surged out to her fingers and toes.

Shauna stepped back, gripping her crotch to throttle another giant arousal while Chenaugh turned away to drown his own in the surge of lukewarm water. Getting back to business Shauna lathered some soap and told him to bend over so she could work on cleaning the grease out of his hair. "Shit Shauna, with this soap, I'll probably have dandruff for the next year or two." They both laughed. He rinsed. "Much better," she said.

They helped towel each other dry as well as they could with the one threadbare, probably unwashed specimen they'd been given. Chenaugh rinsed off the one toothbrush and handed it to Shauna who wrinkled up her nose. "Here goes. I hope the guy – or do you suppose it could be guys - who used this, had respectable germs." She gave her teeth a cleaning and rinsing the brush returned it to Chenaugh. "Toothpaste is for sissies!" he said, following her lead, "We better hurry," said Chenaugh, whispering now, "I have a message to send before Josef arrives." Chenaugh dressed hurriedly, finishing by pulling on and lacing the heavy-duty boots which emphasized how short the pants were. With a black belt in kick boxing and his long powerful legs, the heavy boots made him a formidable weapon but Shauna laughed at the sight. "You look like a tall Charlie Chaplin." Chenaugh stuck his tongue out at her, hiking the pants up even higher.

It hadn't taken Shauna long to put on her three items - the panties, loose shirt and baggy cargo pants. "I'm glad nobody peered in," said Shauna, as Chenaugh grabbed her hand and led by Ilya rushed them back to their confines to get ready to leave. Back to reality. Clean - somewhat.

Finally, Chenaugh was quietly updating Comstock while Shauna was attempting to tame her fly away hair. She finally tied it back with a reasonably clean looking rag she found. Looking around the room she realized she had nothing except the clothes she stood in. *Sure makes moving easy when you have nothing to pack.*

Shauna was excited about starting fresh and new when, KABOOM! The old hauntings about this particular trip smacked her in the head. *This Damn drug must cause depression. I hate the feeling. The next stage of my adventure sure as hell isn't for pleasure. Thank goodness Chenaugh will be with me at least to the airport. I just hope he's on the flight to Moscow with me too.* He'd strongly advised her to pretend she was asleep the whole journey, even though he couldn't know if it would make any difference.

She heard Chenaugh say, "That's correct . . . So the SEALs opened some of the containers and found two large vans filled with women and several luxury vehicles? . . . I doubt Josef has any documentation or proof of ownership," Chenaugh chuckled. "Yeah, I know . . . The SEAL Team was an inspired solution. . . Oh, that's good to hear. Thank Isabella and Richardson for me. I know the likelihood of my flying to Russia with her will make her happy. Anything else I should know? . . . Oh shit, I'm not happy to hear that, but I'm sure Jones and Fin will take every precaution to keep Chip safe on his way to Moscow. . . Isn't that a risky situation? . . . Yeah, yeah, I see. . . Thank you. . . I know. It's good to know we'll be well covered when we arrive . . . Oh, is that right? . . . So, you'll be hiding her in the crowd. . . Yes she does blend in . . . I'll make sure and tell Shauna. Before we sign off, I could use another gun, mine's at the bottom of the ocean. I'll explain later. . . I need to go. . . Yes, thank you. . . Same here. Out."

Shauna waited for Chenaugh to pass on the news - especially about Chip. "Well, Precious, it seems like I'll be going all the way to Moscow with you. Your mother is already there with others in her group who insisted on accompanying her and they should help with the plan. Cameron will also be there. He's making preparations as we speak and will fly there on his private jet, a new Gulfstream G650, which will get him to Moscow well before us. Our people will be monitoring him closely from the time he lands and with any luck we'll know what his next steps will be.

"As far as Chip goes, it's been decided that the safest place to hide him is in the lion's den – Moscow. He'll be on his way soon and will be kept safe in the last place Cameron would expect to find him. Jones and Fin, two of our best, will be with him and the necessary documentation is already in place."

With a look of horror and disbelief Shauna exclaimed, "That's crazy, especially knowing what Sean wants to do with Chip. I just don't get it!" Chenaugh, seeking to reassure her, took her into his arms.

"I totally trust Isabella with my life, and with Chip's, and with yours. I need you to trust me in this. Shauna! Look at me! Our focus is to ensure you, Chip and your mom are protected and safe. Right now you may not see it like that, which is why you have to trust me and my trust in Isabella. Everyone on our team is committed to this and we need you on board."

Looking deep into his intense, dark eyes, plunging to the depths of his soul he'd opened wide to her gaze, she apologized for her moment of doubt.

It was as if he'd always been there, knowing just what to say and really being present. "Hey, you, I think you're remarkable," he added, giving her a warm, moist kiss.

"I know it's no excuse but I'm menstruating. What with the drug and the stress and the worry, my cycle's completely screwed up. Do you think there's a chance of some tampons and Midol any time soon, like before we get on the plane?" "Oh sweetheart, this is great news! Of course I'll do what I can, but I've heard that Josef, for all the bloodshed he causes, is spooked if he gets any blood on him. He'll surely stay away from you for a few days and this should be all over before then."

The sound of the door being unlocked announced it was time for their departure. Chenaugh lifted Shauna again and slung her over his shoulder, becoming Petrov. Ilya and two other sailors stood by the open door ready to take him and Shauna to Josef's waiting helicopter. Chenaugh's heavy boots clunked on the flooring as he toted Shauna, limp and faking sleep, between the grim escorts. Reaching the helicopter, Josef's never-to-be-forgotten ugliness leaned out of the door and commanded Chenaugh to approach and turn around so he could check Shauna's face. Satisfied, he let her head fall back and waved Chenaugh into the rear with his prisoner. Fumbling with the door latch, Chenaugh unceremoniously dumped Shauna on the back seat and hoisted himself in after. Josef barked to the pilot on his right to get a move on. Chenaugh couldn't help but notice the stubby MP5 lying across the pilot's lap. *Wonder what other weapons he has. Obviously a jack of all trades. Bet he can rub his tummy, pat his head and touch his toes all at the same time,* concentrating on keeping his thoughts light as they lifted off.

Into the unknown, thought Shauna. She wanted to get more comfortable but thought better of it and then Chenaugh did it for her. She smiled very slightly keeping her eyes shut. She was breathing in shallow staccato bursts and trembling uncontrollably as her fears began to strengthen. Chenaugh, noticing, touched her lightly, stroked her arm and whispered calming words drowned by the engine noise. Repeating over and over, "I'm not going anywhere. I'm right here. I'm right here."

The trip to Houston's private airport was short and panic-filled for Shauna whose mind-chatter was endless. Setting down the chopper came to rest alongside an all-white Gulfstream G550, and Josef ordered Chenaugh to transfer the sleeping bitch. Two burly men with barely concealed weapons stood guard at the foot of the plane steps and Petrov asked if there was a female attendant on board. Receiving a nod he said, "I need to talk with her now." "And who are you to order us around?" retorted one of the guards. "And keep your guns where they are," continued a gutsy Chenaugh, "I'm an agent for the Russian Government." he finished, staring down the two would-be alphas. Although Chenaugh had papers to prove his identity, he would only use them as a last resort. The way to impose his authority was to own it, to play top dog right from the start.

A little more wary, one of the guards escorted Chenaugh to a rear privacy compartment with an en-suite toilet, sink and closet. Two comfortable bench seats faced each other and Chenaugh chose the one on the right to serve as Shauna's make-do bed, carefully laying her down and loosely strapping her in for takeoff. Walking back to the galley behind the cockpit bulkhead and surveillance compartment he used the same authority tactic with the emotionless female flight attendant, coercing her into handing over a tampon and a strip of Midol capsules. When he returned to the compartment where Shauna rested he ran a glass of water, carefully popped one of the Midol caps and gently pushed it, along with a sleeping pill he kept for emergencies, between Shauna's lips. Taking the hint Shauna opened her mouth a little to receive the water and swallowed. Chenaugh kept the tampon in his pocket for later as he watched Shauna quickly slip into a deep sleep.

The flight attendant came to check on them as the jet engines warmed up, muffled by exceptional soundproofing. Thinking, *I wonder what Josef's up to and have I scared off the two goons?* Chenaugh slid the door closed after she left. Flopping on the other bench he strapped himself in, deciding to treat himself to one drink after they were airborne.

Chenaugh awoke disorientated. Taking a moment, he allowed his memory to re-engage, realizing he had dozed off after drinking a rum and cola. *Damn. What was I thinking!* He stood up to check on Shauna who was lying in the same position as he'd left her. He carefully unstrapped the angelic sleeping beauty, gazing lovingly at the amazing woman in his care. Belatedly it crossed his mind to look for hidden bugs which he did, finding nothing. *I need to be more alert and stay in character* thought a reviving Chenaugh, unaware that he'd missed one vital bug, a microcam that covered the whole room.

"I think it's a shitty, stupid, dumb-assed idea. Why in hell would I put myself in the lion's den? Tell me that?" said an angry and still hurting Chip. Richardson and Special Agent Joe Barclay, who had taken over for Isabella after the killings back in the make-up room, had explained the plan to Chip who wasn't buying it. Isabella was standing by wondering how to handle a fear-filled Chip, concluding that as long as Chip's emotions were running wild it was useless to try. Beckoning the other two aside she suggested they wait for Chip to calm down before trying a new angle. Waiting several minutes, allowing Chip to get over the initial shock, Isabella ventured, "Chip, you're right. It's a crazy, stupid idea, but the truth is that we may need the power of the two of you together to bring Cameron and his network down. We just don't know right now. Although I said at the beginning that we don't just have to take Cameron off the board but have to dismantle his organization too, we're beginning to think we may also need to bury the knowledge of Shauna and her power until what she represents can prevail over anything that would be against her."

"We have put together a plan which we believe will do all of that, but without your help it won't work. While Cameron might not expect you to risk going to Russia to hook up with Shauna, it probably won't surprise him either, particularly if you bumble around like a love-struck amateur while the rest of us stay under wraps ready to pounce. Chip mulled this over for a while and then commented, "So I'm just another piece of bait?" "Yes, you could put it like that." replied Isabella honestly, thinking of Shauna. *My Dearest, I am so sorry we can't think of a better way. What we have in mind will probably be the very worst thing in the world for you to witness but I hope you'll see why soon enough and we can be close again. Please forgive me*

"OK everybody, let's get ready. The plane should be here any minute so be ready to board quickly" Speaking directly to Chip she reaffirmed how key his role would be and suggested he round up anything he'd need for the next several days. She was hoping that his resistance would melt away, the closer they got to Moscow and Shauna. Chip for his part was already focused on seeing Shauna again, knowing he'd do whatever was necessary to make them both safe. *Even if I just get a glimpse of her,* he prayed, thinking, *Here we go again - deeper into unfamiliar hostile territory, the unknown. Thank goodness I'm not alone.*

The surveillance compartment was cramped with the two guards monitoring activity throughout the plane while staying in touch with Josef's larger organization through the secure communications console. Right now, both observers were watching Petrov and Shauna. Petrov was sitting at Shauna's feet with his back to the camera. Leaning towards her crotch between her raised knees he appeared to be playing with her pussy. A sleepy Shauna was watching him, sensuously moving her hips from side to side and up and down. *Gottcha Asshole,* they thought as they rushed the length of the plane and burst into the private compartment, practically breaking down the door as they entered.

Despite being startled, Chenaugh continued working the tampon into Shauna's vagina. *What a pretty little pussy. My dick must be the size of at least four of these. Fuck, I'd love to do a little stretching with my fingers. Come on bro get over it!*

Shauna had been sitting in a pool of blood which Chenaugh had soaked up with toilet tissue. Removing her pants and underwear, he'd left them soaking in cold water in the small bathroom's wash basin. Having slipped a towel under her, he was attempting to fashion a couple of face cloths into a pad to stem any future blood discharge.

The two Russians, disgusted by the bloody residue and steeped in the belief that a woman's monthly cycle made her unclean, backed away. "How barbaric," they agreed before leaving, slamming the door behind them. "You think this is barbaric, you fucking apes!" shouted Chenaugh, not caring whether they heard him or not. He looked down at Shauna who was ready to sleep again and patted her lightly on the cheek. Then wondered where the camera might be.

Finally locating it, he left it in place. Not much point in creating unnecessary problems and he thought he might have some fun with the idiots. Keep them guessing. *And they thought we were having sex! Crap! I wish!*

CHAPTER 26 STOPOVERS

Sean Cameron had settled in comfortably on his luxury jet for the long flight from Houston to a stopover in London. He had brought along six of his toughest and most loyal body guards who were sprawled in the lounge. He was in his private compartment, lying back in a buttery leather upholstered chair. He had been looking forward to being alone and was reminiscing about his time as coach of the Austin Acers. The team had done pretty well considering, but he was more than happy to be through with that part of his life. He wondered how the team and its owner would react when they realized he'd disappeared. Not that he cared, it was just idle musings, a way to pass the time and wind down before focusing on the more pressing business of Josef, Shauna and Gifford.

Smiling to himself, thinking *Oh sweet victory*, he could feel the need to fully express the cunning and dark sadistic passion he'd had to keep in check for so long. Convinced he was born for a greater dominance, he sat thinking, staring vacantly out of the plane window. His mind blurring and whirring to the muffled roar of the jet engines, he reflected on his last meeting with Vlad. *Fuck, I need to find more men like him to extend my reach and power, men who are just as loyal, ruthless and effective.* He didn't yet know that Vlad was gone for good: the real one languishing in Guantanamo, the undercover substitute now flying incognito to destroy him.

Gloating, Sean extrapolated how Josef would perceive the convoy disappearance. *There are no witnesses so he's going to think that his own top people failed him. He'll not just be embarrassed he'll doubt the motivation and integrity of those closest to him which will undermine his whole organization.* And then his thoughts turned sour. Although he'd reamed out his brother the night of the incident he was still seething. *If I could get hold of the idiot, I'd throttle the asshole myself! What was he thinking? I still can't believe he took a shot at Shauna at the barbecue. What part of 'take care of her' did he not understand? When I find out where you're being held I might yet have you killed – or better still, leave you to rot!*

Thinking of his brother led to thoughts of the woman and her boys he'd left behind. He'd not seen them since they'd fled the night he went into a rage after the debacle at the club. He despised them for that, for running away right at the end, not that it mattered. He really hadn't needed her or the boys once his plans for Shauna had been set in motion. She had kept the house looking good and the three of them had given him a gloss of respectability, but that was about it. He wondered in passing why the boys had turned out so spineless, hiding behind their mama's apron strings and avoiding him.

So narcissistic and self-centered he had no understanding of the kind of person he really was. He lived his life to suit his own selfish needs within a fantasy of being hard but fair and caring but not sentimental. He was in fact without morality, integrity or compassion. He'd learnt at an early age that feelings were dangerous and had locked his away forever behind an impregnable hard-pack, solid to the core. He let no one in. Never had, never would. Breaking into Fort Knox would be absurdly simple compared to finding a way into his humanity.

He fixed himself a double-vodka on the rocks. *How appropriate,* he crookedly smiled. *I'm headed to Moscow, my favorite place to be.* He took a long swig. *And a toast to me.* He downed another large gulp. He was looking forward to meeting up with a few of his corrupt billionaire buddies. *Amazing! I know a good proportion of the billionaires in Moscow and every one of them is about as straight as the Moskva River. Which is probably why the city has as much global influence as a pack of jackals – and why it's my kind of place,* he guffawed. *It will be so great to back in my penthouse again, right in the center, perched over the heart of the action. Worth every penny of the outrageous price I paid, it sure as hell beats the squalor of the rundown block houses and cheap apartments that have sprouted like weeds, blighting the view wherever you look.*

Even so, I need to cozy up to the Mayor of Moscow or any other Government official who lives in the Kremlin, see if I can't get a place there. I'd love that. Yeah, the seat of power, exactly where I belong and a perfect center for global domination. I wonder where I'd be now if I'd stayed in Russia instead of moving to Scotland. Oh yeah, I remember, I wasn't too popular back then. If I hadn't left I'd probably be dead, or worse. But not now! And slapping his knee, he drained his glass and moved on to his reason for making the trip.

Josef had agreed to have their showdown in Kremlin Square, Sean's favorite place. And, being superstitious, he figured that would give him an advantage, all but guaranteeing him the victory he deserved. Expecting to reach Moscow first, having left Texas earlier and having a faster plane, he was intent on ensuring his many associates who were committed to his ascendancy would be fully prepared, be in place well in advance and ready for anything Josef might try. Any allies who arrived later would simply add muscle to the cause – he fully expected his supporters to outnumber Josef's by at least two to one. *May the worst of the bad guys win.* A strategy straight out of the medieval playbook. Although neither he nor Josef could be considered royalty, they were kings of their respective empires and demanded fealty of their various allies, and Sean was going to make sure his obeyed or suffered the consequences. *Some things take a long time to change. Some things never seem to change at all.*

Excited at the thought of eliminating Josef as a force, either killing his operation entirely or diminishing it to insignificance, he anticipated Josef's humiliation. *The fat bastard doesn't even know that he holds the golden egg. He thinks he has a beautiful toy to use and abuse and then pass on when he tires of her. I'm dealing with an idiot, albeit a useful one.*

Thinking of Shauna, he considered where to keep her and how to make the most of her exceptional charms while extracting everything he wanted.

The cavernous interior, devoid of any sign of luxury, a few large containers at the far end the only cargo, shook with a constant one-pitched roar that had Chip on edge. The nine of them, Chip and eight agents, Isabella, Dave, Jones, Fin and four others he hadn't been introduced to yet, were lying on thin mattresses laid out on the cargo bay floor. There were makeshift jump seats along each side, but at least some of them knew how uncomfortable they were and they'd all opted for comfort first. Lying there Chip felt like he was inside the belly of a mechanical whale and was as nervous as he'd ever been, finding it difficult to settle down. Seeing him squirming, Dave called, "Hey, bro, this is going to be a long flight and we've barely started our first leg to London. How about a sleeping pill so you can get some rest? It'll sure make the time go faster."

"Sounds good. I can't seem to unwind. All I think about is Shauna and how she's doing." Isabella intervened, "We've gotten word, that she's on board Josef's plane and Chenaugh's with her. She's still sleeping off the effects of the drug, and no doubt will be for several hours more." *No wonder I can't thought-speak with her - the drug will have fried her concentration. I didn't think of that. Damn.* "They should arrive in London a little ahead of us. After all, this is not the sleekest plane." Chip joined the laughter, a relief to them all. "Yeah, seems Chenaugh even managed to get stuff from the flight attendant to help with her period, which I know from personal experience can be tough. She's in good hands for the time being so try not to worry. Now, let's get you comfortable." Dave grabbed his backpack and gave Chip a pill and a bottle of water to wash it down. Closing his weary eyes, Chip let the monotonous shaking and thrumming and the effects of the pill drive him into a fitful sleep.

Later, checking Chip, Isabella, seeing his closed eyes fluttering as he dreamed deeply, decided he'd be better off left alone. *It's probably less stressful for him to find release this way. See if he can ease the load he's been carrying . . . It had been so good to hear him laugh earlier.*

Rolling from side to side, Chip reached out as if to embrace something or someone. He could make out Shauna far away through a crowd. She started rushing to him. He broke free from the people around him and ran to meet her, arms spread wide. But the faster he ran, the farther she got. It was agonizing. He was calling. "Shauna, Shauna, my Love, my Precious Love. Here. Here I am." She tried to come to him, but the crowd held her back. Jolted by a loud crack he looked down to see blood spurting from his chest. Sitting up he looked down to see his chest was unmarked, just as it had been when he'd gone to sleep. Sweat was running down his face and he could feel it trickling down his back. He shook his head and muttered. "Fuck, what a nightmare. It seemed so real, almost prophetic." Seeing his sudden movement, Isabella rushed to him. Reassuring him, she lovingly wiped the sweat from his face before gently easing him back on the mattress. "Would you like some water?" "Please, yes."

Arriving at Heathrow's private terminal, Sean took a private limousine to the main terminal for something to eat and a change of scenery. Looking for a pub with fish and chips and a special Irish beer that he liked, he ignored the stores and their mannequins adorned with the latest fashions, he was still locked into the t-shirt and slacks topped by a jacket with rolled up sleeves look - think 'Miami Vice' from years ago: although he found jewelry on men either effete or vulgar. Spying a likely eatery he checked it out. Deciding it would suit him fine he took a seat at the bar and put in his order. The two guards shadowing him sat at a small table close by - just in case.

Enjoying the greasy, carb-rich meal and especially the beer, Sean thought about traveling for pleasure more. Up to now he'd focused on business. Maybe, now that he had no regular job or family ties - not that that had ever stopped him doing anything – and once Josef was dealt with, he could tour the sex capitals of the world.

Thinking of sex he thought of Shauna and, self-deluded megalomaniac that he was, fantasized about a life with her. *If she really does have the power we've monitored and I can get her on my side she'd be very useful in building my worldwide empire - Hell, a universe-wide one! It would make everything so much easier. What if I could even turn her to my kind of life and my kind of ways? We could then make everything ours, just the way we want it - in every way. Now that would possibly be my greatest triumph. I could be King Sean and she my Queen. I'd toss her in bed like she's never been handled - have her begging for more. She'd become addicted to me.* Titillated by his thoughts, he slapped his belly to confirm his self-approval. Feeling the bulk he thought, *Well, I could get back to working out again and lose this gut but how much more appealing can I fucking get?* He was truly the personification of a self-absorbed asshole. *Or I could cut back on my alcohol consumption. No way! I shall have my cake and eat it too. Yes, my unsuspecting little beauty. You will not only have the pleasure of meeting more than your match, but I can be very, very persuasive. And Gifford, you loser, you chased so much tail without getting anywhere. In fact you lost your wife and children. How could you possibly think you can compete with me?*

Sean's huge ego preceded him as he returned to the limousine eager to continue his journey. His bodyguards scrambled to keep up. "Boss sure is in a good humor," remarked one. "Would be nice if he stayed that way," said the other. "So I guess we'd better shut up and move it," said the first.

Sean and his entourage had long left for Moscow by the time Josef's plane landed in London. Luckily for Shauna and Chenaugh, Josef decided to visit the terminal to eat rather than have food delivered to the plane as he normally would. Chenaugh watched as Josef's gross, bulky body, wobbling like Jell-O, rose and left the plane. As it squeezed through the exit and seemingly rolled down the steps to the waiting limo, Chenaugh approached the flight attendant. Handing her a list and a stack of bills that had been provided, stuffed in the pocket of the pants for just such emergencies, he bribed her to go shopping. She wasn't quite the pushover he'd originally thought she'd be but eventually she agreed.

Waiting till Josef and his guards had left in the limousine the attendant took an airport shuttle, planning to return before her boss to avoid any confrontation. Watching her leave, Chip hoped there was enough cash to cover everything and that she'd have enough integrity to not buy cheap just so she'd end up with more money.

Reaching the terminal concourse, Josef was huffing and puffing ten yards in, pausing for breath in front of a steak and potato place with a long list of desserts. His kind of menu. He entered and ungracefully slumped in a chair that creaked under his weight. He tried to edge it closer to the table, but gave up - too much like hard work. His two guards kept close watch as the 'Bulk' ordered a full meal, heavy on the calories and tucked a napkin into his sweaty collar under layers of chin.

He became angry when he realized there was no bar, taking it out on the first person to come his way; the waiter who brought him his first course. Josef looked at the salad and threw it at the wall closest to him, venomously berating the dumbfounded server. The owner of the restaurant quickly appeared, eased the intimidated and speechless waiter aside and asked what the problem was. Josef bellowed in crude English that he hadn't ordered a salad - he hated fresh vegetables. "I'm sorry that a mistake was made but that's no excuse for your behavior," said the owner, "So I'm afraid I'll have to ask you to please leave." Digging around in his pocket, Josef pulled out a grimy, bulging wallet, opened it, and took out a wad of bills. "Here," he said. "Take this. I don't feel like moving."

This was not the first time, nor would it be the last, that his money would do the talking. His philosophy was that, given the right price, anyone could be bribed. The owner looked down at the bills in his hand. Figuring that there must be at least five hundred dollars, maybe three hundred pounds or more, he cleared his throat and announced, "You can stay, but any more monkey business and you're out of here." Seeing Josef's self-satisfied smirk the owner, having second thoughts, paused momentarily before retreating back behind the cash register. Josef's guards just shrugged, used to their grossly overweight and under-mannered boss buying acquiescence.

The waiter eventually came back, a bit apprehensive, and carefully put a large plate of steak, potatoes and gravy in front of Josef. "Where are my French fries?" he asked pugnaciously. "I'll get them right away, sir," replied the unhappy waiter.

The waiter soon returned with a plate of fries and Josef added them to the heaped plate in front of him before carrying on eating like a mechanical shovel. "Disgusting," muttered one of the guards before he was called over and Josef instructed him, around a mouthful of food, to find a bar close by. Returning, the guard said there was a bar three doors down. Josef grunted a reply, looking forward to a couple of beers to wash down his meal in a more conducive atmosphere.

While Josef stuffed himself, his female flight attendant shopped for Petrov, who would have gone shopping himself but hadn't wanted to leave Shauna unattended in such a vulnerable condition. Checking the list Petrov had provided she went store to store, ending up at a café for sandwiches and coffees, impressed by how the big man seemed to have thought of everything, including a range of toiletries and plus-size tampons.

At the moment the big man was sitting across from the sleeping Shauna, relieved her cramping and bleeding had lessened. *Damn it!* He thought. *She's already been through enough and there's worse to come. I'd like for her to at least have the basic necessities. Hopefully the food and drink will energize her too. Let's just get to Moscow, deal with whatever, and get on with our lives! The mere thought of this slimy pig getting his hands on Shauna makes me want to throw up----or better still, rip his head off. Fuck! Is that me or Vlad thinking?*

Shaking free from following that thread, he thought of Chip, *Bro, You're so vital to this equation. Shauna needs you to do what needs to be done. You know that. And the fact that I've fallen for her too means I'll be with you both through whatever comes up. Count on it, no matter what. But later, Bro.* And he felt the churning of an overwhelming passion for Chip and Shauna both. A sense of connection he'd been totally numb to, like most everyone else, until right that moment. It had been leaching out of his unconscious since meeting Shauna and had suddenly reached critical mass, firing his nervous system.

The flight attendant returned loaded with carrier bags, a tray of coffees and a smile on her normally stern countenance. She and Petrov went through the purchases. "You've done a remarkable job - better than I could have. Thanks so much." Petrov could tell she was pleased by his compliment as she held up a rather drab looking blouse, saying, "I had money left over to buy me this." "Great," was the best response a surprised Petrov could come up with. Given the fashionable clothes she'd selected for Shauna, he couldn't understand why she'd made such a dull choice for herself.

Their business completed, the attendant turned to see a laboring Josef and his guards ready to maneuver up the plane steps for boarding. The guards took Josef by both armpits and literally hauled him into the plane. By which time the attendant was busy in the galley and Petrov had the purchases stowed out of sight.

Josef wallowed through the plane to check on his beautiful prize. Without knocking he lurched into the compartment where Shauna lay sleeping. He took a closer look and grunted with satisfaction. The gross, clammy, disheveled lump never questioned whether he might seem offensive and repulsive or lack sex appeal. This was *HIS* woman. It was that simple. He never, ever pursued any woman. He'd see one he wanted and send a thug or thugs to get her and then she was his until he'd had enough of her. He never considered getting to know his victims. He left, wiping spit from his mouth.

Petrov nudged Shauna. "Wake up, my Precious. I have some things I hope you'll like." Shauna slowly surfaced from a deep dreamless sleep. "First, it's time for a change." He had a couple of hand towels from the kitchen over his arm. He uncovered Shauna and looked at her crotch. "Pretty good my love, your flow has subsided to normal." He took the towel he'd soaped and carefully wiped her. Gently removing the sodden tampon, he wiped her again, and rinsed her off with the other towel. "We won't have to ration these out any more," he said holding up a box of tampons, taking one out and expertly inserting it in her vagina. She felt herself responding sexually to his touch and to the tampon going where a penis would feel right at home. She leaned over and kissed Petrov on the forehead realizing she felt more alive and awake than she had been - for however long it had been since taking that first sip of the drugged drink back at the club. *Hmmm*, she thought, *that feels like ages ago.* "How do you feel?" "Oh, Chenaugh," Chenaugh instantly placed his finger on her mouth. "I'm Petrov for now." Looking contrite, Shauna continued, "I'm so thankful for you. I feel much, much better; like the cobwebs are leaving along with the cramps." She felt an attraction to him that was different for her. "But I'm starving." "Well, well, well. What have we here?" He materialized a bulging sandwich and large cup of coffee topped with whipped cream. Shauna clapped her hands together in delight and her eyes were back to sparkling pools of green. Petrov's spine tingled and his cock twitched.

"Before we eat, why don't we do this," said an aroused Petrov. Reaching behind him he produced new underwear with a box of menstrual pads. "We can't be too sure now, can we," he added, unwrapping a pad and fitting it into the crotch of a pair of green and orange panties. The panties were easy to slip on, but the matching, slightly smallish bra was something else. "Che-Petrov, give it to me and I'll make the adjustments." Shauna let out the straps as far as they would go and then leaning forward, fiddled behind her to fasten the bra. She looked down at her chest. They both broke out laughing. She shook her breasts for the candid camera as the cups slid up exposing her nipples and everything below. Taking one breast at a time she managed to cram them back into the bra cups. "Now, I hope I can breathe without busting something." They both laughed again. Whipping out a bright lavender blouse with a ruffled neck and three quarter length sleeves, Petrov said, "Here, try this on." "Petrov: first of all, it feels so good to laugh with you; second, how did you come by all this; third, I have to pee, and fourth, I want to eat and have some coffee, the aroma is making me drool."

Helping her to her feet he finished putting her blouse on, buttoning it all the way up, and pointed her in the direction of the adjacent bathroom. She came out smiling and content and relieved. Takeoff was announced and they were obliged to buckle up before Shauna could eat. They both snatched up a coffee though, enjoying them as the plane climbed before leveling off and they were free to move around again.

Unbuckling they leaned across the aisle and grabbed their sandwiches, ploughing into the welcome meal unconcerned with manners or appearances. "We're like two vacuum cleaners sucking up food. Here, you have some on your cheek." Petrov took a napkin, interrupting Shauna's feeding frenzy by holding her chin with one hand and wiping her face with the other. "There, that's much better," he said as he planted a kiss on her clean cheek. They sat side by side sipping their coffee, leaning back with their legs stretched across the aisle, feet resting on Shauna's 'bed' opposite.

They were enjoying each other so much - just being together and drinking. No words were needed. Petrov showed her the last of the clothes - slim designer jeans and cowboy boots. Shauna checked the sizes and smiled, pleased. "I've always wanted boots like these so I'll wear them proudly. What a kind and wonderful thing to have done, my Precious," remarked an adoring

Shauna. Neither of them even thought to wonder where the attendant had found such treasures in an English airport, even one as cosmopolitan as Heathrow.

Petrov went to the bathroom to change. Watching through the gap of the not quite closed door, Shauna thought how extremely handsome and sexy he looked in the new long sleeved tan shirt. As he quickly took off his old briefs she caught a glimpse of his super-sized hard-on before he trapped it against his thigh under the new ones. As it strained to come out and play, Petrov tamed it by quickly climbing into new dark gray slacks, adjusting the bulge so it was at least reasonably comfortable if not inconspicuous. Finished, he sat back down next to Shauna and picked up his coffee. Shauna laid a loving hand on his leg as she sipped from her own almost empty cup.

Anybody looking in would never guess they were prisoner and guard. The guards in the surveillance compartment were taking a long break and had not seen what had just transpired. When they returned they never thought to press the replay button as everything looked to be quiet and normal even if both did look refreshed. Why? The guards didn't have a clue – the perfect combination of dumb and unobservant.

As everyone settled in for the final leg of their journey, Petrov got set to tell Shauna about Moscow. She, however, had another idea. She slid down on the bed, laying her head in his lap, and quickly dropped straight off. He looked down at her lovingly, liking the closeness, never wanting it to end.

CHAPTER 27　FIREFIGHTING

Isabella yelled over the engine roar that Richardson was on a CIA jet taking the polar route to Moscow. He would be processed through Terminal A and shuttled over to meet them at the North Cargo Terminal Complex when they arrived. Isabella had felt heartened by the news - knowing her team would now be as good as it could be and that the Russian Government was cooperating. Good to bear in mind going forward and their plans changed, as they inevitably would. So far, every day, sometimes every hour, had added a new wrinkle.

Isabella took a few moments to think about the scope of the operation. Just how many countries, agencies and individuals were combining to bring down Sean and his multinational evil. And that was without including the non-affiliated: the individual risk takers with an excitement for change, bored with normalcy, who could think for themselves; people hungry for new ideas and willing to pursue them, passionate about building a world where it was people who mattered. And it was word-of-mouth that was proving the most powerful magnet. Shauna's sound had been broadcast around the world causing a resonance in those who were ready to hear. Isabella knew this at some level but was leaving nothing to chance and taking nothing for granted.

Waking Chip, Isabella sat beside him and explained that she needed him to listen in as she contacted Shauna through Chenaugh. Using her wrist mic, she called Chenaugh. "Chenaugh. Chenaugh. Can you hear me? This is Isabella. Please respond. Chenaugh?" There was a crackling in her ear followed by a slightly distorted "Yes, this is Petrov." "Thank you Chenaugh. What a relief to hear your voice." "Isabella. I don't want to lose this connection, but I have to be careful, our room is under visual and audio surveillance, so I'm in the adjacent bathroom and can't talk for long. What's up?" "How is Shauna doing? If she's sleeping, please wake her so you can relay what I have to say." A few moments later she heard Chenaugh, "Can you still hear me?" "Clear as a bell," she replied before starting.

"Through informers and known Mafia contacts we've gotten a message to your Mafia boss in America to pass on to Josef about Cameron's actions in having the convoy destroyed. We've also planted the idea that he suggest to

Josef that, in retaliation, he have you, Chenaugh, make her unusable by Sean. With you in control we should be able to trick them both and save Shauna from the worst of their separate plans. With regard to Shauna, please tell her she needs to remember why she's enduring what she is. That her sound of a new way of living is echoing around the world and every person who can receive it seems to amplify its strength. People are coming together from all over in a new biological oneness with a single focus and large numbers of them are on their way to Moscow ready to do whatever they can to assure her safety. What she and Chip have set in motion is a power far greater than any cosmos that increases with everyone who joins them in a oneness . . . and they need to really feel that at a depth of themselves that neither of them have experienced before.

"Now, while I understand how painful it is for them both to be physically apart, unfortunately we have neither the time nor the technology in place to enable the two of them to speak to each other directly at the moment." And then she disconnected.

Feeling Shauna so far yet so close, Chip's emotions flowed freely, as Isabella continued speaking to him, emphasizing that he wasn't just important but was indispensable to the shift that was taking place and must never allow himself to be buried under the weight of anything less - ever.

Stimulated by caffeine, Chenaugh's adoration and gifts, and especially a renewed sense of being close to her love, Chip, Shauna sat back on her bed. Becoming quiet and meditative she let Isabella's words soak in, allowing herself to be penetrated to the depth Isabella had spoken of. Chenaugh, knowing that what she was doing was both necessary and life-affirming for her, remained quietly attentive. *Abundant creativity springs from an undisturbed soul.*

Thankful for Isabella's words, Shauna and Chip were smart enough to know that often it took input from someone else to make the adjustments necessary to stay on course. There was no time, space or place for the vagaries of ego to tarnish what was real and good. Chip and Shauna could spot an ego-driven touch a mile away, within themselves and in other people. They had zero tolerance and faced it down wherever and whenever it showed up, being particularly sensitive to the first signs: never-ending excuses.

Although miles apart in separate aircraft, Chip and Shauna could feel a revived aliveness surge through their bodies. Their eyes became brighter and their skin glowed. Chip dumped his tormenting thoughts while Shauna's drug induced sleepiness was wearing off. They reconnected to their purpose and their undying hunger to live their reason for being here at this moment in time, knowing they could never stop. Knowing they had supporters who would keep nourishing them forward, they experienced a refreshed dedication.

So they hadn't got to speak to each other when Isabella called. They didn't need to. They were forever joined as one anyway. And were once again able to communicate telepathically - such a relief and an excitement, after what had seemed like an unbridgeable distance for so long. Shauna stayed composed, eyes closed and motionless for some time. Chenaugh, observing her, sensed she was communicating with Chip and felt an inexplicable joy of participation.

Landing at London Heathrow, Isabella and her colleagues readied themselves as the plane taxied to the Cargo Terminal where a limovan was waiting to ferry them around the perimeter road to Terminal 3. Looking forward to a decent meal in the relative silence of the busy Terminal concourse, they even agreed that Chip should join them. There were enough of them to ensure he was protected at all times and he certainly deserved the opportunity to clear his head and eat well. Isabella, deciding the plane would be safe on its pad, also allowed the additional four agents to accompany them.

As they neared the turn off to the Terminals, Isabella, who was sitting in the front passenger seat, glanced behind and noticed a black SUV in their wake. Being suspicious, she asked the driver to make the next left turn, away from the airport. Soon enough, a black SUV showed up behind them. Isabella, taking no chances, whispered to the driver, then advised the other passengers to hang on tight. The driver abruptly turned the wheel, skidding the limovan to block the road. Unprepared for the sudden maneuver, the SUV driver, in trying to avoid the limovan, glanced off its right rear fender and ploughed into a hut on the median, demolishing it before coming to a dead halt. Isabella was out of the limovan in a flash, Dave hot on her heels. Jones and Fin joined them while the other agents stayed in the limo with Chip and the driver.

Isabella and Dave were yelling at the driver while carefully advancing from the rear of the vehicle, guns out and aimed at the target. Flipping the driver's door open away from him, Dave screamed, "Hands on the steering wheel now! Let's see both those hands on the steering wheel!" Moving level with the driver he shouted again, "Hands on your head and come out slowly." The white haired driver wearing dark glasses was obviously rattled and pissed off but reluctantly did as he was told. Dave roughly patted him down, removing a gun from a holster under his left arm, while Isabella opened the rear door to check for other occupants. "So," said an aggressive Dave, "What the fuck were you doing following us, who do you work for, and how did you know we were coming?" The trapped man stood tight lipped daring Dave to shoot. Dave cocked his gun, just as a well-dressed man slowly stepped out from the back seat under Isabella's watchful eye. Frisked and questioned, he too stood mute.

"I know this jerk! I've seen him at our basketball games. He's buddy-buddy with Coach." exclaimed Chip who had gotten out of the limovan and headed to the SUV, the other agents in tow. "Shit, Sean has eyes and ears everywhere," said an exasperated Isabella. "We can't discount the possibility of a mole in the Task Force either. One of my constant nightmares," added Isabella. The identified passenger flashed a wicked grin. "Damn it. So Sean knows our moves with Chip. I wonder what else he's figured out?" said an agitated Dave. "And wipe that goddamned grin off your face!" he shouted.

Noting the arrival of the English police, a relieved Isabella welcomed their presence, "Here comes the answer to our prayers. We're wasting valuable time and the police can help us by picking up the slack." She intercepted the police officers, flashing her ID and introducing herself and the others. Deciding to keep it simple she described Chip as an asset who was helping capture one of the world's notorious crime lords, and that the men they'd just seized had been hired to report on Chip's movements, and maybe even kill him. The policeman, after studying their identification and checking with headquarters, looked over the crime scene.

Isabella continued, "We would appreciate you taking these two in for questioning and holding them until we can arrange extradition. I'd also suggest you perform a strip search on them both. Given the organization they're working for, I think you can expect to find one or two if not several bugs – and they can be microscopic. Here's the contact information for me and my boss, who'll want to stay in touch with you." Isabella exchanged cards with the obviously senior officer, noting his name was Radford. "Thanks guys. We have to go. We're due in Moscow by tonight and need to get prepared," said Dave, heading back to the limovan.

As they all piled in they huddled together to discuss Chip's safety. Of all the options they considered, including involving the RAF and the Russian Air Force, the VVSC, they decided that the best one was to continue as planned. Assuming their every plan was being overheard they agreed to institute a localized program of disinformation, feeding the bugs well-dropped tit-bits to direct them on a worthless goose chase. They then continued to Terminal 3 to pick up what they needed and to eat.

They split up into three groups; the four extra agents; Isabella and Jones; and Chip, Dave and Fin. Arranging to stay in contact with each other and meet back where they were standing, each group went their separate way.

Initially forgoing food, Chip had wanted to get some more practical clothes. He was paying for some heavy duty slacks, shirt and leather coat at a small, clothing boutique when Fin and Dave felt something was not quite right. Not sure what they nonetheless closed in on Chip just as he picked up his bags and hustled him toward the rear of the store. Keeping an eye over their shoulders they saw a man come through the front door and draw a gun. The threesome, a bewildered Chip in front, ducked out the rear door into a narrow service corridor.

A few stores down, a clerk taking a smoking break was leaning against the wall by an open door. He paused startled as the fleeing threesome ducked in the open doorway and Dave dragged him in behind them. Drawing his gun, Dave motioned the smoker to stay quiet and pressed himself against the wall beside the door, facing back the way they'd come. They could hear the gunman's footsteps. Dave, now joined by Fin at the door, quickly alerted Isabella to the situation.

The gunman slowed as he neared the still open door. As he fired, Dave shot twice. The gunman dropped, his bullet having lodged in the door jamb where they were hiding. Updating Isabella, Dave watched Fin check the assailant for vital signs. Isabella advised she'd contact Radford, the officer in charge at the scene of the accident and get him to send transport to take the three of them and the other agents back to the plane, ASAP.

After signing off with Dave, Isabella called Radford who said he'd send two vehicles and told her where they should all meet. Calling Dave back she told him to stay put and they'd be picked up. She similarly advised the four other agents of their extraction arrangements and she and Jones went looking for a taxi.

"Holy shit," said Fin - like he'd just walked a high wire across the Grand Canyon. "Good shooting, man. Thank the fuck we're all in one piece. What the fuck's going on?" Looking around, feeling the adrenaline seeping away, they went back inside and crouched by Chip where he had sunk to the ground. "I don't mind being the center of attention, but this is getting a bit much," he said, laughing nervously. Dave and Fin joined in, surprised Chip could find some humor in the circumstances. "I don't like killing anybody, but it's not always easy just to incapacitate them, and it's my heart I want to hear beating after the battle," murmured a shaky Dave.

Helping Chip to his feet, they made their way into the service corridor just as a uniformed police officer came charging through a door at the end. Pounding toward them, he dropped to a knee to check the gunman's body before approaching them. Recognizing Radford, Dave said, "Let's go. We can fill you in on the way." Radford, who'd recognized the dead gunman as one of Josef's most capable killers, kept quiet, just turning to retrace his steps. The four of them exited the service corridor and went down the service stairway to the tarmac where Radford's car, lights still flashing, was parked. Radford had called for backup and a second police car showed up as they were getting into his car. "Hey Radford," called Dave, "Do you have another car to pick up the four other agents?" "They should be being picked up as we speak," was Radford's instant reply. "Let's get the fuck outta here then!" said Fin settling in the back seat with Chip as Radford instructed the officers from the second car to secure the shooting scene for CID.

"Hang on," said Chip "I need to eat before we go anywhere. I'm not going to spend another four hours or so in that fucking rattletrap without some food." Thinking for a minute, Radford said, "I know just the place," and set off. As Radford drove, Dave gave him a run-down of the skirmish.

Isabella and Jones, after picking up some take-out, had caught a cab and were on their way back to the plane. She called Comstock at headquarters to fill him in, speaking low to avoid the cabbie overhearing. The four agents had eaten on reaching the Terminal so were feeling pretty good as they travelled in the other police car, also heading for the plane.

Several minutes after they'd cleared the Terminal complex Radford slowed and swung into what appeared to be a typical English pub - a bit drab, but doable. They scrambled out of the car and entered. Explaining to the bartender that they were in a hurry they all ordered the same thing - shepherd's pie and dark beer - thinking that would help speed up the process.

Radford hung out near the door, keeping an eye on what was going on. The threesome soon discovered that a pub is a pub and not a fast food joint. Waiting impatiently the three became increasingly agitated, eventually agreeing to cancel their order, when finally the food came. "Man this was worth the wait. Good, huh," said Fin as he tackled his loaded plate. "The beer is terrific," commented Dave. Chip was silent as he gulped his food down, reflecting on their fate. The beer helped take the edge off the intensity - and it was certainly tasty, if a bit warm. They would have liked to order refills, but thought better of it, paid up and walked out to the police car with Radford at their side, ever watchful. "I needed that, thanks for stopping. It's sure made a difference to how I feel," said a satisfied Chip. He clung to his carrier bags, sitting back and closing his eyes wondering, *What's next?*

As they circled back onto the perimeter road black smoke from the direction of the Cargo Terminal billowed skywards, bright orange flames licking up from below. "What the Hell!" yelled Radford. His passengers who'd been half dozing jumped alert. Staring at the scene with disbelief and foreboding they almost had their fingers crossed. As they sped closer they could see it was their cargo plane burning. What wasn't obvious until they turned onto the Cargo Terminal apron was the blackened and burning helicopter balanced at a precarious angle upside down on top of the plane.

They drove as close to the scene as they could, scanning the flames as the fire trucks doused the wreckage. "Where the hell are Isabella and Jones?" asked Dave. "I sure hope they're safe." A desperate Fin interjected "I can't believe Sean's network is really this pervasive." Approaching the firefighter's perimeter Chip shouted "Was anybody in the plane when the fire started?" The nearest fireman responded, "As far as we as know, and it's only hear-say at the moment, the pilot and co-pilot managed to get out just in time, sustaining second degree burns." It was hard to hear over the hot crackling fire but they got the message when he followed up with, "You'd better move back now. We don't want more unnecessary casualties."

Turning away they saw a taxi approaching and went toward it praying that Isabella and Jones would step out. They did. The two groups rushed together mirroring each other's horror, collectively mulling a host of questions they wanted answered. "What the hell happened to you?" asked Dave of Isabella and Jones, "I thought you left the Terminal well before us." "Would you believe a flat tire?" said Isabella. "The damn taxi didn't have a spare so we had to wait for a tow and then another taxi. Mind you, if we'd got back straight away we might be burning too." Thinking on that scenario they each turned to watch the firemen as they worked to contain the blaze and snuff it out "I thought another police car was bringing the guards back here." mused a confused Isabella. She went looking for Radford who the three realized wasn't with them.

As they waited, they started getting bits and pieces of information as it passed through the chain of command, reaching them at the firefighting perimeter. Hearing that the helicopter pilots had both died in the crash, Isabella bowed her head, leading the others in a silent acknowledgement and prayer for their families. As she did, she noticed that Radford and his fellow officers were keeping their distance, as if she and her colleagues were in some way tainted.

As the firefighters went about their unenviable task, they continued to supply the four with an unofficial commentary on their operation. "It looks like the pilot and co-pilot were trapped in the cockpit after all. We don't know yet if that was intentional or not. We'll have to wait until the area cools down and the fire inspectors can go through the site in detail." As information continued to trickle in, Isabella consulted with Dave before calling Comstock to advise him of her hunch that they were experiencing the result of a collaboration between Sean and Josef: Sean taking out the plane and Josef setting up the attempt on Chip. She then asked him to run a check on a Ray Radford, supposedly of the Metropolitan Police, and to call their contact at Scotland Yard to have their specialists brought in on the investigation. Switching gears she asked him to find them a US military aircraft that could pick them up and get them to Russia by early morning at the latest, and get them clearance to land in Moscow. Agreeing to make it happen, Comstock then advised her that Cameron had landed in Moscow about twenty minutes previously and was under surveillance. With Josef expected in an hour or so he'd see if he couldn't get Chip and her team in Moscow before morning, local time.

Dave, Fin, Jones and Chip, led by Isabella waited impatiently and with increasing concern for the guards who were still missing. Their bodies hadn't yet been discovered amongst the burnt debris and all Isabella's attempts to contact them had failed. Radford had heard nothing from his end either and appeared similarly concerned, although Isabella had the feeling he was more interested in keeping an eye on her and the others than in finding out what had happened. Finally she heard from Comstock who told her a plane would be with them within the hour and they'd have a fighter escort all the way to Moscow with the VVSC taking over in Russian air space.

Although not as fancy as either Sean's or Josef's Gulfstreams, the G-20H that had been commandeered from the US army was on track to have them in Moscow by sunup. Luckily it had been parked at the Mendenhall USAF base, waiting for the NATO Allied Commander who'd stopped over on his way to Germany. It was also comforting to see a pair of F-16 fighters on each side when they looked out the windows.

Exactly when they passed into Russian air space wasn't quite clear. The fighter changeover happened during the night and all they could see was the navigation lights almost motionless as they continued towards Moscow. As they flew into the breaking dawn each one of the team was struck by the city below them. "Wow! Take a look at that!" exclaimed Isabella. Echoing her sentiment, Fin said, "That is one gigantic city - or one gigantic urban sprawl. I've seen pictures but had no idea." "Be kinda nice to be just simple-minded tourists," said Dave. Chip was still sleeping and missed the view, which would have been fine with him even if he had been awake. His one focus was Shauna.

CHAPTER 28   MOSCOW

When they disembarked, Isabella called Comstock to check progress and received the news they'd all dreaded hearing, passing it on to the others. The cargo plane pilots had burned to death unable to get out because the cockpit door had been jammed closed and all four agents were still missing, presumed captured or dead.

The good news was that the London investigations had been taken over by detectives assigned by their FBI contact at Scotland Yard so they could be confident that that end of the op would be well covered.

Then, ordering them to stay out of sight for next the thirty minutes or so when they would be picked up and given a full briefing, she went searching for a restroom in the private annex where they'd been sequestered.

Dave, Jones, Fin, and Chip were huddled in conversation when an unsmiling Isabella returned. "Hold those thoughts guys. Comstock just filled me in on the latest. Our four agents have been found under a bridge on the outskirts of London. They'd been tortured before being executed so we don't know how much they gave up. For now we're not going to change any of our plans but we need to be even more alert. What is known so far suggests the policeman, Radford, we met at Heathrow is the one responsible. It seems he's been working for Josef for some time, mostly by stone-walling investigations into Russian Mafia activities in Britain." "You know," interjected Dave, "We were just talking about him before you came in. First off, his appearance at the crash site seemed a bit fortuitous, to say the least. And then, when he came to get me, Fin and Chip, it seemed like he recognized the gunman even though he said nothing. And finally, why was he so detached and unhelpful at the Cargo Terminal? Yeah, I'd say he's suspect."

"Well, he's definitely under scrutiny now," reassured Isabella. "Unfortunately, none of this was discovered until after he boarded a plane for Moscow. He's coming this way so we need to keep an extra eye out for him. At least I think we can assume that any agreement their might have been between Sean and Josef is no longer in place, if it ever was.

A large unmarked van pulled up to the Annex and a huge guy in civilian fatigues got out. Entering the building he was met by Isabella who'd rushed across the lobby to embrace him. Leading him back to the group she introduced him. "So, this is Norm - a good guy to stand behind." *He's certainly tall enough and looks tough enough so, yeah, I'm glad he's on our side,* thought Chip. The twenty equally tough looking guys already in the van, identified by Norm as Special Forces, made room for the agents and Chip for the drive to Red Square. As they neared their destination the crowds became thicker. They'd been told to expect hundreds, if not thousands, and were keenly aware that they had no idea who or how many would be on the different sides: although Comstock had relayed that Shauna's mother, accompanied by a large group of supporters from Scotland would be congregating to the south east of the Kremlin behind St Basil's Cathedral, making themselves as inconspicuous as possible.

Richardson was frantic to connect with Isabella. He had arrived a while back and, dressed as a local, had infiltrated the square to try and distinguish who was supporting whom. Those for Sean, or Josef, or Shauna and Chip. Although this last group was more difficult to identify, being a coalition of U.S. government personnel, both from the military and intelligence agencies, all dressed as locals, and a steadily growing swarm of ordinary individuals who were arriving from around the world to help ensure the couple's safe extraction; first from Red Square, then Moscow and finally Russia.

The corrupt Moscow authorities had bowed to Sean's bribes and threats and closed Red Square to all traffic. Guarding the approaches with barriers and armed police, with instructions to only allow access to the square for Sean and Josef and their followers, they had closed Lenin's tomb and the museum and the GUM entrances fronting the square. Although the store was accessible via other entrances, the closures were disappointing, if not infuriating, for tourists and locals alike, and the guards, overwhelmed by the crowds had found it impossible to distinguish followers from others and were letting anyone through, not even bothering to screen for weapons. Richardson wandered the chosen battleground: a gray brick plaza roughly the length of three football fields and one and a half wide. Bounded to the west by the enormous Kremlin behind its massive wall, Lenin's Mausoleum in front, the palace-sized GUM to the east, the State Historical Museum to the north and St Basil's cathedral to the south it was rapidly becoming full and Richardson was becoming more apprehensive at the scale of slaughter that might be in store.

Petrov and Shauna were riding with Josef in the back of his stretch Mercedes. With Josef's favorite guard riding shotgun beside him the boorish chauffeur was plowing through the throngs of tourists and locals without regard for life or limb, clearly broadcasting the Josef philosophy: *Get the fuck out of my way or suffer the consequences.* Pulling to a halt in an alley on the outskirts of the square where a large house loomed old and dirty - the once light gray stone now a mottled black, a few of its smaller turrets crumbling in disrepair – the driver left just enough room for the passengers to squeeze out and through a dark, well hidden doorway to the inside. Several of Josef's loyal followers appeared from upper floors to help him to the conference room. During the trip in the car, and even now, Josef ignored Shauna, not bothering to even acknowledge her presence even while being very specific about what he wanted Petrov to do to her. The guard who'd ridden with them helped Petrov drag Shauna down a corridor towards the back of the house, Josef's guttural voice bellowing behind them. "Make sure Sean knows his 'prize' will never be his!"

Memorizing as much of the house as he could as he and the guard marched Shauna between them, Petrov almost missed the guard's wink as he left them in what seemed to be a mud room. Noticing a door in the wall opposite, Petrov realized the wheels had been greased more than he'd realized and when a light tapping on the other door accompanied the receding guard's footsteps, put a hand over Shauna's mouth to silence her. From the other side of the door they heard, "It's dry in July." Responding with, "Drier in September," Petrov opened the door, gun in hand, ready. A nervous man carrying a large duffle bag stepped forward and embraced Petrov, saying, "It's sure good to see you, man, and not some trigger-happy Mafia killer. I've got to hand it to Comstock. He and his team really seem to be on top of everything, including this little tea party we're about to have." Petrov introduced Shauna to the make-up artist who had turned him into Vladimir.

"You know," said a doubtful, hesitant Shauna, "I'm just not sure about this . . . It seems so degrading and I feel more than vulnerable exposing myself like this." Doing his best to reassure her while at the same time emphasize how vital what she was about to embark on was, Petrov responded, "My sweet precious one, you've been through a lot I know, but unless you do this too, all that could have been for nothing. And there's no telling what you might have to face instead. Following through with this will put us in charge of ensuring the long term safety of you and Chip while bringing an end to Sean and Josef and their empires." Seeing her almost imperceptible nod, the make-up artist opened his duffle bag and started laying out the tools of his trade. He was ready to do what he did best - create magic.

Traveling a convoluted back route to avoid the unusually heavy police presence on the main routes, the panel van with Chip and company eventually pulled in behind a row of mixed-use premises close to the rear of the GUM building on the east side of Red Square. Having dropped off six snipers at the Kremlin so they could set up on the roof, with the blessing of the local administration, and cover the square from the west, it now stopped in front of a faded door. Norm climbed out carrying a package, crossed the sidewalk and quietly unlocked it. Entering he turned and, checking the street was clear first, waved across two of the Special Forces. After the three of them had swept the building making sure it was empty, the rest of the party joined them and got to work.

Norm who'd been charged with taking care of Chip, watched intently as the agents, with the help of a mild sedative, calmed Chip and finished dressing him. Isabella coached him through his performance one last time, suggesting minor tweaks while keeping him focused. Satisfied Chip was as prepared as he was going to be, she nodded to Norm, slipped on a worn coat and babushka and left for her next assignment. Moments later, having made sure the agents and remaining Special Forces were ready, Norm donned his own anonymous garb and departed too.

Isabella made her way through the gathering crowds filling the streets and encroaching Red Square itself. Ghosting through the barriers, pushing people aside and bumping her way through the horde as necessary she forged a path to the Kremlin itself. Reaching the gate nearest to her ultimate destination, she showed her credentials and after a short interaction between the guard and whoever was on the other end of the phone was escorted into the main building. Knocking loudly on a massive door, her escort then stepped aside so that when it opened Isabella came face to face with Yelena Pachenko, the Russian billionaire and wife to the Mayor of Moscow. Taking off her headscarf, Isabella said, "Hi." And the two old friends fell into each other's arms, giggling like school girls. "I'm so glad you came," said Yelena, carrying on without pause. "How long has it been? And don't you just hate what's happening out there? We have to rid Russia of this abomination and corruption." Agreeing, Isabella then asked, "So what's it like, living in the Kremlin with your new husband?" "Different," responded Yelena as arms around each other's waists they went inside. "Now, said Yelena, "Tell me everything."

An impatient man, he paced, he sat, he paced, he sat. One of his associates mumbled under his breath. "Why the fuck don't you stay in one place, you're driving us nuts?" Sean, catching the tone if not all the words, screamed, "Shut the fuck up or I'll shoot you right here!" waving his gun in the man's face. They all knew Sean was an unpredictable time bomb and not to be messed with, so they were warily eyeing the idiot mumbler who was pressing himself into the wall trying to disappear.

Sean was dressed in the gaudy tunic of late sixteen hundred's royalty. A couple of his men had had to help him button the heavily embroidered, ornate, satin jacket with balloon sleeves and stiff, stand-up collar. Thankfully for those around him he'd foregone the matching tights in favor of a pair of dark slacks. A medallion featuring an old coat of arms hung from a wide black ribbon draped around his neck and a sword in its scabbard was strapped at his waist, clanking against his leg as he walked up and down. He'd eagerly taken the hat and carefully put it on, crowned King Sean in his own mind. He looked absurd. But none of his minions would dare tell him that when asked how he looked. They just nodded, seemingly in approval. He'd been strutting around getting used to the attire, wishing that the old place had a mirror and eager for the next phase to begin.

Receiving word that his snipers were in position ready to decimate Josef's people if necessary, the excited Sean exited the State Historical Museum where he'd been waiting and made his way to the center of Red Square facing

Lenin's tomb, his followers streaming into the square behind him to take up position in front of the GUM building.

At Sean's appearance and his passage through the square, Josef moved to meet him. Too bulky and heavy for walking any distance or standing for any length of time, Josef sat on a throne on a wheeled platform and was pushed through the square to meet Sean. The two would-be-monarchs had arranged a classic face-off. Josef, wearing a rumpled, baggy suit over a not-so-white shirt would rather have been at home dining and drinking with his whores, but relished the idea of destroying and humiliating Sean so publicly. Sean's arrogance precluded any sense of possible defeat. And after so many years operating in the shadows building his global empire, he was so ready to be seen as the world leader he believed himself to be – brilliant, ruthless and all-conquering.

The hordes that had simply come to witness the spectacle and participate in the mayhem, if they could do so without risk, were squeezed out to the periphery. Richardson had found a perch near Lenin's Mausoleum and was looking for any advantage for Chip and Shauna. He assessed the two facing forces as evenly matched while Shauna's support seemed weak by comparison. Of course, he wasn't aware of the Shauna supporters from every continent massed with Janet behind St Basil's to the south east, or the contingents that were looping around through the streets to the east and north. Although mostly unarmed they had brought their hearts and their passion for Shauna and Chip and what they represented.

Suddenly, an eerie silence fell over the square and a nervous ripple ran through the massed crowd. Sean had started proceedings.

Puffing out his chest and taking what he thought to be a warrior's stance, Sean unsheathed and raised his sword. Wanting to savor every moment and be the center of attention for as long as he could, he silently held the pose until the people who couldn't see became restless and a gentle murmur disturbed the moment. "QUIET!" he screamed through the bullhorn held by a lackey. As he waited imperiously, composing himself to launch his speech, his second moment was hijacked too.

CHAPTER 29   SEPARATION

Several gunshots echoed around the square, obviously originating from the ranks behind him. Sean was apoplectic as the previously quietening crowd erupted with chatter, turning its attention to a disturbance near the south corner of the GUM building, at the corner of ul Ilyinka where it entered the square.

Above the blood rushing in his ears Sean heard: "Shauna. My Beloved Shauna. Where, where are you? Are you here? Are you here Shauna? I need you. I desperately need you." And he turned to see a ripple of movement as people stepped aside to create a path for the seven foot Chip, face tear-stained, arms outstretched, seemingly headed directly towards Sean. As many argued amongst themselves, surprised or impressed by his courage or stupidity in broadcasting his anguish and grief in the middle of a battlefield in waiting, those closest to him saw his chest explode a fraction before they heard the shot and he dropped. As the crowd froze in shock before pandemonium broke out, the shooter slid down behind the Kremlin wall and made his escape unnoticed while Chip bled into the grey brick.

As the frozen audience melted into movement to go to Chip's assistance they were roughly pushed aside by a wedge of armed men who quickly picked him up and spirited him away along ul Ilyinka. Once clear of the square, the two half-carrying, half-dragging him kept going while the rest of the group blocked the street to prevent pursuit. The square erupted as the witnesses shared their story and those who hadn't seen clamored for news. The consensus seemed to be that he'd be dead on arrival wherever he was going. *Good riddance,* thought some. *Who did this and why* thought others. And many simply wondered what the hell the fuss was about.

With Chip gone, the crowd on both sides of the square returned to the business at hand, waiting for the next act in the confrontation. As the general hubbub began to subside, a new sound intruded. A pitiful, repetitive cry of, "IP, IIIIIP . . . IIP, IIIIIP . . . IP," accompanied by a jangling discordant banging and scraping grew louder as the source progressed through the crowd along the Kremlin wall. People lining the path of this new disturbance were affected to varying degrees - shocked, disgusted, titillated, gleeful – spreading their observations until the square was rife with conflicting opinion.

Isabella, high inside The Kremlin, was following the events through high-powered binoculars. When she deemed the time was right, she handed them to Yelena, exclaiming, "I don't believe this! I really don't. After what just happened to Chip?" A quick look and Yelena handed the binoculars back, saying, "I can't bear it!" Isabella, fully aware of the plan in progress was trying to assess just where Yelena's loyalties lay. Yes, they were old friends but it had been years since they'd last seen each other and she needed to corroborate recent intelligence reports.

Isabella looked through the binoculars again, whispering to herself. "Oh you dear, dear thing . . . What torture it must be. Not just your own situation, but the not knowing for certain how Chip is. I'm sure you had to have heard the last shot fired and will have intuited that he was the one targeted . . . I'm so very sorry." "What was that?" asked Yelena. "Oh, just mumbling to myself. You know, sometimes I really don't like my job," replied Isabella, now completely engrossed in the drama playing out below.

The crowd parted progressively, opening a path to allow a mutilated Shauna to be prodded in Josef's direction by a circle of guards who kept her on course and upright. Arms spread wide, wrists tied to the ends of a massive log that straddled her shoulders forcing her head forward, legs encased up to the calves in buckets filled with cement, she shuffled along, continuing her cries, dragging her pain along with her until the guards stopped her beside Josef's platform.

Her once beautiful hair had been torn out by the roots in front and the rest ruthlessly cut. Her eyes had been stitched closed with two loops of thick thread binding her top lids to her cheeks. Her once irresistible mouth was bleeding, swollen and taped shut. It was no wonder her efforts to call her Love emerged as "IP." Yet she still tried so hard. Her back was like raw meat in places, flayed by severe lashings. She was naked except for a bloodied loin cloth, and the dried blood that encrusted the insides of her thighs. Her large breasts bared for the world to see were covered in the round raw marks of cigarette burns. Her whole body was filthy. Her suffering was plain to see, and hear.

Josef looked on her mutilation with satisfaction, impressed by Petrov's work, the perfect snub. This expensive gift that Sean had gone to so much trouble to deliver to him was now worthless. It sent just the right message: "This is what I think of you and your threats you worthless piece of shit!"

Initially enraged, ready to rip Josef apart on the spot, Sean realized that he didn't need an untouched Shauna to get what he wanted from her. In fact, now she no longer had any allure, he didn't really didn't need her at all. Just as long as she was dead and her power neutralized he could continue as if she'd never existed. And, much as he hated to admit it, he had to admire the way Josef had engineered it too. Not that that would stop Sean from crushing him. He bellowed with laughter, pointing at Josef and Shauna in turn, disconcerting his closest advisors and lieutenants who had no idea what was going on.

Oblivious to his outburst, Shauna stood before the crowd, humiliated, humbled, weak and unstable, fighting her own inner demons. Then, as Sean's demented cackling died, a nearly inaudible chant broke out around the edges of the square. As more and more of Shauna's supporters joined in the sound swelled and the words, "Shaauuuna, Shaauuuna, Shaauuuna, weee loooove yoooouuu, weee neeeed yoooouuu," soared to a crescendo before starting quietly all over again. And wave upon wave of sound built ever-louder above the square to crash ever softer upon the gathered flesh, without discrimination, touching those who loved her and those who hated her with equal impact. Even penetrating Shauna.

The inner pull to dwell on Chip had proven irresistible. How could she avoid thinking of him? Living without him even for such a short time was the worst pain she'd ever felt. It tore at her as if his presence had been ripped from her very flesh. She felt shredded, heavy, dark and powerless. Standing there inert, Shauna felt a call from within replacing her own cries for Chip. Faint at first, as it grew louder she recognized the sound of her core - "We love you. We need you." And the chant penetrated and she knew she would go on. She had to. She didn't know how, she just knew why. Lost in a new determination she felt herself prodded again and shuffled as directed. Dragging one heavy bucket and then the other, she eventually disappeared through an almost hidden door behind Lenin's tomb into the Kremlin itself. At Petrov's command, Richardson who'd left his vantage point near Lenin's

Tomb and caught Petrov's eye, was ushered inside and added to her entourage while two guards were left outside to make sure no one else followed.

Inside the Kremlin walls, the slow death march headed towards a secret underground tunnel, once used in one of the many wars of the 1600's. The passageway had been secretly excavated and ran under the Kremlin wall, and what was now a five lane highway to breach the final retaining wall above the Moskva River. From her vantage point in the Kremlin apartments, Isabella watched Shauna's painful progress. Checking the guards escorting her she was thankful to see Chenaugh in his role as Petrov and Richardson but dismayed by the identity of one of the others. "Sonofabitch! It sure looks like him." She blurted, right before her communicator started beeping. Excusing herself to use the restroom, she waited till she'd closed the door before answering. "Red Wing, this is Blackbird. Do you copy?" "This is Red Wing. Go ahead." "I've come home to roost close to our favorite fledging who is tangled up and can't fly." "Yes, I can see that," said Isabella. "You can?" "Yes and you need to know a double edged predator is on your tail. Black and white speckled head and brown chest feathers. Kill it or our fledging won't be able to fly." "I see it. Consider it done." With the disconnection a nervous Isabella was left hoping she'd really been understood.

Approaching the mouth of the tunnel opening onto the river, Shauna was down to her last reserves. She was spent. Her body ached, especially her shoulders. Richardson wished he could ease her discomfort. Two of the five guards made their way down to the temporary jetty that jutted out from the retaining wall to check on the boat moored there.

Petrov who'd hung back to secure the Kremlin end of the tunnel and talk to Isabella, stealthily made his way through the tunnel darkness towards the river. Sure enough, just as he'd feared, Radford, the salt-and-pepper-haired cop from London, wearing a brown jacket, was already creeping up behind Shauna, garrote stretched tight, ready to pounce. Petrov got to him first and broke his neck. Leaving his body where he'd lowered it to the tunnel floor, he joined Shauna. Looking out over the river, hidden from the guards on the jetty by the tunnel shadow, he was able to let 'Red Wing' know the 'fledging' was safe. A satisfied Isabella prepared to leave her friend and rejoin her colleagues.

Shauna had heard the quiet scuffle behind her but had neither the will nor the strength to turn around to see what was happening. Petrov came up behind her and inconspicuously rubbed her spine to soothe her. The two men at the boat waved for the three of them and Petrov and Richardson guided Shauna into the boat and got her seated. When queried about Radford, Petrov explained that he'd gone to guard the Kremlin entrance to the tunnel to cover their escape and would hook up with them later. The two thugs accepted the explanation with a shrug, revved the engine and headed to the middle of the river. Shauna, who just wanted to get this over with, thought of her darling Chip and cried. Telepathic communication was out of the question for the two of them. There were too many emotions clouding the transmissions.

The sounds of chanting in the square had reached Chip's ears. He was desperate to know what was happening out there - especially with Shauna - but his protectors told him they were clueless and would not divulge a smidgeon of information. Maddened, Chip blurted out, "You guys are useless." And then he apologized to them.

Norm had returned from his assignment on the other side of the square, and was squatted down near Chip, helping Dave, Jones and Fin clean him up. "You don't think you went overboard on that red stuff?" inquired Jones. "Hell no, man," retorted Dave. Remember, we wanted as many people as possible to believe him to be dead, or at least bleeding out. So shut up." "Godammit Norm, That bullet sure packed a hell of a wallop!" burst out Chip.

Pulling a brother of the bullet he'd used to shoot Chip out of his pocket, Norm showed it to him. Taking it, Chip rolled it around in his hand and scrutinized it carefully. "So this is what hit me like a freight train." "Hey, listen, Bro," said Norm, "That's why we gave you two vests. That and the fact that we needed the space between them to install the pouch of 'blood' and trigger mechanism, which I have to say you pulled at exactly the right time.

You did good." They got Chip to his feet and into fresh clothes - the ones he'd picked up at the airport in London. He was wobbly at first, but rapidly regained his equilibrium. "How's that for a guy who has just returned from the grave?" observed Fin. Nobody laughed, everyone feeling the pressure, concerned about getting Chip to safety without a hitch.

A coded knock and a careful Norm, gun in hand, opened the door to Isabella. She rushed by him to wrap her arms around Chip and stand on tiptoes to give him a kiss. Her cheeks were moist from crying. Chip took a long, hard look at her. "Shauna's dead, isn't she? And if she's not dead now, she soon will be. Isn't that so, Isabella?" he probed. She turned her head away as he shook her by the shoulders. "Answer me! Isn't that right?" *If you only knew Chip. Right now is one of the toughest moments of my life. But it has to be this way. You'll learn why later Chip dearest. For right now, please don't turn from me. We are on the same team even if it doesn't look like we're doing our job.*

Shaking off his grip, Isabella turned her back to him. Being ripped apart by her own emotions she couldn't face him. Taking a few moments to compose herself she turned to him and whispered, "Look, we must move. There's really no other choice. So I beg you to believe that you'll soon realize just why we've done what we've done and everything appears the way that it does."

Shrugging into command mode she then said. "We've got to get out of here before everything goes to hell. I've had word that both factions are in for some major surprises. The Russian army is moving in to support the police. They're going to take down Josef and strip him of his holdings in Moscow and around the world. They're hoping with the scale of the arrests they'll severely impair Mafia operations for the foreseeable future. As for Sean, there might be enough to hold him for disturbing the peace or inciting a riot, but that's going to depend on how this plays out and how effective his bribery is. Chances are the worst that will happen is that he'll be run out of Russia and his Russian assets seized. For my money that would be nowhere near good enough. I want that son of a bitch going down," she finished.

Isabella then laid out the plan. "We'll go back to the square and head towards St Basil's. If we keep to the periphery of the crowd, most should be too focused elsewhere to bother us. When we're behind St. Basil's we'll hook up with Shauna's mother, Janet, who is leading a mass of supporters from Scotland and other countries. They'll tuck us in their midst, inconspicuously of course, and then we'll all head towards the Dyuma and the North River Terminal where the recently reopened boatyard is located. Norm, you take the rear and place your snipers where you think best. It's good that the rest of your men are in the van scouting the area - too big a group might have made us too worthy of attention. Dave, you take point. Jones and Fin, you'll join me in protecting Chip . . . So let's get started. The van's been instructed to pick us up a couple miles from here if they think it's safe, if not, we'd better be prepared to do a lot more walking. Everybody clear?" They all nodded. "Let's be safe." was her final remark before opening the door and waving them out one by one.

They cautiously slipped into the street on their way to meet Janet. Norm had a final look round before following, making sure they'd left the house clean. His men had taken the trash with them in the van.

Chip and his protectors drifted along the edge of the crowd, avoiding confrontations, listening to the pompous, amplified Sean throw accusation after insult after abuse at Josef who could have been asleep given his silence. Sean, becoming ever more infuriated with Josef's lack of engagement, screamed, "I WILL HAVE YOUR RESPECT!" And signaled the attack. The deafening sound of exploding grenades and fire bombs was closely followed by the agonizing screams of people being torn apart and burning. Just as Isabella had predicted, all hell broke loose, gunfire and explosions sweeping the square.

Isabella and Norm pushed their group to run to safety with the rest of the fleeing non-combatants, concerned that the rapidly spreading chaos would prevent them from reaching Janet. And then they heard the tanks rumbling in from the north. The army had arrived.

Ignoring their presence, Sean led his men forward until they clashed hand-to-hand with Josef's at which point he ducked out and vanished in the ensuing mayhem. As the mob fought, littering the square with piles of broken and burnt bodies, troop carriers drove into the square from ul Ilyinka to create a cordon in front of St. Basil's. The army commander ordered squads to find Sean and Josef before directing the bulk of his troops, equipped with riot shields, to drive the mob north toward the tanks.

A grim Mayor of Moscow watched from the window of his quarters in the Kremlin. Disgusted by the spectacle he vowed that he would end the corruption - starting with himself. He'd already arranged to seize Josef's shipment of women and contraband cars once it docked. Although, as one last perk, he was still considering keeping one of the cars for himself, a gift he'd been promised by Josef.

Hooking up with Janet and her crowd of Shauna and Chip supporters, Isabella and Norm lead them south east away from the fighting. Stopping after several blocks to catch their collective breaths, Norm confirmed they were not being followed. As they discussed splitting up into smaller groups, Janet wondered whether the presence of her and the supporters had made any difference. She then reassured everyone that despite what they may have seen or heard, she could feel Shauna alive in her body, that their connection, though weak, was still unbroken. That Shauna could still be alive galvanized the gathering as Janet asked them to keep her feelings to themselves and thanked them for their dedication to bringing about a better way of living together. Saying she would continue the work back in Scotland, she said her goodbyes and joined Isabella, Norm, Chip and the agents as they set off for the Boatyard Terminal to ensure their safe escape from Moscow.

Revived by Janet's feeling for Shauna, Chip's heart, which had ached so much, was beating to a new rhythm - *Shau-na, Shau-na, Shau-na* - as flanked by Fin and Jones he followed Dave, Janet and Isabella, while the ever-watchful Norm brought up the rear.

Leaving Red Square they'd left behind the ornate, classical buildings so beloved of tourists for the long featureless blocks of the Stalin era: an ill-conceived attempt to house the masses at the expense of innumerable historical sites demolished in the process. Now, as they hurried toward the boatyard, they passed one of Moscow's botanical gardens. Drawn by the sparkling greenery amidst the grey drabness, Janet wistfully mused, "Wouldn't it be lovely to roll in the grass and stay awhile?" "You'll be resting on a sun-kissed beach soon enough, so let's keep moving and find that van," offered a more prosaic Norm.

Ahead they could hear the steady throb of traffic from a ten lane highway; another Stalin 'modernization' traded for irreplaceable imperial treasures. As they got closer what looked to be their van was just exiting the off-ramp.

Although their instinct was to run toward it, they dared not bring attention to themselves. Norm, hyper-alert as ever, scanned incessantly, machine pistol held ready under his overcoat. Since passing the gardens they'd become progressively integrated with the everyday foot traffic of a busy Moscow and Norm was intent on keeping a low profile. They advanced towards the van, which had pulled off the main highway and parked in a side road. Everyone was ready to take a load off and be driven the rest of the way. "Hey guys, slow down," called Norm. "Wait until I've made sure my troops are the ones inside."

As he approached, the van side door slid open and one of his buddies stared out, a huge grin on his face. "Whew, am I glad to see you," said Norm as he took a look inside, greeting his team. Turning he waved over the small group who'd been awaiting his signal. "OK guys, let's get the hell out of here." Sighs of relief filled the welcome van as they climbed in and made themselves comfortable. Janet warmly thanked Norm for the way he had made sure they were safe. "Hey, lady, it's not over till it's over and we still have to get to the Boatyard Terminal and make it out of Moscow and then out of Russia. You better hold off on your thanks for now."

CHAPTER 30 HORROR

"I'd love to get rid of those two," whispered Richardson, indicating the two thugs in the cockpit near the bow. "They wouldn't know what hit them. Side by side like a couple of ninepins." "I know, man," replied Petrov, "Me too, but we need them as witnesses." The boat was speeding along heading down the ever winding Moskva. Shauna grimaced in agony every time the bow collided with a wave. "Now's as good a time as any," said Petrov and he nonchalantly balanced his way towards Shauna who was sat straddling the bench in the middle of the boat.

Making as if to check her bindings were secure, Petrov carefully loosened the rope holding Shauna's right wrist to the log. Making sure there'd be enough room for her to slip her hand through, he slid a miniature air tank and mouthpiece into the space. Explaining the tank contained twenty minutes of oxygen, he checked that the guards up front were otherwise occupied, and got her to test the arrangement while he obscured their view.

Shauna easily managed to pull her hand through the loosened rope and get a couple of fingers around the tank, giving them both the confidence that she'd be able to do it. Pushing the tank back in place, he activated the built in sonar tracker and arranging the rope to look tight again, whispered for her to remember to take as big a breath as possible when she went overboard. "Richardson and I will make sure there are no distractions while you're being dumped. And the more relaxed you are, the easier it will be." Shauna mumbled, "OK." "I know you can do this," he finished and went back to his seat.

Sean and two of his men climbed into a sedan with black tinted windows - not unusual for a vehicle on the streets of Moscow. Sean had changed into an expensive, well-tailored suit, shirt and highly polished shoes. He looked more like a tourist than a native Muscovite as he contemplated his plan to lie low until the dust settled and he could re-emerge fresh and strong. Sean wasn't worried about rebuilding his empire. He wasn't thinking about starting over.

He was continuing on. He'd easily find the manpower he needed from the underbelly of society and had little concern for the carnage he'd left behind, or the men who'd been killed. He felt no guilt or responsibility for any of it.

In fact he was jubilant. He'd just heard that Josef had suffered a massive heart attack while he was being arrested by the army. *I guess when your time is up, it's fucking up,* he thought. *No surprises with that lard-loaf. I can just see all the vultures and scavengers fighting over his fortune - including some of the most highly placed Government officials. They'll pick his legacy clean. Not that it matters. With that asshole out of the way, there's nothing and no-one to stop me having whatever I want.* Sean rested his head on the seat back and indulged his fantasies, a wicked grin on his face.

But, first things first. He'd gotten hold of his long-time associate, Ramon Hernandez from Argentina, who'd worked his way up the ranks to head Moscow's International Business Center - which just happened to be close to the river on the west side of Moscow - another possible escape route for Sean should the time come. Ramon had come to Moscow obsessed with climbing the ladder of success in the money making paradise of post-cold-war Russia and was now owner of numerous businesses throughout Russia and its satellite states. He had also recently been elected CEO of the Moscow Financial Center - quite an honor for one so young. *I sure know how to pick 'em,* mused Sean. *Ramon has done wonders for me. He's increased my holdings a hundred fold and manages my portfolio for very little return, which is amazing considering how extensive our joint ventures are. Although I haven't seen any signs of him seeking to make any power plays so far, it's probably just as well that I've kept him on a short leash. Maybe he doesn't have the balls to go for total control or maybe he just doesn't think that big. Whatever. I'll ensure his loyalty when I turn my holdings over to him gratis, with the one proviso that I get to use my penthouse whenever I'm in town. He can do the paperwork and whatever else is necessary to keep my name out of the documentation. I'll even pay him handsomely for the privilege. You bet your ass money talks!*

They had arrived at the imposing Financial Center building, a sheer glass needle, seemingly disappearing in the clouds. He recollected that Ramon had a phenomenal office space on the top floor with living quarters in case he ever had to stay late. Part of Sean's plan was to use Ramon's apartment for a short stay. He needed to kick back for a spell and then move on. The car pulled to a stop in front of a huge front entrance that in contrast with the minimalist building was awash with elaborate, ornamental decoration. *So much for city planning. The whole city is a mish mash of styles shoved together. But it seems to work. Maybe corruption does have its advantages.* He got out of the car and gave his two men a wad of money. "Go have some fun. I'll call you when I need you. Probably in a few days." He turned and went into the building.

Sean had no idea how many different elevators it would take to reach Ramon's quarters. He hadn't been aware of any express ones. A funny thought crossed his mind as the elevator took off. *Wonder if this is one way to get to heaven?* Not that he'd ever end up there - nor did he give a rat's ass. When the elevator doors opened on the top floor, there stood a smiling Ramon slicking back his thick black hair. He reached out to Sean, giving him a handshake that would make Olympians quake in their Nikes.

At six foot five, large and commanding, Ramon was a man who won instant respect. He was impeccably dressed and his penetrating, no-nonsense dark brown eyes could easily intimidate the insecure or those who had something to hide. He was large for a Hispanic and many thought he had some other blood mixed in. He had been born and bred into wealth and his Argentinean roots had blessed him with a seductive Spanish accent and a aristocratic presence. He housed a rampant libido which he kept well fed by womanizing at the all-night clubs and bars in the heart of Moscow.

His wife, a gorgeous American, knew well this side of Ramon. Realizing early on that she couldn't change him, and being very wise, she knew she would never be enough for his huge appetite. So, she compromised with herself, settling for living in the lap of luxury, watching the nannies raise their two children, and enjoying the various privileges and titles that were bestowed on her. Both she and her husband considered themselves amongst the royalty of Moscow and made a memorable impression whenever they appeared in public together.

"Hey, man, you're looking fit and sassy. It sure is good to see you, particularly up here. This is incredible, my friend. I bet you can see the whole world. Now, what's it been? Two, three years?" Sean babbled. Ramon put a hand on his shoulder and showed him around the suite. He loved giving tours of his palace. Why not? Everywhere was glass. The office area shone with high-end ultra-modern furniture, including a one-of-a-kind desk that had been specially designed and built to suit Ramon's expansive personality.

"Listen, Sean," Ramon put his hand on Sean's arm while speaking. "I cancelled all my appointments for today when you called. Let's finish the tour, which I know you'll enjoy, and then head to the private restaurant where I've taken the liberty of ordering us a light snack before we go downtown later tonight for some fun. We have business to do and I always work better after I've eaten. What about you?" "Sounds good to me," said Sean, always ready to wheel and deal, and having no doubt hot pussy would be on the agenda, his memories of earlier all but erased. "All right amigo, let's do it!" Ramon went on. "Help yourself to anything you need. I've got just about everything you can think of including an assortment of clothes in different styles and sizes. Take what you fancy. Not that there's anything wrong with what you're wearing." *That's great,* thought Sean. *But what's with the clothes thing? Who keeps clothes in different sizes? Damn, is he gay?* Ramon kept his hand on Sean's arm leading him, way too intimately for Sean's comfort level, towards the living quarters.

The boat, the thugs still in the cockpit, was getting closer to the Boatyard Terminal. Petrov was more vigilant than ever, trying to get a fix on where they actually were, and if the coordinates they'd agreed on were close. He edged around Shauna in the middle of the boat and headed for the cockpit yelling, "Hey guys, slow down. Slow it down." One of the thugs turned around to listen then turned back to talk with his buddy. Petrov, anxious at their slow response yelled again, "Stop the goddamn boat! STOP THE BOAT!"

The thugs throttled it back so quickly that Petrov lost his balance, nearly pitching overboard. "YOU CLUMSY SONS OF BITCHES!" screamed Petrov, stressed and angry. Pissed at being cursed, the thugs went for their guns to show him who was boss. But Petrov was faster. "I dare you," was all he had to say. "It's not safe to get any closer to the boatyard – there are too many people who could see us. So, we're going to dump her here where it's plenty deep enough. Nobody will ever find her. She's too weighted down for the currents and with the help of the bottom-feeders she'll decompose right here with the rest of the crap."

The thugs laughed and stepped towards Shauna and the four of them threw her overboard. As the thugs went back to the cockpit in the bow, Petrov dropped a miniature sonar beacon into the water to mark where Shauna had been tossed, just to be on the safe side, and shouted to the thugs to drop him and his partner off on the bank where they had business to attend to.

Chenaugh and Richardson watched the boat till it disappeared around the next bend in the river, Chenaugh thankfully watching his life as Petrov disappear with it. Once satisfied that they were safe and unobserved they scrambled up the rocky embankment, Chenaugh's thoughts totally focused on the well-being of Shauna. He was praying that everything would go smoothly and according to plan - that at least one of the sonar trackers would do its job.

Shauna could not believe how fast she was falling or how deep the water was. She just kept falling as the weight of the buckets dragged her ever downward. She thanked herself again for her huge lung capacity developed over the course of many years training as a singer. She knew that as long as she was falling she couldn't risk trying to free the canister in case the movement pulled it out of her grasp. Finally the buckets made contact with the river bottom with such a force she thought maybe some bones had been broken. She hoped not. She hoped her muscles had taken the brunt of the impact. Her body was crying out for oxygen and she was intensely aware of the water pressing against her chest. She went to work to free herself from the rope, but what had seemed relatively easy in the boat now seemed exceedingly difficult. She could feel the stirrings of panic as her chest hammered for air and she had to consciously force her mouth to stay shut. She could feel the urge to breathe and willed herself to quiet down, thankful to be alive, and focused on releasing the canister.

Suddenly her wrist came free but the canister was plucked from her grasp by the still heavy log as it was released by the movement. She watched in dismay out of the corner of her eye as the canister tumbled in slow motion to the river bed below her. Despairingly she sucked back sobs. She didn't want to die. No, no, no. Especially not like this - not anytime, really. She had to try something, but the burning in her lungs was becoming unbearable. *If only I could see,* she thought, *but what good would that do?* Shauna could feel herself getting light headed and losing consciousness. Her one last thought was: *Where are my extra-terrestrial saviors?"* Her body went limp.

"Come on. Get that gear over here. We'd better not be too late," he said, pulling at the disgusting, artfully crafted, face mask until part of it detached revealing the water wrinkled mouth of the drowning woman. He then yanked off his own mask and breathed into her mouth, giving her his best attempt

at resuscitation. "Come on. Come on, respond will you!" "P-L-E-A-S-E," chorused three more divers behind their masks, barely able to see her in the murky depths. There was no response. They hauled an extra oxygen tank into position and clamped a diver's mask on her face before slowly increasing the oxygen levels. The four scuba divers frantically prayed for Shauna to respond, a second feeling like a minute and a minute like an hour. Desperate for any sign of life they began to tow her to shore, taking it in turns to do the heavy lifting

Shauna felt like she was in another dimension, weightless and floating wherever she pleased. She was convinced that she had leapt into a different place in space and time. Her shoulders bore no weight. What pleasure to lie where she was - wherever it was - and lean back unencumbered. Her arms felt detached from the rest of her. What was happening? She felt that whatever or wherever she was, this was totally sublime - a soft suspension. She heard her name being called from far, far away and shook her head. She didn't want to be interrupted. But the sound became louder and, lid fluttering, she very slightly opened one eye. She tried to move but couldn't and opened both eyes in panic, silently screaming at what she saw.

Black edges surrounding her face like she was in a small prison with an impenetrable blur outside. Something popped out of her mouth but was as quickly pushed back in and held in place. Totally disoriented she didn't struggle, just relaxed in the buoyancy, feeling herself being propelled forward. And then she was lying flat on her back legs raised and the prison window was removed and her mouth was empty and she was breathing normally

"That was a close call." She heard. "No, don't talk Shauna." And she felt her body being cleaned and gently rubbed with a thick lotion and the pain in her neck, shoulders and wrists began to ease and then her body began tingling, almost unbearably and she realized pins and needles as she slowly came back to life all over. Daring to open her eyes again she found herself surrounded by four figures in wetsuits going about their various tasks and heard a thunk, thunk, thunking as two of them loosened the plaster around her feet by whacking the buckets. Once free, her feet, ankles and calves received the same gentle treatment as the rest of her had.

With her more or less soothed all over, the divers introduced themselves as four of the SEALs who had been watching over her at the docks in Houston: Clyde, Al, John and Ken. They then dressed her with clothes from a large waterproof duffle bag. The slacks and shirt were too big and they'd forgotten underwear, but Shauna thought that was probably just as well. As they'd had to guess at sizes she was relieved that the felt boots fit so well.

Helping her stand, they steadied her as they wrapped her in a large overcoat and tucked her hair into a babushka. "It feels like I have ice in my veins but this coat is wonderful. Thanks so much for what you're doing for me."

Taking turns, so at least one of them could keep an eye on a still unsteady Shauna, they quickly stripped out of their scuba suits and into street clothing, placed the gear and suits in duffle bags, and loaded everything into their nearby car.

"I'm beginning to get the hang of it - this walking thing. I'll have my landlubber legs back in no time," smiled Shauna as she was helped to the car and was driven to the Imperial Hotel where they'd made reservations for a penthouse suite. As they drove, Clyde apologized for the delay in rescuing her, explaining that it was only the sonar trackers that had led them to the right neighborhood, a long way from the coordinates they'd been given. Not that he blamed Chenaugh. These things happened in hostile environments.

The hotel was beautiful, a symphony of understated elegance. Clyde took care of registration as the rest were escorted to their three room suite. Clyde joined them soon after. "You take the master suite and we'll flop here and in the other bedroom with one of us just outside your door at all times," he said. "Hopefully you'll find everything is to your liking, but if you need anything else just holler and we'll get it for you. We think you need to be pampered." "How long will we be here?" asked Shauna. "We have to be at the Boatyard Terminal at four o'clock tomorrow and we'd like for you to get plenty of rest before then." Clyde replied, continuing, "We've arranged for one of the housekeeping staff to take care of you and Al and I are going to find you some real clothes. While we're gone, make yourself at home. Take a bath, eat - I imagine you're starving so order whatever you want – or just relax. We'll be back in no time." Making a note of Shauna's sizes, Clyde and Al left, on their way out the door as Shauna's helper arrived.

Introducing herself, Shauna led her new best friend, Ivanka, into the master suite and they were soon chatting like they'd known each other for years as Ivanka prepared the bath. Climbing into the tub and sinking into the relaxing, hot bubbly water, Shauna suddenly realized just how exhausted she was and, as Ivanka bathed her, drifted into a deep sleep, not even having enough energy to dream. Probably just as well.

CHAPTER 31 ADDITION

Excited, Clyde and Al entered the suite loaded with packages. So many they had to peer round them to see where they were going. As they dropped their purchases on one of the oversized couches, Clyde commented, "It's fun to have a Visa Card courtesy of the Government." "This is Ivanka," introduced John, a subtle warning to Clyde and Al to be careful what they said. Taking the hint, Clyde and Al quickly ran through what they'd bought and where, careful to not to divulge too much, then asked how Shauna was doing. "Well," said Ivanka, "The poor dear fell asleep during bath. Your friends help me get her out. We dried her and put her to bed. I do not think she woke once." "Has she had anything to drink?" asked Clyde. Ivanka shook her head. "Nothing." Clyde and Al checked in on her. Gazing at the sleeping wonder fondly, Al commented, "She sure is beautiful, huh?" "Yep, sure is," agreed Clyde. "Pity we need to wake her to do something about her dehydration."

Shauna had to hack her way through layer upon layer of dense grogginess - it felt like a battle she really didn't want to win. Reaching the final layer, she could feel her body, stiff and aching, before she opened her eyes, slowly lifted herself to rest on her elbows and blearily looked around. Not recognizing anything, even the two men peering down at her were strangers. "I really must have been out-of-it," she observed. "I remember the horror of nearly drowning, which I'd just as soon forget, and some heroic Navy SEALs coming to my rescue just in the nick of time. So I'm guessing you're those blessed rescuers. Now, if you've told me already I apologize, but can you tell me where I am and who you are?" "The Imperial Hotel in downtown Moscow," replied Al. "I'm Al and this is Clyde. Over there is John, the ugly one on the right, and Ken, the even uglier one on the left." Taking the slights in stride, Ken and John, on guard duty, nodded and smiled. Whereas before the four had been shadowy figures stamped from the same mold, now, Shauna could distinguish one from the other. There were still similarities: buzz-cuts, clean shaven faces and lean, muscular frames a couple of inches over six feet, although Clyde, the tallest, was probably closer to six-six than six feet. He was also the good looking one. She felt enormously attracted.

228

Bold, chiseled features and penetrating, sparkling, sea blue eyes: he also seemed to be the one in command.

Shauna felt him drawn to her too. He might be an expert at hiding his feelings from most people, but Shauna wasn't most people. Sitting up, holding the covers against her with one hand, she unwrapped the towel from her head and tossing it tried to arrange her unruly, still-damp hair. "Here, let me help," said Clyde. Sitting beside her and scooting her over to lean against him, he began running his fingers through her hair, gently untangling it in the process. His touch was exquisite and she allowed herself to relax into it. Closing her eyes she almost began purring.

Some time later, her thirst got the better of her and she picked out a couple of juices and sipped at them. The SEALs, crowded around the doorway, chorused that she'd have to do better than that and Clyde stopped his stroking long enough to open a bottle of water and hand it to her. Under the SEALs' watchful eyes, she gulped it down. They clapped when she finished and she smiled, touched by how supportive they were and pleased they were happy to let her process the ordeal at her own pace.

Shauna asked Ivanka if it was possible to make the room a little warmer as she still felt cold. Al jumped to take care of it, happy to fulfill her wishes despite feeling himself sweating in the already hot suite.

"Sounds like you're ready for more sleep," said Clyde, "We'll leave you alone." "Actually, no," said Shauna, "I'm just realizing how hungry I am." "We have chicken soup today," offered Ivanka. At Shauna's nod, Ivanka said she'd be right back and left the room. The four SEALs gathered around Shauna and propped her up with more pillows, fussing with the arrangement until Ivanka returned carrying a room service tray holding a big bowl of soup with crackers.

Taking the tray from her, Clyde rested it on the night stand and proceeded to spoon feed Shauna. Every so often he would gently dab her mouth with a napkin. The others watched longing for a turn so they could be that close. "I must say I'm really enjoying the soup and the attention you're giving me. It seems such a long time since I've been so pampered. Thanks." And she immediately thought of her beloved Chip. "Well Ma'am," said John, who had said very little so far, "right now we only have one mission. To devote every moment we have to you." And snapping to attention he saluted her. "Not sure whether he was serious or having fun, Shauna saluted back, saying, "Right now, I am honored to be your mission, Sir! I couldn't ask for anything better. But, Oh my, I think your mission is a little sleepy . . ." And just like that Shauna crashed into the depths of unconscious. Depths that this time, thankfully, were not watery ones.

The SEALs, her saviors, rushed to make her as comfortable as possible. Removing some of the pillows and straightening the covers that slipped in the process they couldn't help but notice her nakedness. Marveling at the sight, the four stood at this altar of female flesh, a temple of human treasure: heart, blood, bone and an indomitable spirit. The four, and especially Clyde, were so captivated by Shauna's aura that they became impregnated at the molecular level with a fresh sense of the value of life. That doing the right thing was not about being righteous, it was about being human. They tried not to wake her as they re-arranged the covers - one of their tougher assignments.

"I guess our shopping spree goodies will have to wait. Probably just as well. We should get some shut eye too," whispered Clyde as he ushered the team out of the room. Thanking Ivanka they showed her out and then made themselves comfortable, strategically positioned as the first and maybe last lines of defense. Clyde longed to climb into bed next to Shauna. Just to feel her warmth, smell her hair and to hear her deep breathing. He had fallen in love with her fast. He hoped it didn't show too much, but then why should he feel embarrassed? The love he felt was one of giving with no expectation. Although his heart had been broken many times, he still had that capacity to give without measure. Not that anyone would guess it from his demanding, competent practicality. Before he could spiral into dispiriting reminiscences of past heartaches, he was fast asleep.

Once the van had pulled onto the highway heading for the boatyard, Janet had told them about Comstock's plan for them to recuperate in Jamaica. Now, pulled off the road far enough into a stand of trees to be hidden from all but the most alert eyes, the group was taking a break, eating and drinking and talking about life after Moscow. Norm, who'd been huddled with his troops, interrupted to let them know they were way ahead of schedule - it seemed they weren't going to need the time they'd allowed for contingencies – and suggested everyone stay in the van until they could board the boat the next day. Unanimously agreeing, accepting that the undergrowth outside was sufficient to cover bathroom breaks, they set about bedding down. It wasn't easy for them all to get comfortable, but with everyone cooperating they finally managed it and each eventually claimed sleep.

Sean and Ramon were in the heart of downtown Moscow, trolling the upscale clubs and adult lounges, hoisting drinks and checking out the merchandise. Sean was feeling so good, his belly full of fine food, rare delicacies, delectable wines, and now vodka on the rocks. So far he'd had rough and tumble sex with a pretty, young, fiery redhead who'd seemed to like it that way, not that he minded if all women liked was his money, as long as he was getting some - or more. His good mood had started over the business snack with Ramon which had gone far better than he'd imagined it would. All the property transfers were completed and Ramon had promised to at least double Sean's earnings within six months. Their handshake on the deal had involved all four hands and Sean wondered if he was beginning to like this kind of human contact. After all, up till now he'd always been contemptuous of men, and brutal with women.

Now, between venues, Sean, immune to thoughts of danger, was pleasantly buzzed and relaxed with Ramon's touch. When they'd started out, Ramon's arm draped over his shoulder as they walked, he'd been real uncomfortable. Now, having realized that it was common practice in Latin cultures and having consumed enough alcohol he occasionally touched Ramon too. Suddenly, thinking of his two men, he decided to check on them, just because he felt like it. Confirming he wouldn't be needing them for a few days he wished them happy hunting. Glad to be free of his demands, hoping he wouldn't be calling every five minutes, the two flunkies readily hunted happily.

"Well my good friend," said Sean slapping Ramon on the back. "My dick could do with some more pussy. Can you recommend someone who likes it rough and experimental, if you get my drift?" He winked at Ramon. "Sure thing, my friend." And Ramon led them into a nearby bar. Looking around Ramon said, "That one. She's red hot and very much in demand. Let me bring her to you." The scantily dressed girl walked towards Sean with a sensuous roll of the hips, her breasts swinging to the sway. Her brown eyes promised submission, her shiny red, cute mouth spoke of delicious depravity. Reaching Sean she radiated attraction. *And why wouldn't she?*

thought Sean, and turning to Ramon said, "I'll see you in a little while - if I'm still standing." And they laughed.

Lily really was hot. She liked it rough and she played rough too. At that moment she had Sean's prick squeezed between her breasts and was pumping him up and down. She'd started by stripping off his boxers and violently sucking him, using her deft fingers to squeeze what she couldn't engulf. Now he grabbed her and tossing her on the bed, climbed on top. Taking the leather thongs dangling from the bedpost he lashed her wrists to the headboard. She let him willingly. He looked down at her and smirked. "You make one hell of a prisoner, girlie." He wedged a knee between her legs, giving her such a whack that she cried out. This was a turn on for him. Opening her legs further, he reached for her throat, squeezing. She immediately started turning bright red. Knowing many whores faked it and could make themselves turn red on a dime, he carried on.

Why he got such a sexual thrill from dominance and power was a mystery to him, not that he thought about it that much. He only knew that riding the line between pleasure and pain was an erotic button that once pushed could only be reset by release. Grabbing his erection he gave it a few pumps, oblivious to the fact that the girl had gone totally limp in his hand, and poked at her crotch trying to find her hole in the thick patch of pubic hair. "Aha. There you are you little devil." But pushing forward ready to impale her and fuck her brains out he registered the blue-lipped, white-faced, lifeless form beneath him. Leaping back as if scalded, his prick shrank to nothing. At first scared, he hesitantly reached out and checked her pulse, then frantically bent over her mouth to see if she was breathing. Nothing. *Fuck, the bitch has gone and died on me. What the hell? Just as well I pulled away in time. No DNA. I better get out of here.*

He pulled the top sheet over the dead girl's body, got dressed and strolled out to the bar area to find Ramon, making up a story as he went. He looked around the now crowded place and couldn't find Ramon. "Hey, you," he said to the bartender, "Gimme a napkin and pen. Now!" Sean rapidly jotted down a note to Ramon thanking him and apologizing for his abrupt departure, explaining that a business emergency required him to leave town immediately. Sean gave the napkin back to the bartender with a generous tip, telling him to give it to Ramon or else. Just then he remembered he'd left the girl tied up. In a quandary he paused for a moment before deciding: *To hell with it, that's minor.*

Heading for the exit he whipped his phone out. "Hey guys, pick me up at the Moscow Restaurant and Bar, now! It's just east of the Kremlin. Make it snappy 'cos I'll be waiting outside . . . I don't give a fuck! Just pack up your peckers and get here." The call could not have come at a worse time, but there was no way they were going to let their orgasms wither on the vine. Staying to hustle the whores for rapid release they were still out the door, pants flapping, money fluttering behind them and on their way in minutes.

Out on the sidewalk Sean called his pilot, ordering him to round up the crew and make sure the plane was fueled. "File a flight plan to wherever the fuck you like, I'll tell you where we're going when I get on board . . . Yes, yes. I know it's illegal . . . You'll just have to be extra sharp . . . Look asshole, if you don't feel up to it, I'll find someone else and drop you on your head from thirty-thousand feet . . . Yeah, I fucking thought so, you prick." Sean disconnected and paced back and forth to cool down and keep warm until his guys picked him up. "Get to the plane quick." They sped to their destination in uncomfortable silence. The more miles they covered, the further away were any thoughts of the dead girl. Sean's attention had completely turned to his pending trip. He was traveling light in every way.

It was nine a.m. as Isabella, Janet and Dave stood waiting to board the ship scheduled to depart later that afternoon. Isabella had decided it was wise to board early as there were only ten staterooms on the cargo vessel. They'd been fortunate that Chenaugh was able to call in a favor and get them two, but as the voyage had become something of a treat for the local wealthy who enjoyed the isolation and the impeccable food and service, she wanted to be sure a bribe didn't trump there reservations. "I hope Chenaugh and Richardson show up soon with the package," said a concerned Isabella. "I won't relax until we're all on board and headed for Sweden." "I'm with you," responded a jittery Janet.

They had eight tickets for the two staterooms. Chip, Shauna and Chenaugh would be in one, with Clyde and John of the SEALs on guard. Isabella, Richardson and Janet would be in the other. It wasn't an accident that the travelers were the same people who would be going to Jamaica. Jones, Fin and Dave had been flown home and the SEALs, Ken and Al, were going back to their unit.

Norm, who'd stayed to keep watch until the SEALs arrived, had had
to slip away when it was discovered that Chip had lost his papers - not
surprising under the circumstances but exceptionally inconvenient. Chip
himself had been locked away by the port authorities in a cramped, dingy
room. From where he sat he could just make out the boarding ramp through
a small dirty window. An armed guard had been posted outside and every
now and again eyed him warily through an observation window in the door.
As Chip had suspected, Russians in general were not fond of Americans
and especially Americans without papers. Chip looked at his watch, being
careful to not make any sudden moves. *It's already nearly two o'clock, man.
Come on Norm. You can do this, Bro.* Chip was a nervous wreck. Worry about
Shauna had tied him in knots and camping out in the van and the endless
trip to the boat dock hadn't helped. *Why won't anyone tell me about Shauna?
Because she's dead? Because I might inadvertently let on she's alive? I've not felt
her dead though, even in the worst moments. I'll have to trust myself and stick
with that! Damn, what else are we going to be blindsided with? Fucking pull
yourself together!* He finally admonished himself.

When Isabella had informed Comstock about the problem with Chip's
papers, he hadn't been unduly worried. He said he'd work it from his end and
see if couldn't get the Russians to send something through to the boatyard
direct. Everything else seemed to be going smoothly too. So as long as neither
Chip nor Shauna knew for certain that the other was alive before they left
Russia the operation should be fine.

Isolated, Chip wondered if now might be a good time to try thought-
speak with Shauna. He knew distractions of any kind seemed to interfere
with the transmissions but given he had nothing better to do he thought
it worth the effort. Sitting up straight, closing his eyes he made himself
turn inwards, becoming totally focused. He wept when he felt the strong
connection with Shauna again. Unable to stop crying, he released all the pain
and suffering he had been through - the dark pull of doubt, the thoughts that
Shauna was possibly dead and the despair that had grown like a cancer in
response. The tears washed him clean. And he felt Shauna cleansing herself
with tears too. They took their time to re-experience one another. No other
nourishment more potent.

Becoming merged, a seamless form with more power than either one
individually, they felt the depths of their remote communion. Shauna shared
her feeling for Clyde and how Chip would enjoy him too. *"There's unlimited
joy for us and he's such a special and unique person that you and I can now have*

even more together." Rededicating themselves to each other and their purpose, looking forward to being together soon, to fulfilling Chip's promise, with a renewed passion even stronger than before, he blessed her and Clyde together.

Stirring from connecting with Chip, Shauna noticed Clyde awake on the nearby sofa. And then the other three entered the bedroom yawning sleepily and came to stand by the bed. "I'm so sorry if I woke you all up," said a repentant Shauna. "No problem. We're trained to be light sleepers," was Clyde's response, aiming to set her at ease. "How are you feeling?"

"Well, believe it or not, I feel wonderful. I was visited by four men last night who were guided to me by the call I put out. They came to me and worshiped at my side - worshiped and honored the re-birth of a whole new Shauna - humbly paying homage at the sacred altar of my human form. Do you understand? These four wise men could only have done what they did because they were seeking someone like themselves, pure of heart and sacred." Shauna's eyes pricked with tears and her mouth trembled as she spoke through her deep passion. "You each came bearing the greatest gift, yourself, to share you with me. You have helped transform me into a more potent person. I am much stronger now because of your innocent adoration of the real Shauna."

Shauna took a deep breath and continued. "Thanks to you, I'm readier and happier than ever to step up to a greater and more joyful life. I need and want you with me." Pausing a few moments to let this sink in, she then told them her plans. "Once I'm out of Moscow, I'll be going to Jamaica to recuperate. You're more than welcome to come with me. A couple of weeks after that I'll be going on to Scotland where a large group of people from all over the world who have a desire for a completely new life are already gathered. If any of you are married . . ." Three nodded, Clyde didn't . . . "bring your wives with you, if you decide to come and they want to. Whatever you choose though, know what special people you are and how truly thankful I am for you." Shauna wiped away her tears as she looked at each one of them with her penetrating gaze. Spontaneously she got out of bed and standing in her bare feet on tip toes, that had healed nicely, kissed each SEAL on both cheeks. When she stood in front of Clyde, his eyes and heart were so open to her that she reached up and kissed him lightly on the mouth, flooding them both with the heat of a passion far beyond the sexual.

"That's a lot to think about," remarked Al. "Thinking isn't going to do it for us," replied Ken. "Actually there really is nothing to think about," added Clyde. "We delude ourselves with our imperfect thinking so let's keep it simple shall we," said Shauna. "We have a second brain in our stomachs, which may sound crazy but has been scientifically proven. You've all heard the expression, 'I have a gut feeling', well, that's what I'm talking about." "You mean our bodies can override our thinking?" asked John. "Yes," confirmed Shauna. "Our gut feelings never lie. Our heads can talk us into or out of anything." "Let's go with our guts then!" exclaimed an excited Clyde. Of course, they all knew what his gut was telling him.

"Enough talk," interrupted Shauna, "I'd like some food and I'm a wee bit curious about all those packages you brought in. Besides, my feet are cold on this flooring and I'm wondering . . ." Al jumped up and ran to the packages, fumbling in them to eventually pull out a pair of sports shoes. He brought them to Shauna, and had her sit in one of the lounge chairs while he carefully put them on her feet. She smiled and held her legs up so they could all see. "Wow, will you look at those legs!" commented John. They all agreed. Shauna laughed and moved her legs up and down saying, "I agree too." And they all laughed. *What fun it is to be with them,* reflected Shauna who felt lighthearted and simple as a young child. "So is this it then? I go around in my robe and trainers?"

Pretty soon all the packages were open and their contents piled on the bed. Clyde, who had put his arm around Shauna and was stroking her hair fondly and smoothing it behind her ear, suggested, "Now that we're done with the fashion show, let's order brunch." Shauna, who was reveling in Clyde's touch, felt let down when went to get the menu and when they'd all ordered, took him aside and whispered, "I'd like to make love to you, and I think you feel the same about me. But I need birth control pills. Would you get some from the pharmacy downstairs or find some wherever?" Clyde couldn't believe what he was hearing. He felt like he must be dreaming and sat astonished as Shauna continued, "I have a clean bill of health, if you get what I mean, and I just know you do too. Besides I hate condoms." "I-I-t w-wasn't th-that," stammered Clyde. "I-I'm just surprised. Of course I'll get what you want - even if it means selling the shoes off my feet and giving the pharmacist the shirt off my back." He made a dash for the door. "Where's he off to?" queried the others. "Oh he'll be back in just a bit," answered Shauna mischievously.

By the time he got back the food had arrived and everyone was sat round the table eating. "Come get your food," said Shauna. *I'd rather eat you,* thought an excited Clyde. It wasn't food he was craving right now. He picked at his plate thinking that everyone was eating in slow motion and brunch would never end. *I can't stand the waiting,* thought a tortured Clyde. *I've been making myself nervous and irritable. I hope it hasn't shown on the outside yet but I bet that Shauna can feel it anyway. Man, I've got to stop being so damned self-centered. It's such a miserable place to be . . . So how about I just enjoy everybody and jump in.* Feeling his change immediately, proud of him, Shauna was reassured that what she had seen in him really was the raw material that could be transmuted into a higher life.

Relishing her SEALs and the aromatic smell and taste of coffee Shauna began to experience a caffeine buzz. "This stuff sure has a kick to it!" she declared before motioning Clyde to follow her to the bedroom. The others knew what was on the agenda but were happy for Clyde, even if it was because they'd rationalized that he was unmarried and they weren't.

Once in the bedroom Clyde told Shauna how nervous he was. She in turn helped him relax by thanking him for his honesty. Noticing she was somehow different, even more beautiful, he observed, "You look more radiant and beautiful than ever and I don't think it's the coffee either." "Thank you, Precious", replied Shauna as she boldly and fluidly untied her robe letting it fall loose around her glowing body. She eased up to Clyde and started unbuttoning his shirt and unbuckling his belt. Clearing his throat he said, "If you'll excuse me, I need to use the restroom." "Help yourself, but before I forget, let me have the pills so I can take a couple and get back on schedule with them."

Clyde seemed to take a long time in the bathroom, fixated on whether he should return naked or with a towel round his waist. Opting for the towel he finally made his entrance and stood sheepishly, not knowing quite where to look as Shauna lay on the bed naked. She smiled tenderly recognizing his discomfort, then reached out and yanked the towel away in one deft motion. His first response was to cover his crotch with his hands as she started to look him over but he didn't. Standing, Shauna lightly touched his well-toned shoulders with a knowing caress that drifted down to his waist. Boldly dropping to her knees she slid her hands behind his thighs and gently pressed him forward to her mouth. The tip of her tongue came out and gently licked his enlarged and hardened cockhead. Shauna liked the taste and smell of him. She got up and slowly walked behind him, running her fingers around his body, liking what she saw.

He seemed to be perfectly formed in the eyes of this expert. His feet especially pleased her; narrow and long with wonderfully shaped toes. "Clyde, you're in splendid shape and obviously take good care of yourself. I especially like your buttocks and we'll have fun with these beauties," said Shauna, pointing to his feet. She could tell he was pleased by her evaluation.

Clyde had no idea what a ride he was in for. Just the thought of making love to her aroused him, plus getting glimpses of her when he thought she wasn't looking. He looked down at his continually swelling prick. "Let it do what it knows what to do," remarked a light-hearted Shauna. Clyde blushed.

"I've heard pricks are as individual and unique as fingerprints and yours is just the right size and shape for me," said Shauna. Clyde relaxed. "You know just how to make me feel good. And the more you admire me the hotter I'm getting which is great because it's you I want to please," said Clyde. "Oh, Clyde," Shauna beckoned him to the bed where she was half sitting against the head board, her legs spread apart. "You have no idea how happy you just made me feel!" Staring at the big, warm-hearted man who was rough, tough and ripped, and yet seemingly so tender and gentle, she gave in to her arousal.

Becoming increasingly turned on by Clyde's inexperience and vulnerability, Shauna drew him into her erotic orbit. Encouraging him to voice his desires and respond to hers, she showed him the ecstasy of the escalating arousal of two bodies reciprocating desire until they were both consumed by an explosion of release – in her case two.

Clyde had collapsed on Shauna and was about ready to pull out, when Shauna protested. "Oh please leave it in as long as you can." She could hardly speak she was so out of breath. As she felt his penis slipping, she grabbed a nearby towel ready for their juices to flow but very little did. *Well, that will become more abundant the more we make love.* She thought. *Soon he'll be so stoked!* "Wonderful, wonderful, wonderful, Sir Clyde." But Clyde was spent and had fallen asleep. Gently sliding from under him, Shauna turned over on her stomach, still feeling the vibrations of two hefty orgasms and a pulsating vagina. Nodding off fast she thought that next time she'd show him the benefit of a few post-orgasmic niceties to enrich their shimmering sexual experience as opposed to such an abrupt end which tended to tarnish the afterglow.

Woken at noon, Shauna kissed Clyde awake from a sleep born of exhaustion and transformative sex. Careful not to turn each other on too much – a case of mind over matter, Shauna reminded Clyde, who was reluctant to put his clothes on, that this hadn't been a one night stand. And they hurriedly got ready, and walked into the living room where the other three SEALs stopped what they were doing to look at them. Shauna casually asked how everyone was doing. She wasn't embarrassed. For what? Clyde, taking her lead, acted like Mr. Cool, busying himself with packing his belongings into a shopping bag as his colleagues were doing with theirs - the only handy carriers available. Shauna received appreciative comments about her clothes which caused her to smile and she gave each of them a kiss.

CHAPTER 32   TWISTED

After a light lunch they were just about to leave when Clyde got a call. "Hey . . . Fine. How are you guys doing? . . . No kidding . . . Sure we have room for you. Come to our room. Hold on just a minute. What room number are we? . . . OK. It's the Tolstoy Suite on the top floor . . . Yeah, that's right . . . Good deal. See you in a bit." And he disconnected. "You'll never guess who that was." "I bet I can," responded Shauna. "I'll bet you ten bucks you don't know," said John. "I'll bet you twenty bucks I do," was Shauna's offer. "Ok then, who? Smarty pants," jeered John. Shauna wiggled her butt at him, leaving everybody in suspense by not saying anything as she held out her hand for the money saying, "Put it here buddy. And I don't like sore losers." "The names first, I don't trust you," guffawed John. Shauna in a fake huff folded her arms in front of her saying gruffly in a low, low voice, "What did you say?" "Oh darn. I can't remember," responded a gleeful John. "Then this will jar your memory . . . Chenaugh and Richardson!" "Well I'll be damned." And John reluctantly took a twenty dollar bill from his wallet and handed it to Shauna. She grabbed it with great drama and stuffed it down her bosom, patting her chest with great elation. "Oh come on now, John dearest. Don't be a sore loser." She went to John and gave him a hug, saying, "Remember, in future don't bet against the lady with the crystal ball."

At a staccato knocking Shauna rushed to the door and flung it wide open. A brightly beaming Chenaugh stepped through and embraced her. "Sweetie, you look so great," he observed as he spun her around admiring her as she kissed him wherever she could. "Look how you electrify me, my Darling." She said showing him her arms with hairs stood at attention. He took great delight in holding each arm up and liberally kissing them. "And who do we have here?" she asked, pulling Richardson into the room too.

Instantly jealous as Shauna greeted Chenaugh, Clyde gave himself a good talking to. *Come on you idiot. Don't do this. Just let go. Let go. Let go.* And shook himself out of the pit. *Shit! Much better*, he smiled, acknowledging himself. Shauna quickly glanced at him and smiled too. *Change sure is worth it*, he reminded himself - especially after Shauna's recognition of his shift. *I can't keep any secrets from this woman, so why even try. And there's something very liberating about it. I just want to be real with her — no matter where the chips fall. I know she won't leave me even when I fall on my ass. In fact, she'll help pick me up.*

Chenaugh caught the exchange and ambling over to Clyde patted him on the back. "Hey there, laddie. Hast thou caught the spell we nameth Shaunitis? Be of good cheer. We back thee one-hundred-percent." All Clyde could do was stand there, riveted to the spot, turning various shades of red.

With no time to catch up, the boat awaited, they postponed the full reunion until they were on their way. Although Chenaugh insisted on thanking the SEALs for taking care of Shauna who was taking a last look around. Remembering the birth-control pills she left the SEALs scrambling to get their flimsy luggage together to nip into the bedroom and slide the small container off the nightstand and into her jeans pocket. On the way out Clyde left a tip for Ivanka before they all headed for the elevators.

On the way down Chenaugh also mentioned that rumors were already circulating about a girl who wore buckets on her feet and was drowned and then resurrected - kind of like the Jesus thing. Richardson chimed in that there'd already been numerous sightings and she was well on her way to becoming an urban legend.

Reaching the lobby, John went to pay the hefty hotel bill while the others went outside to meet their ride. Richardson continued while they waited. "We're hoping that word about your being alive hasn't reached Sean yet. He took off in his private plane, filing a false flight plan so we don't know exactly where he is. Probably one of Spain, Turkey, Greece or Iraq, because that's where he has the strongest connections and largest holdings. He's now wanted for killing a prostitute and the Moscow authorities believe they have sufficient evidence to lock him up for life. Obviously, we're co-operating in every way we can. As for Isabella, she had a couple of minor problems - including losing Jones, Dave and Fin who are on their way home, Dave planning to retire immediately. But her and your mother sent you their love when I spoke to them earlier and are probably already on board the boat." Lowering his voice, he added, "Keep this under your hat, but Chip's with them too. Seems he had a slight problem with lost papers but that's being sorted."

Hearing the news, tears welled in Shauna's eyes — everyone assuming because of the news about Chip but in fact because of hearing for sure that Janet was well. Chenaugh put his arm around her as Richardson continued to bring them up to date. "Prosecutors are confident that Mark, Chip's ex-chef and Sean's brother, will be imprisoned for killing your father - seems his girlfriend is really planning to nail him when she testifies. But Mark wasn't just placed in Chip's house to keep an eye on the energy thing. Sean wanted to find any excuse to bring Chip down. He just didn't trust him, reportedly envious of Chip's talent and success despite his fucked-up personal life. Just as surprised as everyone else when you and Chip came together, Sean saw it as an opportunity for revenge for having to put up with Chip for so long, and that's when he decided Chip was surplus to requirements and arranged to have him mutilated and you abducted. Then, apparently thinking to kill two birds with one stone, he initiated the confrontation with Josef at the same time, and the rest, as they say, is history."

As he finished, the SUV rolled up curbside ignoring the heavy flow of traffic. They piled in as John came running to join them. Richardson and Al sat in the back; Clyde, Shauna on his lap, Chenaugh and John sat in the second row and Ken rode shotgun. Suddenly, Chenaugh leant forward to get a better look at the driver, and said in surprise, "Ilya? . . . Hey, this is Ilya, one of the guards on the ship where Shauna was imprisoned. Don't you recognize him?" he asked, glancing at Shauna before continuing. "My man, what the heck are you doing here?" Fully alert, they all waited for Ilya to reply. There was only a charged silence.

Finally, Ilya spoke in broken English, "I work for Mayor of Moscow. No longer shipyards. I like. Money better. I got call you need ride. I here to drive you to boatyard. Very good." Something felt wrong - especially to Shauna who knew that the Mayor's wife, Yelena, was supposedly a friend of Isabella's. She couldn't quite put her finger on how that bit of info had any relevancy but it led her to wonder what had happened to the communication with Isabella?

Whispering over her shoulder, Shauna asked Richardson to get through to Comstock. In the continuous throbbing of heavy traffic, despite the vehicle's soundproofing, Richardson's guarded communication with Comstock went unnoticed. Disconnecting, Richardson leaned forward to whisper to Shauna. Catching Ilya watching him in the rear view mirror, he decided to continue his whispered conversation. *Why not? If Ilya was up to no good he'd probably give some sign of it. If he wasn't, it didn't matter if he overheard anything.* "It appears that the Honorable Mayor is using his position to take over much of Josef's private business. He's going to seize the vintage cars and women when they arrive from Houston. Not that we should be surprised. That's how he made his fortune in the first place, before he had political clout. Oh, and his current wife, number three, a billionaire in her own right, is just as corrupt. Whatever's going on here, it's unlikely to be in our best interests.

"Comstock suggests we keep a close eye on this Ilya character; see if we can't use him to our advantage. He also thinks the Mayor is threatened by the same thing Sean is – you. Seems the dark side needs you out of the way so it can stay in business. It won't hesitate to eliminate you or any of the rest of us if we get in the way. The same damn scenario, just with different players. They're like fucking weeds. You can kill what you see but the roots are still there, underground."

Shauna was disappointed to hear about Yelena and was concerned about where Isabella now stood, particularly after Richardson voiced his doubts too. Were they being paranoid or prudent she wondered, grateful for the men with her in the car who she knew would protect her without question.

Hitting the freeway, Ilya accelerated, changing lanes to maintain speed whenever he could, even when it was risky. Traffic was a nightmare and the SUV occupants were edgy. They had become a tightly knit group in a short time and were collectively attuned to the vehicle's progress and Ilya's behavior as he drove. Seeing a sign to the boatyard flash by they tensed until he made the turn on to a six lane trunk route, hoping it was the right road.

With the boatyard exit not too far ahead they almost literally ran into a pile up. An accident involving a van and several cars had blocked all three lanes. Traffic was at a standstill. They could hear emergency vehicles on the way but so far there was only a lone police car, lights flashing, and people had left their vehicles to help provide assistance with the trapped and injured.

Surveying the carnage Shauna noticed a car driving along the embankment to bypass the wreck and bounce onto the roadway, fishtailing as it accelerated away towards the boatyard. And then Ilya was screaming. "GET OUT! GET OUT! There's bomb in car ahead!" And he ran towards the back of their SUV.

Grabbing Shauna from Clyde, Chenaugh crashed out of the door and followed Ilya, the others right behind. A few yards behind their SUV, Ilya threw himself to the pavement and the followers copied him just as the vehicle in front of theirs exploded with a deafening blast, spewing flame, smoke and debris in all directions.

Hitting the ground they'd each instinctively covered their heads with their arms, Clyde and Chenaugh pinning Shauna beneath them. Feeling her shaking Chenaugh could just make out his alias name, Petrov, being repeated over and over again. Realizing he was almost deaf from the explosion, everything was muted to a whisper, he looked around and saw Ilya scrabbling backwards away from the scene frantically waving him to follow. Without thinking Chenaugh grabbed Shauna and Clyde and pushed them after Ilya. Then making sure the others were on their way too, he sprinted toward Ilya just as another explosion drove him forward but not before he noticed Ilya pocket his cellphone, turn and run.

Packed with so much explosive their SUV was punched high into the air to come crashing down almost exactly where they'd been lying seconds before.

Burning debris began to fall around them causing mini fires, singeing hair, flesh and clothing. Watching out for each other, they quickly snuffed them out as they frantically ran for safety. Propelled by the blast, Chenaugh had quickly caught up with his team, and relieving Clyde of Shauna threw her over his shoulder and carried her with him, only too aware of the scrapes and burns on her legs, arms and shoulders from landing on the asphalt and being bombed by tiny slivers of red hot metal.

They eventually caught up with Ilya who had collapsed on the embankment a safe distance from all the destruction. "What the fucking hell just happened?" asked an angry, exhausted Chenaugh, gently laying Shauna down before lunging at Ilya and pinning him down. Rummaging in the man's pocket he pulled out the cellphone and pocketed it himself. Telling Ilya not to move a muscle if he didn't want to be beaten to a pulp, he went to a whimpering Shauna.

Her clothes were torn and smudge-marked and her face was blackened in spots. Checking her back where she'd been burnt, he could tell that the damage was more painful than serious. Holding his hands over the burns to comfort her he explained that while her back probably hurt like hell there were others far more seriously injured who needed more urgent treatment. Shauna raised a hand to caress his face. "I know," she whispered, "I'm not whimpering for sympathy, just for release. Please do what you can and make sure the others are okay. Thanks." Kissing her forehead, he asked Clyde to be with her and went to check on Richardson and the other SEALs. They too had minor burns. Looking towards the scene he could see human chaos and now his hearing was returning, the sound of pain and suffering. *This has to fucking stop sometime,* he thought, and returned to Ilya.

"All right, Ilya. You want to tell me what's going on?" Ilya bowed his head in disgrace. He admitted he'd been ordered to set off the bombs by the Mayor. It seemed like such a small thing in exchange for all that money.

But then, when it came down to following the orders and killing Chenaugh and Shauna, he just couldn't do it. "You didn't seem to have a problem with killing the people in the car in front." "No, no!" protested Ilya. "Mayor told me accident was set up. Car in front was empty plant left by other man."

"So why did the Mayor target us?" asked Chenaugh. Ilya took his time answering. "No sure. Think Mayor want all power his self. Kill lady when heard she still living. Then maybe work for Sean Cameron."

Having bypassed the accident scene, it wasn't long before Yelena was parking in front of the small boatyard office and the chained-off ramp leading to the cargo boat. She was still running on the adrenaline rush of her reckless driving, determined to save her friend from disaster. She asked the uniformed guard standing by the chain at the bottom of the ramp if any passengers were already on board. When he indicated there were, she asked if he remembered anyone named Isabella or Janet boarding, and if so, which cabin they were in. "They are here, but you cannot board the ship. Laws, you know?" he said. Exasperated, Yelena impatiently warned the guard, "I'm the wife of the Mayor of Moscow and I don't have the time to stand here arguing," and she indignantly shoved her ID in his face, totally unaware that just a few feet away, in a small back room in the boatyard office, Norm had just arrived with travel documentation for Chip.

Having handed Chip his own personal papers with the appropriate changes, Norm was explaining that it would have taken too long to get hold of another valid passport and doctor it. "Besides," said Norm, "I'm going to stick around here a while longer and see what I can dig up. It'll be a piece of cake to get more documents made for myself. So take these with my blessings." Chip was very appreciative, but hesitant. "Norm, I don't know how to thank you. But what about Jamaica?" "Well my friend, I have to be honest. It's a great invitation, but sand and sea are not my favorite pastimes. We'll get together another time. In fact I might be interested in coming to Scotland to see how you guys are doing." "I'd love that and I know Shauna would too," responded an enthusiastic Chip. "Great. Now I have to get moving. So, good-bye and be safe brother," said Norm, giving Chip a hug and leaving immediately, ducking out the back, on the side away from the boat ramp. He hated good-byes.

After Norm left, Chip approached the hovering guard and flashed the papers in front of him. The guard took a cursory look and let him go. Chip was rushing up the ramp just as Isabella, Janet and Yelena were coming down. "We were just coming to get you!" exclaimed Isabella. "Come on. We have to get far enough away before it blows up." "What the . . ." began Chip. Isabella grabbed his arm and towed him with her. No time for talk. Chip was insistent. "What about all the others on the ship?" "What about them?" "Don't they matter?" Chip worked himself free of Isabella's grasp and started back up the ramp shouting and gesticulating, "Get off! Ship going to go boom! Get off ship!" He only hoped whoever was left could understand his English or at least some of them could and would translate. Running through the boat, shouting and waving his arms, mimicking explosions, enough passengers got the gist of the crazy black man's message and started hurrying people off. Last one out, as far as he could tell, Chip was sprinting down the ramp when he heard an eerie splintering that became an ear splitting eruption that shot a mammoth plume of fire skyward from the other side of the ship. Chunks and splinters fountained out to rain down across the harbor. Haphazard debris shook the ground and pocked the water as the area was littered with ripped apart boat.

People were scattering across the parking lot and through the gates, frantically dodging flying projectiles. Some struck with burning wreckage opted to jump into the harbor to douse themselves amongst still-burning hunks of wood. Chip felt a strong impulse to stay and help those who really needed attention. Deafened by the blast, he looked around at the injured, realizing that if he stayed he too could easily become a statistic. Wrenched by the choice, he knew his purpose for living had to take priority. That every person he was looking at right now had to make their own purpose for living their priority. His dying would benefit no one, not even Sean. He had to be strong not just for Shauna, his Beloved, but for everything they were to become and would bring about.

Chip ran from the dock, oblivious of several severe burns he'd received-as if he'd been branded. He joined Isabella, Janet and Yelena on the far side of the parking lot where they had retreated after his outburst. "That was close Chip," said Janet. "For a moment I thought we were going to lose you - lose you to martyrdom, a concept – 'It is a far, far better thing that I do', and all that crap - that can seduce any one of us if we're not sharp. There is no one as special as you, Chip. I'm glad that in the end you understood the value of your own life, because in that you understand the value of every life. I'm sure

Shauna will be thankful too. . . Now, there's no time, and it'd be a waste of energy anyway, to re-think your decision, so let's move on." Chip squared his shoulders and smiled at Janet in appreciation. "What next?" he asked.

"Well," said Isabella. "I just finished talking with Richardson. They were nearly here when they got held up by an accident and involved in a couple of car bombings. Don't panic, they're fine. The paramedics are treating them for minor burns as we speak. Yelena's just sent a bus to pick them up and take them to a local airfield where she's put her private jet at our disposal. We'll go straight there to meet them and we'll all leave Moscow together. "Thanks, Yelena. But, at the risk of sounding ungrateful, I can't help wondering why you've gone to so much trouble to help us. Would you care to enlighten me?" asked Chip. Expecting someone to question her apparent generosity, Yelena had prepared herself and had an answer ready. "Well Chip. I recently found out that my husband, the Mayor if you don't know, has been putting Josef's organization back together and what was a threat to Josef is now a threat to my husband - meaning both you and Shauna. He talked of going straight - freeing himself of the corruption he engaged in to amass his huge fortune. But he's basically weak when it comes to changing for the better. In fact there's a rumor that my husband is considering combining power with power and having the evidence against Cameron vanished before joining with him to build an unstoppable global tyranny. I can't just stand by and let that happen, so I'm doing everything in my power to make sure you all leave here unharmed, particularly Isabella who's a longtime friend." "Why didn't you phone her instead of driving here? It would have been a damn sight quicker." "I tried calling, but got no answer and didn't want to rely on leaving a message, just in case Isabella didn't retrieve the voice mail in time. All I could think of was getting to her, so I jumped in my car and drove." "One more question." *This Chip is a pain*, thought Yelena. "Aw come on Chip. Give it a rest and let's get the heck out of here." said Isabella, with a whine to her voice. Chip ignored her and continued. "Did you see our friends when you made your way here?" "No, no I didn't. As I said, all that was on my mind when I heard what my husband was up to was getting here. Besides, all I could see was a backlog of traffic, so I drove over the embankment to get round it and all I saw getting back on the road was a wreck. I didn't see or hear anything that looked like a bombing."

So absorbed in the question and answer duel they hadn't realized that Yelena's car was a pile of burning wreckage until they arrived at the remains of the boatyard office where she'd parked. As they went looking for other transport, the fire reached the fuel tank and Yelena's car went up in flames. "I'd be perfectly happy to never hear another explosion," commented a shaken Janet.

Seeing the boat guard getting into a dilapidated sedan, Chip ran to flag him down before he disappeared. Closing the distance in the nick of time, Chip planted himself in front of the car. The driver brought the car to a slouching halt with the front bumper slightly touching Chip's legs and gesticulated angrily. Chip held his ground and when Isabella and Janet caught up Chip told them to watch both front doors so the guard could not escape. "Do you have any money on you, Yelena?" asked Chip. "I want to see if he'll take us to the airfield if we make it worth his while." Yelena patted first one pocket in her slacks and then the other, drawing out a roll of money. "I never go anywhere without money," she allowed. "What's a tempting amount to get this guy to co-operate?" asked Chip.

Yelena turned her back so no one could see just how much she had. Returning some of the money to her pocket she offered a good sized stack to the guard as Chip asked for his help. He snatched the money and, licking his lips, counted the bills. He agreed to take them.

Squeezing in they were overwhelmed by the acrid smell of stale cigarette smoke seeping out of every nook and cranny of the shabby car. The guard took out a cigarette and prepared to light up. From the back seat Yelena begged him to please not smoke. Chip, sitting up front, reached across and snatched it from his mouth. "Didn't you hear the lady?" Fortunately the disgruntled driver didn't make a fuss. At least he had enough smarts to know he was outnumbered. Besides, he wanted the money.

He messed with the uncooperative gears of the car. Finally getting it in drive he started off to the airfield - a goodly distance for such a jalopy. "Take another route back to avoid the accident," demanded Yelena. *Let's hope Chip realizes how vitally important it is to not let on to anybody else that Shauna is alive,* thought Isabella. Not that she was in a position to control that anymore.

CHAPTER 33 DEPARTURE

Shauna and her group had made it to the edge of the devastation and had received treatment from the paramedics who'd set up a station just inside the barrier. Cars were being diverted to the closest off-ramp but the raggedy-looking group didn't have to wait long before a small bus with darkened windows was waved through the barrier to pick them up. Which was when they realized that Ilya had slipped away. "He must have sneaked off when we were getting treatment," said Clyde. "Just as well. Now we don't have to worry about him learning anything about our future plans. What little he does know shouldn't be a problem. I sure won't miss him."

Shauna was preoccupied, unsettled by the memory of the car she'd seen negotiating the embankment and rushing off in the direction of the boatyard. She didn't know why it had disturbed her so much but she had a feeling it was important. Her stomach was telling her something wasn't right, she just didn't know what. Clyde, sitting beside her, could feel her discomfort and throwing caution to the wind put his arms around her and held her snuggly. She nestled back. Her lips parted. Watching her reflection in the window he was so focused on her beautiful, voluptuous lips that it was only when he bent to kiss her that he recognized the soft, even breathing of sleep.

She had drifted off looking so relaxed compared to what he was feeling. His arm cradling her back began to go numb. Not wanting to wake her, he relaxed his arm rather than move it. Closing his eyes he then attempted to selectively erase the memories of recent events. Eventually he dropped off too, part way through reliving his morning with Shauna.

Chenaugh was up front conversing with the bus driver. He wasn't totally sure why, but some things weren't sitting right with him and he was hoping the driver could ease his suspicions. Ever vigilant and cautious, traits that helped make him such an admired operative he was determined to figure out what didn't jibe.

Richardson was sitting by himself in the back ruminating on the conversation he had just finished with Isabella. It looked like, even though Isabella's long-time friend had all the answers to some serious questions, her responses were too slick, too believable, too reliant on unsubstantiated possibilities, at least to him. Isabella herself hadn't shared any concerns but he was wondering how to get to the truth. *Wait and see what Yelena does next? Perhaps trip her up in her own tangle of lies? What about the truth about her husband?* That sparked a thought and he connected with Norm to have him check a hunch. "It's me, Richardson. Yes . . . that's right. We should be arriving at the airport in perhaps another forty-five minutes, maybe sooner, depending on traffic. What's that? . . . Yeah, she sent a bus to get us . . . Well yes, bro. That's the sixty-four-thousand-dollar question. Why is she doing this? . . . Good. Thanks. And Norm, while you're at it, would you poke around and get me info about her husband too? . . . Yeah, that's good . . . Focus on what his current activities are . . . Excellent! I need this yesterday . . . okay, see what you can do. Thanks. . . That would be good." As satisfied as he could be without doing the snooping himself, Richardson relaxed a little.

Reminding himself to remind Shauna how important it was that she didn't let on she knew Chip when she met him at the airport, he then questioned whether it mattered. The only person he had any reservations about was Yelena and he'd make sure she was in no position to do anything with the information whether she was as dirty as he thought she was or not. Now confident that they'd be able to manage the next phase, whatever might come up, he stretched out along the empty seats next to him, folded his arms over his chest to keep them from dangling on the floor and took a power nap.

The bus trip turned out to be a blessing. All the passengers took advantage of the opportunity for much needed sleep. As for the others in the boat guard's car, sleep was out of the question. They were all wired and watchful. It was too risky to all doze off leaving the guard to his own questionable devices. Who knew? Maybe they would never wake up if they did go to sleep. So they chugged and bounced their way onwards, too busy with their own thoughts and recent memories to carry on any conversation. Yelena was preoccupied with coming up with a better mode of transportation for them. She had a few markers she could call in so took out her phone.

Chenaugh shifted position, trying to get more comfortable, and jarred himself awake when his elbow collided with an armrest. Remembering where he was, he looked through the windshield to see a small guardhouse straight ahead attended by an armed guard with a rifle resting on his shoulder - enough of a statement to say, "Don't mess with me." On either side of the guardhouse were high chain link fences topped with barbed wire winding around the periphery of two large runways and a few dozen private jetliners parked in yellow marked spaces, much like a car parking lot. Behind the jets, low buildings, no doubt for storage and aircraft repair, paralleled the taxiway. The bus driver stopped at the guard house and conversed with the guard, as if they knew each other.

The guard stepped to one side, raised the barrier and motioned the driver to pass. The driver stopped close to space twenty two where a maintenance crew was carrying out last minute checks of a medium-sized business jet. The cessation of motion when the bus stopped brought the passengers awake, one-by-one. Grateful to have arrived and looking forward to being out of Russia soon, they checked their new surroundings.

Shauna yawned and stretched, leaning forward in her seat to see as much as she could. With her weight removed Clyde waited for some feeling to return to his shoulder and arm. "Aren't you coming, Sweetheart?" "You bet I am," replied Clyde, shaking his arm in response to the tingling as she reached out to give him a hand and help him up. He smiled and gave her a kiss and they slowly headed for the exit.

Standing on the concrete, they first heard the vehicle and then saw it. The black Hummer stopped briefly at the guard house before accelerating towards them. "Man, he's going to mow us all down," yelled a panicked John. The Hummer was nearly on top of them before screeching to a halt, protesting the unnecessary emergency stop. A serious Norm leapt out. "Isabella here yet?" he demanded.

"'How are you' or 'hello', or 'good to see you made it here' would be nice," said an irritated Clyde.

"Hey Bro, how's it going? Good to see you too," answered Norm, not intentionally insincere but with more weighty concerns on his mind than the niceties of polite greeting.

"To answer your question, we expect Isabella here soon," said Chenaugh. "In Fact I think that's her right now." And he pointed to the guard house where a bright red Cadillac was just pulling up.

Taking off moments later, it barreled in their direction and Norm stepped away, directing it to meet him.

Pulling alongside him, Yelena climbed out of the driver's seat. "What's got your knickers in a twist, woman?" asked an angry Norm.

"Up yours!" she slammed. "If it hadn't been for me we'd still be piddling along going nowhere fast. You'd be pissed too!" she added, as Chip, Isabella, and Janet piled out to join her.

Unable to help themselves, Chip and Shauna looked longingly at each other as they unthinkingly moved to be close. Ignoring his previous conclusion Richardson cleared his throat and rushed over to shake Chip's hand, breaking the obvious spell between the two, deciding to err on the side of safety – you never knew who might be watching. The two groups were looking at each other in amazement. "Shit, you look like war refugees!" said Clyde, a little shaken by their appearance. "Have you looked at yourself lately?" asked an amused Isabella. "Give me a minute guys," said Norm, "I'll find some place you can get cleaned up with a whole new wardrobe . . . Welcome to the Armed Forces." he finished, chuckling as he took Isabella by the arm to lead her away from the group.

When he judged them far enough away from the others he turned her to face him. The others who had watched them go saw an unusually animated Norm, almost hopping from leg to leg get right in her face, mouth moving a mile a minute. In response Isabella shook her head several times, gaping at the tirade, even turning away in apparent disgust once or twice. Those watching were fascinated, seeing her color rising, wondering when she would blow, like watching a car wreck about to happen in slow motion.

Noticing Yelena somewhat isolated, scanning the area, becoming increasingly restless as if she just wanted to run, Chenaugh, motioned toward her and suggested to Clyde that they keep an eye on her. Nodding silently Clyde then looked around for Ilya, before remembering he'd disappeared at the paramedic's station and noticed Richardson seemed to be as focused on Yelena as Chenaugh. Taking in the rest of them, beat-up, touting burns, smudged faces, and torn clothing he thought they looked more like the walking dead than candidates about to embark on a trip to Jamaica for some well-deserved R and R.

Shauna looked down at what had been, not too long ago, a new outfit she'd been so proud of from Clyde and Al's shopping trip. None of them, it seemed, could hang on to new clothing for very long, their other clothes having gone up in the explosions. "When it comes to a game of shopping, our team seems to have a habit of losing," she laughed. "What so funny?" asked Clyde. "Oh, nothing important: just silly stuff." Clyde pouted. "I feel left out." "Well, Clyde. Get over it," And she laughed again, disturbing the soot on her face, which in turn amused Clyde no end. Punched playfully on the shoulder, Clyde howled in pain, and Shauna gleefully danced around him jabbing the air before standing hands clasped above her head shaking them in victory. "We need more play! Much, much more!" she shouted.

Norm and Isabella rejoined the group, setting off a ripple of rearrangement as various stilted conversations were struck up. Yelena made her way closer to Isabella. Richardson wedged his way between Ken and Norm. Chip and Clyde put themselves close to Shauna. Chenaugh casually sidled closer to both Yelena and Isabella and John shuffled his way behind them. Pieces in place, silence and a sense of uncertainty permeated the group - doing nothing to settle nerves, or clear the air.

The game began, Norm telling Yelena she would be put under guard until the police arrived to arrest her for attempted murder and conspiracy for masterminding the recent serious of accidents and explosions. Although some were surprised, others were not as shocked as might have been expected. Janet and Chip had suspected that her answers back at the boatyard had been less than the truth. Richardson had kept his hunch of her duplicity to himself. And Chenaugh, with his background and connections, always had reservations about anyone with any kind of association with any level of government in Russia.

Yelena admitted her guilt by throwing an arm around Isabella's neck, pulling out a gun and putting it against Isabella's temple. Threating to kill Isabella if any of them moved she started inching backwards dragging Isabella with her, the scared Isabella gagging from Yelena's choke-hold. Yelena loosened her grip a little but kept backing up toward the nearby jet.

As Shauna watched the slow-motion retreat she noticed Yelena's facade slipping away, the woman of class and breeding dissolving to show the years of everyday survival, no-doubt amplified in Yelena's case by her own toxicity, despite her billions. *Every thought releases a chemical*, remembered Shauna, wondering how many toxic thoughts people could handle. *And how many uplifting ones do we have in comparison or need to counteract the negativity that we generate or that surrounds us? It's really true that you can tell where people are, and where they've been if you look closely enough with un-blinkered eyes. There are people I know in their twenties, even younger, who look and act old while others I know in their sixties and beyond who glow with agelessness - so full of living enjoyably. So age is not the determining factor, merely an ingredient – the longer we're here the more negativity we're subject to, both from outside and within. I can't allow myself to be ruled by or subject to the toxicity of myself or others! I have to live with joy! It's who I am!* she declared to herself. A vehicle roaring through the compound gates shook her back to the now and seeing Yelena turn to look its way she spontaneously leapt to kick the gun from her hand.

Too slow she stopped mid-kick, hands raised, looking down the barrel of Yelena's gun. "Aha. Now isn't this just perfect?" hissed a triumphant Yelena. "The bitch responsible for this whole shitty mess is exactly where I've always wanted her." And then Isabella bit Yelena's arm, clamping her teeth as hard as she could. Yelena screamed and Shauna continued forward to push her backwards over the crouching John, who'd been backing up behind Yelena the whole time.

Flying backwards, out-of-control, Yelena whacked the back of her head on the ground ending up in a heap. Released as Yelena fell backwards, Isabella tottered for a few moments before regaining her balance. Norm quickly flex-cuffed the dazed Yelena where she lay, ignoring her cursing protests and violent struggling. "Man-oh-man, you have some mouth on you lady," he said, chuckling, thankful that there'd been no shooting.

Reflecting on the moments before, Norm shuddered at the memory of Shauna's gutsy move and gave thanks to Isabella's timely improvisation. Obviously less impressed, screaming as she writhed on the ground: "GODDAMNIT, MOTHERFUCKING SON OF A BITCH! Do you have any fucking clue who you're dealing with? I'll have your balls in a box for this, you shit ass!" Yelena was beside herself with rage.

Wanting to minimize any self-inflicted damage and ensure she stayed caught, Norm decided to cuff her ankles and short chain her legs too.

Proving easier said than done, he had a venomous snake on his hands, he enlisted John and Ken to help. Even so the three of them were sweating profusely by the time they had her trussed and quietened down some. A relieved Norm muttered, "Let's hope the police get here real soon to pick up this piece of garbage."

As if in answer, they hadn't even finished thanking Shauna and John and making sure Isabella was okay, when the police wagon arrived and two policemen bundled Yelena into the back and slammed the doors on her protests. She could still be heard over the sound of the engine as they drove away. "Let's see if she can bribe her way out of this," quipped a worn-out Norm. "Just when you think you know someone," added Isabella, dismayed

"And now what are we going to do with the rest of you?" asked Norm. John, Al and Ken said they were off back to the States. Richardson said he had been ordered to stay in Moscow for a while to tie up some loose ends, and apologized to them for the change in plans. Disappointed, Isabella, who'd been hoping to have some alone time with Richardson, said the rest of them were going to Jamaica.

"Interesting," said Norm. "I was told to expect six, but if Richardson wasn't unexpectedly staying there'd be seven of you." "Looking a bit sheepish Clyde said he thought he was odd one out who was now in." Nodding slowly as if understanding, Norm turned as an anonymous olive-drab sedan pulled up and Richardson said quick goodbyes, lingering over a kiss with Isabella before climbing in and being driven away.

"Okay guys, let's get you cleaned up and suited," said Norm, and he led them past the line of jets to a blocky brick building facing the taxiway.

Oh, the luxury of hot water streaming over your body and soap to wash the grime away: it seemed like forever since they'd been clean. As they showered, the women taking turns in one locker room, the men in the other, they helped each other clean around burn marks and the other minor injuries, creating a bond amongst them even greater than their experience of shared traumas. Clyde felt frustration, wanting to share Shauna's shower experience, to feel a deeper intimacy with her. And then thought of how Chip and Chenaugh must be feeling and contented himself with listening to the women enjoying themselves together, wishing he could be a women, if only for a minute.

The fatigues they were provided were so starched they could have stood up on their own and, without underwear, irritated every wound and sensitive inch despite the medicated salve Norm had managed to drum up. The boots were just as unforgiving. None of them fit properly and the nine of them clomped a dance of discomfort, unable to contain their laughter at the absurdity of their collective appearance and involuntary twitching and scratching, bursting into a further storm of merriment when Shauna tried cramming her voluminous hair into an undersized ball-cap hoping to tame it

"Okay, platoon, face right," barked Norm, a twinkle in his eye as he marched them to the canteen. "Left, right, left, right, one, two, three, four." The only ones in the facility, they loaded up at the buffet line and sat either side of a long table. "How did you manage to swing this?" asked John. "Connections," replied Norm but, unable to keep a straight face, confessed, "Someone in the DOD called someone in Russia's Ministry of Defence and here we are, at least for today. This op. has driven historical antipathy out the window. Seems everyone wants a piece of Cameron et al. Would that it was like this all the time. But then I guess I'd be out of a job."

Their meal consumed, Norm left them to go finalize transport for the next leg, Jamaica or the States. They sat back and relaxed over steamy cups of coffee. "Welcome to the new order," saluted Clyde. "Yeah, same as the old one," seconded Chenaugh. Saluting her comrades in coffee Shauna said, "Don't knock it, this could be the next fashion trend. Just watch out for the next issue of 'Vogue'.

A thoughtful Norm rejoined them. "Well, the good news, your transport is all set. You guys off to the States will be taken to Sheremetyevo airport where tickets will be waiting for the first flight to D.C. The six of you going to Jamaica are in for a real treat though. We're getting the Russian Military's full cooperation. You're going to be picked up in their stealth jet-copter and flown to Cuba for an overnight stay before taking a boat to Jamaica. "First I've heard that the Russians have a stealth chopper," said Clyde who liked to stay current on military hardware. "I know," said Norm. "It's been kept under wraps and we probably still wouldn't know about it if it wasn't the only machine available that's big enough and can make the trip without refueling. Given Cameron's resources, nobody wants to take that kind of risk, least of all the Russians who right now are responsible for your welfare.

"Anyway; Al, Ken, John: your car to the airport should be here any minute. For the rest of you, the jet-copter won't be far behind but I'll fill you in on the latest about Yelena while we're waiting. "What about documentation?" asked Isabella. "You know, like passports, entry visas for Cuba. Things like that." "Thanks for reminding me," responded Norm. "The Russians are taking care of all that. The driver who's coming to pick up you three for the airport is supposed to be bringing everything you're all going to need with him.

"Now, Yelena. Uncooperative as you'd expect, she has apparently agreed to a deal. Seems she hired someone to kill her husband and his lover - they were found murdered on his yacht, single bullets to their foreheads. The prime suspect for the actual killings is Ilya," "Well fuck me sideways'" blurted Clyde, going red with embarrassment at his outburst. "You know the guy?" asked Norm. "Yes," chorused Clyde, Chenaugh, Shauna, Al, John and Ken. Giving the six of them a queer look, Norm continued.

"Her husband was in the process of cleaning up his act, already having set in motion the return of Josef's shipment of cars and women, undoubtedly pissing Yelena off no end as she was the irredeemably corrupt half of the partnership. It's likely she'd have had him killed even if he hadn't been having an affair. In fact the affair may just have been incidental, you know, the lover in the wrong place at the wrong time. And that's the other twist. The lover was the American wife of Ramon Hernandez the high-flying, Argentinian-born, Russian business magnet. "A real soap opera, or should that be 'Novella'?" snorted Isabella.

"Whatever," continued Norm, "What's real disturbing is that she seems to have been in touch with Cameron right up till her arrest and we don't know what she may have passed on, especially as she's so mad at Shauna, blaming her for everything she's now going through, as if without Shauna she would have been home free. She's totally delusional of course; the authorities already have all the evidence they need to indict her for both the car and the boat bombs." "What a bitch," remarked Clyde. "Right on, bro," echoed Chenaugh. Chip looked at Shauna to see how she was taking the news thinking, *It's always easier to blame someone else than take responsibility for your own fucked up life and Shauna doesn't deserve to be even connected with such bullshit let alone blamed for it. She needs everyone who feels her and who she is to shield her from it. Her safety is not going to come just from power; it's going to take a different kind of togetherness.*

An army driver walked in, a thick envelope in hand, and asked for Sergeant Black. Norm got up and shook his hand. Taking the envelope and emptying the contents on the table, he distributed the paperwork. Making sure they each had the documents they needed, they trooped out after the driver to wish the three SEALs a safe trip, Shauna making certain they understood they would always be welcome wherever she was.

Putting her arm through Chenaugh's as they watched the SUV drive away, she wished she could be as close to Chip right then, knowing he felt the same, both of them heeding their instructions to feign disinterest but less and less certain why.

CHAPTER 34   FLIGHT

Standing outside the run-down building they heard a low pitched whooshing before the jet-copter, like a miniature B-2 with a rotor, ripped into sight and came to a hover about a hundred feet above the tarmac. It slowly descended for a gentle touchdown, a ballet performance in metal.

It was clearly a machine not to be messed with; probably as lethal as it looked. "That's quite something!" exclaimed a very nervous Isabella. "I thought it was the English who were masters of the understatement," quipped Janet, adding, "Does anybody have a Dramamine? I think I might need some." "Nope. Sorry. Only a birth control pill," said Shauna, patting her fatigue's pocket, thankful that in the chaos she'd had the presence of mind to transfer them from her jeans. Chip couldn't help but smile.

Climbing down from the cabin, the co-pilot distributed parachutes to the six, showing them how to put them on and running through a brief safety speech in English with a heavy German accent. Norm took out his cellphone for a group photo before they left and the co-pilot insisted the jet-copter not be in the picture – the Russians might be helping out but they weren't about to have their technology broadcast across the internet. The tight little huddle featured almost believable twenty-first century aviators, displaying a mixture of emotions, against a backdrop of mid-twentieth-century weathered brick. "Well," said Norm, surprising himself with how reluctant he was to say good-bye, "Be seeing you sooner than you think. Have a fun trip and the best to all of you and, hell, I'll miss you." All he got back were waving hands and shouted goodbyes as the co-pilot hustled them on board.

Entering the fuselage, all six were struck by how small the interior was. Much longer and narrower than they'd realized from the outside, at least the seating, single file along both sides, was comfortable enough once they were strapped in and settled. The three men were particularly thankful they could stretch their legs in the aisle.

As there was no cockpit partition, the passengers were able to watch the pilots run through their take-off ritual, their hands dancing over the maze of knobs, switches, diagrams, lights and video screens bringing the jet-copter to life. Once cleared for take-off, gasps filled the black bird as it shot upward with an unexpected G force and headed on its designated flight path. The co-pilot turned around to check on his passengers and told them to put on their oxygen masks. Janet loosed her stop-the-blood-flow grip on Shauna's arm to do so. Shauna patted Janet's other hand reassuringly: the one still clutching Shauna's thigh.

On reaching their cruising altitude the pilot accelerated to maximum speed. Having the honor of being the first non-Russians to not only see the jet-copter – if you excluded Norm - but fly in it, didn't stop them from crashing, emotionally drained and exhausted, still feeling their various hurts.

Sooner than they would have expected they were slowing for the landing in Cuba. The absence of windows made sight-seeing almost impossible but they all strained to catch glimpses through the cockpit windshield of a country that had been off-limits to Americans for so long. Removing her oxygen mask a sleepy Janet commented, "That was fast. It feels like it's taken no time at all. About time we had something going in our favor. And it's so quiet!" The others worked their kinks out in silence but could feel the excitement brewing.

As they felt the craft touch down, its engines whispering to silence, they eagerly unbuckled and removed their flight gear, laying it in their seats beside their discarded oxygen masks. Announcing they had landed at Mirul just outside Havana - an airport abandoned by the Cubans and taken over by the Russians as a base for their Southern operations – the co-pilot informed them that the Russian Military Attache was waiting to take them through immigration and customs and on to their hotel, the Grande de Cuba, in the middle of Havana.

Thanking the pilot, they disembarked, following the co-pilot down the stairs, impacted by the heat and humidity. They each hugged the co-pilot before turning to greet, the good-looking, well-dressed, gray-haired man standing to the side. Speaking English with a heavy Russian accent he introduced himself. "Welcome to Cuba, my friends. I am Dimitri Sokolov, Military Attache." Sokolov shook hands all round, showing no particular interest in Shauna or Chip or indicating that he knew why any of them were there.

"Follow me please to take care of formalities," instructed Sokolov as he ushered them towards a long, low, unmarked, concrete building. Whisking the group through a series of Russian and Cuban checkpoints, Sokolov lead them outside toward a large, white, unmarked van.

It had started to rain and they dashed for the van already discomfited by the humidity. "Sorry about weather," apologized Sokolov. "This time of year is rain season, sometimes hurricanes even. You can feel it hot and sticky, no?" As they all concurred Shauna asked, "Can we stop and get some more appropriate clothes please? These fatigues are really oppressive and we'll need to get some local money too." Sokolov indicated his approval and directed the driver to find a local market when they got to Havana.

When they were finished shopping, with the help of Sokolov, who spoke a ludicrously butchered Spanish, and Chenaugh, who was close to fluent, they carried their purchases back to the van, happy the years of Cuban austerity were over. Carefully stowing their collection of clothes, accessories and toiletries, they completed their journey.

The hotel, although clean, beautifully furnished and apparently well run, was now fading and a little tarnished around the edges on the inside too. While Sokolov checked them in, Shauna wandered over to the hotel shop to check what it had to offer. Chip accompanied her and noticed her looking fondly at a pair of long dangly earrings, a bright bracelet that appeared to be locally made, and a necklace that kind of went with both. Chip memorized her attractions.

"Here are your room keys," said Sokolov, handing them round. "You have two rooms side by side on second floor. Views should be OK. Restaurant is open for food which is pretty good. Not great selection, mainly pork and chicken, but not spicy. Sauces and vegetables are good. I will pick you up at eleven in morning. Breakfast is included, so enjoy. Get good rest tonight. Good-bye." Sokolov was all too glad to get the hell out of there, which the six noted, but at the time were more interested in hastening towards the elevators with their packages, eager to see their rooms, get out of their boots and fatigues and into a hot shower.

"I guess it's going to be boys in one room and girls in the other?" said a not too enthusiastic Clyde. "For now, I think that's a good idea," responded Shauna. "But let's feel free to come and go." Opening the doors they found two suites, not rooms. Similar enough to eliminate bickering, Janet made the decision for them all by flopping onto the large king sized bed of the second suite they checked. The intricately designed brass headboard absorbed Shauna's attention momentarily before she spread out beside Janet with a smile on her face, giving Isabella first dibs on the shower. The men trooped back to the other suite to make themselves at home.

Showered and groomed, Chenaugh found a room service menu and after checking with the woman ordered supper for delivery to the 'girls' suite. "Drinks anyone?" asked Chenaugh already ensconced in the 'girls' lounge with Chip and Clyde, the three of them in loose t-shirts and briefs. "Yes," said Shauna, as she came out of the bedroom towel drying her hair, wearing the one nighty she'd been able to find, perking up the men even more. "WOW. Take a look at YOU!" said an adoring Clyde. Everyone grabbed a delighted eyeful. Shauna happily twirled her assets around requesting, "A glass of their best red wine, please."

All six lounged around the table after the meal, sharing banter, all satiated and mellow having also shared three bottles of wine. Shauna who'd started drinking before eating, was tipsy, abandoned, full of 'amour' looking for fun, going from man to man, sitting in their laps and being a tease. Although fun to watch, Isabella and Janet, wearing rather conservative nightgowns, felt a bit out of their element. But they liked the informality, especially in the humidity and heat as they'd found out that 'Grande' didn't include air conditioning.

Enjoying her freedom, sensing the others weren't as unencumbered as Shauna or even himself, Chip thought about how people put restraints on themselves and then blame others for holding them back. Sitting on Clyde's lap, Shauna, professed her tiredness, shakily got up and wandered through the connecting door into the men's suite, found the bed and collapsed on it. Chip followed, giving her a couple of aspirin before she sank into sleep. About to cover her up with her nightie that had ridden up past her waist, he decided not to. She was safe. None of them would take advantage of her, no matter what the situation. He kissed her forehead and rejoined the others.

Restless but with a purpose, Chip said he was going to walk around for a bit and visit the hotel shop. Clyde and Chenaugh jumped up to accompany him, energy to burn too. Contemplating the pleasure of climbing into bed, closing her eyes and passing into sleep-land, Janet suddenly said, "I'll race you to bed. Winner gets to choose which side to sleep on," and took off running. Isabella, an insomniac and touchy about it, having kept it well hidden, drank the last of the wine and strolled to the bathroom, passing a triumphant Janet sitting on the side of the bed she'd claimed. Staggering a little as she brushed her teeth - that final glass taking effect – Isabella quickly finished and made her way back into the bedroom to find Janet already snoring lightly. *Just my luck*, she thought.

Chip, Chenaugh and Clyde visited the hotel shop where Shauna had stopped to window gaze.

"You guys are sure you want to do this?" asked Chip. "I mean, it's a lot of money and all. Especially buying all three items I saw her eyeballing."

"Give it a rest Chip," responded Chenaugh. "Besides it's not really our money, now is it? And yes, we do want to be part of this - even if it wasn't our idea."

"And using these new bank cards feels wonderful," added Clyde. "I've never been treated by our Government like this before. I could go crazy if I let myself."

"Okay then. I just wanted to make sure," backed down Chip, who was having momentary regrets for having shared his idea with the other two. "Thanks guys for pitching in. We can do the honors together in the morning. Now, how about checking out the bar and having a nightcap before we head back?"

The three friends sauntered into the bar and ordered. Following their recent experiences the three saw everyone as suspicious, particularly if they were caught looking directly at them. "Let's drink up and get the hell out of here," said a nervous Clyde.

Back in their suite, feeling safer, they hid the small packages and quickly got ready for bed. Wiped out and feeling no pain from the additional booze, Chip got into bed next to Shauna and eased her across him, stomach to stomach, one of her arms hanging limp beside the bed, her legs draped either side of him, her flattened breasts tantalizing his chest.

Telling Chenaugh and Clyde that the rest of the bed was for them, he went to sleep, feeling them settling in beside him. Chenaugh and Clyde adoring the beautiful pairing, already transforming themselves through the unspoken encouragement and loving inspiration of Shauna and Chip, feeling so included in the bonding, unthinkingly wrapped their arms around each other, and went to sleep too.

CHAPTER 35   SINISTER

The eastern sky, where the sun was supposed to be, was gray and colorless. A steady drizzle was falling which could be heard tapping on the metal sunshades above the windows, a soothing melody prolonging sleep.

Eventually the noise of cars and pedestrian traffic spilling through the open windows, signaling the early start of a new working day, awakened Janet. She became aware of Isabella stirring on the other side of the bed, as far away as she could possibly be. As soon as Janet started for the bathroom, Isabella yawned and rolled over, spreading out. *I'm not going to take that personally*, thought Janet, changing direction, saying, "Isabella, I'm going to see if the guys are up." Isabella sat bolt upright with dread at Janet's remark.

Janet padded bare foot to the other suite and peeked in the bedroom. She took delight in seeing the three men sleeping in one big tangle of bodies. Not seeing Shauna she went over to the bathroom and took a peek inside. Empty. No sign of her daughter anywhere. A first stirring of fear and panic took hold. Rushing back to the bed she started shaking Chip and calling his name louder and louder until all three guys were sitting up looking at her, blurry eyed. "What! what! Janet?" questioned Chip. "I can't find Shauna and I'm scared," her voice shaking, body trembling. Chip reached out with a reassuring embrace and speaking tenderly said they'd soon find her. Janet was not convinced.

Fearing the worst and visited by rampaging emotions, they continually collided as their search for Shauna became more desperate. They'd checked the hotel – lobby, shop, restaurant, bar – now resorting to rechecking the suites for the umpteenth time: under the beds, in the closets, behind the bar, looking in places for a lost person that didn't make any sense. "She wouldn't have left without letting one of us know. She just wouldn't," repeated a desperate Chip. Everyone was more than wide awake now but had almost become paralyzed by Shauna's disappearance.

Snapping out of his mental turmoil, Chenaugh called Comstock. Unable to reach him he left a message to call back ASAP. Clyde, now stirred, called his SEAL Captain, asking him to have immediate re-enforcements put in place near Cuba. Chip got ahold of Norm to somehow find Richardson and

264

get him to call. He wondered about CIA operatives in the area but, without input from Comstock or Richardson, had no idea where to start with that.

In all the snarl of activity, Janet became suspicious of Isabella's nervousness and lack of participation and approached her. Isabella averted her gaze. "What's going on, Isabella? Is there something you know that could help? Are you involved in some way? Why are you so quiet? What's going on?" and she continued, relentless until Isabella slumped in her chair and hung her head, choking back tears and wringing her hands. Janet didn't want to believe the worst but she was as enraged as she'd ever been, feeling no sympathy for Isabella: as if her daughter hadn't already been through enough suffering. "Dammit woman, we're losing valuable time! WHAT HAPPENED TO SHAUNA?" The men, already aware of the altercation but previously occupied, turned at the shout. Janet waved them off. "Not until she tells us what she knows!"

With all the focus on Isabella now, she was even more reluctant to open up, finding it increasingly difficult to face what she had done. "Come on. Do what you know to be right. Time is wasting! We need you to do this for yourself and for us. Please. I'm begging you," implored a wavering Janet. Chip fell to his knees before Isabella, repeatedly begging her to tell them whatever she knew while seriously considering wringing her neck till she talked.

Cowed, Isabella started to confess, moved by Chip's restraint. "It all happened . . ." "Just tell us where she was taken," said an exasperated Chip. "The Military Attache, who is in fact Sean, and four of his men have taken her by van to an abandoned warehouse near Santiago. His plan is to get the information out of her by any means necessary. He, of course, won't get his hands dirty but will stay close by to ensure a successful outcome." "Enough!" shouted an impatient and angry Clyde before an outraged and disgusted Chenaugh manhandled her into the bedroom and shut the door, advising her in no uncertain terms to not show her face unless called.

The distraught men continued their calls for help with renewed intensity, browbeating whoever they could. Threatening, cajoling or pleading – whatever worked. Comstock offered an additional list of resources to contact and the three fed everything they came up with to Comstock's think-tank. Listening to the back and forth and one-sided conversations, Janet lit up and slipped into the adjacent suite for privacy. Returning quickly, she settled in to follow events with less concern.

Chip was thankful to be occupied with organizing all the information being generated by Chenaugh's and Clyde's efforts. Otherwise he knew he'd be falling apart, or in danger of strangling Isabella. He could feel how counterproductive this split in his being was, that it could lead nowhere except to an impotency of himself and the others; that dredging the depths of his darkness would only endanger Shauna further and hinder any movement to gain her release. It was suppressing his energy and vibrational level to the point where he was becoming totally ineffectual. He broke down and sobbed, helping relieve some of the deep rooted pain and forcing him to open and receive the support of Clyde, Chenaugh and Janet.

A weary but alert Comstock called back with a plan. "It's pretty good considering we've had to put it together on the fly but it requires all of you – and I mean ALL of you, SEAL CLYDE – to stay put, in your suites. Now, we have a SEAL team on its way as we speak. We've retargeted a satellite for surveillance which should come on station in the next five minutes and once we have the warehouse pinpointed the SEALs will move in. Damn, it galls me that we can't intercept the van before it gets to the warehouse, but we can't risk a public take down . . . hold on, hold on . . ." and he was interrupted. Saying he'd call back, Comstock hung up.

Agreeing with Chenaugh and Clyde that they'd give Shauna the jewelry as soon as they reached Jamaica and advising them of his promise to her, Chip felt more composed. That there was a viable plan in place probably helped too. "Now let's find out what's been going on with Isabella," he said. "She seemed so genuine that I'm finding it hard to believe she'd give up Shauna. She must be getting a shit-load of money. I mean, just how much money does it take to align with a fucker like Sean Cameron? I just don't get it and I'm glad I don't. But then again, for some people there's probably only a thin line between integrity and corruption, particularly if you're faced with the dark side every day. Makes my admiration and appreciation for you two so much greater," he finished and the three men embraced, feeling they were experiencing the same thing, thankful to have each other.

"NO! That wasn't how it was," answered Isabella. "I was a good agent - one of the best in fact – but meeting Yelena again somehow triggered a longing I'd always had. To be free, financially. To never have to worry about where the next meal might come from, a constant fear as a child, being hungry all the time. At first I was wary of sharing too much with her about why we were in Moscow, but the more time I spent with her, experiencing the life of abundance she had, the more I thought about the years of service I'd put in, always being at the beck and call of others and risking my life for so little return. I wanted the kind of life she had. Of course, at the time, while I suspected her husband of criminal corruption which she had obviously benefitted from, it wasn't until the airport and after that I realized she was the true source of evil in their partnership. But by then I felt like it was too late. We'd texted each other while being driven from the boatyard to the airport and she'd made the offer: an untraceable numbered account that would enable me to retire when and if I chose in exchange for facilitating Shauna's capture once in Cuba. Not coming clean right away meant that even the life I'd known was over, I would never be trusted again, so I carried on, hoping my duplicity could be kept hidden. Until this morning. When I realized what I had done." Talking, Isabella had felt the knots in her stomach unravel but Chenaugh, less than sympathetic, interrupted. "Okay, so poor you succumbed to temptation. What the fuck happened last night?"

"Well, while I'd hoped that my treachery would be lost with Yelena's arrest – even if she'd mentioned it I didn't expect her to be taken seriously – I wasn't that lucky. At about three o'clock this morning, I was in the living room reading – I have insomnia – when there was a tapping at the door of the suite. When I opened it, five men, the Attaché and four others, pushed their way in. I guess they must have got which suite we women were in from the room service waiter and assumed Shauna would be here. When I told the Attaché she was next door, he sent the four men in to drug the three of you and take her while he stayed to keep an eye on me and boast about the plans for Shauna. That's when I realized he had to be Sean." "What an asshole!" exclaimed an enraged Chenaugh.

Isabella continued, her words pouring out faster and faster. "The men soon appeared with Shauna rolled up in a tightly bound rug hoisted on their shoulders. I was relieved I couldn't see her, more relieved that she couldn't see me even though I knew she was drugged. I remember hoping she could breathe without any problem as they all left quickly, carrying her out without a word. I felt like I'd been punched in the gut. It had been one thing to text about a plan, but another to experience it and feel the consequences.

"I rushed into your bedroom to make sure you were all alright - you were unconscious and breathing heavily - then I ran to the window just in time to see a panel van pull away from out front. I could only assume that the van contained Shauna and her captors. As best as I could tell, knowing how street lighting distorts colors, the van was dark green with a light blue hood. I was too far away and the angle too acute to make out the license plate – even if it had one - but I did notice that the left tail-light wasn't working." "Are you supposed to contact them or are they going to contact you?" asked Clyde.

"The only thing I remember Sean telling me was to go about business as usual and for us, minus Shauna, to board the ship for Jamaica. Sean knew we couldn't do a damned thing with the authorities here and he also knew about our Jamaican plans. He said if we went to anyone for help, we would each be killed, along with our families - we could count on that. He also said he'd left details for accessing the numbered account in a plain business envelope waiting for me at the front desk."

Janet had been listening attentively to everything. In one way, she felt thankful that she was not a light sleeper. After all, what could she have done anyway to help her daughter and still stay alive? She'd be of no use to Shauna dead, but she did have a vital connection with one source that could, without a doubt, save Shauna. She would talk to everyone about it after breakfast and suggested they order, emphasizing that they needed to take care of themselves regardless of Shauna's situation.

Once again they sat around the table, but this time the mood was somber and there was hardly any conversation. They were each in their own way giving to Shauna's safety, silently sending her their undying love and the knowledge that she was not alone, or ever would be, and that help was on the way. Even Isabella, who'd been let out to eat, added to the transmission.

Unbeknownst to them, Shauna could feel their giving and was able to relax a little. She even forgot how thirsty she was and how bad she needed to pee.

Sending Isabella back to the bedroom, Janet addressed the men. Swearing them to secrecy she then told them about the aliens.

CHAPTER 36 HELP

Reminding Chip of Shauna's miraculous healing and the life forms they'd encountered on their space-time travels at orgasm she began to cry. Pulling a tissue from her purse and holding it to her eyes, she lamented, "Oh, Shauna. There are so many things I need to tell you, so many things you need to know. The many secrets you are on the verge of uncovering with Chip. It truly is another world you're headed to . . . worlds I should say. I need you so much my precious Shauna." Blowing her nose, she apologized. Feeling her profound misery they moved to console her, embracing her, Chip tenderly kissing her red, swollen eyes.

Janet quietly continued. "While there's been much conjecture about the existence of aliens, I can tell you quite categorically that they are real and Scotland is one of their primary points of entry and contact. I have been in contact with them for a long time and have trained my chief assistant, Mary, how to communicate with them too. So while you were calling all your contacts trying to move mountains and-or Mohammed, I called and asked her to find them and see if they would come and help. She's just let me know that they're on their way."

Seeing their surprise, she explained that she and Mary were able to communicate telepathically which was also how they contacted the aliens. Mentioning that she understood Chip and Shauna had learnt thought-speak too, she pointed out that it didn't just require all parties to be totally open to revealing their inner depths but that any distractions - mental, emotional, physical, chemical – would impair the process and most likely block it completely. Adding that, given the current set of circumstances, contacting Shauna telepathically would be impossible because of such distractions.

"As for the aliens themselves," she went on, "they have proven both friendly and compassionate, grieving over our continuing conflicts, abuse and mistreatment of each other. In recent times though, unlike in the past, they rarely intervene. They claim that while their intention is to avoid tampering with the evolution of our planet, they get impatient at how slow we are in progressing to a higher life. Now they feel that our fate is coming to a crossroads and are on their way to help and will take whatever action they deem necessary to protect Shauna." Reiterating that the information needed to be kept secret, Janet went on to explain that the aliens were adamant that in order for them to help they had to operate out of the public eye. "Common knowledge of their existence or activities could be disastrous for them and us and particularly Shauna. So, please, keep this to yourselves."

For the first time since discovering Shauna's absence, Chip, Chenaugh and Clyde felt hopeful. Thankful that Janet had sought the aliens' help and the aliens were willing to give it, the three of them sat silently, allowing the significance of her words to percolate through their programmed skepticism, even Chip's, and focused on a Shauna alive and well.

The warble of Chenaugh's phone interrupted their meditation. Quickly taking the call he passed on that Norm and Richardson would arrive soon to pick up Isabella and take her stateside. "After delivering her, Norm will head back to Moscow to monitor progress there and Richardson will go to Spain. Seems he's got a hair up his ass about Sean already having left Cuba for somewhere in Southern Europe," Chip went to check on Isabella.

Entering the bedroom he found her lying face down on the bed surrounded by a field of crumpled tissues. She looked up with puffy, red eyes and recognizing him, started crying all over again. "Don't you think it's a little late for regrets? You might want to take responsibility for what you've done and remember what you said to both Shauna and me right at the beginning – that you were with us one-hundred percent. Well, you're going to have plenty of time to consider what that actually means, because Norm and Richardson are on their way to take you back to the States."

Suddenly Isabella sat up in bed and, putting her shoes on, said, "Chip, Dear, would you do me a favor? Would you accompany me to the front desk to get the envelope Sean left for me?" "Are you kidding?" asked a shocked Chip. "Well you don't have to get so bent out of shape about it," commented an out of touch Isabella. "Isabella, you have no idea what a bent-out-of-shape me looks like. I can't believe you'd even think about taking the payoff money from the fucking asshole who's planning on torturing and killing Shauna. Goddammit Isabella, Shauna could tell him everything he wants to know and he'd have no idea what she was talking about. He's made himself so dense that he doesn't have it in him to grasp anything about Shauna or what she's bringing about. And that good part of yourself that felt her, well that's you and you know it. So no, you're not going to touch the money. Nor are any of us. Maybe some unsuspecting someone will figure out whatever's in the envelope and use the money in the account for good, or maybe it will never be used, I don't fucking care!" Isabella asked quietly, "Chip, can you forgive me?" Chip didn't answer right away and Isabella waited with trepidation.

After what seemed like hours to Isabella, but was in fact about thirty seconds, Chip replied. "Yes, yes I do Isabella. I don't need the burden of being unforgiving. In fact, I can't afford it. But Isabella, I think it's just as important that you forgive yourself, that you're not consumed by remorse and guilt. And be honest with yourself, was it your remorse that caught you or the fact that you were deceitful and full of shit in the first place? And is your guilt genuine? What kind of life you have is completely up to you. Even in prison you can thrive - or you can suffer. It's up to you what you make of what's next. Consider it an opportunity."

Isabella hadn't expected that much from Chip. She was very quiet and jolted to her core. All she could say was, "Thank you." She was thinking to herself, *I can see how Shauna and Chip meet each other. They are so alike: so passionate and nourishing, wanting everyone, not just themselves, to live a higher life. They generate an intimacy that I don't think I've ever gotten close to experiencing with any one person, much less having it with many. That takes more than love as I've ever known it or seen it. I doubt if I could ever be that kind of person. I'm too easily swayed, except when on assignment when I'm single minded. But in my personal life, that's another story. Take away my work and who am I, really?* Chip was about to leave the room when he called back to her, "You'd better get ready to leave." Isabella was all too happy to focus on the mundane. *Enough introspection for now,* she thought.

"How did it go?" inquired Clyde. "Just about what I expected," replied Chip. "I really don't know if I got through to her at all. But I'm not going to waste any more time or energy. I've given her the best of me and she'll do with it what she chooses." "Thanks anyway," said Clyde. "Yeah, thanks Bro," added Chenaugh. Janet, off by herself, aware of everything, enjoyed the closeness between the three men more than her coffee. Her thoughts drifted as she gave her heart and soul to Shauna's well-being.

Their meager belongings packed, the four of them were in the lounge area waiting. Often the hardest thing to do; nerve-wracking. Finally Chenaugh's cellphone rang. Seeing it was Comstock, opting to not put the call on speaker, he accepted the call, raised the phone to his ear and listened. Everything seemed to be proceeding smoothly and on time, although there was still no sign of Sean anywhere. Not even a sniff. But the SEALs had the warehouse surrounded and were ready to move in. Comstock suggested the five of them kick back and rest, not believing for one moment that they would, even though they'd probably have several hours to wait. "Make good use of your time, Chenaugh, and let me know when Richardson and Norm get there to arrest Isabella. In fact call me every thirty minutes, regardless. Got that?"

Chenaugh relayed the exchange to the others before suggesting they order more coffee and snacks, expecting it could be a long wait and he was already getting hungry. "Is there anything worthwhile on the tele?" he asked, hoping to take his mind off the imminent action he had no way of influencing.

CHAPTER 37 RESCUE

The inside of the van was hot and the ride bumpy. Sean and the kidnappers sat in the forward seats and every once in a while one would look back at the rolled up carpet to make sure everything was like it should be - the same as the last look. They had been on the road for hours, or so it seemed. They stopped to take a breather and a stretch. That's when Sean announced that at this juncture he was parting ways with his men, reminding them of their plans for before and after.

The before plan was to interrogate Shauna about her powers, using torture if necessary, until she either told them everything or was dead. The four men were good in this department, knowing just what to do and when to do it. They used mixtures of boiling chemicals to eat away skin, flesh and bones - an extremely flexible process that, if applied judiciously, could cause unfathomable agony, as the body was chemically dissolved, for hours if not days, depending on how much of a hurry they were in.

The after plan was the disposal of the body so it would never be discovered. The four had several options in mind, but would make the final selection based on how far they had to go with the torture.

Beyond that, Sean would disappear while the four men would travel back to the States via Barbados. Sean would then contact them later, having no inclination or intention of providing any possibility of being tracked.

As the van pulled away from the rest stop, the driver looked in the rear view mirror to see a car stop to pick up Sean. The men felt better now that Sean had left them. They never knew what to expect from him except that he would be cruel. He'd lure people into his schemes, preying on their various appetites until they were powerless to escape from his control. Just as he'd done with them. They didn't like him, but loved the money he paid them. Having got moving on the road again, they were eager to arrive at their destination, get the job done and get back to their regular life. That they were going to hurt a human being was not something that concerned them. They kept the Pandora's box of emotions tightly closed and locked within themselves.

Shauna's body was trapped in a very uncomfortable position. Her arms and legs were pinned inside the rolled and tightly taped rug. When they'd tossed her into the cavernous space in the back of the old van, she had landed on her stomach so she had to keep her head to one side or the other so she could breathe. *No wonder they design massage tables with a hole for the face,* thought Shauna, trying to distract herself from the unbearable confinement and increasingly intense pain in her neck.

Distracting herself further, she focused on her lifeline: Chip, her mother, Chenaugh and Clyde and, to a lesser extent, Isabella. Concentrating on gratitude for each one as an individual, for what each one of them meant to her and what she received from them, she felt her pain and fears recede

Although she'd tried to roll on her back before, she now decided to make a concerted effort, empowered by the giving she was feeling from the five. Just as she was girding herself, the van tilted as if climbing a hill. With the additional help of gravity she was able to roll, first onto her side and then onto her back. That felt so good!

I'm beginning to feel there is a way out of this nightmare. I don't know how, but I can feel it! And this feeling is just as real as the nose on my face. In spite of the perilous situation she was in, Shauna was very close to a transformation that would revolutionize the cosmos, not just the planet. An awareness that what was happening inside of her would soon manifest through infinity. *Back to 'As within, so without',* she thought. *Believing that what I give myself to is what I get, I need to watch my every thought, my every emotion, my every feeling, every moment, to be sure that what I'm giving to is life-affirming, not life-destroying. Shit, what a tall order! I've had it up to the wazoo with getting myself and others into these life and death situations. Damn, I don't have answers right at this minute, but the more I tap into this new stuff, new things will come forth. From where? From right out of me. But not just out of me, I'm far from enough. What I can't see and know and feel, someone else will. I sense a whole new dimension that gives greater depth to what I have with the three guys and my mum. We have the beginnings of a powerful intimacy that will grow stronger and more lasting, all-consuming and all-encompassing. Why am I thinking this in the back of an old van while all bound up on my way to who knows where?*

The aliens were pleased with Shauna. If only she knew how close they were. But then, it was impossible to tell if they didn't want you to know. Or almost impossible.

The old warehouse structure was cavernous and dilapidated. A section of the roof had collapsed to leave a sizeable hole through which the rain fell steadily and the gray, cloudy sky could be seen. Accumulated rainwater dripped steadily onto the cracked and crumbling cement floor, adding irregular plops to the continuous pattering. Huge double doors clung to the only entrance. Their usefulness long gone as they hung askew and unmovable on broken hinges - just enough space between for a truck to drive through. Ransacked and stripped of anything valuable, all that remained inside were various lengths of chain scattered on the floor and what looked like a large kids swing with a wide seat that hung a few feet off the ground. Despite the loose and missing boards on all four sides the undivided space was dark and gloomy, especially on a rainy day. Standing in decaying isolation on the outskirts of Santiago, a stone's throw from the bay, it had proven perfect for Sean's needs on several previous occasions, and today would be no different.

The van drove slowly between the battered doors, made its way to the far end where the swing was and parked. The men got out, relieved that this part of the trip was over, and began unloading an assortment of equipment, duffle bags and boxes. They didn't talk much. They concentrated on unpacking and setting up their instruments of torture.

Two iron tripods, each with a large horizontal ring set between the tops of the legs were placed in front of each end of the swing. Burner heads were positioned on the floor beneath the horizontal rings and tubing installed to connect them to a large propane tank that had been unloaded and set to one side. A couple of large portable water containers were stood on the floor near the propane tank. A long portable table was hauled out and unfolded and an array of canisters, ladles and spoons lined up along its top. Various sundries, including two large metal bowls and a few rolls of duct tape, were carelessly tossed on the table, almost like an afterthought. And a stack of old rags and towels were thrown on the floor, handy to both the table and the swing.

Once set up, the men had a brief discussion about where to start. Being lazy and not particularly creative they decided to keep it simple and just use the large bowls. Less preparation or thought needed.

"The bitch might be tall but she doesn't seem to weigh that much so I think the swing should work fine for what we have in mind. Go get her and bind her to the seat so she can't move," instructed the leader, pointing to two of the others. They quickly moved to fetch Shauna while the leader and the fourth thug began preparing the chemical cocktail.

The two men took off Shauna's hood before grabbing the rug and lifting it out of the van. Carrying it towards the swing they purposely dropped the rug and Shauna on the floor. Shauna "Ouched!" as she landed, thankful for the padding of the rug. The two men smiled at each other. "Hey, you bums, don't damage the goods," laughed the leader. The two eagerly started slicing through the tape securing the rug, anticipating the fun to come. Since they'd started working for Sean they'd become addicted to the act of torture. Over time they'd become numb to the effects of inflicting pain, suppressing the nightmares both asleep and awake, and craving the rush of having the power over life, death and pain that torture gave them.

Suddenly the leader called, "Quiet! Did you hear something?" They all paused and looked up at the ceiling, focusing on the gaping hole where the rain was still falling. They listened intently for any suspicious noise but heard nothing. "Okay, probably just a bird, or a slight case of nerves or something. Let's go."

"That was close," whispered the SEAL leader. "Yeah," said the SEAL on the roof who'd been lying motionless for more than an hour, waiting. Having set up their surveillance equipment and positioned themselves strategically around the warehouse, the SEALs were now following developments as ordered – monitor activity and transmit to command. Unless the victim was in imminent danger of serious harm, they were to maintain their positions and observe.

Shauna had pissed several times during the long trip and it had soaked through the inner layers of carpet. Combined with her sweat and cooked by the heat the stench had intensified each mile. Fortunate to have her head separately covered Shauna hadn't been subject to the fumes till now. When the two thugs unrolled the carpet, they gagged and were forced to recoil from the pungent odor they released in the process.

Recovering, the two men held their breath as they hastily grabbed her under the armpits and rushed to tape her to the swing. Opening her mouth to speak as they worked, she was quickly silenced by a smack across the face which jolted her backwards, nearly dislodging her from their grasp. They begrudgingly kept hold of her, breathing in her stench as they continued taping.

It was just as well that she stunk. It kept them from pawing her nakedness through her sodden and steaming nightie. Determined to survive whatever she was subjected to, Shauna passively allowed them to proceed. Having used her time imprisoned in the rug in the back of the van to reconstruct her nervous system with the new life she was experiencing with Chip and their orgasmic travels, she was immune to despair or fear for herself.

She watched intently, more curious than concerned, as the leader finalized the chemical brew in each of the large bowls and the fourth thug adjusted the propane system.

With the two large bowls set into the rings on the tripods and the burners fired up, it was now obvious what they had in mind. A putrid vapor rose as chemicals were heated, the two thugs who had taped her immobile watching intently. "Hey jerks, you planning on getting to the questions anytime soon? Or do you need some encouragement?" asked the leader, drawing his gun and aiming it in their direction. Shaken out of their reverie, the two men visibly flinched and hustled to get started. Pissed at being demeaned in front of the captive bitch they thought to reassert a sense of power with their interrogation.

The larger and uglier of the two began. "So bitch, cooperate and we might make it easier for you."

"I doubt that very much," responded a calm Shauna. "I know that whichever way this goes, you'll kill me."

"Well, well, well, a smart mouth," said ugly and smacked her on the side of the head. "Keep that up and you'll wish we'd kill you," he sneered. Shauna who'd winced with the blow, kept herself steady as a large red welt appeared on her cheek. "Now tell us where you get your power from," commanded ugly.

"I get my power from myself," answered Shauna. "Not that I'd expect you to understand what I mean. You probably think I get it from some other person or persons, or some other source outside myself. And I don't have a crystal ball either."

"Still the smart bitch talking gibberish, trying to confuse us. You think we're dumb or somethin'? I'm going to enjoy listening to you beg to die. Now, one more chance, being as I'm such a nice guy." He sneered again and asked, "Why d'ya wanna rule the planet? Why doncha just go home and do what women do? Be a good wife, take care of your man, make babies?"

"Look, I have no desire to have power over anyone or, for that matter, any thing. What I want is to free people from any limitation that would cause suffering, hardship, struggle or sacrifice - anything that would cause them to sink deeper into darkness and death. I'm not better or worse than anyone else. I'm not a criminal who deserves punishment. Actually, I'm harmless and act from a pure feeling."

Studying their blank expressions she knew that whatever she said would fall on uncomprehending ears, not deaf ones. She'd never be able to penetrate them and momentarily wished for a magic wand to open their minds and hearts, because, right now, she had no idea how to get through to them. Sadly, she decided not to waste her energy any more.

"Fuck. This is getting us nowhere," said the leader, stuffing the gun in the waistband of his pants. "Sean's gonna kill us if we don't get what he wants, so stop pissing around and let's see how smart-mouthed she is when her flesh is melting."

All four of them moved toward the two bowls of boiling chemicals and carefully moved them beneath Shauna's hands which had been left dangling over the front of the armrests when she'd been tied to the swing. She could feel the heat of the boiling chemical mixtures and braced herself for the horrifying experience of being dissolved inch by inch.

Being so finely attuned, Shauna was the first to feel the tremors that began to gently shake the old warehouse. As the tremors increased in intensity, the loose boards began vibrating a symphony of scratches, thumps and rattles. The men looked about warily as the already unstable structure began to shudder violently. The quaking caldrons sent gobs of burning chemicals spattering across Shauna's hands and legs. Shauna's instant, blood-curdling scream pierced the rumbling, magnifying the building's vibrations and bursting outward.

The SEAL was jarred loose from his precarious roof perch. Saved from falling by his safety rope he dangled through the broken roof, offering a perfect target. Although distracted by the cacophony around him, the thug leader was alert enough to take advantage. Removing the gun from his belt he shot the helpless SEAL. Shauna turned away, thinking of Clyde and the other SEALs, wondering if they'd known him. In such a small, tight-knit community it was likely they had. Shauna fought against her restraints now, feeling an abhorrence of killing and violence of any kind.

Realizing that Sean's plan and their safety were now compromised, the group leader, moving to start the van, ordered the others to kill Shauna and get in the van with him. As they moved to comply, the three men plus the leader fell, shot by the SEALs who rushed their positions and secured them. Once they were neutralized, the SEAL Medic turned to Shauna. Seeing the burns she'd endured he instructed his comrades to grab the water jugs and flush her wounds.

As quickly as the tremors had arisen, they subsided, and the SEALs were able to proceed with their task without fearing the building collapsing around them. Tending to Shauna, they seemed unaffected by the rankness that rose from her every pore. Appreciative of the gallantry, Shauna also appreciated the humor in the situation. "Thanks for ignoring my stench guys and being so gentlemanly about it too. Just so you know, though, I won't be offended if you want to choke, gag, or even throw up." She added a laugh, totally dissolving the tension.

"I'm so thirsty I can't even make spit and that water looks so inviting. You want to send some of it mouthwards?"

"Better use my canteen. You never know where this has come from," said one of the SEALs, unhooking his canteen and offering it to her lips. As the SEALs continued the water treatment, she began to feel relief and asked them to continue. After several more minutes, a couple of the SEALs began removing her bindings. The water had helped soften the tape but it was still a delicate task and painful for Shauna, especially where it had been wrapped around her waist. The SEALs smiled reassuringly as inch by inch they freed her.

"Now, slow and easy, let's see if you can stand." With one SEAL on either side and a third behind, Shauna slowly slid off the swing. She gingerly planted both feet on the cold floor. Weak and shaky at first, she was grateful for the support. While she stood, testing her strength, two SEALs kneeled in front of her and started rubbing her legs vigorously to stimulate circulation. Soon, feeling the effects of their well-trained touch, Shauna took a confident step forward, and then another, and another, until she was walking on her own, without a hitch. Stopping every once in a while to shake her legs, she increased her pace until she was running circuits inside the building. "I tell you guys, you have no idea how good this feels. A reminder to not take this wonderful body for granted. Just the simple act of walking, or brushing my teeth, or what it feels like to breathe, or to feel the heart beating. I could just go on and on. Thanks." Shauna shouted with delight.

She tossed back her head and laughed with pure joy. Joining the cluster of SEALs she had a sparkle in her eyes that was irresistible. Enthralled by her infectious persona, they were happy for Clyde, their brother SEAL, who they knew had been released to go to Jamaica instead of joining them for their next assignment. Lucky Clyde.

"OK, let's get you cleaned up, at least a little!" Stripping off Shauna's tattered, filthy nightie, one of the SEALs tossed it as far as possible. A little embarrassed, they all tried to ignore what a strikingly beautiful women she was. It would have been easy to stop and stare, and Shauna was only too willing to let herself be seen. But as at home as she was in her skin, there was no arrogance or coquettishness. She radiated an openness and innocence that allowed the SEALs to relax and enjoy her completeness with wide open eyes, while she enjoyed their adoration. She became a person for them, not a sexual object, and they were able to proceed with their ministrations with open admiration, untainted by sexual fantasies or guilt.

Little by little Shauna felt her recuperative powers being restored as the SEALs carefully washed and rinsed her clean, the tepid water continuing her recovery. Her unruly hair, which was a tangle of curls and frizz, was hard to tame and, since there was no brush or comb to be found, one of the SEALs tied it back with a piece of torn towel. As the Medic dressed her wounds, a team mate hefted a duffle bag toward her, announcing, "Here's the icing on the cake." He opened it and plucked out some clothes. Shauna couldn't believe the SEALs had brought clothing for her. Jumping and clapping with enthusiasm she had them all mesmerized by her bouncing nakedness. Smiling at her response, one explained, "A certain fellow SEAL informed us of the sizes, so it was easy and fun to pick these up before we came." "You guys are the best!" she exclaimed, "I'm so thankful for everything and, as you said, this is the icing on the cake . . ." With tears of happiness and gratitude welling, she kissed each one on the cheek. "Wow!" said one, touching his cheek. "Maybe if we'd gotten you several sets of clothes we'd have merited a kiss on the lips." Shauna wasted no time in making another round and fulfilling his thinly disguised request.

Helping her dress, the SEALs took it in turn to be up close and personal. Each one taking their time adding a garment while the others watched mesmerized, as bit by bit her nakedness was covered. Finally, slipping on the sandals, she stood and modeled her new clothes, strutting around a refreshed woman. "I feel so good. Thanks," she said. "How do I look?" The warehouse rang to their whoops and hollers. "Which reminds me," said one, "when you screamed and the building rocked and rattled more and more wildly, I knew for sure that everything we'd heard about you was true." Absorbing the comment Shauna asked, "So you've heard things about me?" "For sure! Didn't you know you're becoming a legend? You can bet that once word gets out that you were here today, you'll be credited with diverting a hurricane that was headed this way." "Well, guys, that I don't need. Do you think we can maybe keep this to ourselves?"

"Yeah, no problem. Hurricanes change direction on a dime all the time," said one. "What's important though," said another, "is that there are still warnings in place and all air and sea traffic is suspended until further notice." Shauna wondered how that would affect the plan to travel to Jamaica by ship.

While Shauna was being attended to, the four thugs had been treated for their wounds and herded together. Now, a couple of the SEALs picked up their dead comrade and, with the thugs supporting each other, propelled them towards the extraction point for pick up. Not bound by the same weather restrictions as civilian transportation, they'd soon be braving the dregs of the storm on their way to Tampa to drop of the prisoners and return the fallen SEAL to base before picking up a military flight to Austin. There they'd hand over the surveillance records from the warehouse operation. Already transmitted to Comstock via satellite, he wanted the physical recordings for eventual prosecution.

With the rescue mission complete, the SEALs changed into civvies they pulled from the same duffle bag that had carried Shauna's. Piling into an old school bus they'd boosted on their way from the beach, they were eager to get Shauna back to Havana.

No one, least of all Shauna, could have anticipated what was to follow.

CHAPTER 38   SURPRISE

Before departing for Havana the SEALs decided to help the warehouse on its way to its inevitable demise. One of them primed the propane tank and torches with a little dollop of munitions before setting a small fire to get the ball rolling.

The bus waited, engine running, the driver eager to leave. Shauna snuggled against the window in the second row feeling well protected. The fire-starter came out running and dived through the open back door as licks of flame curled from the building's gaping siding. As they drove off they could hear the tortured timbers crackling, grinding and screeching: collapsing against each other. Hitting the road they heard the munitions-charged propane tank blow, disintegrating the structure in a virtual snowstorm of splinters. The shockwave punched the vehicle sideways tilting it momentarily onto two wheels. "Oops," said the demolitionist as everyone grabbed what they could to keep themselves seated.

Cursing the demo man loudly, despite Shauna's presence, the SEALs righted themselves, taking several moments to get settled again for the upcoming journey.

Shauna asked them how they planned to get out of Cuba and was told that what she didn't know couldn't hurt her. Understanding they were protecting her, she asked them for some way to stay in touch. "Ask Clyde," replied one, "he'll know how to get in touch with us." "Of course!" responded Shauna. "But I'd really like you with us in Scotland. Come see for yourselves what we're about and what we're doing. Maybe after your next assignment?" Thanking her they said they'd like to do that and would see if they could swing it. They then settled in for the long ride, silently paying homage to their recently fallen buddy before taking the opportunity to rest.

Shauna opened her eyes to find the bus parked on the side of a small dirt track, somewhere off the main Havana road. Looking around the bus, taking in the still figures of the sleeping SEALs, including the driver who was slumped over the wheel, she wondered if she was dreaming. She shook the SEAL next to her, receiving no response. It felt to Shauna like he was under a deep spell of some kind. Surprised, she remained calm, feeling reassured by a premonition that she'd soon know what was going on. Gentle pulsations in her stomach signaled that someone was trying to tap into her telepathically. Calming even more, she drew herself inwards to be as receptive as possible to this unexpected communication. Sitting quietly, she began to pick up the silent thinking of the transmitter who finally connected with her. Together they communicated beyond the realm of language, exchanging thoughts that could be roughly translated as:

"Hello Shauna. You call me Xetyatowam. Your mother contacted us. She was afraid for you. We pick up her concern though light years away in other universe in a far quadrant of cosmos. We started our journey to you immediate. Your mother we trust in. We go back for centuries together. You and I have a special connection also that started centuries ago. You call it father and daughter. You carry it forward in your DNA as the call to come forth in your power as human has become stronger and stronger. We come at a speed you know not of yet. We watch you and your enemies and your rescuers. We did not get involved till now. We would have if you were in much danger but did not want to be seen here if did not have to be. Our spaceship is cloaked, so unseen. Your rescuers are unconscious until you come join us. They are not harmed. We will wake them and they will continue their trip. We leave them a message about you. Make them feel good about what is happening. Don't worry. Chip knows you are fine. You have questions?"

"No. One thought out of many though. I'm astonished and happy you've come. I feel fortunate and blessed and am ready to join . . . But wait! I do have a question. We are going to get the others at the hotel in Havana?"

"Yes. They are ready. We go pick them up from the hotel roof. We are above you now and for a short time you be with us. Step outside and we transbeam you. No harm for you. There to here in an instant. Don't worry. We do this for centuries of time. It be fun."

Shauna did as she was told and got off the bus carefully so as not to disturb the others, as if she could anyway, and looked up. The spaceship was huge, sheltering her from the wind and rain, either because of its size or because of a force-field it was projecting. Whichever it was, she was thankful. From where she stood, directly under the ship, it looked like it was shaped like a huge donut with a convex indentation rather than a hole in the center. The ship's diameter was too big for her to see anything beyond its outer edge curving upwards. As she processed the sight an opening appeared right in the center of the indentation. A pinhole expanding until there was an opening that appeared to be about six feet in diameter before she realized her sense of distance was completely out of whack. Instead of the ship being almost close enough to touch, it was hovering at least a thousand feet above the ground. Assuming she needed to be in line with the center of the opening to be transbeamed she cautiously moved into position, willing herself to stay calm.

Standing there, looking up, she felt a tingling sensation as her surroundings disappeared and she was standing in the alien craft. She remained still, not sure what to expect or what she was supposed to do next. She could hear a gentle humming which she assumed came from the craft's power source, but it could just as well have come from an air circulation system, or the transbeamer itself. Becoming accustomed to the dimness, she felt dwarfed by the immense interior space that seemed to disappear into an endless darkness. Out of the black a form came, looming closer and closer as Shauna held her breath.

The exceptionally tall, orange-skinned being circled her slowly while Shauna examined he, she or it intently, remembering to breathe as she did so. The being's loose, ambling walk, its extra-long arms, swinging easily with every body movement, as if it were disjointed with very little muscle, suggested a light easy manner, and Shauna released a deep sigh before extending her hand. The alien stared for a moment and then rubbed one of its hands against hers. She was fascinated, not only with the gesture of rubbing, but with the hand itself. The palm was large and wide with five similarly-sized, finger-like, flattened stubs with rounded ends. No elongated fingers with joints and skin folds here.

An oversized and hairless head featured intriguing oval eyes absent lids or brows. Large and dark and devoid of white, it was hard to tell if they housed pupils and irises, although surface reflections animated them with moving highlights. Slightly protruding nostrils which rhythmically flared and receded, as if caused by deep breathing, sat where a human's nose would be. But it was the absence of a mouth that was most disconcerting. Of course, telepathy meant a mouth was irrelevant for communication, but what about eating? What Shauna took to be ears were flattened against either side of the head. Proportionally larger than human ears, the absence of lobes made them circular in shape and Shauna surmised that its hearing was probably very acute.

The body was equally hairless and smooth – iridescent orange skin stretched tight over a slight frame. Sharply squared shoulders topped a thin elongated torso that had a puckered flap, just below where a human navel would be, no obvious signs of genitalia, male or female, and flowed into legs that showed no contours or obvious joints - having the characteristics of two flexible pipes that could bend and twist at will. Large feet had toes similar in appearance to its fingers

Getting a read on how the alien was doing, what it was thinking or feeling, was almost impossible for Shauna at this first meeting. Without the usual indicators of eyebrows, eyelids and mouth, the alien seemed to be in a constant state of wide-eyed wonderment, until she noticed a barely visible intermittent pulsating glow in the middle of its forehead where what we call the sixth chakra would be. She was bursting with questions, adding more to her list as she noticed mores he didn't understand. She wondered what she looked like to the alien - if humans were familiar or foreign to it. And yet-------and yet------she had a sense of deja vu about the encounter-------as if sometime, somewhere, she had been in this same setting------with this same alien. Shauna felt comfortable in its presence, with the friendly waves it was transmitting, and what she felt was a non-critical, non-judgmental appraisal.

Sensing a presence behind her, Shauna turned and met the mesmerizing gaze of a companion alien. The first alien finally tapped her thoughts, letting her know that it was Xetyatowam, Towam for short, who had 'spoken' to her before and that the other was called Etyo. "We both are what you call males." As Towam was considerably taller than Etyo, Shauna was glad for Towam's clarity – she'd thought Etyo might be a female. Towam moved closer and bowed towards her until their foreheads touched, holding the position for what seemed like a long time to Shauna. Having no clue what was transpiring, she maintained the contact until Towam disengaged and Etyo took his place with the same respectful forehead to forehead touching. "Is this your form of greeting?' asked Shauna. After a lengthy pause Towam simply said, "Later."

Towam communicated for Shauna to follow him. He kept his pace slow so she could keep up while she scanned the ship's interior. The donut shaped ring, which she had seen from the underside, was lined by what looked like seating covered with a material she didn't immediately recognize. At the heart of the dome that towered above them was what she took to be the control room. It had a rapidly spinning tubular shaft running vertically through its center and the walls were lined with a myriad panels of different shapes, sizes and colors. Each panel featured a different pattern and seemed to blink at a different rate. And there wasn't a switch, lever, knob or button to be seen anywhere, they were all touch operated. *Of course*, thought Shauna, *the short, flattened fingers! I wonder how they hold anything.*

Shauna's thoughts were interrupted by a soft touch on her shoulder as Towam indicated for her to hurry along. Reaching a new section of the donut ring, Towam stopped beside a half tube positioned open side up that ran along the outer wall. Split into padded sections, each one was just wide enough and long enough to accommodate someone lying down, whether alien or human. Towan gestured for her to climb in. As she lay down she felt the padding adjust to support her comfortably and noticed a series of small holes every foot or so running along the length of the bed just below the lip on either side.

Lying on her back, she could now see three rectangles of a bright shiny yellow shimmering in the uppermost reaches of the dome and she smiled, remembering the light forms visiting her in Austin after the awful attack on the patio. She had been healed and made whole by the flurry of blue-white disks. How could she ever forget that! Shauna snapped back to attention when she saw Towam slide a small device from a shelf above the bed and place it in his hand. He studied it for a moment then tapped different locations on the small box with his thumb. He made it known for Shauna to remove her capris and bandages which gave her a moment of doubt about his intentions before she saw the dim light in his forehead pulsating fast, at which point she let go. Towan was pleased at how quick she was and instructed her, after she had bared her legs, to relax, take some deep breaths, and close her eyes. She did as she was told, finally giving in to a deep relaxation. She just barely felt her hair being tugged out from under her and spread out on the padding. Towam activated a series of panels above the bed, setting off an array of colored lights that randomly penetrated her body via the holes she'd noticed along both sides. Towam then proceeded to carefully move the small box over her, paying particular attention to her hands and the tops of her legs. He made another adjustment to the box and slowly skimmed it over her thick head of hair. Towam again was pleased with Shauna, how quickly and completely she responded to the healing, and how she was more luminous looking than ever. He left her to sleep to let the light rays and light waves do their work.

Leaving a message for them, Towam released the SEALs from their spell, knowing they would never know what really happened. One thing they knew immediately was how much they already missed Shauna.

CHAPTER 39 PICK UP

What a feeling of euphoria. This felt so good that a Please-Do-Not-Disturb sign should be placed somewhere strategically so it would be seen and obeyed. A good body stretch would feel wonderful, or maybe several------like a cat after a snooze in the warm sun following a well-deserved meal. The thought of a meal appealed too. In the meantime, lying wherever she was - thinking nothing, doing nothing - was heavenly . . . *How rude. Whoever you are, please leave me alone. And you can kindly keep your hands to yourself.* She felt a hand on her shoulder again, and this time, it rocked her body side to side. *Well, all right. What is it you want?* She felt the message touching her mind, trying to get through. She wanted to ignore it, but couldn't. "Welcome back." Fully awake, the wonderful state she'd been suspended in rapidly receded. Her surroundings of strange looking metals and materials were dimly lit. She sat up in the tubular bed and everything rapidly came back to her---or was it forwards? Whichever way. *"Greetings Towam. Whatever magic you performed has caused me to feel more wonderful than I've ever felt. Even my head feels refreshed." "That's because it has been, inside and out. Feel your hair."* Shauna reached up to cradle her head in her hands. She casually put one of her hands in her hair and gasped. "Wow! I've NEVER felt my hair so silky smooth-----and it smells so good. Thank you." Towam's forehead was glowing. *"I understood you Shauna, except for the first word."* "Oh, sorry. In this context it's an exclamation of surprise, wonder, pleasure, or similar and I felt all of them when I felt my hair. But Towam, your English is so good." "Yes. Being with you, I have remembered more and more." "Thank you for caring enough to want to communicate. Do you speak other languages?" Not waiting for an answer, she reached up and gently pulled him so their foreheads touched, feeling a surge of energy pulse through her. Releasing him, his forehead still glowing, affection filling his big dark eyes, she felt them a shade or two lighter. Perhaps it was her imagination.

Looking down at her legs she was excited to see them free of injuries. Running her hands over her thighs she felt the skin so soft and hydrated and noticed the backs of her hands just as fresh. Watching her, Towam thought-asked, *"You are very beautiful for an earthling?"* "Yes Towam. I am beautiful." She replied. About to ask where he came from, she was distracted as the spinning cylinder at the center of the ship began humming, rapidly accelerating beyond the speed of light and the ship lifted off.

Feeling like she was in a super-fast elevator, that sense of instantaneous transition from rest to express, her body seemed to momentarily lag before catching up with the movement as she was pressed into the bed, clinging to the sides. Seeing both aliens apparently unaffected she wondered how they managed the tendency of bodies to lose muscle and bone mass in zero gravity – maybe they never had to deal with it, she was certainly not aware of feeling weightless.

As Towam busily stroked the various screens ranged near the central cylinder, a fascinated Shauna watched, admiring his rapid and skillful touch. *"It is often more difficult to make short trips such as this one. It is not easy up and easy down. I hope it is not too wearing on you."* Adding, *"You make me happy Wydir. Your heart brims with Chip and that makes me happy too. Save some room in your heart for me, my Wydir."* She felt a rushing to him - especially after hearing 'Wydir', which she intuited meant 'daughter', but remained recumbent, not wishing to interfere with his concentration.

Arriving over the hotel in Havana, Shauna was so excited she didn't know what to do with her overflowing emotions at the thought of seeing everyone. Towam, having already linked with Janet to explain that her party should huddle together to be transbeamed as a unit, his forehead glowing brightly thought-spoke, *"Pretty soon."* Thankful for his feeling, Shauna got up and walked over to stand near the transbeam pad, stepping back as the five individuals flashed to life before her.

Still huddled together, they paused on the pad to adjust to the experience of their transbeamed selves before stepping off and rushing Shauna en masse, their arms wide open. Their excited movements to embrace one another drove the group off kilter and they all ended up in one laughing heap on the floor. Chip crawled on all fours to where Shauna was lying on her back being smothered with kisses from Janet, Chenaugh and Clyde.

She looked so beautiful, so fresh and glowing as she tried to wrap her arms around all of them at once, while they all tried to get closer to her and each other. Finally, Shauna decided to just let them have their way with her and surrendered to the friendly mass attack. Seizing the opportunity, Chip closed the distance and scooped her into his arms, smothering her with adoring kisses as he rolled her away from the others. She smelled so good. Wow! She looked so irresistible. Chip rolled onto his back with Shauna tightly clutched in his arms and legs. She ended up on top of him, devouring whatever she could get of him with her mouth. Towam and Etyo looked on, their foreheads flashing pricks of light. It was hard to tell why.

Both Shauna and Janet, feeling Towam's need to get moving - out of the city, out of the country, off the planet, the faster the better - quickly sat and strapped in, the guys joining them. Finally headed for Jamaica, it hit them full force that they were actually aboard an alien spaceship and they looked around with awe, soaking up the unfamiliar and mysterious yet intriguing shapes and sounds that reminded them of books and movies they'd each read and seen. Translating Towam, Janet relayed: "If bizarre and futuristic phenomena have been described in books or movie scripts, chances are the authors' ideas and imaginations and dreams are real and will become true someday. Man's unconscious mind contains an unlimited supply of creative ideas that will eventually be made manifest in the physical world." Switching from third person to first, she continued. "In fact, if it weren't for our unconscious minds, our species would have become stagnant and died out long ago. We communicate more through our unconscious than our conscious minds – much as we communicate more through body language than through actual words - even though most people remain asleep to the signals. The unconscious mind is way ahead of the conscious mind in planning and projecting. We could develop much faster and be able to draw on a greater newness and awakened energy from within if we stopped our conscious minds from wearing a rut through our lives by controlling our thought processes and channeling us along the same old knowledge pathways. The way to step up to new dimensions is to take risks. And right now we have an opportunity to take advantage of our miraculous biology – the essence of who and what we really are – and soar to places we have never been!"

Shauna having concentrated on settling her mind so she could tune in fully to Towam's communication had followed along with Janet and now introduced him to her Loves: Chip, Chenaugh and Clyde. She started explaining how the aliens communicated through telepathy, but Chip interrupted her saying Janet had already told them, so she just added that in time they would all be able to use it to talk with each other and the aliens, no matter where in the cosmos any of them might be. As she finished, as if on cue, a few blue-white disks made an appearance. Seemingly curious about the group they went from one to the other checking them out at close range, taking the liberty to go up to, and into, and out of each person. "This is something," said an awe-struck Clyde. "What a treat to be able to see this and be a part of it." Chip was silent, enjoying the alien forms enjoying him and the others. It brought Chip back to when they'd turned up in Austin at Shauna's time of need. Now he could see for himself what she had experienced and felt closer to her, thankful for everything they shared so intimately together. Impatient to get to Jamaica, he drew her close, commenting again on how wonderful she looked, asking her to do a couple of twirls so they could all admire her beauty. The aliens glowed with approval as she stood up and did as asked. "You look so different, so radiant. I'll bet you have a secret to tell us later," laughed Chenaugh. Shauna blushed. "In fact, I'll bet you have lots of stories to tell us," he added, unsmiling, chastened by thoughts of the recent ordeal she'd been through.

Towam, translated by Janet, kept them informed of their progress as the alien ship headed straight for Jamaica, unaffected by the remains of the hurricane. Shauna wondered if the aliens were actually able to transbeam whole ships and were rationing the amount of awe the five of them were exposed to. Moments later, not instantaneous but fast, they were hovering over their final destination - two resort condos on the beach of a private cove close to Montego Bay. Shauna, her mother and her Loves were impatient to land, excited by the prospect of sand under their feet, sun on their skin, sea air in their lungs. Shauna, of course, also had Chip's promise to look forward to.

CHAPTER 40   REUNION

As they said their good-byes, Towam singled out Shauna and they touched foreheads. Once again she was filled with his intense energy as Janet translated his well wishes before directing them to the transbeam station.

Standing together, tightly packed on the pad they felt the first tingling and dematerialized to feel sand and scrub grass under their feet and the still weird sensation of being rematerialized. Automatically checking they had all their body parts and that they all worked, at least those parts they could test in public, it didn't take long before the call of the sea tempted them and Chip and Shauna led the charge across the beach. Stripping to their underwear, mindful of Janet - this time - they ran right into the water, splashing through the shallows before plunging in. Once out in the deep, Shauna stroked into some serious swimming, while the others played and laughed and relaxed.

Swum out for the time being, Shauna rolled onto her back to float under the cloudless blue sky, lost in the glory of the moment until a sudden nudge from below almost panicked her. Resisting the instant urge to move, knowing sharks are hyper-sensitive to vibration and smell to make up for their poor eyesight, she lay as still as she could between the heat of the sun and the warmth of the water. Grasped by the waist and tugged, she took a deep breath before going under to meet the tooth filled mouth of a grinning Chip. Relieved but mad, she was quickly pushed back to the surface by her lover and attacked with hungry kisses.

Succumbing to the kiss attack she responded in kind. Feeling Chip's naked penis bobbing and swinging against her, thrumming with a mammoth erection, she was instantly aroused, nipples popping out like tasty popsicles begging to be sucked. Deprived of each other's touch for what seemed like so long they soon had the ocean aboil. When he fumbled to remove her bra, really wanting to just rip it off, she suggested huskily, voice oozing sex, that they find a bed for this reunion. "Let's make this comfortable, uninterrupted, private and stress-free. There'll be plenty of chances for quickies in the sea, believe me!" And they struck out for the beach and their new home.

Reaching the shallows, he picked her up and pulled her against his very happy cock, her long legs wrapped around him embracing his waist, her arms around his neck. Locked together, his arms under her butt, they made the trek across the sand. Smooching and tonguing, so into each other to the exclusion of their surroundings they didn't at first register the familiar voice shouting for their attention. But then it penetrated and they tore their mouths apart in amazement to see Troy ambling towards them carrying a stack of fresh towels. Chip set Shauna down and they ran to him. "Oh, Troy, I'm so glad you're here! What a delightful and welcome surprise," gushed Shauna, taking his face in her hands and kissing him smack on the lips. Troy blushed various shades of red before Chip enfolded him in a big hug, saying, "It's so good to see you, man!" and then took a towel to hastily wrap around his waist, hoping to corral his erection. Taking a towel to hide her own nakedness, which she'd forgotten in her excitement at seeing Troy again, Shauna looked past him to see Garcia approaching. So excited, she rushed towards her. "I can't believe it! This is so perfect! I never expected to see you again!" she shouted as they came together. "And here is my precious, precious Shauna," said Garcia, melding into a long, emotional hug, their tears mingling with the joy of such an unexpected treat. Gently pushing Shauna to arm's length Garcia looked at her lovingly, took out a tissue and gently wiped Shauna's tears away, saying, "I've been praying for you steady. And you don't look the worse for wear. In fact, you look better than when you left. You have a glow to you which thrills me to see."

Linking arms, the four of them were joined by Janet, Clyde and Chenaugh who'd happily watched the reunion while making arrangements for the accommodations. Deciding that it made sense for Shauna and her men to take the larger of the two condos and Garcia, Troy and Janet the other, they were all ready to check them out, to get out of the sun, relax and enjoy their new living, albeit a temporary one.

Heading across the beach, they agreed to freshen up and take a siesta, not necessarily in that order, before meeting on the veranda of the larger condo a little later. Handing Chip and Shauna their clothes, Janet took off with Troy and Garcia for their condo while Shauna and the men continued on to theirs. On the way Chip noticed two tourist carts parked between the condos. *Handy,* He thought in passing, as he gave himself over to the mingled scents of flower blossom and salty ocean carried on the humid breeze. The pace of island life already seeping into his bones, he felt in no hurry . . . except to satisfy his lust.

Shauna and the three guys crossed the condo veranda, taking note of the outdoor shower at one end, and entered through the sliding plate-glass doors which mirrored the ones in the front at the other end of the living area. With both sets open, the cool, gentle, ocean breeze flowed into and through the expansive interior. They were drawn to the center of the space where a huge, comfortably padded sectional in off-white leather bounded three sides of a large, square, dark wood coffee table - fashioned from one of the local hardwoods. A lush bouquet of local flowers adorned the table top, along with a huge mountain of various tempting local fruits piled in a bowl. While the guys immediately collapsed on the couch, Shauna selected an apricot to munch as she investigated the enormous, kitchen off the seating area. A large, white porcelain sink below a window looking on to the veranda was set in a counter that wrapped around two walls of the kitchen leading to a large, double door refrigerator and an adjacent drinks cooler. A separate peach colored granite slab covered the island unit that acted as a partial barrier between the kitchen and seating area. Checking out the refrigerator, Shauna was impressed by how well-stocked it was and wondered if the resort or Troy and Garcia had provided the goodies. Looking back across the living area she admired the color scheme, so relaxing and cooling - peach, white and a soft blue with accents of dark wood. A few pieces of brightly colored artwork hung on a couple of walls. The flooring, a lighter colored wood, felt good on her bare feet.

Moving on to check out the bedrooms, she saw Chip leaning against an open doorway on the left, beckoning. "Wait till you see the size of this bed." She hurried over and they went in together. "Oh my gosh! I don't believe it! It must have been designed for all of us! I've never seen such an enormous bed." Clyde and Chenaugh rousted themselves from where they'd collapsed on the sectional and went to see for themselves. The immense bed had a light wood headboard with soft lights embedded and there was a huge mirror inset in the ceiling directly above it. "They must have had the bedding made to order," commented Clyde. "Whatever it took," smiled a happy Chenaugh. He went over to the inviting bed and pressed the mattress with his hand. "Yummy."

"Well, I'm very happy we're all so excited about our bed," said Shauna quietly, feeling the tiredness catching up with her, adding, "We'll test it to the max and find out if it's up to supporting all of us, but Chip and I would like be alone together this first time." Understanding completely, Chenaugh and Clyde had already concluded that for Shauna and Chip to be alone after everything the two of them had been through was absolutely vital. It wasn't just necessary for the two of them though, all four of them needed the flow of Chip and Shauna uninterrupted. Wishing them joy and saying they'd be thinking of the two lovebirds, Clyde and Chenaugh went to check out the second bedroom.

Shauna and Chip smiled lovingly at each other as he picked her up, carried her to the bed and, flipping the covers aside, laid her gently on the huge surface. She looked so vulnerable and he tenderly ran his fingers through her still wet hair until she sighed and closed her eyes and asked sleepily, "We are really alone?" "Yes, my Love, we are."

Opening her luminous green eyes she appraised him longingly and then raised her arms to pull him close. "You feel so good," she sighed, "So very good. I want it like this more often - in fact, all the time." "Yes, my Love, me too, but I have to take a quick shower first. I'll be right back." He eased away from her and went into the bathroom. Within minutes he was back at her side, squeaky clean, smelling of pungent, after-bath lotion.

Shauna had rolled onto her stomach, her arms and legs spread out, fast asleep. Chip stood there gazing down at his beloved Shauna. He watched as she slept with her head turned his way, lips slightly parted. He could hear the soft rhythmic breathing as her ribcage rose and fell. He followed the sensuous curves of her body from her firm shoulders, along the line of her back and over the wonder of her buttocks as they flowed into her perfectly proportioned legs. He gazed and gazed. Even sleeping she turned him on. When awake, everything about her was in breathtaking animated motion and he became part of her unfathomable magic, drawn to her being like a bee to a flower. Chip, feeling satisfying exhaustion himself, carefully climbed into bed with his dear Love. Lying facing her, he slowly and carefully slid into her embrace. "Sleep well, my Precious and sweet dreams," he whispered before falling in line with her breathing and nodding off. She stirred, letting out a soft sigh, as if to acknowledge his close presence.

CHAPTER 41 THE PROMISE

The moon's reflection cast a pale light that tinged the room where the lovebirds lay. Leaving sleep, Shauna heard the gentle lapping of waves as they caressed the beach and the soft flapping of the drapes playing in a gentle breeze. Opening her eyes, she was happy to be exactly where she wanted to be. She could feel the warm deliciousness of Chip's sex against her but suddenly started sneezing uncontrollably. Pinching her nose to stifle the attack and burying her head under the covers to muffle the sound, it dawned on her that it was probably Chip's lotion she was reacting to.

Her sneezing fit over, she thought to stay put and enjoy just lying there with Chip, but feeling a fresh nose tickle on its way decided to get up. Slowly working her way out from under Chip without waking him, she walked to the window, wrapping her arms around herself to ward off the coolness. She stood in a deep reverie, abandoning herself to the enormity of the ocean spread out before her. The white foamy crests of endless waves, way out toward the horizon, lined up for their march to the beach. Catching the moon as each one rolled in above the unseen coral beds, fish, sea plants and shells until they expired on the sand with a sigh, an endless cycle of successive generations, hypnotic and soothing. Roused by the soft touch of Chip's arms encircling her from behind, she tilted her head back, puckered her lips and blew him a kiss. He lightly stroked her breasts with his large hands. Drifting lower, his exploring hands tenderly massaged her pussy and thighs. Responding, Shauna turned and rubbed her sex against his enlarged cock. Moving her groin from side to side, she felt the intensifying heat of his swelling hardness in answer, stoking her own fire even more. Her belly turned molten, her sex swelling and throbbing.

She slowly slid around behind him, pressing her groin into his body as she went. Once there she wrapped him with her arms and caressed his chest and abs with feather-like strokes of manicured nails. Teasing his nipples, she ground herself into his back, massaging his buttocks with her pussy. His nipples grew and his cock strained as she alternated her ministrations. Playing with his cockhead a gooey squirt appeared and she spread it, lubricating his already charged erection. Encircling his shaft her hand pumped, fed by both their juices. She could feel her pussy swelling – her lips, her clit, her very core throbbing with anticipation.

Chip knew he would blow if he let her carry on and he wanted to give her more first - an arousal so charged she would be begging him to take her. He wanted her pussy to speak to him. Yet he wanted the escalating sensations to be ongoing. Like the procession of waves across the sea, a steady, inexorable rhythm before the final release.

Overflowing with lust, he picked Shauna up and tenderly laid her on the bed. His smile instantly melted her heart and, ready for more, she spread her legs, placed her hands behind her head and gazed up at him longingly.

Climbing on the bed, Chip poised his prick above her crotch and teased her with its tip. Leaning forward he licked the tips of her nipples till her nervous system sparked with unbridled pleasure.

Pushing her breasts to meet his tongue, her pussy started involuntarily pulsating against his prick. He took a breast in his mouth and sucked with gusto. Feeling her groping to free her clit, he released her breast and slid down so he could help her out. Gently taking her hand away, he found the treasured cherry with the tip of his tongue, sending her into uncontrollable spasms. "Oh YES, YES, YES," she groaned breathlessly, arching her back and squirming all over, not knowing if she could handle any more. Moving his tongue, Chip probed in and out until Shauna was screaming for him to come inside. He jumped to oblige before he exploded, thrusting his erection all the way in, setting her off on an aria of ecstasy. Chip pumped furiously. Shauna moaned and growled and grabbed his prick in ever-increasing waves. Sucking him in even as he plunged, driving them on, clawing his back, the sheets, whatever came to hand, unleashed, panting, "Baby . . . Baby . . . I'm going . . . to have to . . . let go." "Let's do it then . . . Now!" Chip gushed. Semen flooded, mingled and sloshed in the synchronization of supernatural pleasure, two people flowing together in a selfless passion, knowing each other's wants and fulfilling them without hesitation.

Chip had learned well with Shauna and stayed inside her as long as he could, resisting the tendency to slip out with the flow of juices. He was spent, his testicles sucked dry. Lying together, they gently fondled and kissed each other with a sensual tenderness that sealed their rapture, their feelings, and the wonderment of all they had been through together, giving recognition to the magnificence of their bodies as they assimilated the impact of their loving.

Shauna finally emerged from her languor, feeling the wetness underneath her. "I hope housekeeping has a lot of oversized sheets. We're going to need them," laughed Shauna.

Turning to Chip she felt the missing ingredient and could see he felt it too. Where did the lift-off into the cosmos go? Why weren't they jetting through the universes feeling unknown sensations in unknown places? What had happened, or not happened, that they were still in bed? Although they knew they wouldn't travel every time, that each time would be different, somehow they felt that this time they'd been diverted and were looking at each other completely befuddled, when they both sensed a telepathic signal waiting for their acceptance. Taking hands they made themselves quiet and receptive. *"Hello Precious Loves. We happy your sex joining now. You special together. Not good idea to space travel after love making. No want to be obvious here. We wait for Scotland. Then you travel freely. We want take you visit our home. You no need spaceship we think. You have your powers. Very special. Very special. Good-bye now. Enjoy, very much enjoy. We, Towam and Etyo. Love my Wydir."* Chip and Shauna acknowledged them. *"Thank you both. We'll do what you say. Good-bye."*

Neither of them wanted to move, both thinking on being under observation, yet knowing they would not be taken advantage of. It was a miracle they had achieved contact in the first place and they considered themselves to be very, very fortunate. Full of wonder and enthusiasm, with dreams about futuristic adventures yet to be revealed, they could feel themselves both as part of history and of a future in the making, all at the same time.

"Well well," said Chip. "Seems we're so taken care of in so many ways. How about we go take a shower? You're going to love the bathroom setup." "Hang on, I can hear voices. What time is it?" she asked. Replying, "I have no idea," he jumped out of bed and quickly picked up the few pieces of clothing they'd left strewn on the floor and took them into the closet to hang up.

Poising herself, Shauna shouted, "First one in the shower gets a massage!" And jumping off the bed dashed into the bathroom. Chip stalked in behind her, ignoring the beautiful porcelain sink bowls sitting on the immense peach colored granite countertop to enter the open shower stall and lift a triumphant, beaming Shauna so her head was inches from the shower spray. Laughing so hard she soon started choking as the water poured over her face and into her mouth. "Don't expect any sympathy from me, miss smarty pants," said Chip as he let her down, asking, "Are you sorry?" Shauna shook her head no and started laughing again. Chip lifted her a second time. "No, no, please. This is unfair punishment for such a sweet Miss," she spluttered. "It's too much, please except my apologies," she begged, looking sorrowful and suggestively sucking on her lower lip. "Uh-hu, you're so irresistible and so damn beautiful - not to mention quite a love maker. What am I going to do with you?" he asked rhetorically as he released her and she put her arms around his neck to give him a lingering, sensuous kiss. Kissing her back, he voraciously smothered her mouth, exploring it with his tongue until she staggered back against the shower wall, dazed by his steamy assault. "Whew, baby. That's what I call sexy," and she leapt into his arms, straddled his waist and kissed him on the tip of his nose, sliding her legs slowly down his until her feet found the floor.

Stepping away, she left the shower and opened one of the cupboards lining the wall beside it. "Oh my, are we well supplied or what!" she cried, taking shampoos, body wash, conditioner and various types of body scrubbers to lay out on one of many shower shelves. "You're like a kid in a candy store, my Love," laughed Chip. Ignoring him, she lathered a bath scrubber and turned him round to scrub his back with strong circular motions. He winced as she scrubbed over the hieroglyphics she had unconsciously inscribed with her nails. "I'm so sorry, Baby. I fear you're marked for life. I must have been otherwise occupied." He turned to catch her smiling mischievously. "Oh my," she purred, "you're so handsome, especially when you're dripping wet." She continued scrubbing until she'd covered every inch, being very careful around his sexual delicacies that weren't at all private as far as she was concerned. "I love your body, my dearest Baby," she breathed, scrutinizing her handiwork. Chip happily reciprocated, scrubbing and rinsing her lovingly, even washing and conditioning her hair, which took him a while.

Plundering more bathroom cabinets amazed by the quality and quantity of supplies, they didn't know that Comstock had used his influence to have the resort instructed to spare no expense and treat these particular guests as exceptionally special. "I could get used to this," offered a clean glowing Chip. "I think I already am," said Shauna, who was trying on an orange lipstick. "By the way Baby, please stay away from that lotion you used last night. I think I'm allergic to it," she added

Continuing her exploration, uncovering all manner of lotions, creams and oils, Shauna suddenly announced that she wanted to shave her pubic hair. "I think it will heighten my sensitivity and make me more accessible. I'd also like to try one of those really tiny bikinis which show everything except the buttons." Chip laughed, saying, "Whatever turns you on and makes you feel good, my Love. Frankly, I think it's a great idea. And I think Clyde might just be the man to do it for you." "Perfect, Baby. Thanks." "Come on, Love, let's join the others," and Chip led her into the bedroom.

"Mmmm, you smell so good, good enough to eat," he murmured, nibbling at her ear lobe. Dressing in the only clothes they had they opened the bedroom door and hand in hand made their entrance into the living room.

All the others were happily enjoying a feast of fresh fruits, breads, coffee and each other. Janet, sitting on one side of the sectional between Chenaugh and Troy, was the first to notice them. She had both hands wrapped round a coffee mug big enough for three or four people. Grinning a know-it-all grin over it she said, "You both look radiant and satisfied, I take it you had an enjoyable night." Chip and Shauna answered with bright smiles and nods. "What time is it anyway?" asked Shauna. "We don't seem to have a clock in the room - maybe in paradise there's a reason for that." Janet checked her watch. "It's ten-thirty, my dear." "Good," thanked Shauna. "Now I need to eat and have some of that terrific smelling coffee.

"Garcia, what are you doing in the kitchen? And you too Clyde? This is your vacation too, you know." "Well, we got the memo, literally," said Troy, "but the chef we're supposed to have twice a day hasn't shown yet so they're filling in." I appreciate the thought but Chip and I are quite capable of feeding ourselves just fine, thanks. So, go on, out of the kitchen!"

"But I will do your hair when you're finished eating," said a determined Garcia. "Of course you will, Garcia. Thanks." And Shauna gave Garcia a kiss before escorting her out of the kitchen. "You too, Clyde! Out of the kitchen! Come on. Have a cup of coffee or something . . . There, that's better." And she beckoned an amused Chip to join her to help prepare their breakfast.

"What a perfect breakfast," commented Chip as he licked his fingers before picking up his oversize mug of coffee, a satiated look on his face, and settling on the sectional near Chenaugh and Garcia. Clyde, who had finally found a seat facing the others across the coffee table, was nursing his third cup of coffee when Shauna approached him seductively and sat in his lap, draping her arms around his neck. Turning his head slightly he gave her several sensuous kisses. Shauna sighed and reached for her coffee which Clyde handed to her. She closed her eyes enjoying the moment while Clyde savored having her so near and the fact that she'd come to him.

We are creating a togetherness devoid of jealousy or rejection, or any form of hierarchy, the luxury of being together with relaxation and enjoyment without space for self-doubt, moodiness or pettiness. But, then again, if the negative should creep in, we'll all be together to help each other through it, to come out freer, happier and greater. What a wonderful life! thought Chip as he drank his coffee. Putting his cup down he remembered to thank Chenaugh for setting up their security with Comstock before they'd left Havana, asking him, "Can you tell us a bit more about it?" "Sure," responded Chenaugh and went on to explain the four key layers he had put in place: satellites for the perimeter; military grade detectors and trained dogs at all points of entry, a network of locally sanctioned agents strategically distributed around the island; and local law enforcement as backup.

Greeted by an enthusiastic outpouring of gratitude for his efforts and for being such an integral part of the oneness they were creating, he suggested they all relax and enjoy themselves. "How about we meet in half an hour and take the tourist carts into town?" asked Chip, adding, "I know the four of us and Janet could use some new clothes." "Well, actually," said Janet, "I had Towam transbeam our packages from Havana and have them stored in our closet in the master bedroom next door. Maybe you should come get them first before we do that." "I'm on my way!" said Chip immediately, jumping up and heading for the door, hoping against hope that Towam had delivered *all* the packages.

"Let's get you dressed, Love," prompted Chip. "Garcia is eager to get to grips with your hair and try out some of that wonderful stuff you found earlier." Chip already wearing a brightly colored, short sleeved t-shirt watched as Shauna tried to smooth out one of her Havana purchases, a now rumpled, flouncy, multi-colored, midriff blouse. Putting it on, not sure if she liked it or not, she added a pair of bright yellow, hip-hugger shorts. As she slipped into her sandals, Chip whistled, admiring her in the gaudy outfit she was still uncertain about. Shauna received more whistles as Clyde and Chenaugh came in, looking casually gorgeous and extremely attractive themselves in their skimpy attire. "My my! I'm surrounded by beautifully handsome men!" exclaimed Shauna.

Then came the surprise. All three men produced small gift boxes. Clyde opened his first and adorned her wrist with a multi-colored, gem-encrusted bracelet. Chenaugh followed, offering her a choker length necklace with the same design. Lastly, Chip removed a pair of matching earrings, tenderly threading them to dangle from her ears. "Do you recall my Love when we entered the hotel in Havana? You stopped and stared at these earrings in the window of the hotel store. Well, the three of us sneaked out a little later and got these for you. We hope you like wearing them as much as we enjoyed buying them." "I don't know what to say, you are all so good to me and of course . . ." Shauna couldn't continue as she choked up and began to cry, covering her face with her hands. The crying became sobs that shook her body and the three knights encircled her, cradling her in their midst, their arms around each other. Speechlessly they embraced, pouring their love into and through her, amplifying their connection, feeding Shauna with their unlimited passion. While Shauna felt a nourishment she had never experienced before - think Chip times three – the men were equally receiving. None of them were greater or lesser, but as parts of the multiple whole they each expanded exponentially in the oneness of the growing inseparable intimacy they were creating.

"I've never seen you cover your face before, my Love," said Chip, breaking the silence of the moment. "I've never felt the impulse to do it. I've never been so deeply touched - so profoundly penetrated - and it took all of you. Penis to vagina is one thing but it only engages the sexual organs. What I just experienced with you all was a deep molecular penetration that engaged my whole body at every level. I can't begin to explain how I feel but I'm so thankful for your love and devotion to me." Shauna, feeling to cry again, suddenly flashed on a more urgent thought. "Wow, Chip, I just realized we had no birth control last night." "Darling love, don't worry. I called the resort last night and the Doctor on call provided a prescription for the pharmacy to deliver a couple of month's supply. I nudged you awake and gave you one with a few sips of water. You were obviously so out of it you don't remember." "What would I do without you, my dearest baby, you're such a blessing. But on this note my loves, with being on and off the pill, I don't have a clue when my next menstrual period is. But rest assured, when I feel it coming, you'll all be in on it. In the meantime if you want to know a few details, ask Chip.

He's a seasoned pro. Aren't you, Baby?" she finished, giving Chip a mushy kiss as punctuation.

A no–funny-business Garcia came in and took charge. They were happy to let her, particularly Shauna who was still assimilating the recent converging, knowing her DNA and nervous system had been forever altered for the better. Welcoming the change of pace and pleasure Garcia represented, she was soon looking like a beauty queen again thanks to Garcia's magic. Giving her a warm hug Shauna gathered up her meager things and went to join the guys.

CHAPTER 42 EXPANSIONS

The tropical paradise enchanted them and they soaked it up in sheer joy as they progressed to the outskirts of Montego Bay, split fifty-fifty about whether to stop at one of the large hotels or explore the city first. Agreeing to disagree, Chip joined Shauna, Clyde and Chenaugh and they drove to the Bay hotel while the others went exploring.

Shauna and the guys spent the afternoon doing their best to empty the Bay hotel shopping mall of its wares. Shauna excitedly helped her three men expand their taste and style horizons, becoming more enamored with them with every step they took into the unknown. Leading Clyde and Chenaugh out of the conservatism of lives spent undercover and in uniform and encouraging Chip to explore his natural sense of style with greater freedom, she also supported both Chenaugh and Clyde in having their ears pierced, Clyde so proud he started showing off his new earrings to anyone who came anywhere close. Now laden down with their purchases they were heading to meet the others.

They couldn't miss Troy, Garcia and Janet. They were chatting together in a riot of colorful, flowery shirts and shorts, wide brimmed straw hats, neon-framed dark glasses and matching plastic sandals. After an enthusiastic coming together, Garcia and Janet just had to display the swimsuits they'd bought. They were both so happy and excited to get back to the beach and try them out. "How beautiful and colorful," said Shauna, just as excited for them as they were for themselves, and the six of them trekked outside to the valet.

When the carts arrived it was obvious that they'd never be able to get everything into them for the return journey and the valet quickly offered to have a hotel vehicle deliver their purchases for them. Impressed and thankful, they provided a handsome gratuity and asked him to give them an hour start so they could be at the condo to supervise the unloading.

Arriving at the condos, Shauna leapt off the cart, raced inside and stripping at breakneck speed, threw on a robe and headed across the beach as fast as she could. Reaching the water she threw off the robe and high stepped naked through the shallows before finally diving under when the water was thigh deep. "Hey guys, let's go," shouted Chip. "She's left us high and dry so why don't we get ready for her to finish the serious swimming and then surprise her with our new game?" Not waiting for an answer he charged across the beach. Clyde and Chenaugh, immediately took off after him, neither entirely sure what the 'new game' was, but eager for anything that involved a naked Shauna. Arriving at the water, all three stripped and plunged in. "Man, this feels good. I love it," bellowed Chip, splashing enthusiastically as he watched Clyde swim a course away from Shauna.

Both Chip and Chenaugh were impressed as the former SEAL powered through the water - it almost looked as if he were skimming the surface instead of swimming through it. "Man oh man, I have no excuses. I've spent a lot of time on this island but never spent much time swimming in the ocean, and I'm sure wishing I had. Maybe Clyde will give me some pointers so I can impress the lady," said Chenaugh, laughing. Chip clapped him playfully on the shoulder and they waited for the swimmers to finish their workouts. Finally the two started towards shore and the two guys who began wading out to meet them.

As she reached the waders the unknowing Shauna was quickly surrounded by her Loves. The three held hands and walked her back to waist deep water as Chip explained the rules. They then supported the excited Shauna face up in the water, stretched out, her legs apart; Clyde at her head, Chenaugh at her side and Chip at her feet, holding both her ankles. "We're going to arouse you first Love," said a horny Chip. "You're too late!" chuckled Shauna, already pulsing and eager for their combined attentions. They began: caressing her, trickling water over her, kissing her all over, Chip lightly exploring her genitals. At this point Shauna began to spasm, her whole body trembling. "Do you have any idea what it's like to have all of you loving me at the same time? It's making me crazy!" Three hard pricks bobbed in the water, swaying with the waves. Although unable to see them, Shauna was intensely tuned in to their aroused condition, singing inside with their touch and intention.

She felt plugged into a higher frequency, every nerve in her body vibrating as she craved more, her sexual desire increasing uncontrollably with the continuous attention. She began to undulate ferociously and Chip waded between her legs to penetrate her. Thrusting slowly at first, he escalated to fast short jabs until he felt on the brink and pulled out. Chenaugh switched places with him, sliding her gently towards his waiting erection. Shauna felt the difference as Chanaugh's extra girth opened her wider and with a groan she grabbed his hips and with a scream impaled herself completely. Feeling her need, Chenaugh thrust hard and deep as Shauna whimpered and moaned with indescribable pleasure.

"Are you all right my sweetheart?" asked a concerned Chenaugh. "I . . . love . . . it," huffed a trembling Shauna. "This . . . is . . . unlike anything . . . I've . . . felt before. . . I'm . . . quivering inside . . . and I feel . . . like . . . I could explode . . . any . . . second . . . with an . . . orgasm . . . that won't . . . end . . . especially if . . . you start . . . pumping me. . . Oh my Gosh. Oh Gosh. Oh Gosh. It's . . . happening . . . so fast!" Chenaugh was driving like crazy, on the edge himself, powerful sensations rocking his body like never before, and with one final, massive thrust, poured out inside her. Shauna pulsed around him, keeping him close as he stroked her thighs, reluctant to move. "Just stay with me," moaned Shauna, her body vibrating with the delicious echoes of orgasm.

Warmed by her glow, Chenaugh confessed, "I loved you the first time I laid eyes on you. And when we were together on the Russian ship and again in Josef's plane, it was so hard to keep myself in check. But today, you, this, is more than I imagined. And, you know, I'd really like us all to celebrate." "That would be wonderful," breathed Shauna, "but for now, let's call it quits please. And Clyde, you will be my first love tonight." Clyde, a pulsating erection stirring the water beside her head, bent down and kissed her forehead. Chip, similarly engorged after witnessing Chenaugh's performance, but knowing there would be many opportunities later, nodded, saying, "Chenaugh, I am so thankful for you, Bro."

Chenaugh lovingly picked up the, happily glowing, melted Shauna and started towards the condo. "Hey, Clyde, would you get Shauna's bathrobe and give it a good shake before covering her?" he asked as he approached the beach. Clyde, although he'd been momentarily disappointed about having to wait, was more than happy to oblige, seeing just how wonderful Shauna was feeling. Being with her, Chip and Chenaugh was proving to be more exciting and fulfilling than he could have imagined, blue balls and all.

Reaching the condo they greeted Janet and Garcia relaxing in lounge chairs on the veranda. Engrossed in conversation the two of them just waved back as Chenaugh stepped inside to the living area carrying Shauna, Chip and Clyde following. On their way to the bedroom they acknowledged the chef, busy in the kitchen and said hi to Troy, sprawled in front of the TV watching a movie. Chenaugh gently lowered Shauna onto the bed and leaned into her, kissing her lovingly. Shauna looked up, tracing his eyebrows with her fingers, fascinated by the strong, well defined features that worked so well together. His broad flattened nose with the flaring nostrils that complemented his lips. His eyes that drew attention to his bone structure - high cheeks and a broad, high forehead - and his unusual, naturally-rust-colored, free-flopping, shoulder-length dread-locks.

"Thankfully someone brought in all our packages," said Chip. "I think there's enough room in this closet if you guys want to move in here instead of staying in the other bedroom. Up to you, I'm headed for the showers and would love some company." He went over to Shauna, still motionless on the bed, and peppered her mouth, face and neck with kisses. She sat up, putting her arms around him. He picked her up and carried her into the shower stall. Putting her down, he turned on the hand held shower and sprayed her all over including between her legs. "Baby, that feels so good. Do it again," she purred. He gladly complied.

Chenaugh and Clyde soon joined them and all three concentrated on washing her, including shampooing her hair which had her purring all over again. Thoroughly rinsed she was led from the shower and gently toweled dry before being slathered with lotion and given a standing massage as they worked the lotion into her skin. "Thanks so much, my Loves. Garcia can do my hair later, but if you look in the red carrier bag, you'll find the nightie I'd like to wear." Returning with a delightful piece of ruffle with spaghetti straps in splashes of green and blue, Clyde slipped it over her. "You look good enough to eat," he said, taking her arm and munching it with his lips, and then doing the same to her stomach, sending her into peals of laughter. "Thanks, my Precious. I'm so happy you're here and I'm looking forward to later. Now, why don't you go finish getting ready for drinks?" And she blew him a kiss to send him on his way. Eager to join everyone, she quickly put away her purchases, pulled herself together, blissfully aware of her throbbing sex, and sauntered toward the kitchen to grab a drink.

The chef was leaning against the island and asked if he could help her with anything. She studied the extremely handsome guy. Tall, with a prematurely gray-white mustache and head of thick wavy hair, his eyes shied away from direct contact and she knew to be economical with her trust. Shauna looked over at the delectable spread of food he'd been preparing. "Looks heavenly," she remarked. "Would you like to try something?" "Oh! No thanks. I'll wait for the others and then start with your wonderful looking appetizer tray."

Before the chef turned away he scanned Shauna's body from top to bottom, his gaze lingering on her breasts, outlined delightfully by the drape of her skimpy nightie. Unintimidated but instinctively wary of him, she had no intention of taking any chances.

She returned to her quest for a drink, bypassing the large rack of different wines to open the large drinks cooler. Well stocked with reserves, including liquors, champagnes, juices and sodas, she zeroed in on the ample supply of Baileys.

Fixing her drink she stepped outside to join her three scrubbed and shining knights dressed comfortably in loose fitting shorts, nursing beers. She gazed at them in turn, thankful for her lucky encounters with each one - she hadn't been consciously looking, but had certainly found - before joining the chatting women holding down the other end of the veranda, lit by the blazing tints of the fast fading sun.

CHAPTER 43 EXPOSED

The six, comfortably relaxed, watched as the sun, paving the sea with a shimmering path of metallic hues from horizon to shore, quickly sank out of sight leaving a balmy, mellow evening under the looming night sky. As the sky grew darker it seemed as if the ocean became louder, turning up the volume of its rhythmical murmuring, perhaps heralding a higher tide.

On the veranda a third tray of appetizers was doing the rounds and Chip, playing the conscientious bartender, refilled glasses as they emptied, with wine, beer, and, of course, Baileys. Even though she'd been told by more than one person that Baileys was an after dinner drink, Shauna didn't care. Baileys was her drink of choice right now, dinner or no dinner. As long as it came with lots of ice to keep her from getting smashed after just one glass. As Chip came back from the bar holding a frosty bottle of beer, Shauna gave up her chair for him to sit with her on his lap, snuggled close. Chip pulled at the neckline of her nightie to get a good look, kissing her breasts, pure lust on his mind. Shauna playfully protested, and he playfully ignored her. Of course, the booze helped.

Clyde called for Troy to come join them, and Troy responded as he had twice before, "I'll be there when the movie's finished." Adding, "It won't be long now." The chef, who was ready to call it a night, announced that supper was ready and started placing food on the already set table at the other end of the veranda. It didn't seem to matter that the group was already stuffed with appetizers as they ambled over. Commenting on the amazing spread, they dug in as if they hadn't eaten for days. The chef reappeared to ask if they needed anything else. Replying in the negative with a chorus of thanks they wished him a good night. Free to go, the chef asked them to put the dirty dishes in the sink for the maid to clean up in the morning and left.

The table still held a few open bottles and fresh glasses and Shauna asked Chenaugh to please pour her a "teensy-weensy, itty-bitty" glass of any red wine. Chip politely asked if that was a good idea. "Oh yes, a splendid one on this special occasion." "And what is this special occasion?" asked a mischievous Janet. "Weeeelll, it could be any number of things," shrugged Shauna. "You know." So Shauna got her few mouthfuls of wine in a big goblet. She sipped it slowly, in between forkfuls of lobster and fish. "After all, I've only had one glass of watered down Baileys - if anyone's counting." She raised her nose in Chip's direction beside her, causing him to break into a smile and she kissed him on the cheek.

Finished with eating and drinking, Chenaugh suggested a walk along the beach to work off their indulgences and enjoy the sand, surf and moonlight. "We might even find some shells that have been washed up." "Count me in," said Troy, who had finally made it to the table, making up for lost time by shoveling down a huge plate of food, and was sipping a Pepsi. "Oh my," spoke up Shauna, "I don't have the energy right now, even though it does sound inviting." "Hey Honey, no problem. I'll carry you on my shoulders and you can enjoy the ride from greater heights," offered Chenaugh and, unwilling to take no for an answer, took Shauna's hands and with help seated her on his strong shoulders – a process Shauna enjoyed. "Oops, I forgot. I'm not wearing panties," she giggled. "Well, lucky me then. Don't worry though, you'll be safe. Just make yourself comfy and I'll make sure you're well taken care of" said Chenaugh, a far-away look in his eyes. "Ok, adventurers, let's go exploring. And watch out for sea monsters. You'll have to ask someone else to rescue you though 'cause I'm occupied," commented Chenaugh before setting off at a confident clip for the shoreline.

Janet and Garcia opted to retire to their own condo and relax together. It had been a full day and they were ready to crawl into bed, watch the news on TV, and then lights out. But first they cleared the table laden with dishes, stacking them in the sink as requested. As they strolled back to their nearby condo, arms around each other's waists, Garcia commented, "You know, I think I care more for Shauna and Chip than I do for my own children. When your daughter joined Chip in a daily living it was so fast but the best thing that ever happened to him. He's changed so much and she's changing too. And being with them here has really warmed my heart because I feel them so different in so many ways. They have grown more sweet, caring and compassionate, which I would have thought impossible given what they've been through. I'm so lucky to be with them again. They rub off on people, you know. I'm so very proud of them both. Now, with the addition of Chenaugh and Clyde, well, I don't know how they're going to do it but I'm sure they'll find a way as they go."

"Thank you Garcia," said Janet. "Your obvious devotion to my Daughter and Chip touches me deeply. As far as Clyde and Chenaugh go, I know without any doubts that Shauna sees something very special in each of them or she wouldn't have them around her. She's always been a free spirited person with little or no inhibitions, questioning everything, studying everything, observing everything. She's always been curious too, delving into the mysteries of things until she was satisfied with what she discovered. Whatever she does, she plunges in wholeheartedly.

"It was like that with her music. She was young when she became passionate about singing and studied and practiced with discipline and devotion, creating quite a career for herself in a very short time. And now, in so many aspects of her life, she is beginning to harvest what she has been sowing these many years. She will always continue singing, but as far as a career, she has left that behind for much bigger arenas.

"I personally adore how she expresses herself sensually and sexually in such a clean and fun-loving way. I wish I could be that way but I don't seem to have it in me. She makes it look so unsoiled and fun-filled. Whereas it seems to me that, for most of us, sex is so guilt-laden, manipulative, and unsatisfying that it constantly threatens society's stability. There's more screwing in the mind than with the body . . . and this doesn't even include the corrupt imaging of how sex should be! Sometimes I think that the most intelligent and well educated people are the dumbest - that most of us don't have a clue what sex really is. There's too much talk about sex and its perversions and not enough actual participation in healthy pleasurable eroticism."

They walked the rest of the way in a silence that spoke loudly. As they got ready for bed and crawled in, Janet blurted, "I want you to come to Scotland with us, Garcia - if you can swing it. You're needed . . . Good night. I love you."

The weary beachcombers dragged themselves the last few paces up the beach and into the living room. Troy watched them inside before wishing them well and turning for his own condo with an armful of shells. The rest headed for the master bedroom where Chenaugh laid a sleepy Shauna down on the bed as close to center as he could manage. "Thank you," she mumbled sleepily, her speech drifting into incoherence as she rolled onto her back, spreading her legs apart, and sank into a deep welcome sleep.

"Yes," said Chip. "She always likes to sleep with her legs spread out." "That's cool," said Clyde. The guys watched Shauna sleeping, enjoying the vision of her resting. They climbed up on the bed to surround her, partially covering her, cozied to her sides. Chenaugh laid his head between her legs and lightly grasped her ankles. Pretty soon soft snoring could be heard as the men joined Shauna in a well-deserved slumber.

Shauna, still slumbering soundly in an otherwise empty bed, had rolled onto her side in a fetal position, her hands between her legs. Her face wore a smile and was covered by tumbling hair that hid her eyes and cheek. Chip entered quietly to check on her, marveling at her stamina and sexual capacity, lovingly brushing some of the hair from her face. She didn't stir. After lingering with his Love, he left and went back to the beach where the others were having fun with a big beach ball, tossing it back and forth.

They had found the ball earlier in the smaller condo and Clyde and Chip had thought it would be a good diversion for Garcia, maybe help her overcome her fear of water. The guys, including Troy, were standing about knee deep encouraging Janet and Garcia into the water to play, or at least get their feet wet. Both women were wearing their new bathing suits and both looked pretty darn good as far as the guys were concerned. Janet's suit showed off her ample bosom, not quite as well-endowed as her daughter but eye catching nonetheless, while Garcia's, she'd lost weight since Austin, revealed a surprisingly sweet figure. Beginning to enjoy having finally taken the chance of wearing a swimsuit, Garcia had developed a very distinct strut, showing a pride and a sense of being at home in her body, something she found easy to do with this bunch of guys. They'd all told her how proud they were of her and how good she looked. Right now Clyde and Chip were talking to her, allowing her to get used to the gentle waves lapping up against her legs before enticing her further. More talk. And more talk. And then more talking.

Finally some action as Chip lifted Garcia into his arms, walking her further out until he were waist high in the water. Clyde moved around as Chip very slowly laid Garcia in the sea face up, supporting her upper thighs and shoulders while Clyde made sure her head would stay above water.

Garcia started to relax as Clyde and Chip let go, showing Garcia their hands letting her know that she was floating under her own steam. She immediately freaked out, starting to flail about which caused her to go under. The two men lifted her out as she sputtered and choked, holding her nose, blowing out water. Panic stricken eyes articulated her fear. Even Janet, Troy and Chenaugh on shore watching could tell she was upset as Chip and Clyde talked to her, Chip holding her tight and carrying her to dry land. Janet was ready with a towel which she wrapped around her as Chip lowered her feet to the sand. Garcia, now recovered enough to be proud of her first swimming lesson, told them she'd be ready for another later, but at that moment just wanted to relax and have herself a cup of coffee. She thanked Chip and Clyde who thanked her back for being such a good sport.

Waking to find she was on her own Shauna, hearing voices, got up and went to the window, curious to see what was going on. "Oh goody," she exclaimed, delighted to see everyone on the beach. *I think I have time to have some fun with myself.* She gleefully climbed onto the bed, found a relatively clean location and flopped over on her back. Spreading her legs she located her cherry and with long strokes, using a couple of her fingers, began the fun. She pushed deeper between her lips, so ready they'd started swelling almost immediately, and started stimulating her hungry cherry with faster strokes. She had just gotten hold of her breast with the other hand, preparing to fondle, when Chip burst in, closed the door behind him, took off his shorts revealing a very nice hard on, and scrambled beside her. "Hi, Love! There I was minding my own business out in the ocean when I had this strong feeling you wanted to have some fun with yourself and I felt this compulsive desire to help you along. So here I am your humble servant, ripe and ready to serve." He graciously bowed. "I can see you are," said Shauna, looking at his throbbing erection. Sitting up, she bent forward and crammed as much of his prick into her mouth as she could. "OOOOHHHH, Love. Thank you, but what you're doing is going to put me over the edge and I want into you first. So please, let me take charge." She let him go, grinning in anticipation of what was coming next.

He slid her to the edge of the bed, turned her on her side and standing, lifted her top leg over his shoulder and moved the other to totally expose her sex. Confronted with her reddened pussy he asked if she was sure she was up to it.

Writhing about on the bed, she replied, "I adore you and your concern but you'll find I'm more than ready, so please, just fuck me." Pushing forward he let her guide him in, feeling the slickness of her ready pussy. "I love how you fit and feel," she growled and he increased his stroke rate, using the position to penetrate deeper, bringing them ever-closer to completion. He kept her from falling off the bed as her back arched again and again in an erotic frenzy, sucking him to climax too. Unable to stay standing and keep his prick connected, he slowly eased onto the bed and lay beside her trapped between her legs.

Breathing hard and grinning, Chip felt her stroke his heaving chest until he calmed down. She tenderly kissed his eyes, his neck and finally his big delectable mouth - entirely ignoring the spillage dribbling out of her, a leaking faucet the only simile that came to her mind.

They lay there for a while, enjoying the beating of each other's hearts, the depth in each other's eyes, feeling the warmth and closeness. "Whew, that was unexpected. But then how can you predict something that's different every time," remarked a thankful Chip. "Yes Baby. And if we could predict . . . well . . . where's the fun in that? I'm so thankful we don't control ourselves or each other - in love-making, or any other way. I'm sure you'll tell me if I ever try to do that. You'd better!" Chip so loved this person - such a vital part of his life.

Suddenly he scooped her up and half ran, half walked her outside, across the beach and into the ocean and tossed her in. She stayed underwater for what seemed like forever, finally bobbing up several lengths away. "Let's have a swim," she called and headed further out. Up for the invitation, he began swimming in her wake. She slowed for him to catch up and they started tussling before heading back for shore, noticing the others had moved to the veranda out of the sun and were enjoying drinks.

What a blessing the outdoor shower was. Chip and Shauna hurriedly soaped, scrubbed and towel-dried before running into the bedroom to dress, Shauna commenting that she hoped housecleaning would get there soon - the bed was a disaster. Bundling the sheets into a wad she dropped them on the floor at the foot of the bed before scurrying to the kitchen. Eager to join the others but needing to satisfy her hunger for food, she stacked a plate with assorted fruits before fixing a mug of coffee and joining them on the veranda. She called out to Chip, who hadn't shown up yet, asking if he'd like her to bring him some coffee. "No thanks," floated out from between the bedroom drapes.

Enjoying her people enjoying one another, Shauna felt blessed. To be able to relax and have the simple things of everyday living – to not have worries, or struggles, or stress - to simply enjoy. Thinking of her expanded living, she wondered how the four of them would fully manifest. Would she experience the same space-time adventures with Clyde and Chenaugh or was it just her and Chip who could generate it together? Not having an answer just then she was certain that they needed the time here to create a oneness of feeling, of purpose between them all: a connection that could never be broken. She couldn't help wonder about Sean too, sensing that although her coming together with Chip had precipitated recent events, they weren't the complete answer. They couldn't be. Her drawing to Clyde and Chenaugh had felt just as essential and maybe there was more.

Chip plunked into a vacant lounger, resting a glass of orange juice on the floor beside him. Stirred by the interruption, Shauna waited for a lull in the conversation before complimenting the two women beside her on their choice of colorful swimsuits. Thanking her they told her they were planning on going to the Spa for a massage and perhaps a facial, and who knew what else and asked if she'd like to join them. Looking at Chip, who had fallen asleep and seeing Clyde and Chenaugh had almost joined him, she said the four of them were just going to hang out around the condo and have a real lazy day. Janet then asked Troy if he would like to accompany them. While they got pampered he could a look around some more, maybe check out the local bars, and afterwards escort them to one of the live shows that evening, adding, "We'd love your company." "Put that way ladies, you have yourselves a date," said Troy. Janet and Garcia, excited and looking forward to an adventure of relaxation, said they planned to leave at noon.

Happy that Janet and Garcia would be safe with Troy around, Shauna asked Clyde if he was up for the shaving job she'd talked about. "Hey, I'd be honored." He replied. "If you're ready, we could do it now." "All right!" agreed an excited Shauna. "Hey, Bro," Clyde called to Chenaugh, "I'd welcome your help." Janet, Garcia and Troy trotted off to get ready while Shauna, Clyde and Chenaugh adjourned to the bedroom, leaving Chip asleep on the veranda.

Showing Chenaugh where he wanted towels spread on the bed, Clyde went to get his gear from the other bedroom. Returning with a pleased look, holding a small zippered bag, he suggested she lie down and hike her nightie up or take it off. Not one for half measures, she immediately undressed and lay back, asking Chenaugh to go give Chip a nudge and see if he wanted to come be a part of her baptism of pubic nudity. Chenaugh bowed and kissed her already well-trimmed curls before disappearing out the door.

With Shauna lying naked before him, Clyde took his time enjoying the sight. *Will I ever get enough*, he wondered. She looked back at him lovingly, cool and relaxed. Bending, he sensually kissed her welcoming mouth before opening his bag and withdrawing what looked like a sleek, thick cellphone. "What *is* that, Sweetheart? It looks so cute. Where did you get it?" "TV! I was idly channel surfing one night and saw this on an Infomercial. I thought it was so cool so bought one. It works great. Removing hair without discomfort it'll leave you really, really smooth for ages. It's going to be perfect for this because you won't feel a thing. And just to make sure, here comes Chip with a little Bailey's to soften you up." "I get it. You want to get me drunk and then have your way with me," deadpanned Shauna, laughing at the shocked looks. "And just when I'm most vulnerable, naked as a jaybird with my legs spread apart for the whole world to see what's between them. Geez, is this a conspiracy or what?" she continued, laughing even harder. "She's sussed us," said Chip, "but I don't know about having my way with her. I'm not sure I'd want to touch her with a ten foot pole. What do you guys think?" "Okay, enough already," interjected Shauna, "Give me the Baileys and show me your ten foot pole and we'll see."

Downing the Baileys in one gulp, she burped, and handed the empty glass back to Chip, glowing with an instant buzz. "Okay ducky, begin the show."

Not sure if the Baileys would make her reckless, Clyde asked Chip and Chenaugh to hold her legs apart and with skilled, deft strokes, cautiously cleared her hair from outer surfaces to inner, finished. Sitting her up so she could check out the result herself, he said, "I like it a lot, it's hot. How does it feel?" "Oh, wow! I love it! Those new string bikinis I just bought will look spectacular." "Damn right!" said Clyde as he watched her feel the smoothness, a mischievous smile on her face. "It feels so sexy," she grinned, continuing to explore as she lay back down. Clyde excused himself to get

Shauna a mug of coffee. Chip and Chenaugh were transfixed by Shauna's delight in touching herself.

Their staring interrupted by Clyde returning with the coffee, they helped Shauna sit so she could drink. Taking small sips her mind gradually came into focus. Looking at her three escorts in turn she couldn't help but be amazed at what she had created for herself and to wonder again where it was all heading. Overwhelmed with love for each of them, she beckoned them to sit. Chip took her empty mug and placed it on the floor as the four of them embraced and made themselves comfortable. Gently cradling Shauna, with a hand each on her newly naked pussy, the men lay around her unwittingly allowing the bonding she had cultivated instinctively to permeate their depths. Basking in this glow of oneness, they slept.

Waking, Chip rolled over and checked his watch he'd left on the floor. He had to blink several times before his eyes would focus. Nearly twelve. Slipping the watch on his wrist, he rolled back and snuggled up against Shauna again.

CHAPTER 44 FEVER

Everywhere was blackness. Then a myriad lights flashed into twinkling intensity, many of them pulsating with multiple colors, piercing the blackness with rapid-fire hues. A rock storm careened across the sky, like calcified sponges, rolling and turning, tightly-packed. Amorphous wisps of translucent oranges and yellows drifted on invisible currents, their diaphanous swirls dominating the eerie scene as it unfolded until gigantic razor-sharp spikes, ripped through the chaos, spinning wildly, shooting random fiery flares that exploded on impact, throwing off immense chunks of molten metal until a final flare spawned the apocalypse propelling Shauna to sit, shaken from a dream into reality. Another explosion! She drew closer to Chip, unsure if he was alive or dead, as another explosion assaulted her ears. Shaking her head she realized the metallic crashes were coming from the bathroom. Now hearing cussing, she got up and wobbled into the bathroom to find Chenaugh trying to pry the top off a can of shaving cream.

Seeing her distress, he immediately took her in his arms and held her close. "A nightmare, my Precious?" "Yes. And your banging was part of it." She placed her hand on her head and groaned. "A hangover too, my Love? I'll get you some fresh coffee and then a dose of my hangover special and presto, you'll feel good as new." He bent down, kissed her forehead and disappeared to got to the kitchen before she could stop him. This was no hangover, the thundering in her head was a warning, she just didn't know what of.

Joining Chenaugh she took the offered coffee and they grabbed their sunglasses and went to sit on the veranda.

Just after one o'clock the refrigerator was raided as Shauna and the guys, grabbed what they fancied. And there was certainly no shortage of choice. As she ate, Shauna idly flicked through the brochures she'd picked up at the mall the previous day now strewn on the coffee table and suddenly suggested they go for a bike ride. "We can rent bikes in town and ride over to the waterfalls a couple of miles out. It says that there's a steep climb if you want to get to the very top but I think it could be fun. I could certainly do with using some different muscles." Excited by the idea, Chip immediately called and reserved bicycles. Hastily changing, rustling up snacks and drinks, the four were out of the condo and on their way in fifteen minutes.

Picking up the bikes and a more detailed map from the rental office, they quickly made their way through the crowded streets and into the countryside. Once free of the town they were able to soak up the lush colors and rich variety of vegetation that flanked the road as they followed the mainly uphill route under a cloudless sky. The merciless heat and intense humidity had them soaked with their efforts before they reached the falls. "This is one way to detox and clean out the indulgences," commented a dripping Chip. Arriving at the spectacular main falls, they dismounted and joined the many tourists and locals already resting in the cool zone caused by the mist from the plunging water. Catching their breath, they considered the steep climb to the upper falls. "Come on. Let's go for it," urged a still breathless Shauna.

"You do realize, Precious, that there'll be a great deal of nearly vertical rock climbing necessary to reach it," pointed out Chip. "Oh, I do. But it will be worth it for some privacy - if you get my drift." And she beamed. Chenaugh was reluctant. But he didn't want to admit that he was not feeling a hundred percent and he certainly didn't want miss out on the 'privacy', so he psyched himself up for the challenge. Not sure what to do with the bicycles, they ended up leaving them in the undergrowth near the base of the falls with all the wheels tied together with the locks and chains they'd been given. Carrying a backpack each they followed Chip as he started up the narrow trail.

The climbing was slow and almost vertical in places and they had to stop every so often to flex their muscles and catch their breaths. They passed a half-way-marker, the point of no return, and left it behind, dogged in their determination - at least Shauna was. The final stretch of trail leveled out some and they were able to walk almost normally up the now gently sloping path. The same thick foliage that had engulfed them all the way up, suddenly gave way to a patch of almost incandescent green grass leading to a mist of spray that cooled and watered the surrounding vegetation that was even more lush than the rest. They could hear a continuous muted roar before they saw the streams of water spilling from above, pounding the rocky shelf that spread the falling water like a fan as it hit and filling the pool they stood beside before pouring over the edge to feed the falls below.

There was not a person in sight. They happily stripped and stepped naked into the icy, refreshing water, working their way over to where the falls from above forcefully splashed deep into a water eroded hole that seemed bottomless. They looked up as far as they could at the thin cascade of misty water barreling down and worked their way behind the rocky shelf so they were behind the curtain of water in an almost calm pool in a shallow cavern.

Beckoning Clyde, Shauna offered herself to him. He waded toward her, picked her up, put her over his knees and spanked her magnificent ass. There was no struggle out of Shauna. She was happy for whatever he had in mind. Already aroused no foreplay was necessary and they joined quickly, Clyde plunging deep into her from behind.

And they took full advantage with a fresh joy and abandon amongst them. Clyde seemed a new lover, so free in fact that Shauna whispered in her satisfied wonder, "Jesus, Sweetness, that was magnificent. And that gusher at the end, Wow! It seems like you've found your true self. The outdoors must agree with you."

Chenaugh introduced her to anal sex, becoming so aroused by her willing and active participation that he came before she was ready and Chip had to step in to take her to orgasm. Chenaugh dispirited, sulked - until Shauna confronted him and, taking him by the chin, looked him straight in the eye commanding that he stop whatever ego-directed self-pity or measurement he was giving to. "You tried something new for me and I loved it and want more. So celebrate yourself and be thankful. You're not alone Chenaugh, and our oneness demands we each be free of ego in all its guises. Now, let's enjoy one another like never before and honor the moment." Chenaugh instantly understood just how vital he was to her, Chip and Clyde. Not just in their intimacy, but as part of the wider power Shauna and Chip were unleashing.

Drying in the sun, they recharged with snacks, drinks and relaxation, preparing for the journey back. Chenaugh led the descent, Shauna right behind in case she slipped, with Clyde and Chip bringing up the rear. They met two couples who were venturing up the trail and blessed the chance they'd had to have the place to themselves. By the time they reached the lower falls and picked up their bikes, the sun was close to the horizon.

Dropping off the bikes they discussed hooking up with Janet, Garcia and Troy but decided to have a quiet evening back at the condo and an early night instead. Driving the cart home, following the sun, they kept an eye on the heavy clouds building over the ocean.

Crossing the lot from the cart to the condo, the rain started. There would be no walk along the beach. No fireside chats. No gazing at the moon. A full day behind them they were finally ready to just eat and sleep. Foregoing the appetizers the chef had prepared they wolfed down the meal he served and headed straight to bed – they'd catch up with Janet and Co in the morning.

Far, far away Shauna could hear the sound of running water interrupted by sneeze upon sneeze. But it was the coughing that brought her fully awake. Snapping to a sitting position, she listened intently. This time it didn't seem like a dream. The windows were closed against the rain, which was still torrential and loud on the roof, but there it was again, the sound of running water, this time much closer. She looked down at Chip and Clyde sleeping beside her, treasuring their warm muscular bodies sprawled across each other, both snoring softly, their eyelids twitching.

More sneezing. Shauna carefully unwrapped herself from the bed sheet and sleeping bodies and followed the sound to the bathroom where a bundled up miserable-looking Chenaugh was hunched over the sink, bracing himself with both arms on the counter. Placing her hands on his waist she guided him through to the sectional in the living room and had him lie down. Padding barefoot to the closet she quickly returned with blankets and pillows to make him more comfortable before turning on the gas-log fire. "Is there anything you need?" she asked quietly. Chenaugh rasped, in between coughs, "Thanks, Love, some water would be welcome." Shauna quickly gave him a couple of bottles and then went to the bathroom figuring that if they were so well stocked with toiletries, there must be some medications or remedies somewhere. Sure enough, a cabinet rewarded her with Vitamin C, Zinc and a bunch of cold remedies of which she chose two and a cough syrup, just in case. He was a big guy and the sickness might be stubborn.

Returning to Chenaugh she fed him the supplements, one of the remedies and a large spoonful of cough syrup. She then joined him on the sectional, wrapping herself around him to help keep him warm. Chenaugh wriggled his hands from the blankets and she held them. "You feel so good," he croaked,

"I feel better already. I'm thinking that maybe all that time in and out of the water at the falls is what brought this on." "Whatever, Precious, you don't need to figure this crap out. You just need to rest and get better. Just be quiet and enjoy the pampering. And if you need anything, let me know." "Some orange juice would be nice, thanks."

Shauna's dozing was interrupted by Chenaugh tossing and turning as he tried to get comfortable. Testing his forehead with the back of her hand she felt him burning up as he apologized for disturbing her. Unconcerned, she yawned and disengaging picked up a flu remedy from the coffee table, going to the kitchen to prepare it. Coming back with a mug of warm water steeped with the remedy she held it to his lips while he sipped, obediently draining the mug. Shauna placed it on the table and sat for a while stroking his forehead till he fell asleep.

Wakening again, wrapped in Shauna's embrace, a brighter Chenaugh nuzzled her saying, "Not so many layers, Precious. I believe my fever has broken and you were the real remedy." Shauna uncoiled and stood up. She removed a blanket and made another remedy, having him sip while she sat by his side. He stroked her bare legs, beneath her nightie, moving his hands towards her pussy. Stopping his progress she said, "Now my Sweet, hands to yourself. I for sure need more sleep, and you'll shake this flu faster the more rest you get. Or am I going to have to tie you up and throw you out in the rain?" Hiding her smile she snuggled down beside her obviously rapidly recovering patient.

CHAPTER 45   FUN & GAMES

Chip and Clyde were finishing up with their morning routine, wondering where Shauna and Chenaugh were. Last they remembered the four of them had got into bed together. Meandering into the living room accompanied by the thrumming rain, Clyde exclaimed, "My god, it's warm in here! It feels like a furnace." Chip went over to the fire and turned it off before opening the sliding doors to let in some rain-fresh air. Wearing long white hotel robes to keep out the coolness they stood watching the rain for a while. The day was gray and rather gloomy, the sun replaced by low dark clouds, heavy with moisture. The chef was already quietly working his magic in the kitchen. Other than him though, they seemed to be alone. "I thought for sure the guys from the other condo would be here. I mean," Clyde looked at his watch, "it's mid-day already. I hope they didn't float away," he laughed. "Well, to tell you the truth, I'm kinda glad for the rain. I find it soothing and would be quite happy doing nothing but relaxing today," said a still tired Chip. "Yeah, me too, I guess," agreed Clyde. "Lets' turn on some lights and brighten up the place a bit," suggested Chip. "Hey, just a minute Bro. Look at this," responded a startled Clyde in a stage whisper. "Do you see what I see?" Chip joined Clyde by the sectional and looked down on a partially clad Chenaugh and Shauna twined together, breathing rhythmically. "How did we miss them?" questioned Chip. "Maybe 'cause they're sound asleep?" offered Clyde.

Chip gave Clyde a friendly shove in response to the sarcasm, catching him off guard and sending him careening into the coffee table, rattling the empty mug, pill bottles and a vase of flowers which toppled right off the table and landed with a crash on the floor, fortunately not breaking. Chenaugh and Shauna stirred awake as Clyde steadied himself and Chip whispered loudly, "Wow, you can't trust anybody can you. We have our backs turned, our sleeping backs turned even, and these two bozos slip away and do what? Heaven forbid! Naughty, naughty. Hey Bro, do we have a punishment that fits the crime of sex and debauchery?" "Why, let me think. Of course! Twenty lashes on each of their fannies would seem appropriate. Come on. Up! Up! Up! Let's see your fannies."

322

Shauna and Chenaugh, jolted from a deep sleep, were operating far below their peak performance and were still too fuzzy and dysfunctional to figure out what was happening. Retrieving two of the long-stemmed flowers that had spilled from the vase, Chip gave one to Clyde and started flapping the other against Chenaugh's shoulder. Clyde joined in, slapping his soggy flower against Shauna's butt. Which was when Janet walked in and turned on the lights. "Am I ever relieved!" exclaimed Chenaugh. "Now there's some light in here I can see that you're not sixteen, in fact you must be close to forty. Whew, that's a load off." Chip, Clyde and Janet looked bemused as Shauna responded, "Forty, my foot!" and gave him an ineffectual kick. "Here's the deal," continued Chenaugh, "I've done nothing wrong. She assaulted me when I was sick, you can see that right? She's the one who wanted it, not me. She was begging for it." "You are such a liar!" spat a seemingly outraged Shauna, getting into the spirit. "You took advantage of me while I was in a deep sleep and by the time I was conscious, you'd already come, you disgusting pervert!" "Oh yeah? Well it didn't take much to get you over the top, you middle-aged hussy!" And they both burst out laughing.

Chip and Clyde resumed their flower slapping until Shauna protested more forcefully whereupon they jumped on the recumbent couple and began tickling them instead. The four began a free-for-all tussle with Janet and the chef standing by somewhat bemused. As the rough and tumble subsided the four ended up sprawled across the sectional happily relaxed.

Chenaugh, still not fully recovered, though obviously close, went back to bed for more sleep. Chip, Clyde and Shauna showered and, donning robes, joined Janet, Garcia and Troy in the kitchen, the chef having left for the afternoon. With the rain still pouring and the veranda dotted with puddles, they lined up at the island counter to eat a late brunch.

Finishing, they migrated to the sectional for coffee. Relaxing, each wearing a white terrycloth robe - Janet and Co, who'd got soaked in their dash between condos having changed in the second bedroom – inspired Clyde to say they looked like members of a cult. "Best damn cult I know," said Shauna as Chenaugh joined them, a towel around his neck to keep his sore throat warm. Shauna insisted he put on some socks and Clyde went and got him a pair and slid them on his feet. "You know, that's a good idea," said Shauna, stretching her legs out from where she'd been sitting on them. Pretty soon everyone was wearing socks, courtesy of Clyde. He'd also conjured up a selection of relaxing music, turned the fire on low and switched off the main lights to leave a soft glow from a couple of floor lamps.

Shauna invited Troy to keep her company where she lay, scooting over to make room for him to stretch out beside her. "Come, my Pet. Get comfortable. I don't bite," she said, clacking her teeth together playfully. Troy smiled but looked uncomfortably at Chip and Clyde who were chatting idly. Shauna had made sure to pull her robe tight and retie it. "There now, isn't this cozy?" Troy was lying rigid as steel, having a hard time relaxing and enjoying being so close to her. Shauna put an arm around him and rocked gently to see if she could loosen him up and make him feel at home beside her. But it had the opposite effect, Troy sprang up, apologizing in a weak voice, "I'm sorry Shauna. It's not you. It's just that I'm not comfortable being this close to a woman and I don't seem to be able to relax at all. I'm going to pull over a chair and sit close instead." Removing her arm Shauna said, "Of course, Troy. You need to be absolutely at ease. I don't want you doing something you don't feel to. And I admire your honesty. You should never feel like you have to apologize for being true to yourself. I'm certainly not offended, nor do I treasure you less." He leant down and gave Shauna a very quick hug before going to get a chair.

Finishing his coffee, a still sneezing Chenaugh headed back to the bedroom. Troy in his chair was watching the rain through the veranda doors. Chip and Clyde were cuddled up either side of Shauna, almost asleep. So Janet and Garcia huddled together to discuss plans for their next adventure. They flipped through the brochures excited by the choices and enjoying their conversation. In the back of her mind though, Janet was pondering how and when to tell everyone about the information she'd been made privy to: that their stay on the island was only going to be two weeks, not three. She knew how much this vacation meant to the foursome - how much they needed this time to relax and play and help seal their biological oneness. However, so much was evolving and stirring in Scotland that she knew they really needed to focus their attention there.

Already, several hundred people had arrived in the UK to come together with Shauna and Chip. Either out of an awakening in their own bodies from having had direct contact with the two, or from hearing other people talk about awakening to a higher life.

Whenever her thoughts turned to Scotland and the future, she felt overwhelmed by the enormity of the task ahead. The radical, life-changing course they had embarked on, without a map. Janet knew that nothing like this had ever been done before, and her communications with Towam and Etyo had confirmed it. Shauna and Chip were the first to not only feel this new life, but to *be* this new life. Janet had always known that Shauna was born for this purpose. But where to begin? How to organize? What about housing? Plus all the other logistical details? Janet paused her runaway thoughts, knowing she had to let go and trust. To accept that this new way of living was bound to encounter a few hurdles along the way, that it would take total dedication and self-responsibility, but would ultimately be greater and more enjoyable than humankind could ever imagine.

Janet felt the gratitude for her connection with the aliens who were monitoring their progress and would be supporting them in who knew what remarkable ways. Relaxing with that thought, she re-engaged in time to hear Garcia's suggestion of a boat trip around the island

As they continued to discuss the options, making a list and considering the pros and cons, Garcia scanned the room. "Do you realize we're the only ones not sleeping? Do you think if we snuck into the second bedroom and slept for a few hours, anyone would have a problem with that?" "I don't see why they should. It sounds like a marvelous idea to me. I mean, I have no idea what time it is, what with this gray weather. It feels like late afternoon but surely it can't be." "Well, it is! It's going on four o'clock." "My goodness, Garcia, let's go!" Shauna was vaguely aware of them leaving.

CHAPTER 46   NEWS

The wind had picked up and a gust would occasionally cause branches to scrape against the wooden sides of the condo. Dense sheets of rain battered the roof like hundreds of drummers in uncoordinated rhythm, adding to a day that had surely been designed for sleeping. The storm beat a tattoo with anything not tied down or not too heavy to move. Even the crash of the storm-whipped waves was lost in its fury, as was the ringing phone.

A shadowy figure slid through the veranda doors dripping rain. Huge and somewhat portly, the intruder's bulk crackled and dwindled as an outer layer was removed and a regular sized person carrying packages emerged. A rain hat thumped on the kitchen counter awakening Troy, who called, "Who's in the kitchen?" "Crap, you scared the piss out of me boy," said an angry chef. "Don't call me, boy," shot back Troy. "Alright, alright. Have it your way, man." "You can call me Troy." "So give me a break then will you, Troy?" "But what are you doing sneaking around?" "Look, I work here. I'm the chef. I figured given the storm you sleep junkies wouldn't want to eat till late, so here I am to serve you." "Okay, okay. I apologize for startling you and just so you know, we all really appreciate what you do for us." The chef, mollified, set down his packages, turned on a couple of soft recessed lights and got to work. A disgruntled Troy, still angry at the 'boy' remark used the bathroom and then stepped out to the veranda to collect himself.

Chip, disturbed by the short altercation between the chef and Troy, rolled his head from one side to the other and put his hands on Shauna's ass, squeezing gently, before slipping back to sleep. Shauna, feeling Chip's touch, rubbed him with her pelvis, waking him again. Opening his eyes, he turned his head and met Shauna's gaze. He stretched and arched his back, grabbing his hardening prick. Shauna straddled him, well aware of the rising member beneath her, and kissed his lips before jumping to the floor, wrapping her robe snugly and traipsing to the master bath. Chenaugh, who'd been lying awake when she passed, got up and followed her into the bathroom, rubbing sleep from his eyes and blowing a very red nose.

Janet emerged from the second bedroom, gingerly bypassed the seating area and joined Troy on the veranda for some fresh air, despite the storm. In short order though, they came back in, Shauna and Chenaugh arrived from the master and Garcia from the second bedroom. All converging on Chip and Clyde, still laid out on the sectional, like pigeons come home to roost.

"Well, good morning everyone," joked Troy. "Are we up for our little drinking ritual? If so, I'm taking orders. But keep it simple please. By the way, did everyone have a good rest?" Almost all of them replied by yawning. "Make mine a Baileys over ice," said Shauna. "Oh goodie, something new and different for the lady," said Troy, teasing. The rest ordered wine or beer.

The chef, back to his usual mellow self, served a tray of different looking finger foods. "I'm so famished," said Shauna, and I really haven't done a thing today." "My Love, you're always hungry and you had yourself quite a workout most of yesterday," observed Chip. Everyone laughed except Shauna, who blushed. Chip dashed to her side, stroking her wild, frizzy, hair. "I've hardly ever seen you blush, Love," he said as she buried her face in his shoulder. "I'm just feeling extra vulnerable right now. That's all."

Chip held her tighter and Garcia, wanting to help, asked if Shauna would like her do something with her hair. Distracted, Shauna didn't respond and then asked, "Mummy, is there something going on in Scotland I should know about? Something that might cut our vacation short?" "Yes, there is dear," replied Janet, only a little surprised by the accuracy of Shauna's intuition. "I should have known you'd pick up that something was going on and told you yesterday. I didn't because I know how much this vacation means to you, and how much you've needed it. Anyway, I received notice from Scotland that people are arriving from all over the world to join up with you and your Loves. The leaders there are doing their best to get them settled and handle the many things that need to be done, but are beginning to feel overwhelmed. Fortunately, your Navy SEALs, Clyde, said they'll be coming to help us out, once we get there.

"I've agreed that we'll be there two weeks from tomorrow. That means we'll lose a few days here, but they really need us there. Towam and Etyo are aware of the changes and will give us a lift, so-to-speak." Shauna uncurled from Chip's cocoon-like embrace and rushed to Janet, holding her tightly, gently smothering her face with kisses.

Troy switched on the TV and selected the weather channel looking for the local forecast. When it cycled round, the news was encouraging. The storm was moving off to the West and by morning there would be clear skies, slightly higher temperatures, lower humidity and welcome sunshine. "Just in time," observed a reviving Chip. "We'll avoid cabin fever." "I knew there was more to life than drinking and eating," added Clyde. "Well, err, where have you been, my Precious?" asked Shauna, acting the slighted female. "It's alright for you," piped up Garcia, "for some of us it's been so long we may as well have been sewn up. It's probably shriveled from neglect anyway." She chuckled along with the others before announcing she was going to, "put my fat and sassy self to bed."

Janet and Troy were all set to follow her lead when Shauna told all three to stay in the second bedroom instead of sloshing through the pouring rain to their condo. Janet, Garcia and Troy happily accepted the invitation, having been about to suggest it themselves.

The condo was turned down for the night, the two bedrooms soon full, one containing a heap of ready-to-sleep bodies, the other with two figures on the bed and one on the floor, all waiting for blissful oblivion.

Shauna was finding it impossible to sleep with Chenaugh coughing so violently and frequently. Digging her way out of the tangle of bodies she went and retrieved the cough syrup. Filling a large spoon she instructed Chenaugh, "Just take small sips and hold it in your throat for as long as you can." She marveled that Chip and Clyde were not disturbed by the irritating noise. Lovingly covering Chenaugh and tucking the bedding around his throat, Shauna shimmied back under the covers intending to comfort her sick lover, but it was hopeless. The odd blessed moment between barrages of fitful hacking was not going to work. Picking up several spare blankets, Shauna ushered Chenaugh into the living area and made him as comfortable as possible on the sectional near the fireplace. She propped up his head to see if that would help, kissed him good-night and quietly went back to the bedroom for another attempt at sleep.

CHAPTER 47   BEACH

Chip woke just before sunrise. Looking at Shauna looking back at him, he shared a smile and a leisurely fondle before they shambled to the bathroom to pee and brush their teeth, jostling each other playfully, making it challenging to pee in the pot, so to speak.

Clyde joined them and suggested a stroll along the beach where they'd yet to explore. See what was there. Watch the sunrise over the mountain. Just for the fun of it. Shauna and Chip readily agreed. Quietly, they checked on Chenaugh, took water from the fridge and left a note letting the chef and the rest know they'd be back around mid-morning for breakfast. They tip-toed across the veranda into the morning freshness just as the first ephemeral fingers of fragile, colorless light slanted across the beach and into the ocean. A multitude of birds took flight with a flutter and a whoosh and the three congratulated themselves on taking the chance to witness the birth of the new day. It surprised them that the earth had soaked up so much of the rain. The beach itself was firm underfoot and easy walking. Starting at a brisk pace, inhaling the tangy air deeply, Shauna soon broke into an easy jog, her arms out wide, making like an airplane before cupping her breasts to stop them bouncing wildly as she ran. Easing to a more leisurely pace she watched Clyde and Chip running ahead.

Following them along the curve of the shoreline she joined them at the neck of a stubby peninsula jutting into the shallows. Protected from the land by a strip of thick shrubbery they could see that its almost flat surface was covered with a patchy carpet of wild grass, still in shadow from the mountain behind them. In silent agreement they waded out beyond the shrubbery barrier and scaled the peninsula's rocky edge. The grass was lush from the rain, the patches, a perfect size for getting naked and lying down. Stripping off their shirts they did just that, luxuriating in the feel of the thick damp softness against their skin in contrast to the now warming breeze that swirled off the island. They rested on the grass, arms and legs spread wide, and drifted off.

Waking slowly, feeling the sun now bathing her refreshed body, Shauna felt so alive and vibrant. Chip had moved beside her and she met his gaze as he broke the soft murmuring of whispering waves. "I'm so thrilled you decided to shave your pussy my Love. You're so beautiful down there." He idly stroked her, feeling his lust but so much more, a sense of absolute connection, as if they were one and the same. A feeling not unlike he'd experienced in their cosmic orgasms. And he was almost overcome with gratitude. *There is so much more than I would ever have expected*, he thought. He looked around for Clyde and found him watching them. Waving him over Chip pulled the three of them into an embrace that somehow communicated a different value and depth of feeling for the wholeness of bodies together. He felt as if Clyde was becoming like Shauna, was becoming like himself. A revelation that Shauna had intuited and Clyde with his closeness to them was on his way to experiencing.

So completely nourished by the flesh to flesh communion, Shauna suggested swimming back to the condo. Deciding it would be easier to wear their T-shirts than tie them round their waists or carry them they dressed, waded out to where the closest set of waves gently broke towards the shore and dove in.

Clyde, with his strong precise strokes took the lead, Shauna followed and Chip brought up the rear. It felt so good to be slipping through the sparkling water that was almost completely calm after the recent storm. Before they knew it, they had rounded the curve of shoreline and could see the condos ahead. As they swam closer, they could see four figures waving from the veranda. Happy to see a full complement, the swimmers stopped and waved back.

Arriving in line with the condos the swimmers waded to shore, headed for the outdoor shower. The fresh water felt good on their salty, sun warmed skin as they stripped off their shirts and created a pile of them in one corner. They soaped and rinsed each other thoroughly, paying special attention to Shauna's full tresses. Then wrapped in bathrobes thoughtfully provided by Garcia, they joined the others on the veranda. Ready to eat. Ready for coffee.

The three adventurers dug into their food contemplatively. They'd instinctively sat close to each other and the others could sense a difference. Janet was the first to speak, "Good morning. You must have gotten up early looking at how much sun you've soaked up. Pray tell, what you were up to?" Swallowing her mouthfull Shauna said, "It was so worth getting up early to see the sun break across the island. We went north along the coastline, just to see what was there, and we found each other in a new way." She then interrupted her brunch to go sit on Chenaugh's lap. Chip and Clyde quickly moved beside them and the four sat together heads touching, arms encircling.

Cheanugh explained that his sore throat was gone and that, thanks to her, he'd had a wonderful rest but just felt to hang around the condo and recharge. He also informed them that he'd made reservations for later that evening at the restaurant Troy, Janet and Garcia had enjoyed so much the night before. He'd felt it would give them all an opportunity to wear their new clothes. Shauna and Chip couldn't help feeling how in tune he'd been with their morning experience and were looking forward to the four of them being alone.

Which was when Troy invited them to join Janet, Garcia and him on an excursion to Blue Mountain where the scenery was apparently spectacular and where it even snowed sometimes. It was obvious the three were excited to be going.

The foursome gracefully declined, indicating their desire to be together with Chenaugh, maybe to swim, but mostly to take it easy or indulge in whatever else took their fancy close to home. It didn't take a genius to figure out what that might be, especially now that Chenaugh was close to fully recovered.

Followed by well wishes, Troy and the two ladies left for the day. Shauna and her three lovers claimed a lounger each and contentedly sipped coffee, seemingly mesmerized by the tranquility but in reality looking inward at their mingling emotions. Closing their eyes, they enjoyed the gentle, warm breeze, hearing the muted clatter of the maid rinsing the dishes before placing them in the dishwasher. Shauna, seeking the full benefit of the breeze, eased out of her robe and sank into her thoughts, her mind wandering into the unconscious, sort of aware that the men had paralleled her journey in their own minds.

No one heard the phone ringing, or no one could be bothered to answer it. The machine picked up and recorded the confirmation of their evening's reservations. Out on the veranda no one stirred. The maid was in the master bathroom cleaning, hoping to finish and be gone before they awoke. A devout Catholic she was scandalized by their arrangement. A woman with three men! It was just not right!

Chenaugh shifted to release a kink in his neck. Movement enough to knock his coffee mug off the wide arm of the lounger and send it somersaulting onto the tiled floor with a loud crack as it splintered into fragments, only the handle remaining intact. Chenaugh leaned over lazily and carefully picked up the handle. Marveling at its survival, he rotated it, checking its unmarked surface and clean breaks. The three other sleepers stirred groggily wondering what had happened.

Thinking of gunshots, Chip heard the maid scurrying her cart out the plate-glass doors and wondered if she could even handle a gun let alone shoot one. His first impulse to run and check was short-lived, giving way to a lethargy that kept him slumped in the lounger. One lounger along, Shauna stirred. Stretching full length and wiggling her toes she sprang up and headed for the water. Chip, instantly alert, tapped Clyde on the shoulder and gesturing him to follow raced across the beach. Catching Shauna as she was entering the water he scooped her up and churned through the shallows with her.

Slowing as he reached deeper water he stopped when he was waist deep and Shauna's butt was wet. He then lowered her and with a mighty heave tossed her into the air. She went sailing, all arms and legs, landing on her belly with a splat, yelling, "Ouch!" before going under. Chip thrashed his way over to where Shauna was surfacing. "What happened love? Are you hurt?" asked a contrite Chip. Shauna sputtered and spat water before replying. "I'm fine. It was just a less than graceful belly flop that landed me on my sun-sensitized tummy." Suggesting she might find it soothing to sit floating with her belly below the waterline he eased her into position and started towing her by holding her ankles. At which point Clyde turned up and suggested they play 'Pyramid' and then 'Totem'.

Their audience of one, Chenaugh, now sitting at the water's edge, watched, enjoying their enthusiastic acrobatics. Laughing and clapping and occasionally whistling, he encouraged them to keep going, wishing he could join them but knowing not to. They were certainly persistent, trying again and again until finally, the triumphant moment when the three of them were standing straight up momentarily before they all went down together, Shauna diving one way, Clyde the other and Chip falling backwards. "Wow, we should have got Chenaugh to take pictures," whooped an exhausted Clyde. "Next time for sure!"

As the day wore on they continued to play and frolic, engaging in monumental sex involving all three of them with Chenaugh egging them on. Experimenting with two in Shauna's pussy they experienced multiple orgasms between them until the three of them took hands and lying on their backs formed a floating circle, heads at the center. They wanted to sustain their erotic sensations for as long as possible, to let them subside at their own pace until their bodies were flowing normally. "You Lovers are good," yelled Chenaugh. "It was sensational watching the three of you having sex at the same time. A little more of that and we'll all be able to take part, with me driving her mad from behind."

Shauna broke the circle, releasing Clyde's hand and swimming towards shore, pulling on Chip who went along and pulled Clyde in turn. Wading to the beach she sat down next to Chenaugh, arms clasped around her knees. Clyde and Chip joined them, both sensing Shauna's unease.

"Look, Loves, I think it's time to talk about our intimacy. What we have sexually is not just special, it's phenomenal. But there's more. I know Chip has more understanding of what I mean because of what he and I have experienced together, but you're each aware of it or you wouldn't be here. It's not just because the three of you have a feeling for me, it's because all four of us have a feeling for each other. And this demands we think, speak and act beyond our previous experiences.

"As an example Chenaugh, I know you were just being playful, but none of you has any claim over any part of me, and I have no claim over any part of any of you. Nor do you have any claim over any part of each other. We're either all each other's or we're not being who we truly are or who need to be.

"I know we've been fumbling our way collectively toward the manifestation of this through our sexcapades, which are an essential part of this shift toward our ultimate level of being, but with the growing focus in Scotland we need to become indivisible, unstoppable and solid in our movement together before we arrive, or Sean and what he represents will precipitate disaster." Shauna paused, hearing a vehicle pull up in the lot behind the beach, the mountain travelers returning they suspected. The four of them huddled as on the sectional earlier. Their heads touching, arms entwined around each other's shoulders, each one of them allowed Shauna's words to settle deep within and stir their individual desire for the greatness she had alluded to.

Moments later they rose in concert and made their way to the outside shower to rinse off. Troy came over to inform them that their trip up the mountain had been spectacular and that he, Janet and Garcia would come over after getting dressed up and ready to party. Troy looked great, turning a healthy shade of tan.

Sharing the shower, soaping and rinsing Shauna's hair, now revealing highlights from the few days of sun, the three Cs were noticeably less boisterous. Although they still teased and goofed about playfully, there was an element of tenderness amongst them that hadn't been there before.

Leaving the shower they migrated to the master bathroom where Shauna sat on the counter while the three repainted her nails, doing a very passable job much to her delight. Dispersing, they each prepared for the evening with their own little rituals. Arriving one by one on the veranda, they were joined by the three from next door and they collectively relaxed, almost hypnotized by the nearly full moon blazing its silvery path to the beach.

Hoping Troy would offer but reaching the point where hope wasn't enough, Chip asked him if he was up for serving drinks. Troy, who had been staring at Shauna poured into the gorgeous red dress she'd bought on the foursome's shopping binge, said, "Sure." And he wasn't the only one who was drawn to Shauna's appearance. It wasn't just the dress either. Her makeup was immaculate and the exotic hairstyle Garcia had created inspired Janet to comment that she'd outdone herself. Everyone agreed.

Their ride arrived as they were finishing their first round of drinks. Draining their glasses, they made sure the condo was locked and piled in the back. Relaxed and loose, the drive to the restaurant seemed to take no time at all. Long enough though for Janet, Garcia and Troy to recount their Blue Mountain adventure in detail. Animated and colorful, often speaking over each other excitedly, it made following their story challenging at times. But the audience of four was just so touched by their obvious enthusiasm and the feeling for each other the three narrators conveyed.

CHAPTER 48   BLOODY MURDER

The party entered the restaurant, its native décor of bamboo and thatch complemented by local artwork covering the walls. Spacious and already nearly full, the popular venue hushed, eyes tracking, conversations pausing along the path the seven followed as they were ushered to their table for the evening. Shauna was particularly aware of the impact they were making, with her being the central focus. Picking up on some of the surrounding thoughts - *wonder who's with whom, what kind of a group is this* - Shauna smiled and scanned the crowd. *It's one thing to admire and wonder about the beautiful or unusual, quite another to be envious and bitchy about the unknown. Why is it that men don't seem to gossip as much?* thought Shauna.

The food was exceptional. As were the wines their waiter recommended. Each person had ordered a different dish and they were enjoying sampling the delicious variety, especially the local-recipe chicken and pork dishes. Infused with a joy of being together like never before, they sprinkled their conversations with compliments of each other. Chenaugh was particularly glad to be out and about and was experiencing a new freedom to feel each of his companions at a deeper level.

Chip asked Shauna if she'd like to dance and again many eyes followed them as they weaved their way to the floor where Chip spun her around before pulling her close. They kissed sensuously, and then again, and again, and again, and again. Shauna could feel him grow harder and larger as he pressed himself even closer. He whispered in her ear that she'd better be prepared for some great fucking. She whispered back that so had he. And they kissed some more.

Almost lost in the sensuality of the slow dance with Chip, Shauna nearly missed the attention that a very tall black man was giving her. Dancing with a handsome black woman he was following Shauna with his eyes. Shauna stared back. At the end of the dance he came ambling over and extending a large, long fingered hand asked for a dance. Shauna was reluctant, not at all comfortable with what she was feeling around him, but Chip encouraged her, in fact almost insisted, assuring her he'd be close by.

As the man led Shauna across the sparsely populated dance floor, most people having returned to their tables, Chip followed their progress intently. When the music started the man put his right hand on the small of Shauna's back almost covering it and interlaced the fingers of his left hand with those of her right. He introduced himself as Jimbula, a native of Jamaica, an exporter of both fresh and canned fruit.

Soft spoken, he appeared to be a genuine gentleman. He confessed that he hadn't been able to keep his eyes off her since the moment she'd first arrived and told her she was the most beautiful woman he'd ever laid eyes on. Shauna thanked him. At which point he pressed himself close into her crotch so she could feel the size and hardness of his genitals. Thankful she hadn't encouraged him by complimenting his good looks and powerful stature, she tried to create some daylight between them. But Jimbula wasn't about to let her.

"You really need to find out just how good it's possible to feel with my cock fucking your pussy so profoundly, in a way you will never experience with anyone else. I'm a pleaser of women. I have a special place in the back behind the stage where I will have you climaxing and more sexually aroused than you've ever thought possible." *Enough is enough* thought Shauna and called for Chip who had been following their interaction and seen her apparently straining to extricate herself. Enlisting Chenaugh, the two of them quickly made their way across the dance floor. Seeing them coming, Jimbula let Shauna go and fled in the opposite direction.

Having nullified the threat, Chenaugh took Shauna in his arms and held her gently as the three of them slowly made their way back to the table. Watched by the curious, many of whom were whispering amongst themselves.

Chenaugh and Chip sat Shauna between them. A trembling Shauna offered a weak smile, then bowed her head and cried softly. Garcia handed her a tissue to blow her nose while Janet used another to blot her eyes, and face. When Shauna had calmed down, she said, "I should have known better and gone with my instincts. Now Chip, don't protest. I know what was in your heart but as I said earlier, this isn't a democracy. We're each responsible for our own actions. So let's remember in future to follow our intuition, our gut feeling - not what seems to be a good idea or would please another. Our bodies never lie and right now mine's telling me to move on and enjoy the rest of our evening. And guys, each and every one of you, I'm so grateful for who you are and what we have together. Thank you. Now, can I please have some more wine?" A quick scramble and Troy filled her glass.

"I didn't think you'd want to stay after what happened," commented Clyde. "I didn't at first. But then I realized I was fine, nothing serious happened. Yes, it was upsetting and unpleasant but if I allow everything upsetting and unpleasant to take away my joy unnecessarily then I relinquish my power and become subject to every adverse circumstance that occurs. That's not acceptable to me. Besides you all deserve to enjoy your evening, regardless of what happens to me. But that's a whole other subject. Suffice to say, Chip and Chenaugh stepped in and I'm sure, had you felt it necessary, the rest of you would have too. So don't any of you be second guessing what you did or didn't do. In time, we will all learn how to be more alert and how to use more of our powers to protect ourselves. And the more of us who live this life of singular wholeness, the greater our power will be to repel the negative and aggressive. In the meantime though, let's toast to what we have together." Clinking glasses happily, some silently ruminated on her expression – the more astute wondering about the singular wholeness she'd mentioned. Shauna took a mouthful of wine and rolled it around, savoring the taste before swallowing. No longer hungry, she was content to be with her Loves as the seven of them resumed their interrupted meal. To experience the pleasure of their presence, and their interactions, both superficial and deep. This was more nourishing to her than any meal.

Chenaugh nearly choked on a mouthful when his emergency phone rang mid chew. Swallowing quickly he answered. "Chenaugh . . . Yes . . . nine-zero-six-four-five-seven . . . Really? . . . When? . . . OK, I'll be there as soon as I can . . . probably twenty five minutes, maybe sooner if I get an escort." He re-holstered the phone and lowered his head. Having composed himself he faced his companions scanning them in one sweeping glance. "Sorry about the interruption . . ." "Don't be sorry, dammit!" interrupted Janet, "Just tell us what the hell's going on!" None of them had heard Janet swear before and were on the edge of their chairs waiting for Chenaugh to continue. "There's been a security breach to the East, about twenty five minutes from here. They want me there immediately to analyze and assess the situation.

"Please, everyone, take your time. I don't think there's any immediate danger, in fact there may be no danger at all, but go straight back to the condos when you've finished eating. I suggest you all stay in ours as it's bigger. I'll contact resort security and have them send some guards to keep an eye on you. Four of the local police are already on their way. Troy, you'll find a spare gun and extra ammunition in the bottom left hand drawer of our closet. Keep it handy. And Clyde, you'd better take this," he finished, removing a gun from an ankle holster and handing it over.

"Can we assume the security breach has something to do with Shauna and Chip?" inquired a shaken Janet. "Affirmative," replied Chenaugh. "But let me assure you, you will be safe." Not wanting to accept the obvious Janet asked again. "So this is about Shauna and Chip and their safety? Some body or bodies are coming after them and you don't know who?" Chenaugh, considered his response before replying. "Yes and no. Yes, it's about Shauna and Chip. We have one intruder caught on infra-red and satellite camera. We know he's very tall, seems to know his way around, as if he's been here before, and moves like he's military or ex-military. What we don't know is whether he's working alone or who he's working for, although there are indications it could be Sean Cameron."

Chip interjected. "You know, that description of the intruder could very easily fit Norm. Do you think that's a possibility? I mean, to your knowledge, did Norm ever spend any time here in Jamaica?"

"Yeah, he has. Thanks for reminding me. You can be damned sure I'll check it out."

"Wasn't the last time we saw Norm at the hotel in Havana, when he turned up with Richardson to take Isabella back to the States?"

"Yes, I believe so," replied Chenaugh.

"Well then, do you know if anyone has checked to see if Isabella is still behind bars and whether Richardson is alive and well?"

"No I don't, Bro, but I'll find out. Right now though, I need to get going, my ride's outside. Just be sure to keep your cellphones on, I may need to get hold of you fast." A quick peck on Shauna's cheek and a, "Be safe, Loves," and Chenaugh was gone.

Despite Chenaugh's assurances, they decided to doggy-bag the leftovers. Shauna suggested taking dessert with them too. Liking the idea, Clyde asked about adding a baked chicken to the order saying, "I'm still hungry enough to eat a flock." "You and your appetite!" chided Janet. "I also think it would be a good idea to call for the limousine now so we can head home as soon as the food's ready. I think Chenaugh was right. We'll be as safe there as anywhere."

The passengers were lost in their own thoughts as the limousine neared the condos. The guys, who'd become increasingly tormented by the tantalizing aromas emanating from the restaurant containers, couldn't wait to change and get comfortable so they could carry on eating. The driver parked as close as he could and they stepped out into the glare of an unclouded moon that dominated the scene, bathing the shore in a harsh light that brought every nook and cranny into sharp relief.

Asking the others to wait, Troy ran to the shadowed entrance. Finding the key after fumbling in his jacket pocket for a second, he went to unlock the door then noticed it was already ajar. Knowing they'd made sure to lock it when they'd left, he turned to the others and beckoned Clyde and Chip.

Showing them the door, which on closer inspection showed signs of tampering, Troy whispered that he'd go in first and check. Saying it was probably the chef who he'd surprised before bringing in supplies at night, he carefully slid the door open just enough to squeeze through and crept inside, thankful to be in shadow. "Be careful," whispered Chip. Clyde, prepared for the worst, his gun drawn, stood poised at the opening ready to burst in if needed. Leaving Janet and Garcia with the limousine, Shauna joined Chip and Clyde near the door.

Inside, Troy silently eased to his right and into the master suite. Feeling his way to the closet he found the gun and worked his way back to the entrance. Carefully he edged along the wall towards the kitchen then bumped into a side table sending a tall vase rocking and stooped to catch it. The sound was enough.

A tall silhouette suddenly popped up from behind the kitchen island and fired, spraying the living area from left to right and back, scything a path that eventually found Troy. But not before he'd managed to get a shot off. As the barrage of bullets tore through him Troy's lifeless body was punched backwards, hitting the wall beside the entrance door before dropping to the floor and twitching for a few moments. The condo was silent, filled with a haze that filtered the moonlight.

CHAPTER 49   FOUR

"Nooo!" Screamed Chip and Shauna in unison, restrained by Clyde from rushing to Troy. A second thundering split the night. Slightly less intense than the first, it shattered both plate-glass doors, caught Clyde in the leg and Chip in the shoulder as he pulled a screaming Shauna to the floor. She clutched her leg in obvious pain. After the first salvo that had killed Troy, Janet and Garcia had wisely ducked behind the limousine with the driver. Whether a target or just collateral damage, the vehicle now bucked and shuddered under a new fusillade. Lying on the ground, Chip extricated his cellphone and called the resort. Hoping to be heard above the sound of the gunfire, he asked to be put through to security. A few clicks and several rings later he was listening to dead air. After the second try he gave up, muttering that he hoped they were on their way.

A blessed silence. Interrupted seconds later by the sound of the veranda door sliding open. Then the silence continued, this time undisturbed except for their own labored breathing. A few moments later they heard a car door slam further along the beach followed by the sound of an engine and screeching tires. Thinking it was safe to assume the shooter was now gone, Chip rolled off Shauna and called Chenaugh who picked up on the first ring. Chip, almost in tears now, relayed the news of Troy's death and asked Chenaugh to send an ambulance for Shauna, Clyde and himself. Assuring Chenaugh they'd all be okay he advised that the shooter was likely on the coast road traveling like a bat out of hell. Chenaugh said he was on his way to the condo and wasn't that far out so would keep an eye open. *Not that I expect much luck,* he thought. *There's too many side roads leading inland and if I was the shooter, I'd stay off the main routes as much as possible. Maybe slower going but less chance of a road block. Besides, I don't even know what he's driving.* Chip continued, "As far as I can tell the women and the limo driver are safe but resort security was a bust." "I know Buddy," said Chenaugh, "They were all gunned down. I'll get ambulances on the way and check what happened to the local police. Just hang in there, Bro. I'll see you soon." Still reeling from the attack and Troy's death, Chip was even more shaken with the addition of the killings of the security guards. He decided to keep the information to himself. *Let Chenaugh tell everyone else when the situation is more settled.*

Chip called to the women. Janet timidly emerged from behind the car calling back that they were shaken and scared but otherwise okay. "We could do with your help over here," hollered Chip. Shauna, Clyde and me have been shot and Troy . . ." he couldn't get the words out he was so distraught, sobbing with a sense of overwhelming loss. Janet made her way over but Garcia wouldn't budge. She was still terrified and now even more distressed by the news of the injuries to what she still thought of as her charges. Not wanting to become involved more than necessary, the driver stayed to comfort her.

Reaching Chip, Janet helped him set about tending to Shauna and Clyde. Tearing strips from Shauna's already ruined dress, Chip took a few deep breaths to calm himself and knelt beside Clyde to assess the damage. Clyde's leg was bleeding profusely from what appeared to be a half dozen or so bullet holes which ran up his leg from just above the ankle. Chip asked Clyde if it felt like any of the bones were shattered. Through gritted teeth Clyde said he didn't think so, but the pain was so intense he couldn't be certain.

Chip used the strips from Shauna's dress to fashion a make-shift tourniquet around Clyde's thigh. The bleeding slowed and then stopped. Chip held Clyde in his arms and waited for an ambulance. Meanwhile Janet took care of Shauna. Gently shifting her leg from beneath her she examined the injury. A single bullet had passed through the calf, again fortunately a clean in and out – if any aspect of being shot can be considered fortunate. Shauna whimpered as Janet wrapped the wound. "It looks like there's no serious damage and there's not much bleeding, but I bet it hurts like hell," she said. Shauna nodded and called to Chip, thanking him for pulling her down and covering her and then telling Clyde she knew he'd be up and walking in no time.

Janet moved to Chip and checked his bloody shoulder. "It's painful," he said, "but I seem to be able to move it okay and the bleeding's stopped, so I'm guessing I'll be alright." Then Shauna asked if he would find something to cover Troy. "It seems as if wherever I look, he's front and center." And she cried, tears streaming.

Chip left Clyde with Janet and kicking through the shards of glass still hanging from the door frame entered the condo. Stepping around Troy's broken body into the master he collected blankets and pillows. Returning to Troy he looked down, shuddering a little at the pain and disbelief etched on his face. Stooping he closed Troy's eyes and covered him with a blanket. He thought back on the close commitment to each other they'd had for so long. Troy's devotion to him and his appreciation in return, an appreciation that since Shauna had come into his life had become love. Heartbroken, he knelt by Troy's side for a long time, crying from the depths of his soul, feeling an unbearable missing.

Moving outside to Clyde he used a couple of pillows to prop him up in a more comfortable position and then joined Shauna. Kneeling he placed the remaining pillows beneath her head and then crawled to kiss her leg from top to bottom. "You're next," Chip said to Clyde. Their eyes locked and a rush of pure love rose in both of them. Clyde, tears welling, said, "Thanks, Bro."

Janet stood on the beach just above the waterline staring out to sea. Shauna sensed her totally engrossed in communion with Towan. And had a strong feeling what they were communing about. It didn't matter to Shauna who had reached out to whom. The result was the same. Several minutes later, a pensive Janet turned and headed back to the condo.

Chenaugh arrived, slamming to a halt inches from the rear of the limousine. He leaped from his car as the first ambulance arrived right on his tail. Waving urgently, he directed the three medics to get their asses in gear. "Bring the body bag over here," he barked, frenzied and impatient. "But attend to these people, this one first." He pointed at Clyde, having instantly assessed the degree of seriousness of their injuries. The second ambulance arrived soon after, followed by a police car, light bar flashing. "Turn the fucking lights off!" bellowed Chenaugh, as the car doors opened. "The last thing we need is to attract more attention! Think dammit, use your brains!"

Immediately picking up on Chenaugh's manic energy Shauna called him to sit beside her. Saying he didn't have time, he continued snapping out orders. "SIT DOWN, CHENAUGH! NOW!" Shauna's tone as much as the volume stopped Chenaugh short, defusing the adrenaline surge he'd been running on ever since the call from Chip. He sat next to Shauna and buried his head in his hands. Shauna drew him close and held him, pouring her heart into him until he began to calm down. She tenderly turned his head so they were eye to eye. At first unable to meet her gaze, he eventually relented and allowed himself to be captured by her impassioned look.

Finally he spoke, "This is all my fault. Troy, the security people at the resort, all killed. You, my beloved people, wounded. Garcia and Janet, witnesses to the carnage. I can't believe it's all happened on my watch." He lowered his head and sobbed, his whole body shaking in Shauna's arms. She stroked his head and back in a soothing rhythm. "First of all, my Precious, you're NOT responsible for this, any of it. You hear?" He nodded and Shauna continued, "Good. Because you have to understand, this horror story would have played out, perhaps in a slightly different version but it would have played out, whether you were here or a thousand miles away. I don't understand right now the how of all that's happening, I just know that Chip and I are at the core of the why - and now so are both you and Clyde. There are powerful forces in play that want to see us destroyed. It's they who are responsible for this. If there were no offense, we wouldn't even *need* a defense. You are vital and I, we all need you firing on all cylinders, being the brilliant, incisive and indomitable person that you are. Be clear about your innocence, Chenaugh." He leaned in and gave her a gentle kiss. "Thank you."

As Chenaugh stepped away from Shauna, a medic knelt beside her and unwrapped her temporary bandage. Chenaugh scanned the immediate area to see that both Chip and Clyde were being attended to as well. Satisfied, he entered the condo and confronted the destruction. Troy's body had been removed to one of the ambulances – *So much for crime scene integrity. And that* is *down to me.* He thought. The half of the living space, from where Troy had lain by the doors back to the sectional was almost unrecognizable. A broken mess of bullet torn furniture, drywall and flooring. Beyond, the kitchen appeared untouched.

Chenaugh worked his way through the rubble, a policeman behind lighting their way with a flashlight. Although it wasn't really necessary, the moon was doing a fine job pouring across the veranda. Reaching the kitchen he immediately noticed the blood on the floor behind the island counter standing out against the blonde wood. "Don't touch this area." He pointed for the officer. "I'll get forensics to rush the analysis." As he continued looking around he thought of the information he'd uncovered in response to

Chip's earlier questions and began piecing what he knew together, muttering under his breath, as he did so. "I just can't see how Norm could be the one responsible. He was arrested in Barcelona for carrying false papers and is reportedly still in jail awaiting trial. On top of that, even if he's now free, I don't believe the Norm I know would be capable of it. I suppose he could have been bribed but it really doesn't seem likely.

"As for Richardson, if I believe the news that he was killed in a car accident near Barcelona, he can't be involved either - which leaves Isabella. And she seems the most likely. Although she certainly doesn't fit the description of the intruder, she had been reported as being on the island despite supposedly having been escorted back to the States. So maybe it is her and Norm." And he caught himself thinking out loud. Concerned, he glanced around for the officer. Relieved to see him combing through the debris heading toward the master suite, he told himself to be more careful.

Calling the officer to join him, Chenaugh exited the condo via the veranda, and they walked across the beach to the next block along. Unable to trace a specific set of footprints in the sand they headed between the next set of condos toward the parking bays. Faced with an impenetrable growth of vegetation, that bordered the pathway running behind the condos, Chenaugh noticed what looked like partial boot prints leading right. Hardly able to believe his luck, he took the officers flashlight and followed them till they disappeared four feet into the parking lot punctuated by what looked to be a single drop of blood. Against the curb, almost in line with the blood, a wedge of still moist sand held the clear imprint of a tire. Examining the area closer Chenaugh squatted and holding the flashlight close to the ground swept the beam across the asphalt. "Just as I suspected. See? Here, and here?" said Chenaugh, pointing to the vaguest of impressions of what could be small foot prints right where the passenger side of the same car would have been. "Our infamous lady killer, I'm guessing. She must have waited by the car while Norm penetrated the condo. And thinking about it, I'd guess he wasn't expecting any resistance. Just a simple turkey shoot." He stood deep in thought. *I'd guarantee Isabella was here but I doubt those little piles of sand are going to help us much. She clearly didn't pull the trigger.* Looking at the officer he asked him to call in for someone to collect the blood and photograph the partial boot and tire prints and to stay put until they arrived. He wanted to get the potential evidence to the lab right away tagged top priority but knew that wasn't likely to happen. On this small island, law enforcement was meagerly staffed, probably more used to drunks and druggies than hardcore killers.

Janet sat beside Shauna as the medics worked on her leg. Their initial examination confirmed that the bullet had missed anything vital but an X-ray would make sure no bones had been damaged. While Shauna waited to be moved to the ambulance, Janet cuddled closer putting an arm around her shoulder.

Shauna, keeping her voice low so as not to be overheard, began, "Mummy, I already know what you're about to tell me and I'm so disappointed that Sean is still able to target us. I don't believe it has to be, but when will it end? When will the killing end?" "Shauna, love, you already know the answer to that. It's useless to have him killed. Another will just take his place and no doubt be twice the threat. The answer lies with all of us. This is why we must move together. We have to focus on living full out regardless of who's against us if we're to have the unlimited lives we're all meant for, lives without end. If we fight Sean, the resistance will feed his power and weaken ours. Our strength is in our oneness: our biological agreement to be a higher life." "Then why is Troy dead?" asked Shauna. "I'm sorry, my love. I know he was a good-hearted and loyal friend to both you and Chip, but I don't have the answers. Did he save the rest of us by dying? We will never know but that's often the assumption in these situations. That the greatest good for the greatest number warrants sacrificing life.

"I understand that love is often in play in these situations too, but it's a twisted idea of love when dying for another is considered its highest form of expression. The reality is that neither love nor friendship are going to be enough to end this split in and between bodies. If they could, they already would have. What I do know is that Troy was not one with you. Think back to that last interaction on the couch when he couldn't even lie close. Every barrier between us has to go, no matter how ingrained, no matter how painful breaking through it would seem or fearful we are of losing it. There can be nothing between our flesh, ever, if this oneness is to manifest."

Garcia joined them. She'd been told about Troy and had been comforted by Clyde and Chip. Janet pulled her close and continued. "Communing with Towam and Etyo, they told me they'd been in a far sector of the Cosmos when they picked up what was taking place and left immediately. They know it's imperative to get you out of here as quickly as possible and are close. You, Chip and Clyde will be treated on the way to Scotland. Unfortunately, Troy has been dead too long for revival." "When do you expect our alien friends to arrive?" asked Shauna. "They needed to stop off in Scotland but I'd say they should be here, let's see," and she checked her watch, "Oh . . . I would say . . . within minutes. You'd best let Chenaugh know to keep Clyde and Chip here rather than sent to hospital."

"I also need to make sure he comes with us. I'm dreading that he might not and we'll lose him to the investigation and his need to see things through." Glad to have voiced her fear, Shauna called Chenaugh over once again, shouting, "Chenaugh! Chenaugh! Darn it Chenaugh. I know you can hear me!"

"Sorry, Precious, I'm real busy right now. It will have to wait." "It's not an 'It' that's waiting, Chenaugh, it's me. So please, don't be stubborn, and get your beautiful ass over here right now!" Leaving his ego in his pocket, her passion more important than his pride, he strode over, the ambulance drivers watching him, confused. "Look Love, I need to let the drivers know what to do." "Of course, my Precious, but the three of us are staying here." "I figured that," said a resigned Chenaugh.

Quietly relaying orders, Chenaugh kept one of the medics behind to keep an eye on the three and sent the two ambulances on their way - the one with Troy's body heading for the morgue, the other returning empty to the hospital's Emergency and Trauma Center. As he returned his attention to Shauna, she said, "Thank you, my Precious. We don't have much time so let me get to the point. I treasure, love and absolutely adore you. Your natural leadership, the way you command respect, your caring for others, your compassion. I am so thankful for the day we first met and how you've changed so much and come so far in such a short time." Waving him to squat she kissed him. "Any moment now, our alien friends will be coming to take us to Scotland and I need you to come with us." Not giving him space to protest she went on. "I know you're immersed in this investigation and are totally focused on that right now, but I need you to see the bigger picture. You are needed in Scotland. The community we are building is vital to growing humanity out of duality and avoiding an even more devastating dark age. And you are essential for that. I fear that if you don't come with us now, you'll be swallowed up by this case . . . and the next one . . . and the next one, until you are lost in your old life again and what we have to do may never get done. But more important to me than that is that being without you would be unbearable, to be separated from you is now unthinkable, so

I'm asking: If you don't feel like you need to come with us now, do it anyway. Do it for me, simply because *I* need you!"

Chip, who'd been listening intently, broke in. "Look Bro, being without you doesn't compute. What we have together, it's not meant to be broken. Do it for me too." Chenaugh could see the tears in Chips eyes, and felt a rending inside, as Clyde said. "Chenaugh, you don't need to see this through to prove yourself to anyone. Use your connection with Comstock. Get him to do whatever needs doing to get this handled. So what if he gets pissed at you, he's ultimately responsible anyway. Look, much as we might hate to admit it, we can be replaced in any job. Take me. I just retired from the SEALs. I bet they already have a replacement just as good if not better. Thing is, Bro, you can never be replaced with me, with any of us. It's impossible. There is only one you, and I need you just as much as Shauna or Chip."

Chenaugh stood for a moment before going to Chip and Clyde and stooping to embrace them, feeling their passion for him breaking the last vestiges of resistance. Returning to Shauna he wiped his cheeks. "I'm so sorry I made you work so hard. Of course I'm coming with you. Of course I have to be with you. The past days have sealed each one of you so deep inside me that there's just no way I could be apart from any of you. I felt everything. I feel everything." Overwhelmed by the love she felt between her lovers, Shauna wept and Chenaugh held her.

Feeling Shauna's concern subsiding, Chenaugh released her. "I better get a move on," he said. Turning to the medic, who had witnessed the whole interaction, he tossed him his car keys and asked him to take Garcia to the nearby private airport. Explaining that U.S. Marshals were on their way to escort her back to Austin to be re-inducted into the witness protection program to keep her safe, he said he'd call ahead to make sure she was taken care of while she waited. Garcia quickly said her goodbyes, more with intense hugs than words, then climbed in the car with the medic and was gone. Chenaugh went into the condo to pack for them all. Janet drew Shauna close, their eyes meeting, the force of their bodies merging into a single flow that dissolved the distinction between mother and daughter.

CHAPTER 50 TRANSITION

The spaceship appeared, hovering above them. Chenaugh, Chip and Janet helped Clyde and Shauna up for transbeaming. Clyde sensing that wellness was only a space-ship away said, "It's such a relief to be leaving. If you'd told me last night that I'd be saying that tonight, I wouldn't have believed you. The only thing that doesn't seem to have changed is the moon."

The five of them stood waiting, looking forward to being with Towam and Etyo again. Standing on the brink of the unknown they found reassurance in their togetherness, ready to take a quantum leap outside an evolutionary path that had outlived its usefulness. Little did they know what they were in for. All the scientific certainties that had developed over centuries would no longer be applicable. Shauna and her lovers were on their way to replacing the existing order with unimaginable breakthroughs. First they had to be healed though. Physically and psychically cleansed of the evening's trauma.

Materializing on the spaceship Janet quickly greeted Towam, forehead to forehead, their feeling for each other evident. She then greeted Etyo the same. The others followed suite, welcoming in sequence; Towam, Etyo, two hovering light forms and a cloud of blue-white disks that, seemingly delighted, skipped amongst and through them. Clyde and Chenaugh touched foreheads, Chip and Towam high-fived – after a little instruction. A blending of life, completely spontaneous.

Becoming all business they focused on helping Clyde into the healing tube Shauna had experienced. Towam began treatment. He explained, Chip interpreting, that red blood cell production would be increased to improve bone marrow integrity. Then the wounds would be addressed. Once clear of the obvious trauma, his body chemistry, thoughts, emotions and organs would be balanced. He would in fact be healthier than ever. As the procedures progressed Clyde indicated to Chip that when he could quieten his mind he was able to follow some of what Towam was communicating. "Good for you, Bro!" said an enthusiastic Chip.

On the opposite side of the ship, Etyo was treating Shauna in another healing tube. Relaxed in his care she allowed his healing to penetrate completely, so thankful for his loving attention. Sensing her openness, Etyo dialed up the feeling and intensity.

Finished in no time, Shauna lay nearby, letting the session soak thoroughly into every cell. Chip replaced her in the tube to have Etyo treat him. Chip was soon finished too and he thanked Etyo. Even his ruined tattoos were intact again, much to Chip's amazement.

Feeling light-headed but relaxed he eased out of the tube and wobbled over to lie down near Shauna. They were wearing matching shirts of some unfamiliar fiber that came to just below their knees and Chip's was soon tenting around a rapidly rising erection.

Simply aroused by Shauna's proximity but not wanting to interfere with her recovery, he just lay quietly. Shauna turned her face to him. "You know, Baby, I adore it when you're aroused, so don't be concerned." "You really are something," he responded, "Seems I can't keep any secrets from you, my Love. So I guess you know that I want to smother you with kisses and get a little playful." "I certainly do and you turn me on too. You realize of course that Towam and Etyo are picking up on all this, right?" "Fuck, of course they are," replied Chip. "In fact, I bet everyone here is to some degree or other," finished Shauna.

Understandably, Clyde's session was taking much longer than Shauna's or Chip's. Janet had taken over as interpreter when Chip had gone for his treatment and Chenaugh had joined her. They stood by silently as Towam worked, totally concentrating on Clyde who was responding well. As the session came to an end, a happy but exhausted Towam stepped back and appraised his patient. Lowering his head he touched Clyde's forehead with his own and Clyde, feeling a surge of energy pulse through him, opened his eyes and smiled warmly at Towam. Sitting close to Clyde, Towam leaned back and closed his eyes. Now that everyone was whole again, he knew it was time to leave for Scotland. Clyde interrupted his thoughts, asking through Janet what Towam had done in order for him to feel so wonderful. Towam told him to just know that he was better than fine and to rest with that. Clyde closed his eyes again and fell into a deep healing sleep.

Rising from his seat Towam ambled over to Shauna and Chip, indicating for Chenaugh to follow him. He then communed with Shauna that this one, pointing to Chenaugh, needed to learn to switch off his mind and tune into his gut if he was ever going to be able to communicate directly. A must for the future. Shauna immediately passed this to Chenaugh who instantly agreed. He gently shook his body, trying to loosen himself up and then rolled his head around on his shoulders. Towam tenderly placed his hands on Cheaugh's stomach and held them there.

"Towam is saying that your calisthenics are a waste of time and energy. They're still mentality driven. What you have to do is make this so simple that your brain switches off. Lower your energy into your stomach and be quiet, be still. That's it. In the meantime, Towam knows we want to be together right now so he's arranged a space in the dome where Clyde will be able to join us when he feels ready. The disks have graciously agreed to accompany us and look after our needs. Towan has asked that we take care with each other, that we don't over exert ourselves but simply touch one another." Her Lovers, only too happy to follow instructions, thanked their compassionate hosts. Shauna continued, "It's imperative that we quickly rid ourselves of the grief and tragedy and only focus on the present and the future. And we can more readily accomplish this by being close together and gentle.

Janet was happy to stay with the aliens as they powered up and took the craft out of the atmosphere and aimed it toward Scotland. The dome was deliberately left without spin so the lovers could experience being weightless together. It was like being on a new amusement park ride. They floated every which way, a slow-motion un-choreographed dance. They noticed the flock of disks had migrated to the very top of the dome where they seemed to have stabilized themselves.

Left to their own devices the three lovers experimented. With everything a potential handhold, even the pillows on the floor, they played, reeling one another in only to escape and drift off to be caught again. Where they touched was somewhat haphazard, leading to some unusual juxtapositions, the very unpredictability arousing as they tried to pin each other down. Chip finally managed to achieve a measure of stability, and Shauna worked her way over to him and grabbing his hands pulled herself against him. Rubbing gently sent her butt outward and Chenaugh who was maneuvering towards them was slowly presented with a view of her ass.

Already aroused he resisted the temptation to grab her and just drifted past, his erection caressing her cheeks as he did so. A touch that did nothing to curb his mounting sexual desire.

The disks swooped down cavorting amongst them, diverting and loosening them from their handholds to float them in graceful circles around each other, stroking, kissing and caressing as they could. "These guys certainly seem to have a remarkable intelligence," admired Chip. The disks appeared to respond to his compliment, diving in, out and around the four of them, without leaving so much as a trace of feeling. Shauna was tenderly running her tongue around Chip's lips as they briefly floated face to face when weightlessness switched off suddenly and they tumbled into the soft billowing pillows.

The three looked at one another in astonishment and Shauna blurted, "Thank you, Loves. Did you notice how towards the end we were becoming more and more aligned? As if the polarities of every atom were rearranging to make us truly magnetic, indivisible, an integration of mind, body and soul, our true state of being: the source of unlimited adoration and worship of the spiritual and physical as one."

As they were rolling and bouncing on the pillows like they were mini trampolines, tumbling, spinning, twisting and vibrating in harmony, Towam appeared and communed they were hovering over Scotland. An excited Chenaugh said he'd understood at least some of what had been communed and received kisses from Shauna and Chip and a glowing forehead from Towam.

Offering Chip an armload of clothes, Towam turned to Shauna and suggested they get the disks to clean them up before they got dressed. Chenaugh, getting the drift if not the exact wording, snorted, receiving a playful glare from Shauna.

Cleaned, they donned the clothes Towam had provided. What a difference. From the light weight, colorful and skimpy with sandals of Jamaica, to heavy, subdued and substantial with boots and socks! The new clothes reminded Chip of the scratchy fatigues they'd been obliged to wear for their departure from Russia. *Man, a lifetime ago*, thought Chip. *At least these are soft and yielding though.* Stepping to the floor panel Towam had appeared through they were slowly lowered to the ring level in what Chip christened a gravilator – a steel like platform, apparently without support or propulsion, that slid up and down inside a shimmering force field that dissipated when the platform came to rest.

Stepping off the platform that merged seamlessly with the floor as they did so, they were overjoyed to see Clyde up and about. He was strutting around testing his legs marveling at his recovery and feeling better than he ever had. Wearing similar clothes to the other three, he looked made for the Highlands. They rushed together, all four excited to be whole and reunited. Clyde hugged them individually, so grateful to be one with each of them. They ended with Shauna in the middle, the three men surrounding her, heads touching hers, arms encircling the group, feeling the power of their new healing and a sharply focused purpose. Janet joined them and the men parted so she could embrace Shauna and then closed around the two of them. Grateful to the aliens. Grateful to themselves. Grateful for answering the call and choosing to jump into a river of oneness that flowed in all directions.

Saying their goodbyes to Towam and Etyo they stood on the transbeamer pad in the same configuration only looking out instead of in. Which is how they faced their new adventure seconds later, in wide-eyed awe. Wondering what was to come.

LOOK OUT FOR THE OTHER BOOKS IN THIS TRILOGY.
Book Two: 1 Expanding | Book Three: 1 Transcending

ACKNOWLEDGEMENTS

The smartest and best thing I've ever done in my life, was to listen to a deep hungry call in my heart and soul to go to a conference on Physical Immortality in Scottsdale, Arizona from where I was living in Santa Fe, barely hanging on by my finger nails in a near death crippling pain I had created from neglecting my body, and beating myself up with my under-valued self-esteem. This affliction is known in the medical world as Rheumatoid Arthritis. I also harbored anger, which was toxic to my body, covering it up with a protective outer layer of unreal sweetness.

At great risk and determination, not able to physically negotiate an airport, I took my car out of storage and test drove it after finding out that the people I was to drive to Scottsdale with had copped out. Driven by my desire and not listening to many of my concerned friends, I then ventured off into the unknown. I had dreamed about the unknowns awaiting me when a child. I did a lot of daydreaming. So I felt an excitement as I negotiated the roads headed towards Arizona. I recalled that it took me five years to respond to the inner call to get my ass to Scottsdale. In that interim I painted profusely, not having the vaguest idea what was flowing out of me, but liking what I saw. My friends thought I had fallen off the edge of no return. I felt good. And I had several prophetic dreams. Feelings came up in me before my arrival that to die was easy. Just give up. Stop living. Geez, it might take a hell of a lot of balls to keep a fire burning in the belly----to want to be alive.

I experienced the full gamut of emotions and feelings during the two week conference. From wanting to run the hell away from these intense passionate people whose sounds were so new and odd, to being drawn to them by their magnetic pull. Mid-way through my resistance started falling away as my walls came tumbling down and I felt an aliveness of myself I had never had. I ditched my wheelchair and started walking. How good it felt to move my body. A new intelligence was coursing through my body and I was craving closeness with the people. I had never heard in my life anyone say to me how special I am and that I would never be left for anything! To my surprise, I had finally found home----forever flesh! My people.

I drove back to Santa Fe, which took me seven hours versus two days to get there, and started making plans to get back to my people. I collected my paintings of the past five years from galleries. I finally knew what I had been painting. My life.

Time is a crazy thing. I can't believe I have been with Bernadeane and James, the amazing founders and directors of People Unlimited, Inc., since 1987. Leaders in spreading the word about physical immortality, radical life extension and unlimited living since 1960 - when the subject of expanded lifespans was a topic rarely discussed, especially not by mainstream media - being in their presence consistently has caused me to soar to heights above the negativity of the world where joy and weightlessness override the dark pulls of death and aging. I can say that I am here alive and kicking because of the nourishment and support given my flesh by Bernie and Jim and many of the people from around the world who have come to together to generate an aliveness that becomes greater the longer we live. Bernie and Jim have made the bringing together of people seeking an unlimited living their total focus and passion. Nowhere else on the planet can you find this. However, greater and greater numbers of people are waking up to a desire for more and are being drawn. I can't think of a higher purpose than to eradicate death from the planet, starting with eradicating my own.

This book is the first of a trilogy inspired by the life I have with Jim and Bernie and the People Unlimited community they have created. But while they were the inspiration, the characters' personalities, thoughts and language are fictitious and have evolved over the nine and a half years of writing. I have been consistent in doing some two fingered typing through thick and thin every day. Even being in hospital and over two years of assisted living, which was a bitch, didn't stop me from moving ever forward. Now, fresh out from assisted living, I write this from my new apartment where I have my life back sharing a beautiful space with a precious and sweet person who is joyfully here to see to my remaining physical limitations which are dropping away from me daily. I make sure I try something new every day and have a strong knowing I am walking out from all the previous suffering and bad decisions I have made, never to go backwards ever again. I am reconnected with my wholeness, thanks to my people.

I have a strong imagination out of which all the fictitious characters emerged and became real to me. The idea of space travel through simultaneous orgasm and breaking the gender barriers, including the uncanny attraction between Shauna and another strong female in Book Three, are my fantasies.

Sometimes it is hard to tell where I begin or end with my unlimited people, and especially with Bernie and Jim. After all, remember, I have been exposed to this ever-expanding life for twenty plus years. I give thanks all the time for my brave and smart move in coming home to my flesh. Real home. Real flesh. Thank you Bernie and Jim. The words my characters speak are a direct result of the special environment I am in.

And now to my courageous Editor, Doug Morris, who crossed an ocean, coming here for his life from England a couple of decades ago. We created an amazing flow that became faster and easier each time we got together. I am grateful for the way he kept the story on track, keeping the plot moving and removing the non-essential. Often it was so exciting to feel like we were one body moving. We have taken each other on.

I am aware that good editing is the core of a great book. I felt so supported and added on to. Thank you Doug. Thank you for your splendid creativity.

My older sister, Rita Stout, has three published books to her credit of a different genre than mine. I invite you to look her up. She has and is a joyful and positive support of me and my writing in every way. She makes sure I don't stop. That's not in my repertoire. I'm thankful for you Rita

Now comes dear Lorna Collett who wrote "About the Author". Lorna came from England many years ago. Her beautiful prose is legendary to those who know her. I am so honored for her touching words which thrive in the very depths of my soul. Watch for our collaboration on a coffee table book with Lorna's prose supported by my expressive paintings. The magical kind of penetration our never-before-created book will have is monumental and everlasting.

I have to mention all the numerous computer nerds who helped me through many a nerve racking computer mess up. I started my writing using a new computer with a writing program I had never used. I don't recommend this. However, I am fairly computer smart now which thrills me.

Enjoy. May the walls of your body come tumbling down as you are catapulted through many unexpected twists and turns morphing into a new and exciting you.

I welcome your feedback. Lois@LoisAWittich.com

Printed in the United States
By Bookmasters